PR

The Felserpent Chronicles series

2023 National Indie Excellence Awards Finalist in YA Fiction

2022 Foreword INDIES Finalist in Young Adult Fiction

2022 Best Book Awards Finalist in Fiction: Young Adult

2022 American Book Fest Best Book Awards YA Fiction Finalist

2023 Reader Views Literary Awards Bronze Award Winner in Young Adult

"Keridan presents a vivid, teeming fantasy world. . . . Her narrative features sharply etched characters, a chilling portrait of social prejudice, and powerful, emotionally fraught prose. . . . The result is a complex, captivating yarn. An imaginative sword-and-sorcery tale with a winsome love story at its heart."

—*Kirkus Reviews*

"A fast-paced epic fantasy adventure with plenty of thrills and charm. Keridan's writing sparkles and provides the perfect blend of suspense, adventure, and romance that will keep you turning pages long into the night."

—LENORE BORJA, author of *The Last Huntress*

"This story of love, sacrifice, and truth makes for a truly transportive read that pulls at heartstrings and sets the imagination ablaze."

—SATHYA ACHIA, author of *In My Hands*

Realm
United

Realm United

The Felserpent Chronicles: Book Three

Katie Keridan

Published by SparkPress, a BookSparks imprint,
A division of SparkPoint Studio, LLC
Phoenix, Arizona, USA, 85007
www.gosparkpress.com

Published 2024
Printed in the United States of America
Print ISBN: 978-1-68463-272-5
E-ISBN: 978-1-68463-273-2
Library of Congress Control Number: 2024910038

Interior design by Stacey Aaronson

To Sabriel, Kira Nerys, Arwen, Nancy Drew, and Trinity for inspiring me to create my own strong female characters.

THE BLOOD TREATY

We, the citizens of Aeles-Nocens, desirous of more harmonious relationships between those with gold and silver blood, do hereby establish the Blood Treaty, binding and effective from this day forward.

ARTICLE 1:

Seeking to end the fighting between Astrals and Daevals and dedicated to initiating a new era of peace and prosperity across Aeles-Nocens, we, the silver- and gold-blooded citizens of the realm, agree to cease all warfare upon the signing of this treaty. Never again shall Astrals and Daevals take up weapons against one another. Those who commit or attempt to commit blood crimes will be brought before a judicial council where they shall be tried and punished accordingly. We are one realm, with one future, eschewing blood-based hatreds and welcoming conciliation and cooperation so future generations may never know the horrors of living in a realm at war.

ARTICLE 2:

Be it resolved, in order to govern a shared Aeles-Nocens, a silver-blooded King and golden-blooded Queen shall be selected from Daevals and Astrals of marrying age. Candidates may put themselves forward or be named by family or friends. Among Astrals, the woman chosen to become Queen will ultimately be selected by the *Princeps Shaman*, whose decision is final and unalterable. Among Daevals, the man chosen to become King will ultimately be selected by the *Uchel Doeth*, whose decision is final and unalterable. The chosen man and woman will wed, establishing the Felserpent Monarchy and assuming responsibility for the well-being of Aeles-Nocens and all who reside therein. The Felserpent King and Queen shall possess the uncontested authority to govern, appointing councilors and committees as laws are created and enforced for the benefit of all.

Article 3:

On this day, Schatten Rektor, Daeval, Pyromancer, and Commander of the Daevalic military, is hereby chosen by his peers and the *Uchel Doeth* to become the Felserpent King.

On this day, Kareth Arken, Astral, Recovrancer, and healer, is hereby chosen by her peers and the *Princeps Shaman* to become the Felserpent Queen.

In Conclusion:

In this, our beloved realm of Aeles-Nocens, all citizens, regardless of their blood, are welcome to live peaceably. Long may the realm prosper, and long may the Felserpent King and Queen reign.

1

KYRA

I pressed my finger against the doorbell, listening as the familiar three-note melody sang a muffled welcome from the other side of the door. Batty perched on my shoulder, and Sebastian stood beside me, shifting his weight from one leg to the other as his gaze swept back and forth across the porch. Aurelius stood guard near my feet, ears pricked for the first sound of trouble. I was doing my best not to show it, but I was on edge too.

Exhaustion pulsed through me with every heartbeat, and I desperately wanted to take a hot bath and change into clean clothes, erasing any evidence of my captivity in Rynstyn. I wouldn't put it past Tallus to send soldiers after us; he would be furious Sebastian had rescued me before destroying the clandestine experimentation facility. But Sebastian thought our ancient enemy was more likely to respond by targeting my family. Hopefully Tallus would start searching for them at my childhood home or even Demitri's apartment in Celenia; with the blessing of the Gifters, he wouldn't immediately think to go to the home of Demitri's parents. As the only sounds around us were the chirping of crickets and the squeaks and rustles of nocturnal animals, it seemed we'd outsmarted him, at least for now.

Demitri pulled open the door and waved us inside. I'd barely stepped into the house before he threw his arms around me, clutching me as if he'd been afraid of never seeing me again. I returned the embrace. When he finally released me, he turned towards Sebastian.

"Thank you," he said, his tone devoid of the sarcasm he usually employed when speaking to Sebastian. "I know we haven't exactly seen eye-to-eye on . . . things . . . but I'll never forget what you did for Kyra today."

Sebastian dipped his head in acknowledgment. While the interaction was still far from friendly, I hoped it marked the beginning of a change in the relationship between my best friend and my husband from a previous life.

My mother must have been listening around the corner because she rushed into the foyer, a gasp catching in her throat as she pulled me into her arms. Demitri's parents and the rest of my siblings followed, and my fifteen-year-old sister, Seren, embraced me with impressive force just as my mother released me.

"I've been so worried about you!" Seren exclaimed, her white-blonde hair tickling my cheek as she rested her head against my shoulder.

"What in the falling stars is going on?" cried my mother, brushing her auburn curls away from her face. Her Cypher, a hare named Dova, appeared near her feet and anxiously ran her paws over a large ear.

Gently untangling myself from my sister, I looked at Demitri. "Tell your parents what Sebastian told you. I'll share more later, but right now I need to make sure my family's safe."

I gestured towards Sebastian as he conjured a portal. "Mother, this is Sebastian. He has silver blood, but he's helping us. We need to leave, and then I'll explain everything."

My mother gaped at Sebastian before composing herself. Hugging Demitri and his parents, she thanked them for everything, then took my youngest brother Deneb's hand and stepped through the portal, head held high as she instructed my siblings to follow. Enif hurried after her, but Seren hesitated, glancing uncertainly at me. I gave her what I hoped was a reassuring nod, and she stepped carefully into the crackling gateway.

"I'll be in touch soon," I assured Demitri. Turning to his wide-eyed parents, I added, "Thank you for everything, and I'm sorry I—"

Sebastian's head whipped towards the front of the house. I stopped mid-sentence, about to ask what he'd heard, when a sharp knock sounded, followed by someone calling, "Mr. and Mrs. Forenza? It's the Aelian military. We'd like to speak with you."

Sebastian jerked his head towards the portal just as Batty tugged my hair and pointed a wing at the shimmering gateway, urging me forward. I didn't need any more encouragement and hurried through, my heartbeat racing almost as fast as my feet. Sebastian stepped in after me, and while I couldn't help but feel safer as the portal snapped shut, I also hated leaving Demitri and his family to face anything involving Tallus.

I will stay in contact with Halo, said Aurelius, *and let you know what happens.*

Thank you. At least the lynx could communicate with Demitri's Cypher. Peerins couldn't communicate across realms, unless you had a special one approved by the government, which I didn't. Much as I disliked feeling so helpless, there was nothing else I could do to help Demitri, so I directed my attention to the circular receiving room we'd arrived in.

It had been nearing the middle of the night in Aeles, which meant it was close to noon in Nocens. The rain lashing the floor-to-ceiling windows obscured any view of the sun, making it difficult to tell the time. The weak light that managed to shine through the droplet-streaked glass cast a somber grey pallor over the room. Thunder rumbled, and lightning streaked across the dark sky, causing me to squint at the unexpected brightness.

Dunston and Caz were waiting for us, and seeing the Dekarai brothers instantly made me feel better. While I'd never imagined becoming friends with a silver-blooded family who only followed laws when it suited them—while at the same time making a fortune through unscrupulous business dealings—they'd unexpectedly become an important part of my life, and I was grateful for their support.

A woman I'd never met was standing between Dunston and Caz, her grey hair cut into a short, asymmetrical bob that was almost as sharp as the tailored white breeches and jacket she wore. Her expression was equally sharp, and the way she gazed down her nose at our arrival made me feel like a tangled clump of seaweed that had washed up on the beach.

"Welcome to Sea'Brik!" Caz stepped forward with a bright smile. "You're just off the coast of Dal Mar, in the safest place in all of Nocens, which, fortunately, belongs to our sister, Minerva."

So, this was the final member of the Dekarai trifecta, sister to Dunston and Caz and aunt to Devlin and Eslee. Minerva dipped her head in greeting, although the gesture would have felt more welcoming if her expression had softened even the slightest bit.

Deneb clutched our mother's skirt with one hand while he cradled his Cypher, a possum named Hortensia, in the other. Seren's Cypher, Sappho, a black and white sea snake, materialized around her neck, flicking her forked tongue uncertainly as Enif's Cypher, Tiberius, perched on his shoulder, the dwarf owl's round eyes even larger than usual. Seren and Enif stood stiff and unmoving. While they were trying to be brave, I knew they had to be terrified at being so near those with silver blood. Our parents had been far less prejudiced than most Astrals, but we'd still grown up taught to fear Daevals and told to immediately run for help if we ever encountered one.

While Sebastian had spent time with my Astral friends and

even worked with them to rescue me from Rynstyn, this was the first time my family had been around Daevals. I sent a silent prayer to Bellum, the Gifter of Victory. While I didn't think anything terrible would happen, given my own experiences with the Dekarais—plus my mother's unwavering insistence on good manners—I couldn't help but feel this meeting was important, offering a glimpse of how Astrals and Daevals might act towards one another once the realms were reunited.

Returning Caz's smile, I took over the introductions, glad I could do something familiar and assume responsibility for something.

"Mother, this is Dunston Dekarai and his brother Caz. Father met them when he came to Nocens for diplomatic talks. Caz is the one who sent the flowers after his death." Turning to the brothers, I said, "This is my mother, Skandhar, and my siblings Seren, Enif, and Deneb."

"It's an honor," replied Caz with a deep bow, and for a moment the room was little more than Cyphers appearing and introductions being made. Dunston's Cypher, Wayah, materialized, and the Komodo dragon's tail just missed a table holding a delicate vase as Alistair, Caz's porcupine, appeared chewing on a tree branch. Minerva's Cypher was a lovely snowy egret named Thula, with bright yellow feet and a tuft of downy feathers on top of her head. Something about the arrival of the Cyphers helped ease the tension, and everyone began speaking, bowing, and shaking hands.

Seren turned towards me. "Who are you?" she asked Batty, studying the creature intently. Cyphers were traditionally standoffish towards anyone they weren't paired with, and it hadn't slipped my little sister's notice that a Cypher who was most certainly not paired with me was sitting on my shoulder.

"This is Batty. He's Sebastian's Cypher." I purposefully kept my response brief, as I'd be going into detail about a great many things very soon.

From the corner of my eye, I saw Batty draw a wing across his body before dipping into an elegant bow. "It is a pleasure to make your acquaintance," he said to Seren. He then pulled a bag from one of his countless wing pockets. "Would you like a caramel? These are freshly spun, and the salt they use makes them especially delicious."

Seren blinked at the bat, then looked at Aurelius to gauge his reaction to Batty's presence. The lynx ran a paw through his thick silver whiskers. "I can assure you, Seren, Bartholomew—Batty—is a most welcome addition to the family."

I'd never imagined Aurelius championing Batty, much less considering him part of the family. Seren opened her mouth, questions ready to come pouring out, but Caz held up a hand, drawing everyone's attention to him.

"There's a few things I should mention about your temporary home," he said. "Sea'Brik is on an island, but the water around us is spelled to repel unauthorized boats or swimmers, so there's no danger of surprise visitors. The house is spelled, too, and scans everyone upon entry. If it didn't recognize you, it would start shifting staircases, closing off hallways, and employing other defensive tactics, but Minerva has told it you're friends, so it will behave." He motioned to the platinum plate embedded in the floor. "Should you have need of it, the intersector is at your disposal and will send you wherever you like. Anti-portal wards are in place, but your portal signature has been registered, Sebastian, so you can come and go as you please." Everyone nodded their understanding, and Caz's smile turned apologetic. "I do hope you won't judge all of Nocens by this unfortunate weather. Autumn is normally such a lovely time of year, but there's a hurricane at sea, even though it's not the right season."

Sebastian and I exchanged a look. The longer Aeles and Nocens were apart, the more unstable each realm was becoming, experiencing natural disasters such as earthquakes, hurricanes, and avalanches that hadn't been seen since Sebastian and I established the Felserpent monarchy ages ago.

"I know it's the middle of the night in Aeles," said Dunston, patting Wayah's head before straightening, "so we weren't certain if you'd want to go straight to bed or would prefer to eat something first. Rooms and food are both available." He caught my eye. "Eslee's still with Minister Sinclair. They're settling the children Sebastian rescued into a new orphanage—one that isn't a front for an experimentation project—but she'll be here soon. Rennej and Devlin too." He smiled at my family. "Eslee's my daughter," he explained, "Rennej is my wife, and as much as it sometimes pains me to claim him, Devlin is my son."

Minerva guided us into a room where a buffet-style meal had been prepared. The long table was filled with more food than a group twice our size could possibly consume, and I was grateful to see everything was planterian since Astrals didn't eat animals. It was a mark of the Dekarais' thoughtfulness that they'd considered my family's dietary needs in the midst of an incredibly stressful situation.

"Too much has happened for me to sleep right now," volunteered Enif, gazing hungrily at the table, "but I could definitely eat."

Deneb looked up at Enif, then back at the table. "I could eat too!" he exclaimed, never one to be left out when an older sibling expressed interest in something. "Do Daevals eat pudding?"

My mother gave him a nudge, likely hoping to stop any more questions about Daevals before they arose, but thankfully Caz was never one to stand on ceremony.

"I don't know about all Daevals, but I love pudding!" Picking up two plates, he held them out to Enif and Deneb, who promptly joined him. "In fact, I love it so much I always make sure we have at least three types." He studied the table. "Today we have butterscotch, chocolate, and cherry."

"We usually only have one type of pudding," said Enif, wasting no time piling food on his plate.

"Unless it's a special occasion," corrected Deneb, repositioning Hortensia on his shoulder and grasping his plate with both hands before holding it up for Enif to fill. "Then we might have two."

"Well, today *is* a special occasion," said Caz, drizzling sugared syrup over a fruit tart. "This is the first time anyone from Aeles has been in this house, and that's worth celebrating."

I glanced at Minerva just in time to see her grey eyes narrow. While she managed a smile, I sensed she was less than pleased at recent events. Seren kept glancing at Sebastian, clearly waiting for a chance to ask the questions I could almost see perched on her lips. Batty vanished from my shoulder and reappeared on the table, waving Seren over.

"If it is not too much trouble," he said, "would you help me fix a plate? Wings are not the best for managing utensils."

Seren was obviously surprised to see a Cypher interested in food. Her movements were initially wary, but she couldn't suppress a smile as Batty asked her to spoon butterscotch pudding over the top of a chocolate croissant.

Now that everyone was starting to settle in, it was time to face a conversation I'd been terrified to initiate and still wasn't certain how to have. "I know everyone has questions," I said, "but I need to speak with my mother first. Once the rest of the Dekarais arrive, Sebastian and I will tell everyone everything."

"Why don't I show you to your mother's room?" offered Dunston. "That way you can speak privately."

"Thank you."

Enif and Deneb were engrossed in a conversation with Caz, but Seren caught my eye. "Can I come, too?"

"Let me just have a few moments with Mother," I said, "then we'll all talk."

I stepped closer to my mother, knowing she would be worried about leaving my siblings alone while also not wanting to offend our hosts.

"They'll be fine." I squeezed her arm. "The worst that will happen is Caz will let them eat too many desserts."

"That is very likely," Caz agreed, raising a cookie as if he were about to give a toast before taking a bite. My mother drew a deep breath before nodding and following Dunston out of the room.

Will you be alright? I asked Sebastian through our bracelets. We'd barely had a chance to process all we'd survived in the past few hours—Sebastian had overcome Tallus's mental manipulation and faced his deepest fears, rescued me from captivity, saved five kidnapped Daeval children, then burned the vile Astral experimentation facility to the ground. And rather than comforting him or doing something that might have made him feel better, I was now asking him to do his least favorite thing—socialize. While I knew he was comfortable around the Dekarais, this was his first time meeting my siblings, and I couldn't imagine him having much experience with children.

I have zero *experience with children*, he noted, following along with my thoughts. *But I'll be fine.*

That likely meant he was going to slip away and stay in another room until I was done speaking with my mother, but it was probably best if he waited to be around my family until I was there to guide the conversation. I smiled at him and held out my hand as I walked past, grateful for the reassuring squeeze he offered before I strode after my mother and Dunston. Aurelius padded beside me, his presence never failing to make me feel better and serving as a reminder I wasn't alone in facing the obstacles currently threatening to overwhelm me.

Having gotten used to Sebastian's cave, I felt odd being surrounded by so many windows, but they seemed to function in place of walls in the palatial house. The enormous panes of glass must have been spelled together, as I couldn't see any evidence of plaster. On a clear day, I imagined they offered stunning views of the sea and sky, but today they merely took the assault of the pelting rain.

Everything in the house sang of the ocean, from the gentle greys, blues, and greens to the globe-like lighting fixtures suspended from the towering ceiling; strings of trailing lights made them resemble floating jellyfish. There were numerous ocean-themed sculptures, created by Eslee, no doubt, and I admired one in particular; the abstract metal pieces reminded me of a blue and silver wave surging upwards, frozen the instant before it would otherwise break and come crashing down. The wall closest to the staircase had been painted to resemble the rocky basin of a tidepool and decorated with colorful ceramic sand dollars, brittle stars, and sea anemones. As I admired the mural, a brittle star began to move, crawling its slow way forward as a sea anemone waved its short orange tentacles. Even though I knew the objects were enchanted to act as they did, the effect was still impressive.

Catching up to my mother and Dunston, I managed to hear the end of what Dunston had been saying.

". . . sorry your first visit to Nocens had to happen under such unpleasant circumstances. My family and I have loved getting to know Kyra, and we'll help however we can. Please don't hesitate to tell us anything that might make your stay more enjoyable, or at least more comfortable."

"Thank you," replied my mother, although I could tell she

was turning over Dunston's words and wondering just how and when he and his family had gotten to know me.

Dunston kept up a mostly one-sided conversation until he came to a stop before a large wooden door. A sign hung from it, with the words "Coral Reef Room" painted in sweeping brush-strokes. Opening the door, Dunston gestured for us to go inside, although he remained in the hallway.

"When you're done, just tell the house where you'd like to go or who you're looking for, and it'll direct you," he explained. "Minerva says it's just good spell-casting, but I think she's managed to make Sea'Brik at least partially sentient—which is more than I can say for Caz most days." Dunston's grin softened into a more serious expression as he faced my mother. "In my line of work, I've become quite the judge of character." Dunston's dark eyes shone earnestly. "After meeting your husband, I thought, you know, if a man like that can come from Aeles, there might be more to Astrals than just their gold." He ran his palms down the front of his jacket, smoothing the dark blue fabric. "I wouldn't have been nearly so open to the idea of better relations between the realms if it hadn't been for Arakiss. His legacy lives on every time those with silver and gold blood make an effort to understand one another a little more."

My mother reached out and laid a hand on his arm, too overcome to speak, although the grateful expression on her face said enough. Dunston patted her hand, then excused himself, although not before I gave him a hug he happily returned.

Following my mother into what would be her bedroom during our time at Sea'Brik, I closed the door behind me. My knees trembled as my stomach did a somersault, sending my fear spilling through me, and I tried to focus on details of the room to stop my racing thoughts.

True to its name, the space was decorated to resemble a coral reef. Starfish were carved directly out of the crown molding, and elegant paintings of black, white, and yellow fish decorated the pale pink walls. My mother sank into a wingback chair covered with small, embroidered cuttlefish, rubbing her fingertips against her forehead as Dova hopped up on the blush-colored sofa beside her.

I considered sitting, too, but doubted I'd be able to remain still. Crossing the room, I wrapped my arms around myself and gazed outside. The rain had let up just enough for me to see the ocean below, white-capped waves crashing beneath heavy grey clouds, and I swallowed to wet my increasingly dry throat.

How in the falling stars was I going to tell my mother the truth?

2

KYRA

Doubt swirled through me, filling every space not already occupied by fear. My mother had to believe me; after all, I was her daughter. But then again, given what I knew of Sebastian's father, just because someone was your parent didn't mean they supported you and had your best interests at heart.

What if she didn't believe me?

It will not make anything you say untrue, said Aurelius, situating himself in front of the fireplace where a cheerful fire had sprung up. *You cannot control her response; you can merely speak your truth.*

"I don't know where to start," I admitted, turning to face my mother and clutching the hem of my tunic. "Let me just try and get everything out, and then I'll answer your questions."

Taking a deep breath, I decided to start where my entire life had changed. "There are some things about Father's death I need to tell you." I explained about accidentally going into Vaneklus while trying to heal my father, as well as the research Demitri and I had done in the Archives and how I'd ultimately discovered I was a Recovrancer, able to recover the shades of those who died before their appointed times.

The blood rushed from my mother's face, making the freckles I'd inherited from her stand out more than usual.

"I wish you had told me sooner," she frowned, although her

expression was more worried than angry. "But I can also understand how it might not have seemed like the right time, given everything with your father. I'm so sorry, Kyra. You shouldn't have had to bear this by yourself. Perhaps Healer Omnurion knows how to break such a curse. We could—"

"It's not a curse." Normally I wouldn't interrupt my mother, but she needed to understand this. "It's a gift. I love being a Recovrancer. It's part of who I am . . . who I've always been."

My mother's eyes widened. "Are you saying you've actually recovered a shade?"

"A few shades."

I told her about Laycus, how shades were ferried to Ceelum for rest or Karnis for rebirth, and how I could use my *sana* bracelet to tell when it was a shade's appointed time to die. While my mother had likely believed in the Shade Transporter the way all Astrals had been taught, I suspected most of my kind didn't think about him very often; I certainly hadn't, not until I'd learned death would be an ever-present part of my life as a Recovrancer.

My mother clasped her hands in her lap. "But recovrancy is against the law in Aeles. How have you been doing this without anyone discovering you?"

I pressed my sweat-dampened palms against the tops of my thighs, heart pounding. "Because I only use my recovrancy when I'm in Nocens."

My mother's reddish-brown eyebrows shot up towards her hairline.

"Remember when I accidentally fell through that portal with a Daeval?"

She nodded, everything about her going incredibly still, as if she already knew whatever I was about to say would force her to reconsider things she'd thought were settled. I proceeded to tell her the truth about meeting Sebastian: how Batty had misdirected his portal, how I'd healed him from the potion he'd taken to disguise his blood, how that had resulted in him setting off the Blood Alarm, and how I'd seen *The Book of Recovrancy* in his pocket and saved him from the Aelian military to ensure I didn't lose access to the book.

"He and I stayed in touch," I said, preparing myself for what I considered the second most unbelievable thing I was going to ask my mother to believe. "In fact, we're in a relationship."

"You're in a relationship . . . with a Daeval." My mother's blue-grey eyes were unblinking.

"Yes. Daevals are nothing like we've been taught to believe." And now it was time to tell her the truly most unbelievable thing I hoped she would accept. "Also . . . this isn't the first time Sebastian and I have been in a relationship."

My mother's expression shifted from disbelieving to confused.

"In a past life, I was an Astral woman named Kareth, and I agreed to marry a Daeval warrior named Schatten to stop the constant bloodshed between Astrals and Daevals. Aeles and Nocens haven't always been separate. They used to be one realm, and our marriage brought peace, ending centuries of fighting. But we were betrayed by a man named Tallus, who overthrew our kingdom and divided the realms." Heat rushed into my chest at the memory of Tallus's evil deeds. "Schatten and I couldn't fix things in that life cycle, so we bound our shades, promising to return when the time was right to find one another and reunite the realms. Through binding our shades and reconnecting, we've been able to recover some of our past life memories, which is how I know the things I'm telling you. And now that we've returned, it's time to bring Aeles and Nocens back together."

My mother looked more stunned than I'd ever seen her, but I pressed on.

"The reason you had to leave Aeles was because Sebastian

and I aren't the only ones who've returned. Tallus is back, too, although everyone in our realm knows him as Senator Rex. He tricked me into going to Rynstyn, then held me prisoner so I'd help him end the existence of Daevals. He wants me to use my healing and recovrancy powers to change Daevals from the inside out, turning them into Astrals. Sebastian rescued me, but things are going to get worse before they get better—which is why we're here in Nocens where everyone will be safe."

My mother stared at me, and I held her gaze, waiting for her to say something; instead, she leaned forward and rested her elbows on her thighs before dropping her face into her hands.

My heart drummed in my ears as I struggled to master my rising panic. I knew my mother had to come to terms with things in her own way, but at the same time, I wanted her to wrap her arms around me and assure me she would always love me no matter what. The seconds ticked by, and eventually she lifted her head.

"It's all true," I said. "I promise." Regardless of the realm, there were always consequences for lying, and they could range from inconvenient, like not being able to perform a particular spell, to downright terrible, making you ill or preventing you from using your *aleric* gifts. I hoped reminding my mother what might befall me if I wasn't telling the truth would make what I was saying more believable.

"My issue isn't that I don't believe you." She frowned, her eyebrows knitting together. "It's that you're just now telling me!"

"I'm sorry. I wanted to tell you sooner, but it seemed like there was always something more pressing to attend to. And"—I gestured helplessly with my hands—"these weren't exactly easy things to share. I didn't want to upset you. I also didn't want you to be mad at me. I didn't want to lose the only parent I have left." My voice broke, and I pressed my lips together, doing my best to contain the emotions swirling through me.

"Kyra, you will always be my daughter, and I will always love you," said my mother. "But what you're saying is serious. Life-changing! If the government finds out about your recovrancy or your relationship with Sebastian, you could be in a lot of trouble."

"I'm not trying to hide from the government. I'm trying to change it," I explained. "I'm working to bring back a united realm where Astrals and Daevals can live side-by-side without fearing for their safety."

"While that's certainly admirable, how can you expect Astrals and Daevals to interact peacefully when all they've known is hatred?" asked my mother.

Hearing the overly patient tone my mother often used when speaking to Deneb, I couldn't stop my shoulders from slumping. What I was attempting to do wasn't *admirable*—it was realm-changing and would alter everything everyone had ever known, rewriting the past while offering a chance at a completely different future.

"Remember when Caz sent those flowers after Father died?" I tried to keep my voice from betraying both my disappointment and my rising annoyance. "You said Father's kindness must have overcome the prejudices between Astrals and Daevals. If more of us would put aside what we've been taught to believe and give those with different blood a chance, there's no telling what a united realm could accomplish!"

"But what about internship and taking your father's place as the *Princeps Shaman*?" A stricken look flashed across my mother's face. "What about a courtship with Demitri?"

Of all the things for my mother to focus on.

"Mother, even if Sebastian wasn't in my life—which he is—I was never going to court Demitri. He and I are friends, and there will *never* be romantic feelings between us. I know that's not what you want, but you're going to have to come to terms with it."

My mother shook her head. "This is just so much to take in; I can barely make sense of it." I hated knowing I'd caused the betrayal flickering in and out of her eyes. "I feel like I've been excluded from some of the most important parts of your life. I know you and your father had a close relationship, but that doesn't mean I don't love you just as much as he did."

"I know that. I just—"

"—I'm also terrified for you," continued my mother. "If this Tallus is as horrible as you say, you're in danger. Is there any way you can seek asylum in Nocens until this blows over?"

"It's not going to blow over. Don't you see?" My voice rose, my frustration refusing to be contained any longer. "I'm not a child anymore, Mother. I know from personal experience the world can be a dangerous and cruel place. But I also know it doesn't have to be that way. It *wasn't* always that way. Because of my past, I have a responsibility, and that doesn't end just because my life cycle does."

My mother exhaled loudly, but at least she seemed to be taking me more seriously.

"Aeles and Nocens are in my care," I said, standing up straighter as I felt the subtle weight of a crown on my head. "I chose to become the Felserpent Queen. I chose to rule because I was willing to do whatever it took to bring Astrals and Daevals together. I changed things for the better before, and I can and will do it again."

My mother blinked as if she no longer recognized me, and something shifted between us, giving me the courage to speak my next words.

"I desperately want your support," I said. "More than anything, I want to know that not only do you believe me, you believe *in* me. But as much as I want your blessing, I'm not asking for permission. I know what has to be done, and I'm going to do it." I took a step forward. "I also know this isn't how you wanted to learn about things, and I'm sorry for not telling you sooner. I understand if you need time to process it. I'm just trying to do what I've been taught all my life—to use the privilege I have to make things better for others. You and Father always stressed how important it is to speak the truth even when no one wants to hear it. That's all I'm trying to do."

A tear slid down my mother's cheek, and she brushed it away before bringing her gaze back to mine. "I've already lost your father." Her voice was strained. "I don't want to lose you too. What you're describing—it's so dangerous. But as the Gifters said, the rightness of an act is never determined by the ease with which it can be performed." She drew a shaky breath before pushing herself to her feet. "Thank you for telling me everything. I believe you, and of course I support you. I don't have to like what you told me or when you chose to share it, but the point is you told me." She gave me a tight smile. "What happens next?"

I couldn't stop myself. I crossed the distance between us and threw my arms around her. "I'm so sorry about Father!" Words I'd kept to myself for weeks rushed from my mouth, desperate to be shared. "I wanted to save him more than anything. I did everything I could, and I hate that it still wasn't enough."

My mother wrapped her arms around me, and I sank into her embrace, clinging to her as we cried. For the first time since my father's death, I didn't feel so alone with my grief. While I didn't think the pain of losing him would ever go away entirely, the constant ache I'd experienced since his passing throbbed a little less sharply.

"You're not alone, sweetheart." My mother ran her hand over the back of my head, smoothing my hair. "I'll do whatever I can to help you." She pulled back and gazed into my eyes. "And Sebastian . . . he's good to you?"

I nodded, wiping the wetness from my face. "I've never been happier."

Of course, I still didn't know what reuniting the realms meant for my bond with Sebastian. I'd bound our shades so we would find one another when the time was right to rejoin the realms, but would accomplishing what we'd set out to do also mean the end of us finding one another in future life cycles? Unfortunately, that was a conversation for Laycus, and clearly there were things I needed to handle in the realm of the living before I could visit Vaneklus.

"I'd like to meet him properly," said my mother, "now that I know who he really is and what he means to you."

I pressed my fingertip against the bracelet, asking Sebastian to join us, then explained how our bracelets worked until a knock sounded at the door. Judging by how quickly Sebastian had arrived, there was a good chance he'd followed us upstairs, positioning himself nearby in case I needed him or to simply avoid conversation downstairs.

"Come in," I called.

Sebastian strode into the room, and if I hadn't known him better, I would have thought him the very picture of collected calmness. As it was, I could tell by the set of his shoulders and the way his eyes immediately sought mine that he was nervous, which surprised me. Given that he'd been the most powerful man in the realm at one time, his anxiety over speaking with my mother was more than a little endearing, although it also struck a protective chord in me. While my family's reactions were beyond my control, I still wanted them to offer him a warm welcome.

"Mother, this is Sebastian." I took his hand as he stopped at my side. "Also known as Schatten, the Felserpent King, my husband in a past life, and the Pyromancer my shade is bound to."

While my mother was naturally one for hugs, she was also

skilled at reading others, and she correctly sensed Sebastian was not inclined towards hugging. Extending a hand, she offered him a warm smile. "Thank you for everything you've done for Kyra—in the past, as well as more recently."

Sebastian shook her hand. "There's nothing I wouldn't do for her."

Sincerity rang out in his words, which he'd proven true countless times in this life as well as our shared past. While I knew Sebastian's experiences with his own parents had been fraught with terror and loss, I hoped he would eventually come to enjoy being part of my family, accepting and perhaps even appreciating the additional opportunities to be loved and supported.

"I'm looking forward to getting to know you," continued my mother, "although I suspect that may have to be postponed, given what Kyra has told me about Tallus and the need to reunite the realms." Her expression turned worried. "Speaking of Tallus, do you think Demitri and his parents are in danger from helping us? I wish we had a way of knowing if they're alright."

"Peerins can't communicate across realms, unless you have a special government-approved one, but Cyphers can," I explained. "Aurelius, do you have any news?"

Aurelius shifted his position in front of the fire. "According to Halo, Demitri and his family are fine. The Aelian military questioned them, but since they didn't know our plans, they could honestly say they had no idea where we went." He flicked his short tail. "Demitri did tell Halo there's something he'd like to show you, but he's not certain how to send it to you."

Sebastian reached into his back pocket and handed me a copper peerin with a large sapphire set in the top lid. "The Dekarais have a few government-sanctioned peerins that will allow you to communicate with anyone in Aeles. Caz is working on getting you one of your own, but he said you can use this in the meantime."

My mother smiled approvingly. While anyone would have viewed Sebastian's gesture as a thoughtful one, it was also far bigger than that. He was actively helping me communicate with Demitri, recognizing my best friend was important without viewing him as a threat, which was huge for him.

"Thank you!" I clutched the peerin to my chest, and one side of Sebastian's mouth rose in a pleased smile.

My mother placed a hand on my shoulder. "Why don't you go contact Demitri while I take a moment to collect myself, and then I'll join you downstairs?"

I placed my hand over hers, enjoying the comfort of a loving touch and feeling lighter than I had in a long time, relieved I no longer had to keep so many important things to myself. I was also looking forward to developing a deeper relationship with my mother based on who I was now, and I offered a silent prayer of thanks to the Gifters for having been given not one, but two, loving parents in this life cycle.

3

KYRA

Stepping into the hallway with Sebastian and Aurelius, we walked a little distance before ducking into a circular alcove. Flipping open my borrowed peerin, I rang Demitri, and Aurelius was kind enough to tell Halo it was me calling since I was using a device my best friend wouldn't recognize.

"Are you alright?" I asked, my stomach clenching as I searched Demitri's face for any signs of what he might have experienced since I'd left.

He nodded, and while I knew he was a skilled actor, I was glad to hear nothing but sincerity when he spoke. "I told Senator—I mean, *Tallus*—the truth. I'd known you were going to Rynstyn as part of your work with him, but when time passed and I didn't hear if you'd made it back, I started to get worried. I contacted your family, and they came over to my parents' house. No one could reach you, and we didn't know where you were. You and Sebastian showed up here without warning, Sebastian opened a portal, and you left with your family without telling us where you were going." The corners of his mouth rose upwards. "Thank you for that, by the way. Even though I still very much want to know everything—and I mean *everything*—it's clear my family and I are safer with less information, at least for now."

"I'm so sorry," I said, hating that Tallus had taken an interest in Demitri and his parents because of me.

"Mother did an excellent job of being irate over not knowing what was happening," Demitri added, a broader smile stretching across his face. "It was actually fortunate Tallus arrived when he did—I hadn't told my parents anything yet, so their reactions were genuinely upset and confused."

I hated to ask, but I also had to know. "What did they say when you finally told them the truth?"

"They know I'm not lying, but I'm not certain that's the same as believing me," Demitri admitted, running a hand through his layered brown hair. "They love you and your family, but it's a lot to take in. That much I can understand."

I nodded. "It's definitely a lot. I just told my mother everything. She wasn't happy I kept so much from her, but she's supportive."

"Well, that's a relief. We're going to need all the support we can get." Demitri drew a deep breath and leaned in closer. "The entire government is convening first thing in the morning. I think Tallus is going to try and assume emergency powers so he can begin making unilateral decisions for Aeles."

I certainly wouldn't put it past the conniving man to do such a thing, but the thought of him having uncontested power over the citizens of my realm—not to mention control of the military—was a terrible thing to consider.

"He probably wants to order soldiers to invade Nocens so he can bring me home and force me to help him," I said. Since Demitri wasn't aware of all that had occurred in Rynstyn, I added, "Tallus wants to erase Daevals from existence, and he wants to do it by turning them into Astrals. Because I'm a Recovrancer and a healer, I might actually be able to change them, even though I would *never* do such a thing. But now that Tallus knows it's at least possible, he's going to do whatever he can to find me."

Memories of the experimentation facility flared in my mind, things I'd witnessed as well as what I'd seen through the dreams and memories Sebastian had shared. Daeval children had been tortured, restrained while their blood was taken and their bodies treated as experiments, viewed as nothing more than specimens to be studied until all available information had been extracted, at which point their bodies were unceremoniously burned, leaving behind no record of their short lives. I would never let Tallus perform such atrocities again, much less assist him.

"You might be more right than you know." Demitri's expression darkened. "I'm going to send you a government brief that's been playing at regular intervals on every communication device in Aeles."

My heart lurched as Demitri shared a series of moving images, but I forced my hand to be steady as I pressed a fingertip against the frozen scene.

Tallus appeared on screen, his voice streaming out from the peerin and making me tremble, even though I knew he wasn't actually nearby. Sebastian stepped closer, and the slight pressure of his arm against mine made me feel safer if not necessarily happier about what I was watching.

"Citizens of Aeles." Concern sobered Tallus's elegant face. "I must ask you to prepare yourselves for what you're about to see. While we know those in Nocens are nothing like us, it seems we have underestimated the depth of their hatred towards those with golden blood. It is my unfortunate duty to announce that just a few hours ago, Kyra Valorian, beloved daughter of Arakiss and Skandhar Valorian and the future *Princeps Shaman* of our realm, was kidnapped by a Daeval."

The image shifted, and I saw myself standing in the room Tallus had locked me in at the experimentation center. The feed fluctuated between clear and grainy. While there was no sound, there was no denying it was me, especially not with Aurelius, an especially recognizable Cypher, at my side.

"Ms. Valorian was attending an internship meeting in Rynstyn," explained Tallus from somewhere off screen, "and while I never would have imagined such a thing to be possible, it seems our wards are not as strong as we believed."

Sebastian appeared, leaping into the room with me after destroying the door, and a portal snapped open. From the angle of the hidden captum recording us, you couldn't tell he was kissing me. Instead, it looked like he was grabbing me, and it wasn't a stretch to imagine him threatening me as well.

"Nocens sent their best, a mercenary named Sebastian Sayre, and I'm sorry to say he was successful in his mission," continued Tallus. On screen, Sebastian's hand was still wrapped around my arm, and he shoved me through the portal before quickly closing it. At that point, the captum feed ended, and the scene cut back to Tallus, whose expression deftly shifted from anguished to determined.

"Rest assured the Aelian government is doing our best to find Ms. Valorian, and know that we will do whatever it takes to ensure she is returned to her realm and her grieving loved ones."

His pale blue eyes held mine as the communication ended, and even though I was viewing him on a device a realm away, my heart was racing. I'd been right. Tallus was actively looking for me, and he had no qualms about lying to everyone with golden blood, which should have been unthinkable for an Astral. Fear flooded my torso, although it was quickly replaced by anger. I pressed the lens again, returning to Demitri.

"Thank you," I said, even though part of me wished I'd never seen the vile propaganda. "I'll figure out a response to this. In the meantime, please be careful."

Demitri nodded, and I snapped the peerin shut before turning to Sebastian. How dare Tallus skew the truth for his own selfish purposes!

Astrals always gave one another the benefit of the doubt, assuming someone was being honest until proven otherwise, and Tallus was purposefully playing on that tendency while also inflaming deeply instilled fears about Daevals.

"He shouldn't be able to do this!" My voice echoed off the windows before me, and I clenched my hands into fists, only releasing them when the sapphire on top of the peerin began to dig painfully into my palm. I shook my head before looking at Sebastian. "That's not what happened, and that's *not* who you are."

He shrugged, and I wasn't certain if he was simply trying to appear unbothered or if Tallus's portrayal of him wasn't all that different from how he saw himself—or at least how he'd seen himself up until I'd reentered his life. "It's not a bad strategy," he said, purposefully avoiding a discussion of how he felt about what he'd seen in favor of focusing on the facts as we knew them. "Tallus knows he needs you to help him alter Daevals, so he can't turn Aeles against you. It's better to say you were taken against your will than you fled the realm for your life."

"I want to tell my kind the truth," I pressed. "If we record a response, do you think Caz or Dunston could ensure it played in Aeles? There must be something we can do. I can't stand letting him get away with this!"

"That's why he did it," explained Sebastian. "He's trying to goad you into revealing yourself. We can't take the bait. It's exactly what he wants."

I crossed my arms, gazing out the rain-spattered window at the churning ocean. Even though I knew Sebastian was right, I still hated to see the man I loved portrayed in such a manner. I also hated that Astrals were receiving even more incorrect information about Daevals, making my goal of bringing everyone together that much more difficult.

"Nocens isn't going to like this, though," Sebastian said. "They'll either say it never happened or I was acting on my own without the support of the government."

"Do you think the Dekarais could postpone a response?"

"I'm not certain it matters; I can't imagine Astrals will believe anything coming from Nocens right now. We should still show Dunston and Caz, though, so they're aware, even if they don't take immediate action."

"One more thing to tell everyone," I groaned, trying to summon any remaining strength I hadn't already utilized. "Do you think we should consider getting Demitri and his parents out of Aeles?"

"Tallus clearly isn't trying to make you look like a traitor," Sebastian reasoned. "Everyone knows you and Demitri are friends, so I imagine the average Aelian citizen will be concerned with how he's holding up. That will keep him in the public eye, which means everyone will be suspicious if he suddenly disappears. Your realm loves you, and their concern for you will ensure Demitri and his family are safe, at least for now."

I was about to ask Sebastian how long he thought we had until Demitri and his family were no longer safe, but he spoke again.

"I've been thinking about something." He shoved his hands into his back pockets. "And seeing how Tallus is using that recording makes me even more certain." His dark eyes were hard as they met mine. "I think he let us escape the facility in Rynstyn."

I gaped at him. "You overcame Tallus's spell that made you face your greatest fears. You fought four guards outside my cell. You destroyed the entire facility. How can you think Tallus let any of that happen?"

"Years of experience." Sebastian's voice was calm but certain. "It wasn't easy to get you out, but it also wasn't impossible. Remember, Tallus knows what I'm capable of. He could have made it more difficult."

"Are you saying he wanted you to rescue me? Why? So he could twist what you did to make it look like I'd been kidnapped by someone with silver blood and drum up even more hatred against Daevals?"

"I think that's part of it," Sebastian agreed. "I'm not certain if he planned to let me rescue you from the beginning or if something changed his mind, but regardless of when he made the decision, he decided you were more valuable to him not locked inside a cell."

"But why would he let me go if I'm so important?"

"I don't know," Sebastian admitted. "I just want you to keep it in mind. If he sacrificed his experimentation program for footage and let you go in exchange for a story to tell Aeles, you can bet he has a reason. We just have to figure out what it is."

I stepped closer, wrapping my arms around him and enjoying the momentary respite of feeling sheltered. At the same time, I couldn't ignore the fear Sebastian's words had planted, a fear I knew would only keep growing until we'd managed to stop Tallus for good.

4

SEBASTIAN

Not knowing why Tallus had let me rescue Kyra was like having a pebble in my boot during a fight—it would irritate me until I could do something about it, even though right now I *couldn't* do anything about it. In fact, I had to purposefully ignore it, at least for a little while, so I could focus on telling the Dekarais the truth about myself and my past, as well as the plans Kyra and I had for reuniting the realms. I hated talking about myself as much as I hated being the center of attention, but here I was about to do both. As Kyra and I headed to rejoin the others, I steadied myself the way I would before any contract I'd been hired to complete, tightening and loosening my muscles, controlling my breathing, and focusing my concentration on nothing more than the task at hand.

As we waited for the rest of the Dekarais to arrive, Kyra made herself a plate from the buffet. Although I'd been hungry earlier, my appetite had vanished. I settled for sitting next to her on an oversized ottoman, stopping myself every time my leg began to bounce or my fingers started to twitch, my anxiety seeking any available outlet. Kyra's mother had come downstairs while we'd been speaking with Demitri, and she'd just asked Dunston a question about his work with the Nocenian government when the door opened and Eslee swept into the room. Kyra jumped up, and the two hurried towards one another.

"Thank the Fates you're alright!" cried Eslee, pulling Kyra into a hug and looking prepared to single-handedly fight off any further dangers that might appear. While I'd initially wanted the two to become close so Eslee could replace Demitri in Kyra's life, I now found myself less motivated by that particular desire and simply grateful the two had formed a genuine friendship.

Kyra handled introductions, and while Seren gave Enif a sharp nudge, it didn't stop him from gazing at Eslee as if he'd never seen anyone more beautiful. Kyra and her mother both fought down smiles as Eslee pretended not to notice the impact of her arrival, instead welcoming everyone and complimenting Seren's blue velvet breeches. While she made the most of her appearance the same way Devlin did, I'd always sensed it was because doing so made *her* happy and not because she craved attention and needed to be publicly fawned over like her brother.

As the general conversation resumed, Eslee took a seat close by and leaned towards me, keeping her voice low.

"The children you rescued are safe. They were all orphans, like you suspected. Minister Sinclair did what he could for them physically, but it's going to take a while for them to heal mentally and emotionally from what they've been through." She shook her head. "That littlest one, the girl who wouldn't stop screaming—her name's Raethe, by the way—I overheard her describing her nightmares to Minister Sinclair. I don't know if she was recalling actual experiences or if it was just her way of processing things too terrible for words, but they sounded awful. She talked about feeling like she was falling and drowning in dark water as someone stood nearby wearing a black hood."

She shuddered, and while her words briefly made me think of Laycus, I knew from firsthand experience the Astrals at the experimentation facility had regularly employed water-based torture. Thank the Fates Raethe had survived, postponing any journeys with the Shade Transporter and keeping her shade safely inside her body where it belonged.

"I also removed the collars the children were wearing," added Eslee, "but I kept them, in case you needed them."

"Thank you." I appreciated her foresight. To my knowledge, those collars were the only way for someone with silver blood to bypass the Aelian Blood Alarm other than suppressor medallions. Since Tallus had destroyed all but one such medallion, it was good to have another option for getting into Aeles without alerting the entire realm.

"The children wouldn't stop talking about you." Eslee grinned. "Someone with silver blood, appearing out of nowhere with a fiery sword, opening portals, and rescuing them—they aren't entirely certain you're real. Once things calm down, you might consider paying them a visit. I know they'd love to speak with you."

While I was glad I'd spared the children from further cruelty and eventual death, I couldn't imagine what in the burning realm I'd say to them. I worked hard to avoid thinking about my time in Rynstyn. I certainly didn't want to sit around and compare stories of being tortured. Then again, given that things weren't going to calm down anytime soon, speaking with the children didn't seem like something I needed to worry about.

Before I could form a reply, the door opened again, and Rennej and Devlin strode into the room. Rennej's Cypher, a lemur named Loris, grunted as soon as she saw Caz and hopped onto the arm of a sofa before turning her back to him. Rennej and Caz had never been fond of one another, probably because Caz never passed up an opportunity to annoy Dunston's wife, often through ill-conceived practical jokes, and Rennej viewed Caz as an imbecile she couldn't have me eliminate and was therefore forced to tolerate.

Devlin's Cypher, an enormous panther named Onyx, surveyed the group and looked as if he was considering dematerializing until Devlin shook his head. The panther let out a low growl and slunk off to a corner, although not before he and Aurelius exchanged respectful nods. While Onyx generally viewed anyone other than Devlin as undeserving of his attention, apparently that didn't extend to another feline.

Kyra oversaw introductions, and this time it was Enif nudging Seren as she all but melted at the sight of Devlin. Her eyes were wide as they took in his black leather breeches, the inked drawings crawling over his arms, and the gold hoops in his nose and ears. She finally regained control of herself and directed her gaze to the floor, although her face remained flushed as she fidgeted with the ends of her long, pale hair. She must have felt me studying her, though, because she lifted her eyes, and I found myself surprised when she didn't offer me a smile. Kyra was so friendly, I'd just assumed her siblings would act similarly. Judging by the way Seren's expression hardened as she studied me, clearly my assumption had been wrong. Hopefully once she knew more about who I was and what I meant to Kyra, she'd be more welcoming, or at least less hostile.

Once everyone had taken a seat, Kyra looked at me, and it was all I could do to nod over the thudding of my heart. Objectively, if the Dekarais weren't going to believe me or simply didn't want to get involved in a fight that wasn't theirs, I needed to know sooner rather than later so I could begin making plans. But try as I might, I couldn't be objective or detached, not in this situation. As much as I had anything approximating family besides Kyra, the Dekarais were it—along with LeBehr, I supposed—and I didn't want them to bar me from their lives or think I was crazy. In fact, I found myself realizing just how much I liked being a part of the Dekarais' lives and how much I valued their opinion of me.

I wanted them to believe me, not just because I needed their help, but because they cared for me too.

Kyra cleared her throat. "Now that everyone's here, there's a lot Sebastian and I need to tell you."

I placed a hand on her knee, although whether it was to support her or comfort myself, I wasn't entirely certain.

I'm happy to start, but will you add anything I forget to mention? she asked.

Of course. Thank you for doing most of the talking.

She smiled at me before facing the others and plunging in. "I'm going to start by saying everything I'm about to tell you is true. I promise. It might sound like something from a bedtime story, but it's all real."

Eyes widened and a few glances were exchanged. From being around Kyra, I'd learned Astrals were much more comfortable than Daevals invoking the *aleric* consequences of making promises. Those with silver blood were far less quick to say the words "I promise," preferring to use everything short of the contractual language while allowing plenty of room for creativity. Kyra's promise would certainly make whatever she said be taken more seriously, but while believing us was a necessary first step, it also wasn't the same as supporting us.

Kyra proceeded to share what I'd told Demitri, Nigel, and Adonis, describing the constant fighting between those with silver and gold blood, and how the citizens of the realm, in order to stop the warfare, had instituted a monarchy comprised of a silver-blooded king and a golden-blooded queen. She told them about Kareth and Schatten, how they'd met and ruled, and how their kingdom had been overthrown by Tallus before he divided the realms.

Shock spread over the faces around us, and I could see questions forming, but Kyra held up a hand. "Before Schatten and

Kareth died, they bound their shades together, promising to return when the time was right to find one another again and reunite the realms." She smiled at me. "Sebastian and I were Schatten and Kareth, and we've returned to reunite Aeles and Nocens." She gestured to Batty, who was attempting to squeeze between two bowls on the buffet but was blocked by his belly. "Batty knew us both in our past lives—he was my royal advisor—and he's worked tirelessly over the centuries to ensure we found one another again."

Batty quickly stuffed the last bite of a pastry in his mouth before nodding. I tried not to be frustrated with the sweets-loving creature, even though as a Cypher he didn't need to eat.

I'd prepared myself for outcries or exclamations, but the complete silence that followed Kyra's words was more unnerving than if someone had stood up and accused us of lying or being out of our minds. Dunston stared at me before pulling a red silk handkerchief from inside his jacket and wiping his face, shaking his head as if the act might loosen his tongue and help him find the words he wanted to say. Caz ran a hand along his jaw, considering how to use what he'd heard to his advantage. Minerva's grey eyes were calculating, and Kyra's siblings were staring open-mouthed at her as if she'd suddenly transformed into an entirely different creature. Devlin and Eslee shared a look that seemed more curious than disbelieving, and Rennej stroked her jeweled necklaces before gazing down at her painted nails, her red lips pursed.

"Now," continued Kyra, "as for what's been going on more recently . . ." She spoke about her father's death, which I knew was still painful for her to revisit, and how it had led to her discovering she was a Recovrancer. While that revelation nearly caused Caz to leap out of his seat with excitement, he managed to calm himself, refocusing as Kyra described taking her father's place on a project with Senator Rex that turned out to be an experimentation program focused on Daevals. Heads shook in disbelief, and Kyra's family sat incredibly still, obviously ashamed at what their kind had done but also uncomfortable learning about it in a room full of Daevals.

When Kyra shared how her father had actually been working to shut the experimentation program down, she spoke proudly, and I was certain I was the only one—aside from Aurelius—who knew how truly frightened she'd been over what her father might have been doing. Aurelius must have been thinking the same thing because I glanced over to see him already looking at me. A silent understanding passed between the two of us. We, more than anyone else in the room, knew what Kyra had lost, sacrificed, and survived. While at one time I hadn't wanted to share Kyra with anyone, I'd become grateful for her Cypher and his unwavering devotion, particularly since he was perpetually concerned with her safety and, like me, never thought she took her safety seriously enough.

"Having me go to Rynstyn was a trap," Kyra said, and Aurelius twitched his whiskers as if to say he'd known all along going to the snow-covered province was a bad idea before reassuming his usual stoic demeanor. Kyra shared how Senator Rex was really Tallus returned, as well as how I'd worked with her Astral friends to rescue her after she'd failed to assume control over Tallus's mind. When she was done speaking, the only sound to be heard was the deep rumble of thunder across the dark sky.

Just when I thought the fire inside me might start burning through my skin, Devlin raised a hand. "Does this mean I have to call you *Your Highness* now?" he asked me, a smirk breaking out across his face.

"Absolutely not!" I snapped, but something about his question broke the uncomfortable silence, and everyone began talking at once.

Batty waved a wing from the buffet. "Devlin, I will offer you a generous candied incentive if you will only refer to Sebastian as *Your Highness* from this day forward."

"Well," grinned Eslee, "that certainly explains the connection you two have! I'm not entirely surprised."

"In all my years, I've never met a Recovrancer!" Caz rubbed his hands together. "How does it work? Can you recover both Astrals and Daevals? More importantly, have you thought about the financial benefits of being able to recover loved ones? Oh, if Raks Nemoya knew about this, he'd be livid!" Caz let out a gleeful laugh, his violet-blue eyes practically sparkling as he pictured the reaction of the Dekarais' most infuriating rival.

"How exactly do you plan on reuniting the realms?" asked Dunston. "I can't believe they were united at one time. I had no idea!"

While things could still take a turn for the worse, my earlier fears were slowly being replaced by a cautious optimism. No one had accused us of being delusional, and the Dekarais hadn't insisted we leave or barred me from their lives, which seemed to bode well.

"No one had any idea Aeles and Nocens used to be one realm," Kyra agreed. She explained about the *Ligarum Incanta*, or Binding Incantation, in the Chronicles and how LeBehr was helping us find the book. "LeBehr knows the truth about us because we needed her help finding information on the Felserpent monarchy," Kyra shared. "Once she locates the Chronicles, Sebastian and I will go to the ruins of our former home—which are in Aeles—and find the Cor'Lapis stone, the heart of Aeles-Nocens. We'll prove we're Schatten and Kareth returned and reunite the realms."

"Does reuniting the realms mean rejoining them physically?" asked Minerva. "That could mean flooding for those who live near the coasts. Many Daevals make a living fishing, kelp harvesting, or oyster farming, you know."

From the corner of my eye, I saw Kyra blink, and thanks to our connection, I felt the jolt of surprise that ran through her, followed by annoyance. It was true Dunston and Caz were more immediately supportive of ideas they liked, whereas Minerva took her time, asking questions and considering all options. While such behavior made her an asset to the family business, when it came to *our* plans, I suspected Kyra wouldn't see it that way. Minerva's question was worth considering, though.

Batty materialized on the low table in the middle of the semicircle we'd formed and brushed a few lingering crumbs from his fur.

"It is true the breaking of the realm allowed the sea to fill the space between Aeles and Nocens," he said. "That cannot be undone, and bringing the realms back together will not displace the ocean or rejoin the land masses that are now Aeles and Nocens. Instead, reuniting them will exert a healing effect on the realms, in addition to allowing folks to sail freely between the two. Currently, ships can only go so far before they are forced to turn back, but that will change when the realms are reunited."

While it was odd seeing folks impressed by something Batty said, I couldn't deny I was grateful for his knowledge.

"Well, that's good to know!" grinned Caz. "Shipping between the realms will certainly offer interesting new business opportunities." He looked between his brother and sister. "We should start acquiring ships—quietly, of course, but first to market is first to profit."

"You always have to make everything about money," frowned Rennej, who'd made it clear on more than one occasion she found Caz's willingness to discuss finances in public irrefutable evidence of his low breeding.

"And it's lucky for you I do," retorted Caz. "That's a lovely necklace by the way. Purchased using money, I presume?"

Rennej glared at Caz as she pressed a hand against the strands of rubies and pearls, but Kyra skillfully redirected the conversation.

"There's also more to reuniting the realms than Sebastian and I simply doing what we think is best," she added. "The natural state of Aeles and Nocens is to be together." She explained about droughts, avalanches, and other natural disasters occurring as a result of the realms being divided. "Regardless of what we do afterwards, the realms have to be reunited. It's the only way to ensure a future for both Aeles and Nocens."

That certainly got everyone's attention. As Kyra pulled out the peerin Caz had loaned her, I couldn't help but think about what reuniting the realms would mean for our bond. There was still a part of me that maintained if rejoining Aeles and Nocens meant the end of us finding one another in future lives, I'd gladly let the realms be destroyed. Of course, that meant Kyra and I would only have one life together, which wasn't nearly enough. The fire stirred unhappily in my veins, and I hoped Kyra would speak with Laycus soon. We needed to know more so we could choose the best course of action. While I did my best to keep my emotions out of my decision making, how I felt about Kyra would always carry more weight than facts or logic.

Kyra angled the peerin towards the far wall. "Tallus is clearly doing his best to increase the animosity between Astrals and Daevals," she said before projecting the lies he was blanketing Aeles with. When the broadcast was over, the Dekarai brothers shared a look I took to mean one of them needed to reach out to the Nocenian government.

"I'm sure you can anticipate everything you've shared will be difficult information for both realms to hear," ventured Dunston.

"What, exactly, is your plan for *after* you've reunited the realms?"

"One of the reasons I wanted to begin meeting Daevals who were open to better relations with my kind was to start the process of uniting Astrals and Daevals on a social level," Kyra explained before telling her family about the party the Dekarais had thrown for her a couple of weeks ago. "After the realms are united, I'd love to see a coalition formed, a government where silver and gold blood are equally represented and everyone can have a say in how the realm functions moving forward."

"I cannot imagine it will be that easy." Minerva shook her head, echoing sentiments Aurelius had expressed to Kyra on more than one occasion.

"I don't think it will be easy at all," Kyra agreed, "but that isn't going to keep us from doing our best to accomplish it."

I nodded. Even though the gesture was far less eloquent than anything Kyra had said, I wanted everyone to know she had my full support and the two of us were in this together.

Eslee leaned around me and caught Kyra's eye. "It's so obvious you used to be a queen," she grinned.

Kyra beamed appreciatively in response, a faint blush coloring her cheeks. While I could have endlessly admired how lovely she was, my appreciation was interrupted by Seren leaping to her feet. I stiffened at the unexpected movement as my body demanded further instructions, ready to set the room ablaze, direct a weapon towards a target, or make a calculated retreat. Seren's bottom lip quivered, and then she bolted from the room, not even bothering to close the door behind her. I watched a stunned expression spread across Kyra's face as her eyes followed her sister's path. Skandhar started to rise, but Kyra was instantly on her feet.

"Let me talk to her," she said before glancing at me. "And then I think we should visit LeBehr."

5

KYRA

As I made my way around the furniture, Minerva reached out and placed a hand on my arm.

"She's in the observatory."

I blinked at her. How could she know such a thing?

"I am intimately connected to Sea'Brik," she said, an expression hinting at untold secrets flashing across her face. Gesturing with her head, she added, "The house will show you the way."

White lights appeared on the tile floor, and I thanked Minerva before following my silent guide up two flights of stairs and down a long corridor with closed doors on either side. Seren must have run blindly until she'd found an unlocked door, but I was glad she'd known better than to try and take the intersector somewhere. I wasn't certain if Minerva's intersector functioned like the one in Caz's office, allowing untraceable entry into Aeles, but my siblings needed to remain inside Sea'Brik where they were safe. While I didn't want to frighten them further, it was probably wise to ask my mother for help in impressing the seriousness of our situation upon them.

The glowing lights stopped before a partially closed door. Stepping into the room, it seemed not only were the walls made of glass but the ceiling was, too, offering what I imagined would be a breathtaking view of the night sky. Different sizes and styles of telescopes were situated around the room, and instruments used for tracking the courses of stars and planets were neatly arranged on a table, reminding me of the items we'd had in the Astronomy Tower in Velaire. Tempted as I was to run my fingers over the sleek metal tools, that wasn't why I'd come upstairs.

My sister was standing in front of a window, watching lightning streak across the sky as waves rose and fell below.

"Seren?" I said quietly, not wanting to startle her. "What's wrong? Why did you leave like that?"

Seren turned to face me, and I could tell by her red-rimmed eyes she'd been crying. She wasn't crying now, though, and the look on her face made my heart stutter. I couldn't remember the last time I'd seen her so angry.

"I can't believe you kept all that from me!" she cried. "We used to tell each other everything, even things we didn't tell Mother and Father. And now you tell me life-changing news along with Daevals I just met! You should have told me sooner."

"It wasn't exactly easy," I tried to explain, "figuring out how to tell family who've know me my entire life things that sound too outrageous to be true."

"But I've always believed you," protested Seren. "You didn't trust I could handle the information."

"I didn't want any of you to deal with something that wasn't your burden to carry," I corrected her. "I was trying to protect you while I figured out the truth about Father and Daevals and myself." I stepped towards her, but she stiffened and crossed her arms over her chest, her amethyst eyes narrowing. "I'm sorry I didn't tell you about everything sooner. But now that everyone knows the truth, we can all work together to bring peace between Astrals and Daevals again."

"Of course you'd say that!" shouted Seren. "You've always gotten what you've wanted, and you expect the rest of us to just stand by and be happy while you have everything handed to you on a golden platter!"

"Nothing has been handed to me on a golden platter," I assured her, surprised she could think such a thing but happy to clear up at least one misconception. "I've lost and suffered and been broken in so many ways. I—"

"Poor Kyra." Seren's voice dripped with false pity. "It's not enough you're the most gifted healer in the history of the realm or that you're a Recovrancer, wielding a power Aeles hasn't seen in centuries. On top of that, you were the first queen of Aeles-Nocens, you performed an ancient spell to bind yourself to your husband, and now you're in love with someone I don't even know and the two of you are going to reunite the realms." She shook her head, her face flushed. "It's not fair. You got everything, and I got nothing."

"That's not true. You're brilliant—especially at math—and you make everyone in the family laugh. You bring us together. You notice everything, you're a wonderful listener, and you're beautiful. You—"

"I've always been in your shadow," Seren interrupted. "Every teacher I've ever had started class by saying what high expectations they had for me, given whose sister I was. Astrals—and now apparently Daevals—are only nice to me because they like you."

"That's not true," I said, but Seren barely paused for breath.

"You're so perfect, you can't even see it!" she wailed. "I'll never do anything as important as the things you've done. And now you're going to be the savior of the realm, and everyone will hug me and tell me how lucky I am to be your sister." Her eyes flashed. "I'm tired of constantly being compared to you and knowing I'll always fall short. Even Father was disappointed I wasn't more like you."

"That's ridiculous! Father loved each of us for who we are.

He never compared us to one another or thought anyone was better than the others."

"Believe what you want," spat Seren. "You'll never understand. Anything I do is immediately compared to how you would have done it, and you always would have done it better. Just once, I want to do something without anyone mentioning *you*!"

"Seren, I had no idea this was happening." I hoped my efforts to stay calm might exert a similar effect on my sister. "It's clear you've been feeling like this for a while. Why didn't you say anything?"

"Maybe I just wasn't sure how to tell family who've known me my entire life things that sound too outrageous to be true," she said heatedly, using my own words against me. "You wouldn't have cared anyway."

"Of course I would have!" I hadn't meant to raise my voice, but I couldn't keep my frustration in check any longer. "I love you. Whatever else happens, we're family, and I only want the best for you. I know you're hurt I didn't tell you the truth about things sooner, and I'm sorry for that. But you can't be upset with me over feelings I didn't even know you had until this very minute."

"Apparently we weren't as close as we thought." She tossed her head. "Good to know."

"Seren . . ." I reached for her, but she took a step back. "I'm not perfect," I said, fighting to keep my voice level. "I've made mistakes and second-guessed so many decisions, and I've tried to navigate things I didn't even know were possible. All I want is to be with those I love and work as Aeles's *Princeps Shaman*, but I can't do that because I'm responsible for the realms and all the Astrals and Daevals who live there. I'm doing my best, even though it might not be enough, and I wish you could see that instead of thinking I have it so easy."

Seren turned her back to me. "Just because the realms need you doesn't mean I do. Someday I'm going to do something so important, everyone will be saying how lucky *you* are to be *my* sister."

Her words stung with the sharpness of a paper cut, but I forced myself to swallow the reply that sprang to my lips. Saying cruel things just to hurt my sister's feelings wouldn't help the situation. I'd never suspected she resented me so much. I hated hearing she'd ever felt compared to me or pressured to live up to anything I did, but at the end of the day, we were sisters—we'd always supported one another and we always would.

"I already know I'm lucky to be your sister," I said, wishing my gaze could soften the angry tightness in Seren's shoulders. "It's not a competition between us, and anyone who ever made you feel that way was wrong. I'm going to LeBehr's so she can locate the Chronicles, but we can talk more when I come back, if you like."

"Go get your precious book that probably says what a fantastic queen you were and how everyone who knew you loved you," sulked Seren without turning around.

Fire stirred in my belly. "Clearly not everyone who knew me as Kareth loved me or the realms would still be united!" I said hotly before spinning around and striding out of the room, my breath coming faster than usual.

Seren could feel however she liked, but there was no reason for her to take out her feelings on me. It was so easy for her—and my mother—to say I should have told them the truth sooner, but at least part of my hesitation had been fearing what might happen to my family if someone in Aeles discovered I was a Recovrancer or involved in a relationship with a Daeval. Yes, I could have done things differently, but I'd made the best choices I could at the time. At some point, those who weren't happy with my decisions needed to try and see things from my perspective, just as I was working to understand things from their point of view.

Closing the door behind me, I pressed my hands against my hot cheeks. I hated fighting with my family, especially now when I needed their support more than ever. Hopefully giving Seren some space would allow her to calm down and realize she hadn't been accurate in all her assessments.

Aurelius appeared beside me, rubbing his head against my knee, and I ran a hand over his back before touching my fingertips to the gold bracelet.

Are things alright with your sister? Sebastian asked.

No, but they also can't be fixed right now, so I'd rather go to LeBehr's and focus on something else. It's a lot for Seren to process, but she'll come around.

At least, I hoped she would. There was already a chance reuniting the realms would mean the end of the bond I had with Sebastian, forcing me to find a way to connect our shades again. Surely it wouldn't also cost me my relationship with my sister . . . would it?

6

SEBASTIAN

The crooked sign hanging outside LeBehr's bookstore creaked as it swung gently back and forth. The late afternoon sun coated the squat wood and plaster building in a golden light that made it appear enchanted, like a spelled cottage from the stories my mother had read to me as a child. Lamps shone invitingly through the grime-edged windows, and I dipped my head respectfully towards Mischief, sprawled on her side in the open doorway, before stepping carefully over the cat.

LeBehr's Cypher responded with an unhappy yowl, which was a good sign, as it was always better for a cat to be annoyed with you than to ignore you. She offered Kyra the same disgruntled welcome, but when the black cat spotted Aurelius, her ears perked up and she twitched the tip of her tail. The two must have engaged in a silent conversation because Aurelius rolled his eyes and shook his head, causing his furry jowls to sway. As Mischief let out a raspy chuckle, I couldn't help feeling like the creatures were discussing Kyra and me—or possibly just me—and not in a positive way.

You have learned an important lesson, said Batty from his position on my shoulder. *Had you taken me with you more places, watching two Cyphers having a discussion would not be such an unfamiliar experience for you.*

I exhaled my annoyance as the bat added, *Most likely they are complaining about the change in their schedule. Mischief takes a nap after lunch, and based on Aelian time, Aurelius should be asleep right now, so they are not pleased we have interrupted their routines.*

LeBehr hurried out from behind the counter, hugging Kyra and grinning at me as she adjusted her oversized chartreuse shawl, the color making her short white hair look bright as fresh snow. While LeBehr knew the truth about who Kyra and I had been in our shared past, she wasn't aware of all that had happened in Rynstyn, and Kyra quickly caught her up. I still hated to think of Kyra being held captive in the experimentation center, and I couldn't wait to run Rhannu through Tallus's chest and watch the light leave his eyes as he took his last, labored breath.

"All the more reason to locate the Chronicles!" LeBehr exclaimed when Kyra had finished, darting across the room and forcing Mischief to dematerialize as she closed the door. LeBehr grunted as she struggled to fasten the rusty latch, even though the powerful spells she kept applied to the building would prevent an intruder far better than the half-functioning lock. Whirling around, the bookseller gestured for us to follow her to the back of the shop, leading us between teetering stacks of books, which somehow stayed upright, until we reached a storage room I'd never been in before.

A table was situated in the middle of the room, the only items on it a blank piece of cream-colored paper and a small vial filled with a pulsing blue liquid.

Aurelius rose onto his hind legs, resting his oversized paws on the edge of the table, and Mischief arranged herself on top of a large wooden crate. Batty hopped down from my shoulder, landing on the table with a grunt and just missing the glass vial. Reaching into a wing pocket, he withdrew the page he'd managed to remove from the Chronicles before it had been taken from him hundreds of years ago. Setting it down, he grinned hopefully at Kyra. The bat was never one to waste energy flying when he might be transported by other means, and she quickly picked him up and placed him on her shoulder.

"Now," said LeBehr, "I'll drink the locating potion while holding the page from your book, and a map will be created, which will appear on this parchment." She tapped the blank paper.

From the corner of my eye, I saw Kyra grip the hem of her tunic, excitement and a slight current of apprehension running through her. Reaching out, I took her hand, and she interlaced her fingers gratefully through mine. While I wasn't naturally given to unnecessary physical contact, I was also pleased I was learning—or relearning—ways to take care of the woman I loved, which made me feel unexpectedly proud.

LeBehr tipped the vial into her mouth and swallowed the blue liquid in one smooth gulp. She then picked up the page from the Chronicles, holding it with both hands as she closed her eyes. A white light began to shine upwards from the blank paper, and Kyra squeezed my hand.

The light quickly spread to cover the entire piece of paper. There was a loud pop, and then the light disappeared, leaving the paper covered in a veritable sea of stars, silver shards glistening against a black night sky. Kyra and I stepped closer for a better view just as the stars began to rotate, as if we were moving through them. Even though we were standing still, for a brief instant, I had the sensation of flying, as if I were really streaking past comets, nebulas, and glowing constellations.

The stars soon turned into an ocean, and I swore I felt a spray of saltwater against my face just before the ocean gave way to land. Small buildings were grouped under the names of towns, and clusters of trees marked various forests. The word "Vartox" scrolled by in heavy cursive letters before the map shifted, taking us south. We sped over the territory of Doldarian, where my cave was located, continuing on a straight course until the names of oases began to appear, some of which I recognized from completing contracts in the unforgiving desert land of Jaasfar. A town came into view, but rather than seeing it from overhead, we dropped down into the middle of it. Stucco buildings with rounded archways sported red or blue doors, the bright colors startling against the otherwise bland brown and white backdrop.

A street wound crookedly through the buildings. We sped along it until we left the town behind, arriving at a sprawling complex surrounded by dark red sand as far as the eye could see. The complex resembled a fortress more than a house, although fountains bubbled in the courtyard, and thick rugs created a carpeted path across flat, oversized stones. Coordinates appeared on the parchment in dark ink. I quickly memorized them, even though they didn't appear to be in danger of fading.

LeBehr swayed where she stood, and Kyra moved to steady her until she'd regained her composure. Handing the page from the Chronicles back to Batty, LeBehr peered eagerly at the map.

"Well, thank goodness the book is in Nocens!" She ran a hand across her forehead as if wiping away invisible sweat. "That should make it easier to retrieve than if it were in Aeles."

"Do either of you know what that building is?" asked Kyra. "It looks like a military outpost."

I wasn't aware of Nocenian military outposts in that part of Jaasfar, but that didn't mean there weren't any. Pulling out my peerin, I spoke the coordinates into the chormorite lens. Thanks to my work with the Dekarais, I had access to government data that would tell me if the coordinates belonged to a business or private residence, which would inform the plan we made to recover our book.

Text quickly appeared on the lens, and I read it out loud: "Private residence of Raks and Win'Din Nemoya."

My words were followed by silence. LeBehr ran a hand through her short hair, ruffling the thick strands as was customary for her when she was thinking, and Batty scratched the golden mantle of fur around his neck before gazing at his feet. Mischief shook her head as if we'd just received an ominous foretelling, and Kyra glanced around, assessing our reactions. "Is that a problem?" she finally asked.

I made a face. "The Nemoyas are the Dekarais' biggest rivals. The families despise one another." I'd never done any work for the Nemoyas for that very reason, as there was no question my loyalty lay with Dunston and his family.

"They used to order from my shop all the time," said LeBehr, "but I never sensed a true love of books from them. They're collectors, and they like to have things precisely so others can't." She frowned, clearly disapproving of such behavior. "Let's just say what I told them was available didn't always match what was on my shelves. Of course, that could be why they rarely order from me anymore."

"I wonder how they came to have the Chronicles." Kyra studied the map. "LeBehr, can you tell where the book is in their house? Is it out on a shelf or is it locked away somewhere?"

LeBehr squinted before shaking her head. "Unfortunately, the map won't reveal that level of detail until I'm physically closer to the book. Once I'm inside the house, though, I can tell you exactly where it's located, whether it's packed away in a trunk, sitting on a nightstand, or hidden beneath a floorboard."

"That's wonderful!" said Kyra.

It was wonderful, aside from one small detail. "That means we need to get into the Nemoyas' house," I pointed out. The Nemoyas weren't known for extensive security, but given what I'd heard about their home itself, they didn't need it. Getting in and out wouldn't be easy and might not be possible, even with my burglary skills.

"The Nemoyas throw almost as many parties as the Dekarais," offered LeBehr. "Perhaps we can finagle an invitation to one."

I'd rather take my chances breaking and entering than depending on someone else to get me into a party where I'd be forced to utilize my underdeveloped social skills, but it was always wise to have a backup plan—even one I doubted we'd use.

"We'll speak with Rennej and Minerva," I said, knowing they kept close tabs on their rivals' social schedules. "We can figure out our options from there."

"Sounds good to me," nodded LeBehr. "I'm going to go home and rest—that potion always takes a lot out of me—but let me know once you've found a way in." Her mismatched green and yellow eyes sparkled. "Something tells me this will be the finest book rescue of my illustrious career!"

I certainly hoped so. The future of the realms depended on it.

7

SEBASTIAN

Kyra and I returned to Sea'Brik just in time to see Minerva press a hand against a wall. A chime sounded. When it had fallen silent, Minerva said, "Dinner will be served in the Oyster Hall." She'd spoken at a normal volume, but I heard doors opening and closing as folks responded to her announcement. Being able to transmit her words to specific locations was certainly an effective way of communicating across such a large house, although I didn't like the idea of being in my room and unexpectedly hearing a voice. I hadn't spent as much time around Minerva as the rest of her family, since she preferred her privacy and running the business from behind the scenes. But based on the little I knew, I suspected she valued efficiency over any preferences her guests might have.

"If you'll excuse us," said Aurelius, "Bartholomew and I have some research to do." I glanced down at him in surprise, and he shrugged a black-spotted shoulder. "We need to know more about the spell Tallus cast on himself," he said, as if it weren't unprecedented for him to voluntarily spend time with my Cypher, when most days he barely managed to tolerate the bat.

"I'd love to know more about how he's keeping his past life memories intact," Kyra agreed. "Shades aren't supposed to remember every detail from every life they've lived, but he obviously found a way around that." Either she wasn't surprised to see her lynx choosing to work with Batty or she was simply better at hiding it. "Where do you plan to start?"

Batty proudly patted one wing with the other. "While Tallus was focused on forcing Sebastian to face his fears at the experimentation center, I managed to grab a few hairs from his head. The hairs will contain traces of any spells he cast on himself, which means when we place them in the right potion, we can uncover the spell he cast to preserve his memories. Mischief is going to meet us back at the bookstore to help us find the recipe for such a potion after LeBehr is settled."

The bat was still on Kyra's shoulder, and I scowled at him. "Why didn't you tell me you might have a way to uncover that spell sooner?"

"Because you already have enough to deal with, and you don't need to do everything yourself," he replied, twitching his oblong black ears. "This is a way I can help you."

While it was true the bat was being helpful, he also knew far more than he let on, parceling out the truth as it suited his needs —which, I realized with a start, was also something *I* did. I'd spent so many years distancing myself from my Cypher and not wanting anything to do with him that it came as no small shock to see we were actually quite similar in certain areas.

Batty chuckled, following along with my thoughts, but thankfully he refrained from saying more.

"Well, may the Fates and the Gifters favor you both," Kyra said to the Cyphers.

Batty kissed her cheek, then waved a wing at me before he and Aurelius dematerialized together, truly a sight I'd never imagined seeing.

Blinking white lights appeared on the floor, guiding Kyra and me to a large formal dining room with walls covered in yards of grey satin. The Oyster Hall was aptly named: the high-backed chairs situated around the long table were covered in thick brocade the color of charcoal, and two silver chandeliers bathed the room in a soft light made brighter by the numerous platinum candelabras positioned across the table. The table itself was truly a sight to behold, created by fitting different-sized pieces of grey and white driftwood together. I couldn't imagine how long acquiring the materials must have taken, but the Dekarais were nothing if not patient when it suited them.

Folks began to file in. Seren purposefully avoided looking at Kyra, which I knew upset her. Minerva slid into the chair at the head of the table and gestured to her right.

"This seat is empty, Seren," she said. While Seren momentarily appeared stunned to have been addressed by the Dekarai matriarch, she nevertheless made her way to the chair and sat down. Kyra's family and the rest of the Dekarais also claimed seats, although Devlin was noticeably absent, likely either sleeping or off searching for more excitement than could be found at Sea'Brik.

Once everyone was seated, Kyra rested her hands against the edge of the table.

"LeBehr found the Chronicles," she said. "The book is in Jaasfar, thank the Gifters, because I can't imagine trying to get back into Aeles right now, *but* it's in a house that belongs to . . ." She hesitated and turned to me.

"Raks and Win'Din Nemoya," I said, causing a chorus of groans to fill the room.

Concern swept over Kyra's face. "Are they really that terrible?"

"They're the worst!" exclaimed Dunston, slamming his wine goblet down and causing Minerva to frown over his treatment of her table. "They're always nipping at our heels and trying to horn in on our business!"

"They're completely disreputable!" agreed Caz, tearing a bread roll in half. "There's nothing they won't do to make a profit. No standards, no rules." He scowled as he grabbed a knife and slapped butter onto one half of the roll before taking a large bite.

Minerva brushed back a section of grey hair that had fallen across her forehead. "They're the worst sort of Daevals—new money." She made a face as if the scent of new money was particularly foul. "Their fortune buys them everything except class."

While I unquestionably supported the Dekarais on this issue, I did think it was interesting how differently they saw themselves from the Nemoyas. Technically, it was Rennej who came from old Nocenian money. Dunston had married into it, and while he and his siblings had made fast work of expanding Rennej's wealth, some might consider marrying into a fortune a particular type of new money. I would never say such a thing, though, and instead focused on my roasted potatoes.

"How did they make their money?" asked Kyra.

"Horse racing," replied Dunston. "They've got quite a stable, built from capturing those wild horses in the desert and breeding them for racing stock."

"That's barbaric!" Kyra's eyes flashed. "We learned about that in school. Racing destroys horses. It's terrible for their bodies, and once the animals are past their prime, they're discarded or slaughtered."

While I knew the Dekarais didn't feel strongly one way or the other about horse racing, I could tell they enjoyed seeing Kyra so angry at the Nemoyas.

"They also have unregulated gambling over the horse races," added Caz, clearly trying to add fuel to Kyra's fire, even though I knew she only cared about the animals. "The government doesn't like it, but the Nemoyas are smart enough to make frequent political donations, which keeps them out of official trouble."

After we reunite the realms, we're outlawing animals being forced to perform or compete. Kyra's voice was tight in my head. *They'll never be made to do anything for someone's entertainment again.*

I didn't support horse racing, either, as I'd attended a few races to gather information or perform surveillance on targets, and I'd seen how cruelly the animals were treated. At the same time, Kyra and I couldn't simply force our personal beliefs on the realms—that would make us monarchs or even dictators. But we could discuss our plans for improving animal welfare later.

Eslee sprinkled brown sugar over the cooked carrots on her plate. "The Nemoyas won't buy anything from my gallery, so they clearly have no taste in art. No taste in clothes, either—every time I see them, they're wearing every gem they own. They're even more ostentatious than Devlin!"

"Who's more ostentatious than me?" Devlin sauntered into the room, a wide grin on his stubble-covered face.

"The Nemoyas," Dunston practically hissed before taking a long drink of wine.

Kyra told Devlin what we'd learned from LeBehr, and he took a seat next to Seren, who promptly turned a furious shade of red and kept her gaze fixed on the food in front of her.

"Of all the places for the book to be," lamented Caz. "I mean, yes, it's certainly better than if it were in a government building in Aeles, but getting it won't be easy. In fact, I'm not certain how we're going to pull this off."

"The Nemoyas are having an auction tomorrow night," volunteered Devlin. "We could attend. That would at least get us into their house."

"Their auctions are invitation only," Minerva pointed out. "I know because *my* auctions are invitation only, and when I refused to invite Win'Din, she started hosting her own knock-offs and never once invited me." She made an injured noise, although I couldn't tell whether she was upset over Win'Din copying her or not inviting her to an event she'd never attend in the first place.

"I can get us an invitation," Devlin assured the table.

"How?" demanded Dunston. "I'm not certain even Caz could call in enough favors to warrant an invitation."

Caz frowned but nevertheless nodded his agreement. One of the first things I'd come to appreciate about him was his ability to provide an honest assessment of how much power he wielded in a given situation; he didn't minimize what he was capable of, but he also didn't overestimate his connections or leverage. I'd learned to take him at his word when he said he could or couldn't achieve a particular outcome.

Devlin looked around, clearly enjoying being the center of attention. "Wait, does this mean I'm the only one capable of getting us something we need? I'm able to do something no one else in this family can?"

"So it would seem," replied Minerva in a clipped voice as Eslee rolled her eyes.

Dunston threw his hands into the air. "Burning realm fires, Devlin, just tell us how you plan to get an invitation to the auction!"

"Let's just say I don't find Win'Din as unbearable as the rest of you," smirked Devlin. "She and I are *old* friends."

Groans and other sounds of disapproval rose from the Dekarais. I certainly didn't want to dwell on such an ill-conceived dalliance, but at the same time, I also couldn't say I was surprised.

Kyra politely ignored the Dekarais' response to Devlin's revelation. "Could you reach out to Win'Din and see about getting us an invitation?"

"Of course!" Devlin replied breezily, as if we were discussing something as inconsequential as getting tickets to the theater. "How many should I tell her to expect?"

"I will not be going," sneered Minerva.

"Rennej and I wouldn't be welcome," said Dunston. "Definitely not Caz."

Caz laughed under his breath, no doubt picturing what a scene his presence would create.

"I wouldn't be welcome, either, but I'm available if you need me," volunteered Eslee. "I never imagined saying this, but it's probably better if Devlin is the only Dekarai there."

Devlin looked from Kyra to me, a wide grin on his face. While my hand was steady as I placed my napkin beside my plate, my mind was racing. I didn't like this. Using social connections was far too risky when it came to something as important as the Chronicles, especially when it meant trusting Devlin, of *all* Daevals. I was far more confident in my own skills, whether that involved covertly breaking in and stealing the book or confronting the Nemoyas directly and using whatever threats or force were necessary to ensure they gave me what was rightfully mine.

At the same time, I was fully aware of how much effort the Dekarais were expending to help me and Kyra, leading me to choose my words with care. "I'm not certain attending the auction is the best course of action. It might be better if I retrieve the Chronicles myself."

Kyra swiveled in her chair to face me. "There's no need for you to do something dangerous when Devlin can easily get us an invitation."

She switched to speaking directly into my mind. *I thought you weren't going to be involved in things like burglaries and interrogations and harming others any more. You told me you were open to changing careers.*

I am open, but a career change might have to wait until after we get the Chronicles back, I replied, causing her frown to deepen even though she didn't immediately disagree.

"The Nemoyas' house is practically a fortress," said Devlin. "It's in the middle of the desert, and security can see anyone coming for miles away. There are anti-portal wards in place, and the inside is practically a maze." He grinned and offered a carefree shrug. "But if you want to try your luck sneaking in, I'll tell you everything I know. Thank the Fates I'm here to share such important information."

Annoyance stirred in my chest. "You'd be surprised what I already know about the Nemoyas' house," I said, even though my knowledge had been gathered from bits and pieces of gossip over time and not from personally visiting the house, as Devlin obviously had. "I agree breaking in will be challenging, but I'll just need to plan things carefully."

"It's too dangerous," Kyra insisted. "If you're caught and the Nemoyas are truly as awful as everyone says, who knows what they might do to you? Plus, they'd probably move the Chronicles, and then LeBehr will have to brew another locating potion and that could take weeks."

I was about to tell Kyra that even if the Nemoyas captured and tortured me, I would never reveal I was searching for the Chronicles when Dunston spoke. "Kyra makes some good points, Sebastian. I think we should give Devlin a chance to get an invitation."

"You do?" Devlin spoke before I could, his butterscotch eyes wide as he gazed at his father.

"I do," replied Dunston. "If you can get an invitation to the auction, great. If not"—his expression hardened, as if he were already imagining Devlin failing, and the change in his demeanor caused Devlin's throat to bob—"then we go with Sebastian's plan of acquiring the book by any means necessary."

I still didn't like the idea of pinning our hopes on Devlin, but aside from making me uncomfortable, there was no other reason not to at least let him try. If, or more likely, *when* he failed, he could tell me everything he knew about the Nemoyas' house in detail, and I'd devise a plan from there.

"I'm fine with that," I conceded.

"Gee, thanks for the vote of confidence, you two." Devlin crossed his arms. "So, what's the final number I should tell Win'Din to expect?"

"Three," said Kyra. "You, me, and Sebastian."

I shifted in my chair. Kyra wasn't going to like what I was about to say, but we had to be strategic.

"There's a good chance you'll be recognized at the auction," I said slowly. "I don't think that's a risk we can afford to take."

Kyra's eyes snapped with barely contained anger as she realized where I was headed, and while I hated knowing I was upsetting her, I forced myself to continue.

"I think it would be better if I went with Devlin and LeBehr joined us."

"But I wrote the Chronicles!" she protested. "I have as much right to be part of getting that book back as you do."

"Of course you do," I assured her. "If anything, you have more right. But *how* we get the book back doesn't matter as much as getting it back. If you attend the auction, it'll raise questions and draw attention we don't want. I wouldn't put it past the Nemoyas to leak information about you being there to the Aelian government if they thought they could profit from such a disclosure."

"That's exactly the sort of thing they'd do." Dunston jabbed a finger into the air as Caz and Minerva voiced their agreement.

The Dekarais' reaction made Kyra hesitate.

"It makes sense Devlin would bring a bookseller to an auction," I added. "No one would believe he'd be buying a rare book for himself, but LeBehr can say it's for someone he's trying to impress."

"That's completely believable," Eslee nodded.

Kyra cocked her head to one side. "What reason will you give for being there?"

"Private security. No matter how 'friendly' Devlin and Win'Din are, no one will be surprised to see him with a security detail, given the history between the families."

Kyra looked down at her plate, a storm of emotions crossing her face. Through our connection, I felt her disappointment and anger as she silently railed at the unfairness of the situation. Slowly, however, her frustration faded. Even though traces of sadness lingered in her eyes, I could tell she'd accepted the situation as best she could.

"You're right," she agreed. "I don't like it because I want to be there, but we don't want to do anything that might make its way to Tallus. Getting the book back is all that matters."

"I'll reach out to LeBehr after dinner," I said, although I'd bet a small fortune the bookseller would be overjoyed to participate. "You know if anyone cares about the Chronicles almost as much as you and I do, it's her."

Kyra's face brightened, making me glad of my words. "That's true."

"What's your plan if the book isn't part of the auction?" asked Minerva.

"Thanks to LeBehr, we'll know where the book is. Since I'll already be in the house, I'll steal it," I replied.

Devlin set his fork down so hard, it clanged against his plate. "If something is stolen after I was in the Nemoyas' house, they'll assume I had something to do with it!" he objected. "I'll never be invited back."

I gave him a look. "Once we reunite the realms, it'll be common knowledge Kyra and I wrote the Chronicles and are its rightful owners. No one is going to care how we recovered it. They'll have too many other things to think about."

Devlin stroked the gold hoop in his nose. "I suppose that's true. Let's just hope the book is up for auction."

"Let's just hope you can get an invitation to the auction," I said, fixing him with a pointed look.

Thankfully, dinner progressed without any more uncomfortable conversations, and I could feel recent events starting to catch up with me. I hadn't slept since long before rescuing Kyra from the experimentation facility, and then we'd retrieved her family, come to Sea'Brik, and visited LeBehr. As a rule, I didn't require much rest, but if I was tired, Kyra had to be nearly asleep on her feet.

Pushing back her chair, Kyra rose and offered the table an apologetic smile. "I'm sorry to eat and run, but I'm exhausted. If you'll excuse me, I'm going to turn in early."

I rose, too, and said my goodnights before following Kyra out of the room. As we headed towards the sweeping staircase, the bracelet on my wrist vibrated, and I touched it, surprised to hear Kyra's voice in my head when she was walking right next to me.

I know we agreed to talk about things, even when it's awkward, she said, *so . . . do you want to sleep in the same bed tonight?*

I stopped and looked at her. Although redness tinted her cheeks, her gaze was hopeful.

Of course, I replied. *Why wouldn't we?*

I don't know, I just . . . well, I do know . . . I've never shared a bed with someone while my family was in the same house. But I want to. She reached out and took my hand, as if gathering strength from touching me, which I quite liked. *We're a couple, and everyone knows it, and whatever they think about what we do together, it doesn't matter.*

It didn't make sense to me, but I suspected Astrals had different views about things like sharing beds prior to being married.

I want to sleep in the same bed with you, I said, *but if it makes you uncomfortable with your family here, we don't have to.*

Kyra leaned over and rested the side of her head against my shoulder. *Thank you for always working so hard to take care of me. Let me just grab a few things, and I'll meet you in your room. If anyone knocks on my door and I don't answer, well, they can have the house find me or wait until morning.*

This seemed like a bigger deal to Kyra than I'd expected, but I settled for kissing her forehead and heading to my room. Designated the Kelp Room by a sign on the door, the bedroom was nearly as large as the main living space in my cave and decorated in shades of green and silver. One entire wall was fitted with metal pieces shaped like stalks of kelp. Even though I knew the fluttering leaves were the result of a spell, the effect was still soothing, making it feel like you were underwater watching the long plants sway in the ocean current. To my surprise, Aurelius was curled up on the dark green sofa, and Batty was leaning against him, the back of his head propped against the lynx's leg. The bat's wings were folded over his belly, and he let out a snore that should have been far too loud to come from such a small creature.

Pulling out my peerin, I contacted LeBehr, who was ecstatic about attending the Nemoyas' auction. She rarely left her bookstore, so the fact that she would close it to help us spoke of how seriously she took recovering the Chronicles.

Tomorrow, I'd go to my cave and retrieve my own clothes and toiletries, but tonight I appreciated the well-stocked dresser full of sleeping clothes, as well as tunics, breeches, undergarments, socks, and a host of other items. They were fancier than the clothes I usually wore, which were about comfort and not getting in my way when I was working, but these would be fine for now. I had just finished changing when I heard a soft knock at my door.

It's open, I said to Kyra through our connection. Even though her coming to sleep in my room wasn't a surprise, my heartbeat sped up anyway, darting right past my attempts to control it.

8

SEBASTIAN

Sharing a bed with someone was still new enough that it felt like a big deal, even though it was also familiar, as Kyra and I had done it every night for most of our lives as Kareth and Schatten. I ran a hand through my hair, trying to appear nonchalant as Kyra slipped inside, the smile on her face making her look like she couldn't quite believe she was getting away with something but was nonetheless pleased about her success. She was wearing a long-sleeved sleeping shirt and loose pants she'd no doubt found in her room, and for a brief moment, I imagined the two of us getting into bed wearing less clothing, or perhaps no clothing at all.

The fire stirred beneath my skin, enjoying the direction of my thoughts, but before I contemplated being completely unclothed in front of Kyra, I first needed to be comfortable taking my shirt off around her. I didn't want the unsightly scars on my back and chest to upset her or make her feel less attracted to me, even though I sometimes still found it hard to believe she was attracted to me in the first place. While I wanted to work on being more comfortable in my own skin, I was also exhausted, which was never a good time to try something new, so I ultimately kept my tunic where it was. Once Tallus was defeated and the realms were reunited, Kyra and I could devote endless amounts of time to becoming comfortable around each other in various states of undress.

Still, there was no denying it was getting increasingly harder to put aside what I *wanted* to do in favor of what I *needed* to do.

Kyra paused at the sight of Batty and Aurelius sleeping against one another on the sofa, happiness lighting up her face and making me glad my Cypher had played a role in giving her a reason to smile. Perhaps I'd pick him up some of the Dal Marian caramels he was so obsessed with, although I didn't know how I would surprise him, since as my Cypher, he was aware of my every thought. Tiptoeing past the animals, Kyra moved to the far side of the bed and pulled back the blanket. Running a hand over the bedding, she made a face.

"These sheets aren't nearly as nice as yours," she noted as she crawled between them. "You've spoiled me."

"I want to go to the cave tomorrow and get some things, so we can bring some of my sheets back with us," I said, wrapping an arm around her and pulling her close. As the back of my head hit the pillow, I blinked at the ceiling, missing the familiar brown and tan stone and feeling out of place sleeping in an actual room. As Kyra snuggled against me, she let out a deep sigh, allowing the enormity of our situation to surface.

"I still can't believe everything that's happened since I went to Rynstyn." Her voice was soft. "Thank you for arranging our stay with the Dekarais. I couldn't function if my family wasn't safe."

I squeezed the arm wrapped around her. "There's nothing I wouldn't do for you."

"I know," she returned the hug, "and I feel the same way. I haven't forgotten about recovering your mother."

"She's not going anywhere, and it'll be safer to bring her back after Tallus has been dealt with and the realms are reunited." Even though that was the best course of action, I couldn't stop the ache that flared in my chest, the part of me that was desperate to see my mother alive again disliking any delay.

Kyra nodded, her body tensing against mine, drawing my attention to whatever she was about to say. "Tomorrow I'm going to ask Laycus what reuniting the realms means for our bond."

Fire surged through my veins, and Kyra lifted her head from my chest.

"Reuniting Aeles and Nocens can't really mean the end of us finding one another in future life cycles, can it?" she asked.

The small note of fear I heard in her voice was more than a little unsettling, but I forced the feeling down, wanting to be strong for her. "You didn't bind us together *until* the realms were reunited," I pointed out. "You bound us together so we would find one another and reunite the realms." It was a slight difference, but I knew from years of contracts how important even a single word could be.

Kyra gazed down at me, her long black hair framing her face. "If reuniting the realms means the end of us being able to find one another again, there's a part of me that doesn't want to do it. And that goes against my desire to do what's right for everyone else who lives here." Her mouth turned down. "I knew doing the right thing would be hard, but I didn't expect it to impact *us* so much, which in hindsight seems incredibly naïve of me." Sorrow filled her eyes and threatened to spread across her face as she clasped one of my hands. "There's a chance who I am and what I'm going to do will cost me my relationship with my sister. There's a chance it will cost me my bond with you. Those weren't sacrifices I was expecting to make." She swallowed. "And I'm not certain they're sacrifices I want to make. It also makes me wonder what other things we're going to be asked to give up that I failed to anticipate."

As someone who worked incredibly hard to anticipate everything, good or bad, I also hated not knowing what our actions might bring about even as I suspected Kyra was right to be worried.

"You know how I feel," I said. "I don't want to sacrifice my connection with you for some nebulous greater good. I only care about you and being with you."

Kyra smiled. "Sometimes I like how single-minded you are about us."

Unfortunately, being me, I couldn't help but consider all the facts as we knew them. "That being said, the realms are growing more unstable every day they're apart," I reminded her. "If we avoid reuniting them because of how it will affect the two of us, at some point there won't be a realm for us to return to."

"That's true." Kyra sighed. "It's really not even a question. We have to reunite the realms. If it means the end of the bond I created between us, I'll create another." Determination filled her blue eyes. "I bound our shades together once; if I need to, I'll do it again. We've overcome death and outlasted time, and I'll never live another life without you."

I reached up and tucked her hair behind her ear, grateful for the ferocity I felt pulsing through her. "As long as the realms continue to exist, we can figure everything out," I said. "Our bond, your relationship with your sister, and anything else that comes our way."

Kyra kissed me before returning her head to my chest. As I did my best to put all thoughts of reuniting the realms from my mind, I was struck by a realization. It was like I'd been staring closely at individual puzzle pieces, unable to make anything out until I'd taken a step back, at which point the bigger picture had suddenly become clearer. I shook Kyra's shoulder, prompting her to lift her head again.

"That's why Tallus let you go. He needs us to reunite the realms."

"What?" Kyra sat up straighter, doing her best to follow along.

I pushed myself into a sitting position. "Tallus can't continue his campaign against Daevals if the realms cease to exist," I explained. "His own safety—not to mention his plan to get rid of Daevals—depends on the realms continuing to function. He's retained all his past life memories. Even if he doesn't know he caused the instability by dividing the realms, he has to know so many natural disasters aren't normal."

Kyra cringed, and I could tell she was forcing herself to face whatever painful truth she'd just recalled. "I might have mentioned that to him in Rynstyn," she said, keeping her eyes on the blanket. "I don't remember my exact words, but after he revealed himself, I think I yelled something along the lines of how his actions were the reason the realms had become unstable."

Rather than being a cause for concern, Kyra's words only made me more certain. "The last thing Tallus said before I left Rynstyn was that he knows what you and I are planning to do." I touched Kyra's hand, prompting her to look at me. "You've fought with him for centuries across different life cycles . . . it's not as if our wanting to find one another and reunite the realms has ever been a secret."

"That's true," she admitted.

I gazed at the wall behind her, letting my thoughts fall into place. "I think he finally realized his plan of having two separate realms won't work. Part of that is because dividing Aeles-Nocens made the realms unstable, but even if they could continue to function separately, Tallus has proven he can't be happy in a world where Daevals exist. He wants silver blood wiped from existence. At Dunston's party, Camus said he's been worried about a potential Astral invasion. It would certainly be easier for Tallus to launch an attack with the realms united. Right now his only way into Nocens is through intersectors, which can be shut down, or portals, and portal-making is one of the rarest abilities there is. Reuniting the realms is the best way for him to get everything he wants."

Kyra ran a hand over her face. "Do you think he knows we need the Chronicles to reunite the realms? He didn't mention it when I was in Rynstyn."

"He has to know. He's a historian. He wrote most of the Blood Treaty. I'm not certain he knows the spell to reunite the realms is inside the Chronicles, but think about it." I leaned towards Kyra. "He's spent every life cycle telling Astrals it's impossible for those with gold and silver blood to live peacefully together. As long as the Chronicles exists, it proves he's wrong. Wouldn't he want to find the book and keep it from being read, even if Batty's spells prevented him from destroying it?"

Understanding sparked in Kyra's eyes. "You're saying he wants us to find the Chronicles. Just like he wants us to reunite the realms."

I nodded. "He let us leave Rynstyn. The only reason he would do such a thing is because he needs something from us—something he can't get by any other means *or* something he knows it's easier for us to accomplish. He wants Aeles, at least, to continue to exist, and we're the only ones who can ensure that. He wants the Chronicles and knows we do, too, and we're far more likely to find that book than he is." Of course, there was a chance I was giving Tallus too much credit, but it was always better to overestimate your enemy than underestimate them.

"What do you think he's going to do next?" Kyra asked, curling her fingers into the green and grey blanket.

"I think he's going to give us time to find the Chronicles and reunite the realms."

I opened my eyes, my heart racing, my lungs sucking in air as if there might suddenly be a shortage. Pushing my hair off my face, I wasn't surprised to find sweat clinging to my hairline. I sat up and swung my legs over the side of the bed. Resting my elbows on my knees, I dropped my face into my hands.

It was only a dream.

I *knew* that, and yet I still found myself reacting to the nightmare as if I'd been right back in the midst of it, helpless as my Astral captors pressed a hot poker against my skin, studying the pain tolerance of someone with silver blood.

Even though there was no reason to be embarrassed, given that Kyra was fully aware of my past, a small part of me briefly wanted to create a portal and disappear. It wasn't surprising I'd had a nightmare as this was the first time I'd slept since going back to Rynstyn. Still, I'd secretly hoped going back and facing my past—not to mention eviscerating the experimentation facility—would mean I wouldn't be so bothered by the memories and might stop having nightmares altogether.

Apparently destroying the past wasn't the same as forgetting it.

Lifting my head, I looked over my shoulder. Kyra was sitting up, watching me closely, traces of interrupted sleep still clinging to her face. She held out a hand, and I took it, more than a little surprised to find myself not only accepting the comfort she offered but being grateful for it. Letting the fire inside me settle, I turned towards her, making it clear I wasn't going anywhere. There was no need. Even though my instincts told me to run and hide my vulnerability before someone could take advantage of it, in this instance, my instincts were wrong. I understood why they were saying the things they were, and without them, I would have died countless times over the course of my almost twenty-one years. But Kyra would never use anything from my past or present against me, and that truth was stronger than my self-preserving instincts.

Kyra's eyes patiently searched my face, ready to hear whatever I wanted to share but also content to simply sit with me.

"I suppose I can't expect the nightmares to stop just because we ended Tallus's program," I said.

"Healing always takes longer than destroying," Kyra agreed. "Getting rid of an illness or fixing a wound is only the beginning of the healing process. I'm so sorry you keep reexperiencing what you went through in Rynstyn. It's easy for me to say it'll get better with time—and once we put an end to Tallus for good—but it's far more difficult to live through the healing, day in and day out. *That* I know from experience."

I nodded, grateful she didn't expect me to no longer be bothered by what I'd endured. Then again, Kyra was far more patient with me than she was with herself.

Shifting into a cross-legged position, she toyed with the sleeve of her sleeping shirt. "There might be a way I can help," she said hesitantly. "Before everything in Rynstyn, I was working with Healer Omnurion on using my *alera* to alter the mind. With the right combination of *alera* and my *sana* beads, I can help someone stop thinking about painful things." Her eyes found mine. "It's possible to remove or destroy memories so they don't continue causing harm. I wanted to learn how to do that because . . . I thought it might be helpful for you."

I'd never heard of being able to permanently get rid of memories, but I was certainly intrigued.

"In Aeles, someone who wants their memories removed meets with a counselor, to ensure they truly understand what they're asking a healer to do," Kyra explained. "But if they understand, and they're making the choice of their own free will, it's possible for a healer to help them forget certain memories or destroy them beyond recovery."

She made a face. "Unfortunately, in some instances, no matter how skilled a healer is or how successfully they work, a mind still won't let go of a particular memory. So, there's a chance I could do everything correctly and you'd still have memories of being tortured in Aeles."

"But there's also a chance I'd never recall those memories again?"

"Yes."

I gazed down at the evergreen-colored sheets. I'd lived with nightmares for so long, it was difficult to imagine being without them. What would it be like not to dread falling asleep? I thought of all the nights I'd woken myself from a dream screaming or crying, too frightened to close my eyes again, prompting me to distract myself with weapons and books or by completing contracts. While such activities kept the nightmares to a minimum, I also never got enough sleep and lived in a state of perpetual exhaustion I refused to acknowledge. Could I truly be free from such dreams forever?

At the same time, for better or worse, my captivity in Rynstyn had provided some of my most transformative life experiences. They'd given me the foundation for who I had become and what I had become capable of doing. Who would I have grown up to be without my determination to prove my captors wrong through my survival? If those memories were removed, would I lose an integral piece of myself, something I hadn't known I'd possessed until I'd lost it? Would there be a gaping space in my memories, a dark hole whose edges taunted my desire to move on from my past?

"There's no need to decide anything now." Kyra's voice was gentle. "Obviously I have more work to do before I've mastered the procedure, but I wanted you to know it exists."

"It's definitely tempting," I admitted. "No one would love an uninterrupted night's sleep more than me. And I don't think replaying things from my past is actually helping me deal with them. Every time it's like I'm back there again, and even though I know what's going to happen, I can't stop it. I can only keep surviving it." I rubbed the back of my neck. "But I also worry about destroying any memories that might involve us. I became who I am today because of those experiences, and who I am today is with you. What if removing those memories changes something about me in a way you or I don't like? Who we are together is made up of who we are individually, so what if changing *me* changes *us*?"

I hadn't really known myself to possess such a philosophical bent, but Kyra nodded. "Those are valid questions I don't have an answer to. That's why it's something only you can decide for yourself. Just know I'm here and I love you and I'll do anything I can to take care of you."

I leaned forward and kissed her. "I'll think about it. It's definitely not at the top of our priority list right now."

"It involves you, which makes it a priority to me!" Kyra insisted.

"I just meant the dreams aren't going anywhere, so we don't need to rush. Let's stop Tallus, reunite the realms, and recover my mother, and then we can decide what to do with my memories." At this rate, it felt like there would never be a time when we weren't attempting to figure out or fix something, but that was just a feeling. The reality was Kyra and I would continue to handle whatever came our way.

"Alright," Kyra replied, even though I sensed there was a part of her that wanted to start removing my terrible memories right then and there. "I'll work on it more while you're at the Nemoyas'. It'll give me something to do besides wishing I was with you." She glanced up at the ceiling. "House, will you please wake us when others start heading down for breakfast?"

A soft two-note chime sounded, and Kyra grinned before slipping back against my side. Wrapping my arms around her, I found it difficult to remember there'd ever been a time I'd slept by myself. Even so, it took me a while to fall back asleep, partly because I didn't want to face another nightmare but also because I couldn't stop wondering what it would be like to fall asleep without being afraid of my dreams.

9

Dear Journal,

Today marks the one-year anniversary of the Blood Treaty. I've just been notified I'll be publicly reading the cursed document in celebration of this momentous occasion, and while I won't risk my court position by refusing, I shall perform the task with a heavy heart.

I confess there were times this past year when I didn't know if our newly united kingdom would survive. Not for anything lacking in the treaty itself, as I still consider it some of my finest—if most disagreeable—work, but because of the inherent impossibilities of forcing Astrals and Daevals together. The Felserpent monarchy attempts to convince us we can live as a realm at peace, but we are not a realm at peace, and we never will be so long as Daevals are allowed to live among those with golden blood.

I will never forget the night silver-blooded soldiers descended on my village. I can still see the fire, smell the smoke as it stung my nostrils, and hear the cries of my friends and neighbors. My mother screamed and my father pleaded, and I lay hidden in the root cellar where they'd shoved me, praying to the Gifters I wouldn't be discovered as I obeyed their last instructions and attempted to save myself rather than them. I waited nearly a full day before leaving my hole, long after I'd heard the horses' hooves ringing against the ground, still not trusting the bloodthirsty marauders were gone even though my ears told me as much.

The images that greeted me when I emerged haunt me even now. The dead were everywhere, and flies and carrion birds were feasting on the bodies the fire hadn't consumed. Even though I had no reason to hope, I still wept over my parents' remains. I buried them together and was kneeling at their grave when my aunt and uncle arrived. They were overjoyed I was alive, and while I was grateful to be welcomed into their home, my life would never be the same.

As I grew and watched relationships worsen between Astrals and Daevals, I thought the time might finally be right to rid Aeles-Nocens of those with silver blood once and for all. I never imagined leaders agreeing to share the realm, dividing rulership between an Astral queen and a Daeval king. And who did they select for the Daeval king? None other than Schatten Rektor, the commander of the Daeval military.

I don't care that he didn't personally attack my home. He must have known about it, to have spent hours planning the massacre. How can I ever trust such a man? I hate everything he stands for, and I loathe myself every time I must pretend to support his reign.

It's a shame our Astral queen is so besotted with him. Kareth is a uniquely powerful individual, and I'm disappointed she continues to be so intent on strengthening relationships with Daevals. I can only hope, given enough time, those with silver blood will reveal their true natures; they cannot keep their depravity hidden forever, and then we can banish them from our borders for good.

Since the institution of the Blood Treaty, there have been a few incidents of violence, but they've been dealt with swiftly and severely, and as a result, they seem to be occurring less frequently. I've paid for some and personally instigated others, but so far nothing has tipped the scales in Astrals' favor. Thankfully, there are others who maintain a hatred or at least a distrust of Daevals, and I will do everything in my power to reverse the increasingly terrible decisions being made for our glorious realm.

T

10

KYRA

I woke to the gentle melody of a wind flute, the song the house had chosen to rouse us gradually becoming louder as I opened my eyes and stretched. Leaning over to kiss Sebastian, who was already awake, I forced myself to leave the warmth of the bed in favor of a more thorough shower than I'd taken the night before, when I'd been too exhausted to do more than run a bar of soap over myself.

After a good scrubbing, I wrapped myself in a thick white robe and began combing my hair as Aurelius materialized beside me.

It's difficult to catch you alone these days, he said, *so I'll get right to it. I know what you're considering regarding Tallus, and I do not support it.*

Given his intimate connection with me, I wasn't surprised Aurelius was aware of the half-formed plan I'd stumbled upon while being held prisoner in Rynstyn. If I could remove Tallus's shade from his body, I could force him to appear in Vaneklus before his time. When a shade appeared before their appointed time to die, Laycus had the option of consuming them, ending their existence forever. I hadn't mentioned the possibility to Sebastian yet, as I wasn't certain such a thing was even possible. But now that we'd figured out Tallus was waiting for us to reunite the realms, I needed to know everything I could about shade removal so we could stop him before bringing Aeles and Nocens back to their rightful state.

I have no doubt such a thing is possible. That is not the point! Aurelius stomped an oversized paw against the rug, a rare display of anger from the normally reserved creature. *It will destroy you to commit such an act, and I cannot let you.*

I'm not looking forward to it. Impatience flared inside me. *But Tallus has to be stopped, and if that means I have to live with the consequences of ending his existence, I'll do it.*

The lynx shook his head. *There has to be another way. What about making Tallus forget his past life memories? If he didn't remember hating Daevals or wanting to turn them into Astrals, wouldn't it be safe for him to be reborn?*

I'm not strong enough to assume control of Tallus's mind, I argued. *Making someone forget a memory is difficult enough when the patient is participating willingly, and even then, sometimes the mind still won't release the memory. Tallus won't be a willing participant; he'll actively fight me every step of the way. Since he's retained all his past life memories, he knows spells to protect his mind I've never even heard of and wouldn't have the first idea how to counter.*

Aurelius twitched his whickers unhappily. *What about breaking the spell Tallus cast to preserve his past life memories?*

If we had unlimited time, of course I'd prefer to figure out how to break his spell. I heard the exasperation leaking into my voice. Why did it seem like everyone was against me when I was only trying to do the right thing and live up to the responsibility I'd accepted centuries ago?

I am not against you, Aurelius said, moving his head to catch my gaze. *It is my privilege and my duty to take care of you, so I'm trying to determine how best to support you.*

I let out a shaky breath. I wasn't mad at my Cypher. I was upset at the situation with Seren, disappointed I couldn't participate in recovering the Chronicles, afraid of whatever Tallus was planning, and terrified of what I might have to do in order to stop him.

Once we have the Chronicles, we'll need to move against Tallus as soon as possible, I said. *But if you and Batty can find out how to break the spell he cast on himself before then, I'm all ears.* Aurelius nodded, and I crouched down to give him a hug. *I'm sorry. I don't mean to be short with you. I just feel so overwhelmed.*

With good reason. Aurelius propped his chin on my shoulder as I held him close. *You can accomplish anything you put your mind to, Kyra, but just because you are capable of doing something does not mean you should have to. Given everything you're facing, I must say, I'm grateful for Sebastian's presence in your life.*

Coming from Aurelius, that was a resounding endorsement, and I hugged him tighter, as grateful for him as I was for Sebastian.

After dressing, I asked the house to direct us to where the others were gathering. White lights appeared on the hallway floor, guiding us to the room where Sebastian and I had told everyone the truth about ourselves, which, according to a sign I hadn't noticed the day before, was called the Driftwood Lounge. As I stepped inside, I looked around, only to have my heart sink. My sister was nowhere to be seen.

"Is Seren eating in her room?" I asked my mother.

"No, last night after dinner Minerva asked her if she'd like to help with a project, so she was up early."

"Oh." On the one hand, I was glad Minerva had found a way to keep Seren busy, giving her something to do besides stew in her resentment towards me; at the same time, there was something unsettling about my little sister learning anything about the business of the most notorious family in Nocens.

"Sebastian and I are going to get some things from his place after we eat," I said, "so I'll be gone for a while. If you need me, you can have Dova reach out to Aurelius."

If my mother was surprised to hear that I'd been to where Sebastian lived or that I was keeping some of my things there, she did an admirable job of hiding it, although she might have been distracted by Caz hurrying in, carrying an assortment of pails and shovels and covered head to toe in a tight-fitting black warmsuit.

"Am I the first Dekarai downstairs?" he asked. His chest was rising and falling as if he'd run all the way from his room, and when my mother nodded, he let out a relieved wheeze. "Oh, thank goodness! I was worried you'd already been talked into some ridiculous activity by Rennej."

He volunteered to take my family down to the beach just as Rennej arrived, looking put out Caz had beaten her.

My mother waved Caz and my brothers away. "You go have fun. It's not every day I have the chance to speak with a mother from Nocens." She smiled at Rennej and gestured to a chair, inviting her to sit down. "I have so many parenting questions I'd love to ask you!"

Rennej shot a triumphant look at Caz before settling across from my mother. Casting an expectant glance around the room, her expression turned confused and then concerned when no servers appeared, but either Minerva ran her home with a handful of attendants who kept out of sight or the house was so enchanted staff weren't required. A look of helplessness flashed across Rennej's face. When my mother poured coffee from a silver carafe and offered her a cup, she let out a relieved sigh and gratefully accepted the steaming drink. Loris appeared beside her, and the lemur patted her arm as if to express her deepest sympathies that Sea'Brik fell so short of the lifestyle Rennej enjoyed in her own home.

"Caz, do you know if Devlin's made any progress on getting an invitation to the Nemoyas'?" Sebastian asked. "Of if he's even awake?"

Caz chuckled. "House, can you tell me the location of my favorite nephew?"

No blinking lights appeared on the floor to direct us to Devlin; instead, a pleasant voice said, "Devlin Dekarai is not currently at Sea'Brik."

"Hopefully that means he's off visiting Win'Din," said Caz before giving an exaggerated shudder. "May the Fates favor his efforts."

With my family settled and breakfast eaten, Sebastian opened a portal, and I found myself happier than I'd expected at being back in the cave. Running my hand over the rock wall, I savored the familiar coolness of the smooth stone even though I'd never imagined anything about a cave feeling familiar.

"I'm going to get Rhannu and a few other weapons before I pack up some of my things," said Sebastian. He'd secured Rhannu in his weapons vault after rescuing me from Rynstyn, before we'd gone to Demitri's to get my family, and I knew he was eager to be reunited with his favorite weapon. "Good luck in Vaneklus."

He likely thought I was seeking out Laycus to ask what reuniting the realms meant for our bond, and while I certainly planned to do so, that wasn't the first question on my list anymore. More than anything, I needed to know if I could stop Tallus by removing his shade.

I smiled at Sebastian as I settled my shifter cloak around my shoulders and pulled *The Book of Recovrancy* from my dresser drawer before making my way to the sofa.

Aurelius twitched his long silver whiskers. "Bartholomew and I are going to continue our research into the spell Tallus cast on himself."

The lynx was clearly all the more determined to uncover the spell after our conversation in the bathroom, and, knowing how single-minded he could be, I almost felt sorry for Batty.

As the Cyphers dematerialized, I ran my fingertips over the blue cover of *The Book of Recovrancy*. Before I spoke with Laycus, I wanted to see what the book knew about removing someone's shade, as it often shared things Laycus either didn't know or didn't want to tell me. Bracing myself for what I might discover, I opened the cover and placed my palm flat against the first page.

Is it possible to remove a shade from a body before the shade's appointed time to die?

Lifting my hand, I gazed down at the white paper. One beat passed, then another, and still no text appeared. It didn't usually take the book so long to respond, and I wasn't certain whether to ask again or wait. How long was an appropriate time to wait before repeating myself? Just as I considered reaching out and asking Aurelius for advice, black ink rose to the surface of the page.

Why do you seek to perform such an act?

My stomach did a somersault. The book had never asked me a question before. Pressing a fingertip against the edge of the page, I let my mind fill with what I recalled of Tallus's destruction, his cruelty towards Daevals, and his undying insistence on finding a way to rid the realms of silver blood. *He has to be stopped*, I told the book. *If Sebastian ends his life, that won't keep him from returning with his memories intact and sowing discord for all eternity, thanks to the spell he cast on himself. I want to remove Tallus's shade from his body, force him to appear in Vaneklus before his time, and have Laycus end his existence for good.*

I blinked at the page, trying to breathe evenly as I waited for a response to the terrible act I'd proposed.

As a Recovrancer—and a healer—you are charged with saving lives, not ending them, the book finally replied.

The book was right, and while I certainly would have preferred not to take such gruesome measures, I also wasn't *just* a Recovrancer and a healer. As the Felserpent Queen, I'd been responsible for the safety of those in Aeles-Nocens, and that hadn't changed simply because the realms had been divided and I existed in a different body with a different name.

More text appeared, and I realized my fingers had still been pressed against the page, conveying everything I'd just thought.

Very well. Text began to appear more quickly. *There have been instances throughout history when a Recovrancer needed to perform such an act for the safety of others. It is possible to remove a shade before its appointed time of death, but there are important things to consider.*

When it came to anything involving my recovrancy, there were always important things to consider.

You must first discuss what you wish to do with the Shade Transporter, the book directed. *While Laycus is permitted to consume shades that appear in his realm early, the choice is up to him. He must willingly agree to consume the shade.*

I couldn't imagine Laycus taking issue with consuming Tallus's shade, but more words appeared.

When the Shade Transporter consumes a shade, he experiences the life of that shade as if he lived it himself. He will experience every act the shade performed, every decision they made, as well as every feeling they felt, and these memories will remain with him for eternity.

I gazed at a cluster of yellow quartz sprouting like a stone bouquet across the cavern. If Laycus consumed Tallus's shade, he would feel everything Tallus had felt, not just with regards to Daevals but with regards to *me*. Laycus would be forced to live with Tallus's hatred of me, holding within himself the rage Tallus felt towards the work I did and the causes I supported. Would seeing me through Tallus's eyes change the way Laycus felt towards me?

I certainly hoped not. He'd been the Shade Transporter for so long, surely he could differentiate between memories of shades he'd consumed and memories he'd made himself. At the same time, according to *The Book of Recovrancy*, I wasn't just asking Laycus to consume a shade . . . I was asking him to carry a burden for the rest of time. Was it fair to use our relationship, the knowledge that he cared for me, to ask him to do such a thing? Part of me thought reuniting the realms was unquestionably worth whatever the sacrifice, but the rest of me wasn't so certain. While I was concerned for the Shade Transporter, I was also concerned for myself. There was already a chance I'd lose my bond with Sebastian, not to mention my closeness with my sister. Would I have to give up my relationship with Laycus too?

I'll speak with Laycus, I eventually told the book. *The decision will be up to him, and I'll respect whatever he decides.*

Should the Shade Transporter agree to do as you'd like, return to these pages, and further instructions shall be given, replied the book, managing to sound both promising and ominous at the same time.

11

KYRA

Making my way out into the open space of the cave, I sat down on the stone floor in a cross-legged position, arranging my shifter cloak around me.

"*Bidh mi a'dolh a-steach*," I said, running my fingers over Tawazun and Rheolath on my *sana* bracelet and feeling more anxious about going into Vaneklus than I had in a very long time. The cavern disappeared, and I found myself standing in the grey river, the wooden dock jutting out to my left, enormous boulders lining the banks and marking the boundaries of Laycus's domain. Since sharing my blood and establishing a closer relationship with Death, I was better able to discern the moods of the realm, and I appreciated the water lapping a friendly welcome around my knees. Bending down, I trailed a hand through it, hoping my action would be perceived as affectionate since I wasn't certain how else to show my fondness other than perhaps patting a boulder.

Laycus's boat emerged from the perpetual fog bank just as I straightened.

"Thank the grey waters of Death you are safe!" exclaimed the Shade Transporter as I dried my hand on my breeches. Once his boat reached me, he stuck the end of his staff into the river, bringing the vessel to a stop as his eyes settled on mine. "Bartholomew has kept me appraised of your whereabouts since

Rynstyn," he explained. "My regards to your consort for such a successful rescue."

"I'll be sure to pass that on," I replied, too distracted by the thoughts swirling in my head to muster the appreciation Laycus's rare compliment towards Sebastian deserved.

Laycus tilted his head inside his cowl. "I don't recall seeing you so preoccupied before. Dare I ask what's on your mind?"

"I have two questions for you, and I'm not looking forward to asking either of them." There was no point delaying the inevitable, and even though my mouth went dry, I forced myself to speak. "Tallus has to be stopped," I began. "But ending his life won't prevent him from returning and attempting to undo whatever good Sebastian and I are able to achieve. The only way I can think of to stop him for good is to end not only his life, but his shade."

Laycus's garnet-red eyes flickered. "I told you before, Tallus has always appeared on my shores at his appointed times. I would have consumed him by now, if I could."

I drew my cloak tighter around myself. "According to *The Book of Recovrancy*, it's possible to remove a shade from a body and force them to appear in Vaneklus before their appointed time of death." I gazed up at Laycus. "The book said it's happened before, so I'm assuming you know it's possible. You probably remember the Recovrancer who did it. I'm not asking you to tell me if it was me, but it *is* at least possible."

Laycus tapped his skeletal fingers in a rhythmless motion against the front of his black shroud. "It is certainly possible," he agreed. "What you're facing must be dire indeed if you were willing to ask that book about such a thing."

I told him the lies Tallus was spreading, how he was working to take control of Aeles, and how war between Astrals and Daevals was practically inevitable.

Correctly guessing what I was leading up to, Laycus studied me. "Why are you so conflicted over asking me to perform an act I would happily do anyway?"

"Because I'm worried it will change our relationship. According to my book, when you consume a shade, you remember everything about their life, forever. And since Tallus has retained his memories from every life he's ever lived, you'll be forced to carry all his memories with you. I don't want that to change how you see me."

Laycus leaned forward. "And if I said I did not wish to carry such a burden for all eternity?"

"Then I would respect your choice, and I'd find another way to stop Tallus," I replied without hesitation.

Laycus continued to gaze at me, and I hoped my stronger connection with the realm would allow him to know the decision really was up to him. He didn't seem to have the luxury of many choices in his role. While I could plead, I couldn't threaten him, nor would I, even if I'd had the leverage to do so.

"Fortunately for us, I have consumed my share of despicable shades," Laycus finally said. "I am not worried about being influenced by Tallus's perception of you."

"Really?" My heart was hammering so loudly, it was a wonder Laycus hadn't commented on it.

"Really."

"So . . . that means you'll do it?" I'd always valued my relationship with Laycus, but I hadn't realized until this very moment just how much I loved the enigmatic figure before me.

"I shall," he nodded.

"Thank you." My voice caught as I gently placed a hand on his boat. "I wish I could convey how much I appreciate this, but please know, I'm eternally grateful."

Laycus smiled, although his expression quickly turned curious.

"While I have no qualms about consuming a shade, I have to ask: How will it affect *you*, knowing you aided in ending the existence of someone, even someone who deserved it?"

I shivered despite my efforts to control myself. "I don't like it, but if that's my burden to carry, I'll bear it as best I can. We're all making sacrifices to unite Astrals and Daevals."

Laycus rested his hands on the top of his staff. "You are not the same woman you were when I first met you."

"I'm not," I agreed, sad at the innocence I'd lost but also proud of the strength I'd discovered. "If I have to live with performing a terrible act for a good reason, I'll do it."

Laycus dipped his head. "I shall be ready when you have mastered shade removal. What was the second unpleasant question you wished to ask me?"

"I bound my shade to Schatten's so that when the time was right to rejoin Aeles and Nocens, we would return and find one another." I told him about LeBehr locating the Chronicles, bringing us one step closer to successfully rejoining the realms. "Will reuniting the realms mean the end of our shades being connected, or will Sebastian and I still continue to find one another in future life cycles?"

Laycus stared down into the water eddying around his boat. "This is all so unprecedented, I'm not entirely certain. I could make a case either way."

"Are you saying we'll just have to wait and see?" If I'd been a Pyromancer, flames would have sprung from my hands. "That's entirely unacceptable!"

The edges of Laycus's smile were sharp. "I am not a subject in your kingdom, your Majesty."

I glanced down at my shifter cloak, unaware I'd been clasping the velvet fabric. The garment was spelled so that when I touched it and thought of a particular color or pattern, it changed to what

I was picturing. Right now it appeared to be made of black and grey scales, identical to the cloak the Felserpent had given Schatten to wear as king. I dropped my gaze in apology, although I left my cloak as it was.

"Well, if even *you* aren't certain, I'll need to find a way to bind our shades again, just in case," I said. "Perhaps Batty knows where the Pelagian Scroll is, since it worked so well the first time."

Laycus shifted his staff from one hand to the other. "I will speak with Suryal about this. Life and returning in different lives are really more her area of expertise than mine."

"Thank you," I said, surprised at Laycus's offer.

"We both know if I don't reach out to her, you'll attempt to, so I'm merely saving myself a headache," he shrugged.

Part of me wondered if Laycus was speaking metaphorically or if he actually had the capacity to experience headaches. I almost asked him but decided against it. He'd already been incredibly helpful, and I didn't want to push my luck.

I returned to the cavern to find Sebastian packing a bag of clothes from his wardrobe. Rhannu and a large roll of what I assumed were other weapons rested on the dining table, and Sebastian motioned towards the dresser he'd purchased for me.

"I laid out a bag for you," he said, "if there's anything you want to bring to Minerva's. I already packed sheets."

"Thank you." My thoughts bounded over one another as I tried to decide where to begin.

Sebastian turned towards me, brushing his hair off his forehead. The gesture was so familiar it made me smile; one of the only things he'd liked about wearing a crown was how it had kept his hair in place. "What did Laycus say about how reuniting the realms will affect our bond?"

I told him what I'd learned, and he scowled, clearly unhappy we still didn't have a firm answer. "Now that I've found you, I can't imagine a life without you," he said. "I *won't* live another life without you."

I felt the same way, but I was also confident we could deal with that when the time came. Right now, Tallus was a more immediate concern. While I hoped Sebastian would care more about having a way to destroy our enemy forever than being the one to end his existence, I also knew he yearned to exact vengeance.

"I spoke with Laycus about the possibility of ending Tallus's life for good." The words practically exploded from my mouth.

Sebastian's eyebrows rose, but he nodded for me to continue.

"You could easily kill Tallus," I said, "but ending someone's life isn't the same as ending their shade, the same way destroying a building wouldn't have been the same as truly ending the experimentation program. I only know a little so far, but apparently it's possible for a Recovrancer to remove a shade from a body before the shade's appointed time to die. If I can remove Tallus's shade and take him into Vaneklus early, Laycus can consume him, ensuring there's no way he can ever be reborn."

I sensed a variety of emotions churning through Sebastian, and he reached up to rub the back of his neck, a gesture he often made when thinking.

"Is Laycus willing to help?"

"He is." I shared my fear that having Laycus consume Tallus's shade would change my relationship with the Shade Transporter. "Fortunately, he assured me he's consumed plenty of despicable shades over the years and it won't affect how he sees me. *The Book of Recovrancy* told me it would share more if Laycus agreed to help. Since he has, I can start learning about shade removal, which I plan to do this afternoon."

Sebastian crossed his arms over his chest and widened his stance.

"You're right about me wanting to be the one to end Tallus's life," he admitted. "But we can't risk him being reborn and continuing to sow discord between Astrals and Daevals. I don't like it, but ensuring he can't return is more important than getting to be the one who kills him. You gave up going to the Nemoyas' so we'd have the best chance of getting the Chronicles; it's only fair I give up killing Tallus so we have the best chance of stopping him for good. It's a smart plan." He stared intently at me. "Are you comfortable with it?"

I dragged my hands down my face. "Laycus asked me the same thing. I don't like the idea of ending anyone's existence, but if that's my burden to bear, then so be it. Astrals and Daevals are my responsibility, and I'll do whatever it takes to keep them safe. That's what I agreed to when I became the Felserpent Queen. It's not just about using my gifts to heal individuals anymore. I'm trying to heal two broken realms, and one Astral shouldn't be allowed to pose so much danger and cause such rampant destruction."

"It's not just *your* responsibility." Sebastian reached up and rested his hands on my shoulders. "We're in this together. Just as you would never ask Laycus to do something that made him uncomfortable or might change him, I would never ask you to do something you didn't want to live with. We can always find another way."

"Thank you," I said, stepping forward and wrapping my arms around him. "There probably is another way, but we don't have time to find it, which makes this the best course of action available. I don't want to live with it, but I can. That's what leaders do. They make the best decision at the time and keep moving forward."

Sebastian rested his chin on top of my head. Part of me wanted to ask him what it was like to end a life, even though I knew it was different from ending a shade, but I couldn't bring myself to form the question.

"I remember you told me before sometimes there isn't an easier or better option," I said instead. "You act, and you get through it. That's what I'm going to do."

He hugged me tighter. "And that's why you're the Felserpent Queen. I would do it for you, if I could."

I pressed a kiss to his lips, wishing I could let him handle Tallus before pushing such futile thoughts away and strengthening my resolve to perform the act the realms needed from me.

"Nerudian's here," Sebastian said when we pulled apart. "I told him we'd stop in before we left."

Making our way down the moonstone-embedded tunnel, I smiled as Nerudian lifted his head from the chasm housing his treasure cache.

"Thank the ancients you're safe!" the dragon called as his yellow eyes landed on me. "With the realms divided, I couldn't fly to Aeles and help rescue you, but I told Batty I would come through a portal the instant I was needed." He shook his head, smoke curling out of his broad nostrils. "I would have taken immense pleasure in destroying that facility—although from what I heard, you did perfectly fine on your own, Sebastian."

I walked forward and stroked the black scales on the side of the dragon's face, appreciating his love and support. Something stirred behind me, and I turned to see Aurelius trotting over as Batty materialized on a nearby rock, a wide grin on his furry face.

"We have returned with news!" the bat crowed happily. "Mischief helped us find a book that directed us to a potion; when poured over the hairs I took from Tallus, it revealed his secret. He cast the *Memoria Aeterna* spell on himself, and *that* is how he has kept his memories intact."

"I'm so impressed you figured that out!" From the corner of

my eye, I could see Aurelius watching me closely. I wasn't certain if he'd been following along with my thoughts as I'd spoken with Sebastian, given that I hadn't confined the conversation to our bracelets, but he might also have been too busy with Batty and Mischief to pay attention. "If we can find a way to break the spell soon, we'll do it. But, if not"—I winced even as I forced myself to meet Aurelius's gaze, knowing he wasn't going to like my next words—"I have another way we can stop Tallus."

I shared my plan, and while Aurelius gave his head a rough shake, I appreciated that he refrained from outright disagreeing with me.

Nerudian lashed his tail against his sea of sparkling treasures. "I'm more than happy to gobble Tallus up if you need him out of commission for a while. I realize it won't stop him for good, but it would certainly be enjoyable." He swung his gaze between Sebastian and me. "If I can be of assistance in stopping him, please don't hesitate to ask."

"I think we'll start by trying to get near Tallus undetected," said Sebastian, "but if we need a distraction or assistance on a larger scale, we'll certainly let you know."

"I shall be here." The dragon gave a satisfied nod as he resettled into his canyon.

Aurelius's whiskers turned down in a decidedly disapproving manner. "Well, then I shall do what I can until it is time to confront Tallus. I will be learning about the *Memoria Aeterna* spell at LeBehr's if you need me." He quickly dematerialized, followed by Batty.

I smiled at the space where Aurelius had been, grateful for his devotion. While part of me suspected we'd already identified the only way to effectively defeat Tallus, I was certainly open to another option. Despite my brave words, I had no idea how I would live with myself after participating in destroying someone's shade.

12

SEBASTIAN

Back at Minerva's, I asked the house to locate Devlin.

"Devlin Dekarai is not currently at Sea'Brik," replied the pleasant voice we'd heard earlier. Pulling out my peerin, I rang Devlin but he didn't answer, which only served to chip away at the fragile confidence I was trying to maintain in him. We only had a few hours until the Nemoyas' auction. If we weren't going to get an invitation, I needed to start planning exactly how I was going to retrieve the Chronicles, whether that meant stealing them during the auction or waiting until the guests had gone and those in the house were asleep.

Deciding we might as well have lunch as we waited for news from Devlin, Kyra and I headed downstairs. While I'd planned for us to take our food back to our borrowed bedroom, we met Kyra's mother at the bottom of the staircase.

"What perfect timing!" Skandhar exclaimed. "I wasn't certain how long you would be gone, but since you're back, why don't we have lunch together?" She turned a broad smile towards me, and I froze, feeling like an animal that had been spotted while attempting to slink back to its den undetected. "Deneb and Enif just got back from the beach with Caz, and they're so looking forward to getting to know you better, Sebastian."

I glanced at Kyra, and while I kept my facial expression neutral, I knew she could sense my apprehension. What in the burning realm would I talk about with her family? The list of things we couldn't talk about was far longer. We couldn't talk about what I did for a living or had done for a living until now. We couldn't discuss my cruel father or my childhood spent being tortured in Rynstyn. I supposed we could talk about Kyra planning to recover my mother, but that would lead to questions of how she had died in the first place, and describing my mother's murder didn't seem like the kind of thing you discussed over a meal.

"Lunch together sounds wonderful!" Kyra agreed. As her mother headed off to collect her siblings, she squeezed my hand. *It'll be fine. I'll keep the conversation incredibly focused.*

Alright, I replied uneasily, my gut assuring me this was a very bad idea. *I just don't want to say anything that upsets your family—or you.*

Batty materialized on my shoulder. *I can also serve as a distraction if the need arises*, he offered. *I am more than happy to fall into a souffle or take a swim in the soup dish.*

While I certainly hoped it didn't come to that, I nevertheless appreciated the bat's support.

Kyra and I filled our plates from the seemingly ever-present buffet. I wasn't surprised at the abundance of planterian options, but I hadn't expected the Dekarais to do away with meat-based dishes completely, although their observance of Astral dietary preferences was certainly kind. Now that I thought about it, I'd been around Kyra so much lately I couldn't even remember the last time I'd eaten a steak. I supposed I'd find out at some point if there were any adverse effects of deviating from my usual fare, but so far, I didn't feel any different and, if I was entirely honest, I wouldn't have known some of the things I'd eaten at Sea'Brik were planterian based simply on taste or texture.

Kyra and I took seats at the table as Skandhar, Enif, and

Deneb joined us. Seren was conspicuously absent, and even though Skandhar said she was working with Minerva, I felt Kyra's disappointment. While my knowledge of sibling relationships had been gathered solely from books and observing the Dekarais, I thought Seren was overreacting. Kyra hadn't done anything to intentionally hurt her; she'd merely kept information to herself until the right time. I supposed an argument could be made that a fifteen-year-old wasn't mature enough to understand such things, but I'd started my assassination business at fifteen. That had been far more complicated than dealing with difficult information.

As Kyra's mother and brothers took their seats, I readied myself for their questions. I understood their interest in me, given my importance to Kyra, but a small part of me resented them for knowing her longer than I had in this life cycle. I didn't want to be jealous and possessive like my father had been, but recognizing how I *didn't* want to act was only the first step towards actually changing my behavior.

Nevertheless, acknowledging the need to change is an important first step, noted Batty approvingly.

I'd just taken a bite of seasoned mushrooms when Enif leaned forward, his nutmeg brown eyes wide with excitement.

"I can't believe you were the first king of Aeles-Nocens!" he exclaimed. "What was it like? Did you have a sword? Did everyone have to do what you told them?" He grinned. "Did you punish anyone who disagreed with you, or was everyone too afraid to disagree with you?"

"Enif, perhaps we can start with something else," Skandhar suggested.

"But you said asking questions was a good way to get to know someone," protested Enif.

"I did have a sword." At least there was at least one topic I could easily address. "It belonged to the leader of the Daeval military, and when I became king, I was allowed to keep it. Its name is Rhannu."

"You must have fought so much." Enif's voice had a breathless quality to it. "What was the best battle you were in? Did a lot of soldiers die?"

"Enif, we *are* trying to eat." Kyra's voice held a warning her brother quickly recognized because he gave her a sheepish grin that might have been apologetic if his natural countenance hadn't been so mischievous.

"I did fight a lot," I said, thinking that wasn't telling anyone at the table something they didn't already know. "But I was glad when we signed the Blood Treaty and there could be peace between Astrals and Daevals."

"What happened to your sword?" Enif was clearly more interested in weapons than peace treaties, and I couldn't entirely blame him.

"I still have it. Before we died, Kareth hid it in Vaneklus. The Shade Transporter kept watch over it until we returned."

I'd thought mentioning things like the Shade Transporter and his sister going into the realm of the dead might lead Enif to change the subject, but his attention wouldn't be swayed. "That's amazing!" he practically shouted. "Where's Rhannu now?"

"Upstairs in my room." While I was surprised by his enthusiasm, I was also pleased, as the sword deserved such admiration. "I can show you sometime, if you'd like."

"Can we go now?" Enif started to rise, but his mother motioned for him to sit back down.

"Let's finish lunch first," she said.

"Okay," he replied, turning his attention to his plate.

Deneb asked, "Did you wear a crown when you were king?"

"I did."

"Did you wear it a lot?"

"I wore it all the time."

"Even when you were sleeping?" Deneb's eyes widened.

"No," I corrected myself. "I wore it a lot of the time, but not when I was sleeping."

Deneb nodded, obviously a stickler for accuracy. "Did you have a throne?"

"Kareth and I both had thrones."

"I bet yours was bigger, though," said Deneb. "Since you're bigger."

"Kyra's had to be smaller," volunteered Enif around a mouthful of rice. "Otherwise she would have needed a ladder to climb up and take her seat." He and Deneb laughed, and I stiffened, causing Kyra to place a hand on my knee under the table.

He's just teasing, she assured me before rolling her eyes and making a face at the boys that caused them to laugh even harder.

I appreciated her insight, as it was taking all my concentration to keep up with the fast-moving conversation.

"I think that's enough about the past for now," noted Kyra's mother. "Let's talk about *this* life cycle. Sebastian, where did you grow up?"

"I lived in Vartox as a child," I said. "Then my mother and I moved to Doldarian when I was seven."

"Why didn't your father move with you?" asked Enif.

I chose my words carefully. "He wasn't a part of my life. He . . . wasn't a nice man."

"But he was your father!" protested Deneb, passing Batty a blueberry. "He should have been nice to you."

"He should have been," I agreed. "But he wasn't."

"Where's your father now?" asked Deneb.

"He's dead."

"How did he die?" asked Enif.

"In a fight."

Enif's and Deneb's eyes widened, although I couldn't tell if they were impressed or concerned. Thankfully, Kyra skillfully redirected the conversation.

"Sebastian went to school with Devlin and Eslee. He's known the Dekarais his entire life."

"I like Eslee," said Deneb. "She's going to show me how she makes her sculptures this afternoon." He looked at his brother, a taunting smile spreading across his chubby face. "Enif likes Eslee too. He goes like this every time he sees her." Deneb proceeded to bat his eyelashes and make kissing noises. While I wouldn't have stood for such teasing even as a child, Enif didn't contradict Deneb's impression of him, instead simply grinning and shrugging.

"Eslee's wonderful," smiled Kyra. "I've loved getting to know her better."

"Devlin said his aunt has her own gymnasium on her island," offered Enif. "He told me he'd take me there this afternoon. I think he spends a lot of time in gymnasiums."

I'd never known Devlin to enjoy being around children, but it was clear all the Dekarais were working hard to make Kyra's family feel welcome, which I appreciated. And Enif was right; Devlin spent copious amounts of time at any gymnasium with a mirror. Still, muscles earned in the comfort of a climate-controlled building were different from those earned through daily use, when your life quite literally depended on your strength or flexibility. Then again, would Kyra prefer I look more like Devlin? I'd always been on the lean side, favoring speed and endurance over bulk, but I wasn't opposed to installing gymnasium equipment in my cave. Considering the logistics of such an endeavor caused me to miss whatever Enif said, although I heard Deneb's next question quite clearly.

"Are you and Kyra going to get married?"

I had no idea how to respond and swung my head towards Kyra, whose cheeks were turning red. "It's a bit early to be thinking about that," she said.

"Why? You were married before. It makes sense you'd get married again," noted Enif, polishing off a small bowl of greens and turning his attention to a platter of grilled eggplant.

"One of my friends was a ring bear in her sister's wedding," said Deneb. "I could be a ring bear in your wedding!"

"It's a ring bear*er*," corrected Kyra with a smile, "and you would be the best one ever."

"Aurelius could walk you down the aisle," suggested Enif.

"I will oversee the catering!" Batty exclaimed, raising a wing before biting into a candied walnut helpfully supplied by Deneb.

"I'd always pictured you having a traditional Aelian wedding," admitted Kyra's mother, "but that was when I assumed you'd be marrying an Astral. I'd love to learn more about Nocenian wedding customs! Judging by the clothes the Dekarais wear, weddings in this realm must be quite the fashionable event."

"Let's stop Tallus and ensure the realms are reunited before we attempt anything else," said Kyra. "We've got enough to focus on right now."

"True, but weddings *do* bring folks together," Skandhar pointed out. "I agree it's not the right time, but what a lovely event for those with silver and gold blood to look forward to!"

While Kyra swiftly moved the conversation to what Deneb and Enif had been learning in school, my thoughts remained where they were. Enif was right. It did make sense Kyra and I would get married, and while I didn't know the first thing about Astral betrothals, in Nocens, one member of the couple generally took the initiative to ask their partner to marry them, either during a private moment or at an event attended by loved ones. Many marriages in Nocens—like the one between Duston and Rennej—were arranged for a purpose, powerful families uniting to gain wealth, land, or status, but marriages also happened for love. When Kareth and I had first married, it had been purely political, to stop the constant fighting. I liked the idea of marrying Kyra again in this life cycle, not because we were doing our duty to the realm but because we loved one another and chose to be together.

Kyra squeezed my knee, drawing my attention back to the table.

"Sebastian graduated at the top of his class," she was saying, possibly repeating something she'd already said for my benefit as I tried to catch up. "He started his own business years ago, but what with all the . . . changes . . . taking place between the realms, he's going to have a lot of new opportunities. It'll be a good time to figure out what will be the most profitable venture but also the most sustainable."

I nodded, hoping Kyra's ability to use a lot of words without divulging much information would allow the conversation to flow to another topic. Unfortunately, Skandhar tilted her head, a considering expression moving over her face.

"What sort of business are you in?" A faint awareness she might not like my answer flickered in her blue-grey eyes.

As I tried to find the least offensive way to describe being an assassin, Batty spoke. "Sebastian has specialized in threat neutralization, item reclamation, and information acquisition," he said smoothly. "But he is looking to transition into customized security and asset protection."

I nodded, silently thanking my Cypher. While there was a good chance Skandhar would ask more questions about my profession later, Kyra could handle whatever objections her mother raised, even though I felt bad she'd have to do so because of me.

We managed to finish lunch without venturing into any truly

unpleasant topics, and I agreed to show Rhannu to Enif soon. Just as I was pulling out my peerin to contact Devlin again, the door flew open and there he stood, an ear-to-ear grin on his face and a piece of paper in his hand.

"And you didn't think I could do it!" he all but shouted. Crossing the room, he handed me the paper. "A gift for you, *Your Highness*."

The auction invitation was thick and glossy, and the blue-green ink spelling out the names of Devlin, myself, and LeBehr shone in the light of the chandeliers. Even with the invitation in hand, I still had trouble believing Devlin had really succeeded. While I didn't want to discover the trust I'd reluctantly allowed him had been misplaced, I also couldn't keep from considering alternative explanations for how he'd acquired the invitation. The parchment couldn't have been stolen, as the names wouldn't have been right. Could Devlin have forged the auction invite? I knew how strongly he wanted to prove himself to his family, particularly his father, and regardless of his romantic diversions with Win'Din, it was just so unlikely the Nemoyas would allow a Dekarai in their home.

"So, we present this, and we'll be allowed into the auction?" I asked.

"Yes," Devlin replied, his earlier smugness slipping into an unhappy frown over my less-than-enthusiastic response.

I considered asking him to promise the invitation was real, but that wouldn't necessarily tell me anything useful in the limited time we had—whatever consequences Devlin suffered for lying might not take immediate effect or they might be so minor they could be ignored or hidden, at least for a while.

Kyra leaned forward. "What Sebastian means is, he's sorry he underestimated you and he'll try to do better moving forward. That's fantastic, Devlin. Thank you so much!"

Even though I knew Kyra was attempting to smooth things over, my mind refused to quit racing. Simply flashing an invitation couldn't be enough to guarantee entry to the auction, as anyone sufficiently motivated could create a believable facsimile. That meant the Nemoyas would have a way to test the document to ensure it was authentic, and authenticating documents traditionally involved Barantula dust. I'd seen the lie-revealing dust used before, as Dunston and Caz regularly employed it to determine whether a written agreement was genuine. They also had a few mines that produced the black rocks, which, when ground up and combined with other spelled ingredients, created the forgery-revealing powder. If Devlin's invitation was indeed a fake, the Barantula dust would cause the paper to disintegrate, and we'd be turned away before we ever made it inside the Nemoyas' house.

"You got this from Win'Din herself?" I pressed, causing Kyra to frown at me.

"Well, I certainly didn't get it from her husband," retorted Devlin, crossing his arms.

I know you're not used to trusting others, Kyra said, *but Devlin did what he said he'd do. He went to a lot of trouble for us, and you're not being grateful or even particularly nice.*

Unfortunately, there was nothing I could do to authenticate the invitation. I could coat the entire thing in Barantula dust, but without having an original to compare it to, I wouldn't know more than I did now. That meant we'd have to wait until we reached the Nemoyas to determine whether the invitation was real, which was a risk and not at all how I preferred to run my operations. Well, if the worst-case scenario occurred and it turned out Devlin was lying, I'd do what I would have done without an invitation and figure out another way to acquire the Chronicles. I'd also let Dunston deal with his son, which would be a punishment far more severe than anything I could dream up.

I passed the invitation back to Devlin. "Kyra's right. I'm not used to working with others. Thank you."

Dunston entered the dining room before Devlin could respond, and seeing the invitation, a surprised smile broke out over his face. "Well, Devlin, I must admit, I'm impressed."

"Given the low standards you maintain towards me, I doubt that's saying much, but I'm always happy to prove you wrong," quipped Devlin. "Now if you'll excuse me, I promised to show Enif the gymnasium, and then I need to decide what to wear tonight."

As everyone went their separate ways, Dunston caught my eye. "May I speak with you and Kyra for a moment?"

13

SEBASTIAN

Kyra and I readily agreed and followed Dunston into a room I hadn't been in before, which turned out to be a beautiful library filled with books of all colors, shapes, and sizes. My fingers twitched, eager to touch spines and pages, but such a diversion would have to wait. Dunston motioned for us to sit. As he sank into a dark brown armchair, he cleared his throat before drumming his fingers against the arm rests. It wasn't like him to hesitate over a conversation he'd initiated, and the fire flickered uneasily beneath my skin.

"Let me start by saying I truly believe everything you've shared about your pasts and the history of the realm," he began. "And I'm committed to helping you for both personal and professional reasons. But, there's a good chance other Daevals will need more convincing."

I wasn't surprised at his assessment, and for once there was an easy solution to a problem we faced. "Once we've recovered the Chronicles, LeBehr can make copies so everyone can read the truth for themselves."

"It's not just the information," admitted Dunston. "It's the delivery. I can tell government officials everything you shared, or they can read it themselves, but it's far more convincing coming from you."

I knew what he was going to say before the words left his mouth.

"It could go a long way towards ensuring support from those in power if you two spoke to the Nocenian government."

I forced myself to sit calmly while Dunston finished, even though I wanted to immediately insist I would never do such a thing. It had been hard enough telling folks I'd known my entire life about my past as the king of Aeles-Nocens . . . I couldn't imagine trying to tell Daevals who didn't know me—or who knew me and disliked me—who I'd been at one time.

Kyra moved closer and placed a hand on my leg, aware of my discomfort. "What would we tell them?" she asked.

"Exactly what you told us." Dunston scooted to the edge of his seat, clearly pleased Kyra was at least considering his suggestion, which was no doubt why he'd made it with her present. "You don't need to mention being a Recovrancer. It's probably best if we keep that to ourselves for the time being. Just talk about who the two of you used to be, how you reconnected, and how you're going to reunite the realms—and what will happen to Aeles and Nocens if the two aren't rejoined."

Kyra looked at me before turning back to Dunston. "I'm not opposed to it, but could we have a moment to discuss what you're proposing?"

"Of course!" Dunston hopped up and bustled towards the door, his dimples drilling holes in his cheeks even though we hadn't agreed to anything yet. "Take all the time you need, and just ask the house to direct you to me once you're done."

The instant Dunston closed the door, I shook my head. "I'm not telling the entire Nocenian government who I used to be."

Kyra ducked her head, tucking her hair behind her ears. "I'm certainly not excited about it. Given the lies Tallus has been spreading, Daevals probably won't believe a word I say. But given who we are, I don't see how we can avoid being in the public eye, at least for a while."

"I don't want to be in the public eye."

Nothing good ever came from being noticed. Being noticed had meant being teased by my classmates for stumbling over words as I read out loud. Being noticed had resulted in my father killing my mother so he could force me to hone my skills at the Nocenian military academy. Being noticed had caused me to be tortured and experimented on by those with golden blood.

Being noticed came with terrible consequences.

"We don't need anyone's approval for what we're planning," I snapped. "What are they going to do—vote on whether the realms should continue to exist?" I scoffed at such a thought.

"We don't need anyone's permission," agreed Kyra, "but it would be nice to have their support."

"Astrals and Daevals can live in a reunited realm without needing to know we were the ones who reunited it," I insisted. "If we tell the Nocenian government our plans, they're going to say I shouldn't be involved because of the things I've done. I'll have to assure them I'm changing careers, and I shouldn't have to tell anyone anything about what I plan to do for a living."

"But you've already decided to change careers." Confusion surfaced in Kyra's eyes.

"I did. But I'm doing it for me—for *us*. I'm not doing it for anyone else. And I don't want anyone thinking I'm doing it because I have no choice."

I had a choice, and while I was certain I was making the right one, a heavy sadness nevertheless swept over me. I'd worked hard to build my business. It had made me feared, as well as respected, in addition to keeping me fed and clothed and able to live without worrying about my finances. Thanks to Dunston's advice, I'd invested in profitable ventures that meant I wouldn't need to work for the foreseeable future. Even though I knew I could build another successful business, this was still a loss—and one I didn't intend to speak publicly about.

"Wouldn't addressing the government be a good way of clearing up any confusion about what you intend to do for a living moving forward?" asked Kyra.

"It's none of their business!" I all but roared. Taking a deep breath, I tried to calm myself. "It's different for you. You've spent your entire life preparing to be your realm's *Princeps Shaman*. I've never wanted to hold a public office or be anyone of note. I agreed to return when the time was right to reunite the realms. I did *not* agree to become a public figure again!"

I got to my feet and stalked across the room, summoning a flame to my hand and gazing into it, wishing I could burn every government building in Nocens to the ground even though that wouldn't actually solve anything. After a moment, Kyra came to stand behind me.

"Just because I've always planned on holding a public position doesn't mean I like everything about it," she said softly. "But you're right that I've had a lot more time to adjust to the idea of living in a constant spotlight. For me, the benefits outweigh the aggravations. But it's always been my choice, and I'm sorry you're being put in this position just because of who you used to be. It's not fair."

She fell silent, and I pulled the fire back inside me before turning to face her, appreciating her understanding how difficult this was for me. At the same time, I knew what she wanted us to do.

"You think we should address the Nocenian government, though. The way you see it, because of our pasts, we have a responsibility to help change things in Aeles and Nocens for the better."

My words brought a mildly embarrassed but also pleased smile to Kyra's face. "Am I that predictable?"

"I just know you."

"You know me better than anyone. And you're right, that is how I feel. While the thought of telling complete strangers who we used to be and what we're planning to do is absolutely terrifying, we're the only ones who know the truth. We can't expect the realms to move forward without guidance, and because of our pasts, we're uniquely positioned to guide them. I don't want to be involved in running a united realm forever—I want to focus on healing and recovrancy—but I don't think I can be happy doing what I want to until I've done what I need to."

Studying Kyra as she struggled to find a habitable space between her desire and her duty, I wondered if Astrals and Daevals would ever truly appreciate the woman who had once been their queen. I doubted it, which made me even more dismissive of addressing them.

"Dunston clearly thinks it's a good idea for us to address the Nocenian government," Kyra added. "He's done so much for me and my family—all the Dekarais have—I'd hate to let him down."

As much as I cared for Dunston and felt I owed him for everything he'd done for Kyra, I didn't see myself paying him back by speaking to ostentatious Daevals who had more money than sense. But this wasn't only about me. If Kyra believed addressing the Nocenian government was the right thing to do, she would do it, even if she had to stand before them by herself. I couldn't abandon her like that. A mixture of emotions tangled in my chest as I thought back to our conversation about the cost of reuniting the realms. Kyra had feared we would be forced to make additional sacrifices we hadn't anticipated, and she'd been right.

It was one thing to change professions, but it was something else entirely to give up my privacy, telling folks who I'd been in a past life and assuring them I would no longer be an assassin moving forward so they wouldn't be worried I'd end their lives if they didn't do as Kyra and I wanted. This was a change I hadn't expected being forced to make. I valued my privacy more than anything—well, anything except Kyra, of course. I supposed if I looked at it from that perspective, becoming a public figure was a way I could support her and our relationship. Thinking about it that way made the idea of turning my past life into public knowledge no less terrible, but at least doable.

"Tallus is doing everything he can to foster hatred between the realms," Kyra continued. "This is a way we can directly counteract his lies. And even though we don't need permission or approval, everyone has a right to know what we're doing. They live here too. Whatever we do affects them."

"I hate how you always have to be the one sharing such big news." I scowled at the toes of my boots, but Kyra took my hand, drawing my attention to her.

"I don't mind," she said. "I think we each do whatever we find easier, and we take turns supporting one another. I enjoy public speaking, and I'm a stickler for making sure everything is clearly understood, so I don't mind answering questions."

I envisioned myself pulling a knife on someone who dared question me about reuniting the realms, and Kyra smiled, following along with my thoughts through our bracelets. "It's definitely better to let me handle the questions," she agreed. "But I mean it, Sebastian . . . if you don't want to do this, we don't have to."

"I don't want to do this," I said, "but I also think we have to."

Kyra rested the side of her head against my shoulder, and I leaned over and brushed a kiss against her hair. I still wasn't happy about giving up my privacy and losing the anonymity I'd worked so hard to maintain, but if I had to become some sort of recognizable public figure, at least I would do so with Kyra by my side.

"Let's go tell Dunston our decision," I said.

14

KYRA

Dunston was thrilled we were willing to address the Nocenian government. Before he hurried away to organize everything, he handed me a silver peerin with a sparkling topaz set in the top lid.

"Compliments of Caz," he grinned.

Given how tightly governments controlled peerins that could communicate across realms, I couldn't imagine the favors Caz had called in to acquire the device, but I gratefully accepted the gift and offered Dunston the peerin Caz had been loaning me in return.

Back in our shared room, Sebastian grabbed Rhannu and headed off to find Enif. I briefly considered asking if he wanted me to accompany him, but if there was one thing Sebastian could speak comfortably about, it was his sword. He could excuse himself from any conversation that became too uncomfortable.

Even though it was just after the middle of the night in Aeles, I wanted Demitri to have my new contact information when he woke. I rang him, intending to leave a message, but he accepted the communication, sitting up in bed and rearranging his burgundy pillows behind his back.

"I'm sorry to wake you," I said, but he quickly shook his head, his mussed hair falling into his eyes.

"I was still up. It's not like I'm sleeping great these days." His expression softened. "Besides, I'm grateful for any chance to speak with you. I miss you."

"I miss you too. How are you? Has Tallus met with you or your family again?"

"No, thank the Gifters. He's officially assumed emergency powers and has the military on stand-by. He's clearly pushing Aeles towards a war with Nocens. I'm not certain if it's a ploy to try and get the Nocenian government to hand you over or if he's actually serious about a potential invasion, but Celenia is more tense than I've ever felt it."

Demitri dropped his gaze. "It's probably nothing," he said, choosing his words with the care of someone picking their way across a floor of broken glass, "but I ran into Healer Omnurion when I was leaving work this evening. She was on her way to meet with Tallus and said she couldn't visit because the specimens shouldn't be out in the open for long. When she realized I had no idea what she was talking about, she opened the box she was carrying and—it looked like it was filled with little bottles of golden blood."

I felt as if someone had upended a bucket of ice water over my head. Sebastian had ended the experimentation program. What in the falling stars was Tallus doing with golden blood? Did he still have silver blood hidden somewhere? Was he somehow continuing to compare the two? Even though I believed Demitri, his observation didn't make sense. Why would Tallus continue that line of research when he knew Daevals couldn't be turned into Astrals through their blood?

"Healer Omnurion wasn't happy about whatever she'd been summoned for," continued Demitri, "and she's incredibly worried about you. I've been doing everything I can to remind Astrals how important you are and how sickness will inevitably run rampant if you aren't here to heal us." He smiled. "At least this is one time in my life I don't have to pretend. It's not an act to be your incredibly concerned best friend."

I wanted to tell him about my plan to remove Tallus's shade and end his existence forever, but I also didn't want him to possess any information that could potentially get him into trouble. I settled for smiling back at him.

"Thank you," I said, "and please be careful." Even though I knew he would be, I felt better reminding him since there was nothing else I could conceivably do to protect him.

"How are things in Nocens?" Demitri asked. "How's Sebastian handling . . . everything?"

"Thank you for asking." Sebastian and Demitri had started out despising one another, barely able to exchange a civil word and acting like I was something to be fought over; thankfully, Tallus kidnapping me had given them a reason to work together, and they were making a concerted effort to get along. "It's a lot for him, but he's really trying. He had lunch with my mother and brothers today."

A sharp laugh escaped Demitri's mouth before he could stop himself, and he coughed in an attempt to hide it. "And how did *that* go?"

"Surprisingly well. We discussed everything from him opening a new security consulting business to what it was like being king of Aeles-Nocens to having Batty oversee the catering at our wedding."

Demitri's mouth fell open, and I knew exactly what part of my statement he was fixating on, so I quickly shook my head.

"We have absolutely no plans to get married any time soon. It was just something Deneb and Enif brought up, mostly because Deneb wants to be a 'ring bear,' also known as a ring bear*er*. But Sebastian handled the entire experience very well. He didn't draw a weapon and he didn't run out of the room, so I consider it a success."

"That's definitely worth celebrating," agreed Demitri.

"He's going to attempt to recover the Chronicles tonight." I explained about the auction and the roles Devlin and LeBehr would play. "I'm still disappointed I'm not going with them, but we can't risk anyone recognizing me."

"Staying behind has to be so hard," lamented Demitri. "After all, you wrote the Chronicles! But it makes sense. Even though Tallus probably assumes you're in Nocens, there's no need to confirm your whereabouts."

I considered pointing out that Sebastian had said the same thing, making this a rare but noteworthy occasion where my best friend and my chosen partner actually agreed on something involving me. But they were both trying, and that was enough.

"I'll let you know once we've got the Chronicles back," I said instead. "Try to get some sleep. I love you."

"I love you too," said Demitri, blowing me a kiss before ending the call.

I gazed at the peerin for a moment, sad I couldn't be in my own realm and worried over Demitri's safety but also grateful I had a way to speak with him and see with my own eyes he was as well as could be expected.

Setting the peerin aside, I picked up *The Book of Recovrancy*, determined to make the most of the afternoon. Glancing at the empty cushion beside me on the seaweed-colored sofa, I wished Aurelius was there. It was so odd to sit and read something without him curled up next to me, twitching a paw or ear as he slept. At the same time, I appreciated the work he was doing. Just a few short weeks ago, he'd been as prejudiced against those with silver blood as most Astrals. I was pleased his experiences with Daevals and their Cyphers had made him content to judge those in Nocens based on their actions rather than their blood. My family's Cyphers and those paired with the Dekarais seemed to be acting similarly, and I hoped their behavior was an indication of how most Cyphers would react.

As I opened *The Book of Recovrancy*, excitement laced with nervousness made my hands shake. Laycus had agreed to help me dispose of Tallus, which meant I was ready to know how to remove a shade from a body. I placed my palm flat against the title page.

Laycus is willing to consume Tallus's shade if I can get him to appear in Vaneklus before his appointed time of death. Will you teach me how to remove a shade from a body?

Unlike my previous conversation with the book, this time text appeared almost immediately.

Yes.

I lifted my hand and the pages fluttered forward, coming to a stop as text and pictures appeared on the white paper. The title at the top of the page read, "*Anima Remotionem*," which the book translated as, "Shade Removal."

> *Removing a shade from a body is quite difficult, as shades are always harder to manage in the realm of the living than in Vaneklus. This procedure will require the precise and coordinated use of Rheolath, Zerstoren, and Tawazun. Be advised that this sound combination is especially challenging to manage as Rheolath and Zerstoren will each seek to be dominant, which is why Tawazun must be included, to balance the powers of the other two notes.*
>
> *In order to remove a shade, you will need to be within six feet of the body you are removing the shade from. You will use Rheolath to assume control of the body, ensuring it does not*

run away or attempt to fight you. Once you have control, you will say the following:

Permitte mihi videre quod est absconditum (Allow me to see what is hidden)

You will then have the ability to see the shade separate from the body it has inhabited. Once you can see the shade, you will say:

Pono imperium tuum et umbram tuam (I assume control of your shade and your self)

Praecipio animae tuae ut facias mandata mea (I command your shade to do my bidding)

After this, you will add in the sounds of Zerstoren and Tawazun. Zerstoren will allow you to destroy the connection between the shade and body. The same way you use your alera *to destroy harmful growths connected to a body, you will direct your* alera *around the shade, severing its connection to the body it has inhabited. Tawazun will ensure balance between Rheolath and Zerstoren while also protecting the shade from harm.*

You will then take hold of the shade and bring it with you into Vaneklus.

Perhaps the most challenging part of this procedure is that there is no way to practice it, as it is far too dangerous to go about removing and reinserting shades at will. As with all aspects of being a Recovrancer, much depends on the will of the woman attempting the procedure. Whether you believe you will succeed or fail, you will be correct.

When no additional text appeared, I gazed across the room. Even though I was nervous about performing such a complicated procedure, I'd also come to trust my recovrancy skills and didn't doubt I could do it. The most troubling part of the whole process was that I needed to be within six feet of Tallus in order to assume control of his shade. How would I manage to get so close without him trying to capture or harm me? Thanks to our suppressor medallion, Sebastian could open a portal to anywhere in Aeles without triggering the Blood Alarm, but with the military on alert and the entire realm poised for war, I couldn't imagine the two of us simply strolling into Tallus's office in Celenia. Thankfully, if anyone could organize a successful strategic operation, it was Sebastian. After he retrieved the Chronicles, he could turn his full attention to getting me close to Tallus.

I practiced repeating the provided shade removal spells until I could say them smoothly from memory, coordinating the words with the beads of my *sana* bracelet. Having accomplished that, I glanced at the door. Sebastian hadn't returned, which meant this was a good opportunity to read about recovering his mother. I could certainly read about it with him present, but seeing him every time I looked up from a page would also be an inescapable reminder of exactly who would be heartbroken if Grace's return wasn't successful.

Pressing my palm against the smooth paper, I asked, *How do I recover a shade from Ceelum?*

Lifting my hand, I couldn't keep from smiling as the pages flipped forward. I'd never imagined interacting with a book in such a way, but as new text appeared, I found myself grateful and more than a little awed by this unexpected benefit of being a Recovrancer.

You are already aware recovering a shade from Ceelum is one of, if not the most, complicated procedures a Recovrancer can attempt to perform, far more difficult than removing a shade. You may only use this spell once in your current life cycle. Are you certain you wish to proceed with learning how to recover a shade from Ceelum?

I pressed my fingertips against the edge of the page. *Yes.*

Very well.

I felt as if I was in my kadac being lifted by an ocean wave, rising upwards and speeding across the water's surface, and my heart drummed in my ears as I read the words appearing before me.

In order to recover a shade from Ceelum, the shade must have died before their appointed time. They must be residing in Ceelum, and they must wish to be recovered.

This was information I was already familiar with, and I nodded my understanding, even though the book couldn't see me. I'd journeyed to Ceelum to speak with Grace, and I doubted I would ever forget the desperate hope that had flooded her face at learning there was a chance she might be reunited with her son. Despite the dangers I'd carefully explained to her, she'd given me her blessing to attempt her recovrancy after I had acquired the necessary knowledge to perform such a feat.

More text appeared.

After these requirements have been met, someone else must die at their appointed time. They must possess the same gold or silver blood as the shade you are seeking to recover possessed in their last life. They must also be willing to have their body used to house the shade you wish to bring back to the land of the living.

While no two recovrancies are the same, we have found it best if the shade who is willing to donate their body has some connection to the shade you are attempting to recover. This is not a requirement for a successful recovrancy, but past experience consistently demonstrates a better outcome when the shade is already somewhat familiar with the body that will be housing them during their return to life.

Well, that certainly complicated things. I tapped a finger against the edge of the page. How was I going to find someone who had known Grace when she'd been alive, not to mention someone who still remembered her even though she'd been dead for thirteen years *and* would agree to donate their body to house her shade? It wouldn't be so difficult if Laycus possessed an almanac listing the dates and times Daevals were scheduled to die; I could share the names with Grace and see if she'd known any of them, identifying possible body-donating candidates. Unfortunately, Laycus had said before he wasn't aware of a death until the shade appeared in Vaneklus, which meant I would have to go to Vaneklus each time a Daeval arrived and speak with them to determine if they'd known Grace.

The book continued.

Once the shade who died at their appointed time has given you permission to use their body, you will perform the Incolens Corpus Novem *spell.*

You will begin by going into Vaneklus and summoning the shade you wish to recover from Ceelum, using Rheolath and Tawazun as you say:

Quiete te accerso (From rest I summon you)

De morte mittam te (From Death I will send you)

In terra viventium (To the land of the living)

Tibet licet redire (You are allowed to return)

The shade will appear before you. Instruct them to hold onto you as you coordinate a four-bead combination: Rheolath, for control over the shade; Tawazun, for balancing Rheolath's appetite for power; Saund, so the shade may be at peace; and Lleiaf, so the shade's memories from the last life they lived will remain intact. You will say:

Id quod mihi permittitur facere (That which I am permitted to do)

Libenter facio (I do willingly)

Ut haec umbra iungere cum hoc corpore (May this shade join with this body)

Cursus vitae, ubi mors (Ensuring life where there is death)

You will then return to the land of the living and wait for evidence the tethering was successful. We find it best to avoid having all family members of the recovered shade present as they return to life, as you cannot predict how the shade will behave.

Making sure my fingertips were touching the page, I thought, *What if the recovrancy isn't successful?*

The book answered quickly.

If the procedure is not successful, the shade will begin to panic, or worse. There have been instances where shades formed enough of a connection with their new body to attack those around them; hence, caution should always be exercised when dealing with a newly recovered shade.

As if that wasn't enough cause for concern, the book added,

While bringing a shade out of Vaneklus depends entirely upon the skill of the Recovrancer, it is up to the shade to accept the new body they have been given, making the abilities of the Recovrancer no guarantee of a successful recovery.

I gazed at the seahorse-shaped lighting fixture across the room, grateful I knew more about the complicated procedure even though I didn't like some of what I'd learned. It wasn't fair—I could do everything right and Grace still might not adjust to being alive again. Why couldn't the result depend on me as much as the process? I'd much rather accept full responsibility for something and have my efforts fail than do everything correctly and still not be able to ensure a given outcome.

Even without Aurelius there to make the point, I didn't miss the parallels between recovering Grace and removing Sebastian's traumatic memories. Why were two of the most important things I wanted to do—both of which involved making Sebastian's life better—ultimately beyond my control, no matter how hard I worked? My stomach knotted. Even though I knew I wasn't all-powerful, I couldn't keep from wishing I was, pointless as such wishes were.

Still, forewarned was forearmed. I needed to find a shade who had died at their appointed time, who recalled Grace from thirteen years ago, and who was willing to have Grace take over their body as they journeyed onwards with Laycus. I wasn't certain what presently seemed more impossible: recovering Grace, reuniting the realms, or removing Tallus's shade. But such was the way of impossible tasks. They were only impossible until you mastered them—or at least survived them.

15

SEBASTIAN

Showing Rhannu to Enif had gone surprisingly well. Kyra's brother had been fascinated with the weapon, and I'd shown him how to hold it and even how to perform a few simple blocks and parries. The sword was too large for him, of course, but that hadn't deterred him, and the afternoon had sped by faster than I'd expected.

Returning to my room to prepare for going to the Nemoyas', I found Kyra reading, although she put aside her recovrancy book to tell me what Demitri had shared about Healer Omnurion taking golden blood to Tallus. While he didn't have any more Daevalic children to draw blood from, it was at least possible he'd stored silver blood somewhere other than the experimentation facility. If I hadn't hated Tallus with every fiber of my being, I might have been impressed at his unwavering commitment to searching for ways to get rid of Daevals.

Putting Tallus from my mind, I turned my attention to preparing for the auction. Thankfully, unlike the party the Dekarais had thrown for Kyra a few weeks ago, this event wouldn't require me to dress up; there was no reason to deviate from my usual clothing if I was accompanying Devlin as security detail. I'd likely be asked to surrender any weapons I brought, so there was no point in taking Rhannu, but even without a weapon, my fire and fists were usually enough to give folks a second thought about engaging with me.

Kyra and I made our way to the Driftwood Lounge, and I didn't miss the disappointment intermittently surfacing in her eyes. I knew she hated staying behind, even though she was trying to remain upbeat. Opening a portal to LeBehr's bookstore, I schooled my expression to be perfectly neutral—or what passed as neutral for me—and tried not to stare at the bookseller's outfit. LeBehr was never one to attempt to blend in. Her floor-length dress appeared to be made entirely of pink and purple feathers, aside from the silver plumes perched on her shoulders like soft epaulettes. The entire garment was spelled to occasionally flutter, and as was customary for her, she'd laced a black corset over the dress instead of under it. Holding up the hem of her feathery garment, she grinned as she lifted a foot, showing off her no-nonsense boots.

"I've learned a thing or two from you over the years," she said. "These are in case we need to move quickly."

"That was good thinking," I agreed, surprised she'd paid such close attention to something I'd said, much less acted on it.

"I've also got the map to lead us to the Chronicles"—LeBehr patted her handbag—"but I cast a spell so anyone else looking at it won't see a map. They'll see a list of books I'm searching for at the auction."

"Excellent." I nodded approvingly as Mischief materialized on a shelf and used a paw to open the cover of a book. "Are you coming as well?"

While my tone had been respectful, the cat hissed. "I would rather become a mortal animal forced to hunt in order to feed myself!" snarled the Cypher. "I will not be setting a paw outside of this shop. Aurelius and Batty are in the back room, and we are still searching for how to break the *Memoria Aeterna* spell."

I shall meet you at the Nemoyas', Batty said. *There's a chance we may be onto something.*

"Thank you for your assistance in that matter." I bowed low to Mischief before following LeBehr through the portal.

Kyra rushed to welcome the bookseller, marveling over her attire just as Devlin arrived, Onyx at his side. Studying my clothes, Devlin sighed unhappily but didn't press the issue, since tonight the less noticeable I was, the better. Instead, he turned his attention to LeBehr, and the two moved to embrace one another.

"I swear you get more handsome every time I see you!" exclaimed the bookseller. "Now, if only I could get you to read more. I know all those books your parents order from me are gathering dust somewhere in your room, probably under a pile of clothes."

Devlin grinned. "Not all of them. I've given some as gifts, and they've always been very well-received."

"Well," LeBehr considered Devlin's words, "I suppose regifting a book is the next best thing to reading it."

"You look marvelous!" Devlin took her hand and spun her in a circle, causing LeBehr to laugh. "I'm not used to spending an evening with someone who's both beautiful *and* brilliant. This is going to be quite the adventure."

LeBehr made an exasperated noise, even though her smile only grew wider.

Devlin turned to face me. "Like I said before, the Nemoyas' house is warded against portals. I thought it might seem suspicious if I asked Win'Din to make an exception for us when it's already such a big deal I'll be there." He handed me a piece of paper. "I've arranged for a carriage to meet us at this location. It's the town nearest to the Nemoyas', and this way we can arrive in style."

I rolled my eyes but nevertheless consented, as Devlin admittedly knew far more about the rules of Nocenian society than I did. And he was right . . . we didn't want to arouse suspicion. Concentrating on the written coordinates, I opened a portal. As LeBehr, Devlin, and Onyx vanished through the gateway, I turned to Kyra, who stepped forward and gave me a hug.

"I'll find the book," I assured her. I couldn't help feeling guilty leaving her behind, but at the same time, it was also a relief knowing she'd be safe at Sea'Brik, allowing me to focus my undivided attention on acquiring the Chronicles.

"I know." Her voice was muffled against my tunic. "Be careful. And try to be patient with Devlin." We pulled apart and she took a step back, wrapping her arms around herself before offering me a final wave.

As I strode through the portal into Jaasfar, a hot gust of wind hit me squarely in the face, which was exactly the sort of greeting I'd expect from the harsh desert territory. Even though the sun had set and the sky was dark, the heat of the day still lingered over the oasis town, making me glad we wouldn't be walking to the auction.

Devlin gestured proudly at a nearby carriage. "Our ride awaits!"

To my credit, I managed to bite back my initial reaction. We weren't trying to sneak in, we were trying to make an entrance, which had to be the *only* explanation for why Devlin had secured what had to be the most ostentatious carriage in the entire realm. The body was crafted from hammered silver and fitted with ebony doors. I could see my reflection in the polished wheels, each spoke studded with jewels that glinted in the light cast by a nearby street lamp. The carriage was enchanted, meaning it didn't need to be pulled by horses or mules, and polished gold lanterns shone from each corner. Grasping the silver handle, Devlin grinned at LeBehr as he opened the door.

"Ladies first."

LeBehr's eyes sparkled as Devlin helped her into the coach.

"I don't usually think of myself as a lady, but I could get used to this," she said as she made herself comfortable.

I took a seat opposite her as Onyx curled up on the floor and Devlin pulled the door shut with a gentle *click* before settling beside the bookseller.

Inside, the carriage was even nicer than out. The plush bench seats faced one another and were so thick you could hold a drink without spilling even if there were bumps in the road. The walls were lined with black silk, and small cabinets were built into the sides, containing miniature bottles of things to drink, as well as tins of chocolates and other candies. There was an option to have spelled music play. You could even fill the carriage with a variety of different scents, although I couldn't imagine why anyone would want to.

Cupping his hand in front of his mouth, Devlin spoke the address of the Nemoyas' house, then pressed his palm against the side of the carriage. The silk-paneled wall rippled as it absorbed the directions. The coach gave a slight shudder, as if shaking itself off after a long sleep, then slipped forward without so much as a lurch, the wheels gliding smoothly over the stone road.

"And we're off!" cheered Devlin.

Raising the shade, I glanced out the window, taking in the endless red sand stretching to the horizon. Given my fair complexion, I generally avoided the desert. When I did complete contracts there, I added a surcharge for the hassle—the sand rubbed blisters inside my boots, the wind tore at my face, and it was easy to get turned around in the dunes and lose your way. At night, however, even I had to admit it wasn't a terrible landscape. With no large cities nearby, the stars shone luminously overhead, and I thought of how much Kyra would have enjoyed seeing the Nocenian constellations.

Whether it was something about my expression or just that

easy to guess who I'd be thinking about, LeBehr leaned forward, a smile on her face.

"You probably haven't had the chance to show Kyra much of Nocens, but when the time is right, I bet she'll want a full tour. From what I've read about Aeles, there aren't any deserts there, so she's probably never seen anything like Jaasfar."

"She'd love the stars here," I said. "She's always been fascinated by the night sky, even when she was Kareth."

LeBehr's eyes lit up excitedly. "The Rhai Lla'khar meteor shower is in a few weeks. This would be a wonderful place to bring her to watch it."

"She would love that," I agreed. It was difficult picturing the two of us doing something as ordinary as lying on a blanket, watching stars stream past us, given how focused we were on stopping Tallus and reuniting the realms. It certainly sounded nice, though, if for no other reason than it would mean we'd accomplished what we'd set out to do and could enjoy some well-deserved time by ourselves. Filing away LeBehr's suggestion, I nevertheless put such pleasant imaginings aside, as entering a dangerous situation—like the auction—with a distracted mind only invited injury, if not death.

"We should discuss our strategy before we arrive," I said. While I usually planned out my jobs by myself, you could never have too much information about a location or target. I looked at Devlin. "How do you think we should proceed?"

Devlin sat up straighter, clearly pleased at having his opinion sought. I couldn't remember ever directly asking his advice about anything before, but I gathered information where it was available, not where I thought it should be.

"Once we arrive, we'll present our invitation." He tapped the lapel of his jacket. "I expect most of the house will be off-limits for guests, but we'll have the run of whatever part is open to visitors. Security will be present but not obvious. If the Nemoyas have to choose between making an impression or being safe, they'll go with making an impression."

I couldn't fathom being so stupid, but I supposed it was fortunate for me so many others were fine with it.

Devlin stroked one of the numerous red silk ribbons hanging from the sleeve of his jacket. "With the blessing of the Fates, the Chronicles will be up for auction. I think LeBehr and I should do the bidding, and when we win, I'll pay for the book."

"I'll pay you back for the book," I corrected him, in no need of his financial assistance and not about to be any more indebted to the Dekarais than I already was. Remembering Kyra's admonishment to be patient with Devlin, I added, "But I agree, you and LeBehr should do the bidding. In fact, you should buy or at least bid on a few other items besides the Chronicles. It will seem odd if you only express interest in one book."

Devlin nodded.

"No one ever accused me of being a shrinking violet," chuckled LeBehr. "What's our plan if the book isn't up for auction?"

"We'll still know its exact location, thanks to you," I said, "so I'll steal it while everyone else is socializing." If the book wasn't up for auction, the next best scenario would be if the Nemoyas were keeping it in a library or bedroom. Even though the anti-portal wards would prevent me from moving as freely as I pleased, I was adept at using shadows and other aspects of my surroundings to avoid being seen. The worst-case scenario would be if the Nemoyas had some idea how valuable the book was and were keeping it locked up under heavy guard. That still didn't make retrieving the book impossible as I could pick locks, counteract alarms, and deal with paid security, but it would be significantly more challenging.

"The fact that a Dekarai is attending a Nemoya party will

ensure everyone's focused on you," I said to Devlin. "If it comes to it, I have no doubt you can hold the attention of the room while I search for the book."

Devlin grinned. "It's nice to have my talents recognized. If that's what we have to do, I can guarantee no one will be looking anywhere but at me."

I didn't necessarily like the idea of trusting Devlin more, but given our situation, I didn't see a better option. Putting my faith in him would have been significantly easier if I'd known the auction invitation was real. While I wanted to believe him, I also couldn't keep from worrying what the Barantula dust would reveal. He didn't appear the slightest bit worried, but that could be an act. My instincts still told me a burglary in which I depended on myself would be easier than depending on others, but I'd also learned from being around Kyra that my instincts weren't always correct. Sometimes choosing a different response resulted in a better outcome.

I just hoped I'd made the right choice and would be rewarded with the Chronicles.

As Devlin opened a drawer and pulled out a mirror to check his reflection, something else occurred to me. "While we're there," I said, "you need to keep a clear head and be aware of your surroundings. Stay away from the wine."

"You can't attend an event like this and not have a drink!" scoffed Devlin. "It'll seem rude if I went to the trouble of getting an invitation and then won't even enjoy the refreshments. No host would appreciate being slighted in such a way."

I couldn't have cared less about slighting the feelings of folks like the Nemoyas, but Devlin was probably right about us needing to blend in with the vapid society we were forced to interact with tonight. "Fine," I said. "But if I have to choose between carrying you or the Chronicles out of the auction—"

"—I know, I know," interjected Devlin. "You aren't the only one who wants this to be a success, alright?"

He replaced the mirror, satisfied his appearance hadn't changed since the last time he'd inspected it, and a loud buzzing sound rang out, prompting us to reach for our peerins. The government rarely sent out mass communications. Nervousness zipped alongside the fire in my veins, and even before opening the hinged copper lid, I suspected this might have something to do with me and Kyra.

Text scrolled across the lens:

By order of the government, the borders of Nocens are hereby closed until further notice. Due to unrest in Aeles, intersectors have been reset to issue an alarm should they detect golden blood, and any Astrals found in the realm should be reported to the authorities immediately.

My stomach clenched. Daevals had never outlawed Astrals from coming into our realm before. Aeles had their Blood Alarm, created by Tallus during one of his many life cycles to sound the instant it detected a drop of silver blood, but Nocens kept Astrals at bay through fear, through the knowledge of what would happen should they enter our realm uninvited. I'd been hired to deal with a few such Astrals by the Dekarais as well as other government officials, interrogating or eliminating suspected scouts for the Aelian military or those attempting unsanctioned trade. But this decree was unprecedented, at least in my current lifetime.

I slipped my peerin back into my pocket. Thank the Fates Kyra and her family were with the Dekarais and not in a place where someone might detect their golden blood and report them—or worse.

Devlin caught my eye. "My family will keep Kyra safe. Her mother and siblings too."

I nodded, not questioning that, simply annoyed I needed help yet again to ensure Kyra's safety. It made sense relations between the realms would get worse before they got better, but I hadn't expected things to start deteriorating quite so fast.

Devlin ran a hand along his jaw, his expression thoughtful. "This is probably the last time you'll go somewhere without being noticed. Once you and Kyra reunite the realms and everyone knows who you are—and who you used to be—you'll be joining me in the perpetual spotlight." He grinned. "I'll welcome the company, but it's going to be quite the change for you."

While Devlin's assessment was accurate, it was also an unwanted reminder of the direction my life was taking. "It ought to be enough I'm changing careers." My voice was almost as sharp as Rhannu's blade. "It's absurd I have to become a public figure again."

"It's so much to put on the two of you." LeBehr's expression was apologetic, and the feathers on her shoulders drooped, prompting me to wonder if she'd spelled the garment to correspond with her mood. "Please remember we're here to help however we can. You and Kyra aren't alone, even though I'm certain it feels that way."

"Thank you." Most of the time it did feel like we were alone, but the fact that LeBehr and Devlin were there with me, that they'd believed me and were helping me, made it clear Kyra and I were supported. Then again, given the announcement the government had just made, I couldn't keep from worrying that the support we had—strong though it was—wouldn't be enough to overcome the trials Kyra and I were facing. Unfortunately, as much as I disliked it, there was nothing I could do aside from trusting those around me and hoping for the best—behavior that would have been difficult for me even in the best of times, which these most certainly were not.

The carriage began to slow, and Devlin grinned as he touched his oiled hair. "I have to say, I'm disappointed you'll be giving up espionage. This is exciting!"

I supposed it could be if your life wasn't on the line, but seeing how mine typically was when I completed contracts, I couldn't quite share in Devlin's enthusiasm. Still, I didn't need to squelch it, either, so I simply remained quiet as we rolled up the smooth drive, coming to a stop before an arched doorway with an open gate.

Peering out the window, I recognized the courtyard from LeBehr's map. The open space was surrounded by a high wall. You wouldn't need to post many guards, given the unobstructed view of the desert the house offered, allowing even one or two sentries to see anything coming at them from miles away. I still preferred the impregnability of my cave, but if you were going to be so out in the open, this was a good setup.

Someone opened the carriage door from the outside. I exited first, followed by Devlin and Onyx. As Devlin helped LeBehr out, I studied the space before us, which was helpfully lit by numerous spelled lighting orbs.

Fountains filled the courtyard. Water bubbled, cascaded, pooled, and spiraled, an exorbitant display of wealth in a land where water was more valuable than gold or gems. Devlin had been right about security . . . guards were scattered here and there, but they were wearing party clothes and doing their best to fit in. To trained eyes like mine they were as obvious as candles in a dark room, but I doubted the other auction attendees would even notice, simply assuming they were treasure-seeking guests from across the realm if they didn't recognize them from Vartox society.

As I'd suspected, an attendant was waiting just inside the

courtyard, and next to him was a tall stand supporting a ceramic bowl. Devlin fished the auction invitation from his jacket pocket and presented it with a flourish completely in keeping with his larger-than-life personality. The attendant accepted the paper with one hand while he dipped the other into the bowl. When he lifted it, black Barantula powder glittered across the fingertips of his white glove.

My pulse surged forward with a speed that would have put a desert racing horse to shame. This was it. We would either be allowed inside, or I would learn beyond a shadow of a doubt trusting Devlin had been a mistake.

As the guard's dust-coated fingers made contact with the invitation, a hissing noise sounded. The fire writhed in my veins as it always did when I was anxious, reminding me I wasn't powerless regardless of what happened next. All the same, I still found myself holding my breath as the thick parchment was enveloped in a cloud of black smoke. The smoke vanished almost as quickly as it had appeared, and I blinked to make sure my eyes weren't playing tricks on me.

The invitation was unharmed.

Devlin had been telling the truth.

I allowed myself a silent exhale of relief as the attendant passed back the invitation. It seemed my trust, despite being given begrudgingly, hadn't been misplaced after all.

As we continued deeper into the courtyard, I moved beside Devlin. Keeping my voice low, I muttered, "Well done."

He smirked as he slid the invitation back inside his jacket. "It's not trust if you only believe me *after* I've proven myself. But thank you, and I accept your unspoken apology for doubting me." He offered LeBehr his arm before walking along a path formed by thick carpets leading into the house. I followed, memorizing what I could.

Up close, the house looked even more like a fortress than on LeBehr's map. Smooth stucco would make climbing the walls challenging, and the various levels suggested a maze of twisting staircases that would be difficult to navigate while running or trying to evade someone familiar with the layout. Most of the windows I could see were small and set towards the top of the walls, making them hard to slip through. While I certainly hoped retrieving the Chronicles didn't involve climbing walls or going in and out of windows, I liked having as many escape routes as possible.

Raks and Win'Din were greeting guests just inside the open front door where they wouldn't be bothered by the lingering heat. Low ceilings featured heavy wooden beams, and filigree lanterns were everywhere, hanging overhead, arranged in rows on shelves, or glowing atop tall stands. While they were strategically placed to cast a soft light flattering to guests, the shadows they created would also make it easy to move around unnoticed.

We stopped in front of the Nemoyas, and Devlin bowed as Raks spoke.

"When my wife told me you were coming to our auction, I was certain I'd misheard her." He extended a hand to Devlin as he offered a smile that didn't quite reach his eyes. Raks was short, with a neatly trimmed beard. His earrings, necklaces, and rings were almost as extravagant as his clothes, which featured hundreds of tiny diamonds sewn into geometric patterns along his sleeves and down the legs of his pants.

"I was grateful for the invitation," replied Devlin before turning his attention to Win'Din. She extended her hand to him, and he immediately pressed it against his lips, causing her to giggle as her already rouged cheeks flushed a deeper shade of red. Her wavy blonde hair shone in the lantern light, and she was wrapped in layers of pale pink silk that reminded me of spun sugar. Dark blue sapphires the size of eggs dangled from the woman's ears, matching the sapphire pendant hanging from a gold chain strategically placed to draw attention to her plunging neckline.

"I assume you both know LeBehr," said Devlin, gesturing to the bookseller.

"Of course!" exclaimed Raks with a fawning bow. "We're honored to have you at our little gathering."

"When someone says 'books' it's hard to keep me away," said LeBehr, the silver feathers on her shoulders fluttering excitedly.

Win'Din said something to the bookkeeper as Raks's eyes moved to me. He knew who I was. While hiring me for something as routine as security was over-the-top, it also wouldn't be entirely unexpected given the animosity between the Dekarais and the Nemoyas as well as my closeness with Dunston's family. Raks gave me a silent nod, which I returned just as LeBehr asked, "Any chance of seeing the items before they come up for auction?"

Devlin and the Nemoyas laughed.

"Exactly what I would expect from Nocens' foremost bookseller," tittered Win'Din. "Everything is laid out just around the corner. I'm afraid there's no touching until after you've completed the purchase—that way if you break it, you've already bought it—but please, enjoy looking at what's available."

Devlin thanked her, and I didn't miss the way Win'Din's eyes lingered on him as we walked away. I was grateful for her interest, as it had gotten us into the auction, but I didn't enjoy seeing it with my own eyes, especially when her husband was standing right next to her—although he didn't seem to care.

LeBehr pulled the map from her handbag. While she'd told me about the spell she'd cast on it, I was still briefly surprised to see nothing more than a list of books she hoped to find at the auction scrawled across the paper.

"It's here," said LeBehr, keeping her voice low as her eyes

swept over the parchment. "On a table at the far end of the room."

"I'll follow you," I said. "But let's not go straight there. Start at one of the other tables and work your way over." I didn't want it to appear as if we had a goal in mind or were searching for something in particular.

Devlin grabbed a glass of red wine from a passing tray and gave me a silent toast before taking a drink. While I would have enjoyed throwing something at him, I couldn't do more than hope he'd stick to our agreement about keeping a clear head.

LeBehr headed towards a table featuring several paintings. As she wove in and out of the other attendees, servers passed us carrying overflowing trays. I couldn't recall the last time I'd seen so much food outside of an eatery. There were bowls of apricots and dates, small plates of olives and almonds, lamb kebabs and colorful vegetable skewers, pans of roasted pheasant, stacks of warm flatbread covered in butter and garlic, platters of grilled tomatoes, and tins of salty anchovies.

Arriving at the first table, we made our way past the priceless antiques, most of which appeared old, ugly, or merely useless to my untrained eye. Devlin and LeBehr did an admirable job of considering the items laid out on the white tablecloths, pointing, asking questions, and keeping up a running dialogue. Gloved attendants stood behind the tables, trying to appear bored and uninterested but keeping a close watch as Daevals perused the miniature statues, pottery, glass vases, and other priceless relics of bygone eras. As we reached a table covered with books, I felt my senses sharpen, the awareness of being near the object I was searching for sending a rush of adrenaline to mix with the fire inside me.

Would I recognize the Chronicles when I saw it?

I remembered a hard cover with green binding, but nothing

beyond that as the book had really been nothing more than a journal—albeit an incredibly important one.

About halfway down the table, LeBehr stiffened before folding the map and slipping the parchment back into her handbag. I stepped closer, peering over her shoulder. She didn't have to say anything.

I knew.

There before us was the Chronicles.

16

KYRA

I joined the others for dinner, even though most of my attention was on what Sebastian, Devlin, and LeBehr might be doing at the Nemoyas'. While I agreed the approach we'd taken was for the best, I still wished I were there and could be the first to hold something so important to the two of us, not to mention instrumental to the history and future of both realms.

After eating, I'd planned to pass the time by learning more about removing memories, but as I pushed back my chair, Minerva caught my eye.

"Could we speak privately for a moment?"

My stomach tightened. "Of course," I replied, hoping I didn't sound as nervous as I suddenly felt.

I followed Minerva out of the dining room and down the hallway until she came to an abrupt stop. There appeared to be nothing but a wall in front of us until she placed her hand against a section of the seashell-patterned wallpaper and a doorknob appeared. When she grasped the knob, a door came into view, leading into a previously hidden room that turned out to be a small sitting area with a breathtaking view of the ocean. The room was positioned so the water flowed directly underneath it, and I half-expected a wave to lap against my feet.

"Please, make yourself comfortable." Minerva closed the door before settling gracefully on a white settee.

I chose an armchair across from her, my mind racing to identify what she wanted to discuss. Had one of my siblings done something to upset her? Was she going to ask us to leave? Where would we go? I couldn't picture my entire family in Sebastian's cave, although we might not have another option.

While my nerves made me want to say something, I held my tongue, thinking what Sebastian would do in a similar situation. He wouldn't start talking just to make himself feel a false sense of control over the conversation. He would wait and let whoever had initiated the meeting speak first, allowing him time to consider a response. While it wasn't my natural inclination, it seemed appropriate for the situation at hand.

"I'll get straight to the point." Minerva rested her hands in her lap. "Dunston told me you're addressing the Nocenian government tomorrow. You'll need to be prepared for their questions. Since I'm not as certain about reuniting the realms as the rest of my family, that makes me the perfect Daeval to practice speaking to."

While I'd suspected she wasn't as enthusiastic about our plans as the rest of her family, I also wasn't pleased to hear her say as much. At the same time, I couldn't expect everyone to welcome such enormous change without voicing at least *some* questions or even disagreements, and I'd much rather address them directly. Doing my best to keep a friendly expression on my face, I held the woman's scrutinizing gaze.

"It's a lot to take in," I agreed. "If someone told me everything Sebastian and I shared with you, I'd have questions too."

"I'm glad you can appreciate that. What, exactly, are your plans for after the realms are reunited? You can't imagine everyone will welcome being forced to live with one another."

"I don't plan on forcing anyone to do anything," I assured

her. "Folks can live in whatever part of the united realm they wish, and they'll be given the choice to interact as much or as little as they want. I'm not going to insist Astrals and Daevals suddenly start courting one another."

I'd meant my last words to be humorous, given that I was, in fact, an Astral courting a Daeval, but Minerva didn't offer so much as an indulgent smile.

"The act of reuniting the realms is forcing folks to accept what you believe to be best simply because you have the power to enforce your wishes," she said. "It makes me wonder what other changes you plan on making."

I blinked for lack of a better response, taken aback. Put that way, she made what Sebastian and I were attempting to do sound so selfish.

"Sebastian and I don't intend to form a monarchy and rule the realm ourselves," I tried to explain. "As I mentioned before, I'd like to see a new government formed, comprised of both Astrals and Daevals. I want everyone in Aeles and Nocens to have a say in how we move forward and to be involved in creating what a reunited realm looks like on a day-to-day basis."

"And how do you plan to establish such unity, much less enforce it?" pressed Minerva. "You can't simply have Sebastian eliminate anyone who disagrees with you, not if you wish to have goodwill among your subjects."

"No one is going to be my subject," I bristled. "I don't want to rule Aeles-Nocens. I want to be Aeles's *Princeps Shaman* and improve the care healers are able to give to both Astrals and Daevals."

"You cannot do something as monumental as reuniting the realms and then simply step aside and hope for the best." Minerva shook her head. "Whether you like it or not, you're tied to this, and you'll be the one citizens look to for guidance. That also means you'll be the one they blame when violence inevitably breaks out, diplomatic talks fail, and Astrals and Daevals struggle to live in any sort of proximity."

"Just because I don't plan on ruling doesn't mean I'm going to completely step aside," I said, annoyed at how she was interpreting my words. "I intend to be involved until the realm can function without me." I considered telling her everything Sebastian and I were giving up precisely so we could help guide a united Aeles-Nocens, but I kept my sacrifices to myself and instead asked, "Are you worried what reuniting the realms will mean for your business?" Given how the conversation was going, I saw no reason to be delicate. "Because this could benefit you and your brothers more than anyone else. You could lead the way in government-sanctioned commerce between Aeles and Nocens. You have the operational capacity, and you also have what no one else does: advance knowledge of how things are going to change."

"It's not that simple," she replied. "Of course we can pivot the business and do well. It's the fact that we have no say in such a thing and will be *forced* to pivot that bothers me." Calculations swirled across her grey eyes. "How, exactly, is your reuniting the realms different from Tallus dividing them?"

"*Excuse* me?" I had to have misheard her.

"Based on what you said before, Tallus made the decision to divide the realms, then took action and did it. You've decided to reunite the realms, and you have the power to act. It seems we are trading one individual making decisions for the realms for another."

"It's not like that at all!" I insisted. "Tallus destroyed families; he killed and tortured Daevals. I want Astrals and Daevals to live peaceably and happily together."

"Because that's what you think best," said Minerva. "Tallus likely thought he knew best as well."

I couldn't believe what I was hearing. How could this woman

possibly compare me to someone like Tallus? "It's true Tallus wielded power just as I'm capable of wielding power." I clasped my hands in my lap to keep them from shaking as anger spread through me. "But he chose to use his power for evil, whereas I'm choosing to use mine for good. And before you say good and evil are matters of perspective, he killed those who didn't agree with him; I've never done such a thing, nor would I."

Minerva dipped her head, allowing me that. "True, but you still aren't giving them a choice."

"What would you rather us do?" While I could have asked the question in a gentler tone, I was ready to hear whatever point Minerva wished to make sooner rather than later.

"It seems we are past the point of choosing whether or not to reunite the realms, given their instability," she said. "But simply because the realms have to be reunited does not mean the same must go for Astrals and Daevals. After you and Sebastian rejoin Aeles and Nocens, citizens should be allowed to vote on whether they would like to live and interact with one another."

I stared at her, fully aware I was doing a terrible job of hiding my frustration, and she continued.

"The only way to truly ensure the reunification process is successful is to allow everyone a say in the matter. If the vote passes, at least those who voted against it will know their voice was heard. And if the vote doesn't pass, then it's clear those with silver and gold blood are not ready to share their lives with one another."

"How a reunited realm functions is far too important to be left up to a vote," I protested.

"Because you're afraid those voting won't make the same decision as you?"

"I'm not certain they know the right decision to make," I said. "When you've been raised on lies, how do you recognize truth? I grew up being told Daevals are cruel, untrustworthy creatures barely capable of speech and thought. I didn't know such things weren't true until I interacted with those in Nocens for myself. Nothing short of interacting with one another is going to change how Astrals and Daevals view those with different blood."

"I agree firsthand experience is the most compelling," said Minerva. "But I still don't like that you're going to force everyone to have such experiences. That's implying you don't trust those in either realm to make the right decision."

"Then I suppose I *don't* trust them to make the right decision," I replied in a heated voice. "When you grow up on nothing but government-approved propaganda created for the sole purpose of being divisive, how can you know unity is even possible? Each side thinks they're right because of what they've been told their entire lives, so I can't trust them to be informed enough to know they're wrong."

"Spoken like a true monarch," observed Minerva.

"Spoken like someone who has had opportunities other Astrals and Daevals haven't," I countered. "I've seen and experienced more than most, and that gives me a different perspective. I would be failing in my duties as someone capable of bringing about change if I didn't use what I'd been through to make things better and safer for those in Aeles and Nocens."

Minerva was silent as she considered my words. "It still bothers me, though," she finally said. "When the realms were divided, the average citizen had no say, and it appears they will continue to have no voice as the realms are reunited. I trust you see the similarities?"

"I see returning the realm to its rightful state," I replied firmly. "But . . . I also see the wisdom in what you're saying." Gazing out at the ocean waves rising and falling beneath the night sky, I offered silent prayers to Acies and Bellum, the Gifters of Wisdom and

Victory. "I don't necessarily like it, but we *could* hold a vote after the realms are rejoined," I conceded. "You're right that, regardless of the outcome, at least everyone would have a say. Citizens could choose to integrate, or they could choose to create separate living areas for those with silver and gold blood. For all I know, the majority in either realm will want to remain exactly where they are and ensure their lives are as uninterrupted as possible."

Minerva crossed one leg over the other. Unlike her brothers, who were far more expressive, she didn't appear to make a move unless it was on purpose. I couldn't imagine being so still all the time, although I recognized the same controlled physicality in Sebastian.

After a moment that seemed as if it would never end, a shrewd smile softened Minerva's otherwise impassive face. "Your passion will serve you well so long as you remember this: being a diplomat is as much about listening as it is convincing others why you are right. I will support what you are proposing, and I suspect even the most recalcitrant Nocenian politician will do the same."

"Thank you," I said, trying to let my anger melt into relief. It didn't matter that what I would be proposing was more Minerva's idea than mine; what mattered was gaining the support of the Nocenian government, and wisdom was wisdom, regardless of where it came from. "I wish I could address both realms at the same time, but it's clear we need to deal with Tallus before telling Astrals more since he's proven he'll twist anything involving me for his own benefit." I shook my head. "It's not going to be easy, but things that matter rarely are. I'm not afraid of hard work."

Minerva made a noise of agreement. "I suggest you remember that when it comes to mending your relationship with your sister."

I stiffened. Was the rift between us that obvious?

"I know a thing or two about sibling relationships," continued

Minerva. "I understand you sharing things when you did, but I can also understand Seren struggling to come to terms with such revelations. I can't imagine being your sister has always been easy for her."

"We were so close growing up, and I thought I'd done a good job of including her," I said, surprised to find myself speaking freely to Minerva about something so personal. Then again, sometimes it was easier to speak about family matters with someone who wasn't family. "I had no idea how much she resented me. I never meant for her to feel like she was in my shadow. I certainly don't see her that way."

"She doesn't resent you," said Minerva. "She adores you and looks up to you, and she's hurt because she doesn't know what her place will be in this new life you're creating."

I thought back to a conversation I'd had with Aurelius, about how Sebastian was afraid I wouldn't find building a new life with him as attractive as continuing the life I'd established before the two of us had reconnected. I would never leave Seren behind. Regardless of what position I held in the future or who I'd been in the past, there would always be a place for her in my life. She had to know that—didn't she?

As they tended to do, my thoughts must have shown on my face, because Minerva leaned closer. "Whatever you're thinking, it might be helpful to share that with her."

"Thank you," I said, ashamed over my previously unkind thoughts towards the woman across from me. "And thank you for finding ways to help Seren stay busy while she's here."

"It's really selfish on my part," replied Minerva, raising and lowering one shoulder in a gesture that reminded me of Eslee. "She's a quick learner and exceptionally good at math. She's also eager to make a place for herself. I wasn't so different at her age." She studied the pearl bracelet around her wrist before bringing her gaze back to mine. "Once the realms are reunited and we've established whatever our new normal is going to be, I'd like to see her continue working with me. I've never had an apprentice, but if she's interested, I would welcome it."

"That's incredibly kind of you," I said, surprised again by Minerva's words. "The decision is Seren's, but I'd certainly support it. As long as she isn't involved in anything dangerous, of course."

"Once the realms are reunited, I suspect we'll need to create a new division within the business to handle the increase in—how did you put it—*government-sanctioned* commerce," said Minerva, and I appreciated her making it clear Seren wouldn't be involved in anything unsavory. "It will go a long way for Daevals, at least, to see those with silver and gold blood working so closely together. It's also nice to have someone who's actually interested in the family business," she offered in what I suspected was for her a rare moment of vulnerability, "since the interests of my niece and nephew lie elsewhere."

She rose swiftly to her feet, indicating our meeting was over, and I did the same.

"Thank you for your time, Kyra. I appreciate your dedication to the realms and those who live in them. Since I suspect you would be an impossible politician to buy off or trade favors with, I'll be glad to see you continue your career in healing."

"Coming from you, that's quite a compliment," I smiled. "Thank you."

17

SEBASTIAN

As I studied the green cover of the Chronicles, a memory from my past life resurfaced, of a warm summer afternoon in the castle of Velaire a few years after Kareth and I had married. Kareth was sitting at a desk in the study, afternoon sunlight shining through the large window behind her as she recorded the days' events in the Chronicles. I was reading in a chair nearby but kept turning to look at her. She was so focused on what she was writing she didn't notice my observation, and I enjoyed watching her thoughts play out across her face as her pen sped over the parchment, documenting things she was determined to keep from being forgotten.

I blinked, and while the memory disappeared, thankfully the Chronicles was still before me. Even though I knew I couldn't simply reach out and snatch up what was rightfully mine, it took more self-control than I'd anticipated to continue moving down the table, acting as if one of the most important books to ever exist was nothing special. Devlin and LeBehr finished examining the antiques before moving into the crowd, helping themselves to food while chatting with the Daevals around them. I was glad to see Devlin switching to mint tea after his glass of wine, which in my opinion was a far superior drink to begin with.

Standing behind him and LeBehr as they laughed and gossiped, I let my gaze move slowly around the room. I recognized a handful of the Daevals. Some I'd purchased information from, others I'd completed contracts for, and a few I'd seen at the Dekarais' recent party for Kyra. Thankfully, those who had hired me knew better than to make a big deal of our past interactions. While I saw their eyes widen or their lips press together, they either gave me only the briefest nod or simply ignored me.

Devlin, on the other hand, was impossible to ignore, sweeping around the room and attracting the eyes of every partygoer. I had to admit, his ability to hold a crowd's attention was impressive. Part of me couldn't help picturing what I might look like acting similarly; no matter how hard I tried, though, I couldn't imagine ever being so comfortable in the spotlight.

Just because you will be assuming a more public position does not mean you are expected to turn into Devlin, Batty said, materializing on my shoulder before stuffing an olive he'd swiped into his mouth.

Well, that's a relief, I muttered, still unsettled by the thought of holding any position of note. *What took you so long?* I tried not to sound peevish, but when it involved the Chronicles, I preferred having the bat close by.

It's nice to know I have been missed, grinned Batty before pointing a wing towards a tray of small bowls filled with crystallized apricots. I was about to tell him to knock it off when he added, *I find I am most helpful with a little something in my stomach.*

Grabbing a bowl from the startled server who'd been too busy gazing adoringly at Devlin to notice me, I held it up, and Batty swept the candies into a wing pocket. At least he had the good sense to brush away the sugar that had fallen on my shoulder.

I was trying to comfort Aurelius, the bat said by way of explaining his late arrival. *We were not able to find anything about breaking the* Memoria Aeterna *spell, even with Mischief's help, and Aurelius is not taking our lack of progress well. He does not want Kyra forced into participating in the destruction of a shade, even one so vile as Tallus.*

I understand where's he coming from, I replied. *I don't want her to have to do such a thing either, even though I know she can and will. But I also don't know of another way to stop Tallus for good.*

Batty made an acknowledging noise, his mouth full of candied apricot, and I continued surveying the room, stopping when my gaze landed on Minister Sinclair.

The man's golden-brown eyes flashed with recognition. He excused himself to the Daeval he'd been speaking with before making his way over, although I was glad he made it appear as if he were simply coming to get another drink from the nearby table. I hadn't seen my realm's highest-ranking healer since the party the Dekarais had thrown introducing Kyra to Nocenian society. Thankfully he'd been more polite to her there than when she'd taught him to uncover trace memories in a Nocenian morgue, but I still couldn't say I was pleased to see the pompous government official.

"By yourself tonight?" he asked.

Since it was obvious I was there with Devlin and LeBehr, I assumed he was asking about Kyra. I nodded. "I'm here on business."

"Interesting," replied the minister in a silky voice, "although that seems to be a common theme these days, as I've heard more than a few *interesting* reports coming from Aeles in the past few hours."

I narrowed my eyes, daring him to be difficult, but fortunately there was no malice in his gaze. "Is Kyra alright?" he asked quietly.

I hadn't expected him to be concerned over Kyra's safety, and while I appreciated the sentiment, I still chose my words with care. "She's fine. I doubt whatever you heard is the truth."

"I doubt it, too," he agreed, "which is likely why the two of you will be addressing the government tomorrow. I assume it's also related to the decree that was just issued outlawing anyone with golden blood from being in our realm."

"One of the senators in Aeles is preparing to make a big move." While the minister was aware of the unrest in Aeles, if he didn't already know one individual was behind it, he'd appreciate the information. I didn't collect favors like Caz, but it was never a bad idea to have someone indebted to me, particularly when it didn't cost me anything to share information. I grabbed a small glass of tea and took a sip of the warm, sweet liquid. "The senator needs Kyra for what he wants to do, but she's safe."

Minister Sinclair nodded. "And I take it whatever you're doing here has something to do with the Aelian senator and his big move."

His words hovered somewhere between a question and a statement, and I merely blinked, not about to provide him with a direct answer.

He smirked. "For you to let Kyra out of your sight tells me she's someplace you aren't worried about her, which most likely means she's with Dunston or Caz. And since you're here, there must be something at this auction important enough for you to willingly leave her side."

The minister was clearly more observant than I'd initially given him credit for, which was irritating, but I remained silent as he continued.

"You know, ever since learning about trace memories and *aleric* tags from Kyra, my healing skills have been more in demand than ever. It turns out being able to identify past illnesses and injuries is quite helpful, as is being able to pinpoint where in Nocens an injury was received. *That* service, in particular, has proven useful in more than one legal dispute." A self-satisfied smile slid over the minister's square face. "Of course, it probably helps I'm the only healer in our realm capable of performing such an advanced procedure."

I scowled at him. "Kyra would expect you to share the knowledge she gave you with other healers so more patients could be helped."

Minister Sinclair had the audacity to laugh. "Yes, well, I suspect she and I will always have differing opinions when it comes to various aspects of being a healer," he said. "But I must admit, I find myself exceptionally curious to know more about the healing procedures Astrals are capable of." He took a sip of his tea. "To that end, I've grown rather attached to the idea of better relations between Astrals and Daevals. Did you know no healer with silver blood has set foot in Aeles for hundreds, if not thousands, of years? What a wonderful opportunity for a Nocenian healer bold enough to take it." Desire flashed across his eyes. "I'd hate for whatever is happening in Aeles to disrupt that. If there's anything I can do to ensure progress continues to be made between those with silver and gold blood, do let me know."

I considered his offer. While attempting to steal the Chronicles would be a risk if it came down to such an act, trying to win the book in a bidding war was no less risky in its own way. There was always the chance someone would become intrigued simply because they saw Devlin taking an interest. While he had been instrumental in getting us into the auction and close to the book, when it came to acquiring it, the guest of the hour might be more of a hindrance than a help. Having another option was a smart move. Minister Sinclair was self-absorbed and pretentious, but he'd made it clear he supported Kyra, if for no other reason than he wanted to be the first Daevalic healer to visit Aeles. He'd tipped his hand by making what he wanted so obvious, and although I wasn't certain whether he'd done it on purpose or by accident, for my purposes it didn't really matter.

"There might be a way for you to continue supporting improved relationships between Astrals and Daevals," I said in a low voice. "I'm here with Devlin to purchase a book, but there's a chance others will become interested once they see him bidding on it."

Minister Sinclair's upper lip curled into a sneer. "Yes, Raks has quite the history of being the highest bidder at his own auctions."

I hadn't been talking about Raks, but a frisson of apprehension charged up my spine. "What do you mean?"

"This isn't like one of Minerva Dekarai's auctions. Here, the host bids freely and has no qualms about beating any of his guests."

That would make acquiring the Chronicles even more difficult, as no one would be paying closer attention to Devlin than Raks, except perhaps Win'Din, although not for the same reasons. I finished my tea and handed the empty glass to a passing server.

"It seems our interests are aligned tonight," I said, and my words sparked an eager smile from the minister, although he quickly assumed a more detached expression. "I know Kyra would appreciate your assistance in securing this particular book. As would I."

"How will I recognize the book?"

"It has a green cover. And Devlin will keep raising his bid against anyone who competes with him for it."

"Is there an upper limit I should be mindful of when bidding?"

"No."

Minister Sinclair appeared surprised at the lack of a budget but quickly gave a single nod and sauntered away, calling out to someone else across the room. While part of me insisted I'd merely been putting a backup plan into place, it was still odd choosing to rely on someone other than myself or Kyra. It was inevitable at some point for someone to fail me or attempt to double-cross me, but I'd also seen trusting others didn't always have to be a last resort or something to be avoided at all costs. I'd trusted LeBehr to find the Chronicles, and she had. I'd trusted the Dekarais to take in Kyra's family, and they had. I'd trusted Devlin to get us into the auction, and he had. I hoped Minister Sinclair came through, but even if he didn't, that was a reflection on him and not the other decisions I'd made to accept help when I needed it.

Batty tugged on a lock of my hair. *If we are emptying the bank account, I maintain a list of things I would like to purchase.*

We're doing whatever it takes to get the Chronicles back, I corrected him. *I'm not tossing around money for fun, and I'm certainly not looking to invest in the Dal Marian caramel business.*

If we owned the manufacturing and controlled the distribution, we would make a fortune! insisted my Cypher, resurrecting an argument he'd made numerous times over the past few years.

Thankfully, a bell sounded, ending our conversation, and chairs were brought in so quickly it was clear the process had been choreographed and rehearsed. The auction attendees began to take their seats as eager murmurs filled the air, and I chose a spot directly behind Devlin and LeBehr.

"Thank you all so much for coming," beamed Win'Din from the front of the room. "I hope you're as excited as we are about the incredible pieces available tonight." She spread her arms wide. "Let the bidding begin!"

The crowd cheered as the auctioneer made her way to a mahogany podium decorated with swirling ribbons of gold and an attendant stepped forward, presenting the first item.

While I wished the auction would pass faster, we made steady progress through the antiques—patterned pottery, colorful glass vases, and a small bronze statue, followed by a slew of books—and the bids came fast and furious. The average citizen in Nocens made roughly fifty thousand skoiyas a year, and while those in attendance made far more than that, a few items had already reached double that amount.

At one point, LeBehr made a show of whispering furtively to Devlin and he instantly bid on a book, following the plan we'd made in the carriage. While Devlin raised his bid a few times, he ultimately conceded with a dazzling smile and affected shrug, earning himself scattered applause and comments of how good-natured he was. Someone near me murmured, "Better behavior than I'd expect from a Dekarai." While part of me wanted to drag the man outside and remove his tongue, that wasn't what we were here for. Clenching my jaw, I forced my attention back to the auction, even though I memorized the man's face for future reference.

Thanks to my conversation with Minister Sinclair, I wasn't surprised when Raks occasionally bid on an item, although it wasn't clear whether he was trying to raise the amount ultimately being paid or if he genuinely wanted the object. He tended to stop bidding after two or three rounds, and with the blessing of the Fates, that pattern would continue once the Chronicles came up for purchase.

Other items went by, and then at long last, the attendant stepped forward holding the Chronicles.

"This is quite the interesting find," said the auctioneer. "We don't know much about the book, other than it's incredibly old and there's a spell in place to keep anyone from opening it, meaning this will be a decorative item rather than an interesting historical read."

Was that your work? I asked Batty.

It was. He shoved a chocolate-covered date into his mouth. *Not only did I ensure the book could not be destroyed, I also made certain not just anyone would be able to read it. Unfortunately, given the setting we now find ourselves in, I fear my efforts will only make Devlin's interest more obvious. After all, why would anyone want to purchase a book that cannot even be read?*

It was still incredible spellcasting, I said. I could feel the bat's happiness at my compliment, which was rare enough to be considered notable although I was getting better about expressing my appreciation to him.

Devlin turned to LeBehr, making a show of asking her opinion on if he should cast a bid. She shrugged, then spoke just loud enough for those close by to hear. "It has a nice aged look to it. I generally believe books are for reading rather than decoration, but you aren't always one for reading."

Devlin chuckled. "It's true. Sometimes I just don't have the patience to see how the story will turn out. But I do like pretty things." He flashed a grin at Win'Din, who smugly tucked a blonde wave behind one ear. "Why not?" Devlin raised his hand. "It might make a nice present for my mother."

The crowd roared with laughter picturing how Rennej would react to receiving something purchased at a Nemoya auction. A few other hands went up, but Devlin continued to raise his bid, the lazy smile on his face indicating he wasn't taking any of this too seriously, which was completely in character for him. I'd clearly underestimated him as an actor.

Another hand went up, and to my annoyance, it belonged to Raks Nemoya.

18

SEBASTIAN

Surprise rippled through the crowd at Raks's unexpected bid, and he smiled. "If a Dekarai is interested in the book, there must be more to it than I initially thought," he said. Devlin responded with a good-natured laugh, but I didn't miss the way his eyes hardened. While he was different from Dunston in many ways, they both hated being denied something once they'd decided they wanted it.

Given that the book couldn't even be opened, the bidding started low, although it quickly reached twenty gold skoiyas, then fifty, then one hundred.

"Five hundred," said Devlin.

"One thousand," replied Raks.

"Five thousand," returned Devlin coolly.

"Ten thousand," smirked Raks.

Devlin studied the man, a wide smile breaking out over his face. "Fifty thousand," he said, causing a hum of admiration to rise from the crowd.

Not to be outdone, though, Raks raised an eyebrow. "One hundred thousand."

The fire stirred inside me; I hated seeing something that belonged to Kyra and me treated as nothing more than an object. Devlin drew a deep breath before running a hand through his hair, hiding the glance he shot me from the corner of his eye to confirm I was fine with him spending more. I gave him a barely perceptible nod.

"Two hundred thousand," Devlin called in a loud voice.

"Two hundred and fifty thousand," retorted Raks.

"Three hundred thousand!"

"Three hundred and fifty thousand!"

Devlin glared at Raks, who returned the expression, and just as it seemed like the two might come to blows, a voice at the back of the room called out, "Five hundred thousand!"

Gasps filled the air as everyone turned to see Minister Sinclair calmly sitting with his arms crossed over the chest of his blue pinstripe suit.

Devlin and LeBehr exchanged a horrified look; while I could have told them my plan, I needed their reaction to be genuine. As heads swiveled amidst not-so-whispered conversations, Devlin's wide eyes found mine. I gave my head the slightest shake, making it clear I didn't want him to raise his bid against Minister Sinclair. He pressed his lips together but didn't argue. LeBehr had covered her mouth with her hands and looked ready to grab the Chronicles and run for the door, but Devlin reached over and whispered something, prompting her to settle for running her hands over her corset, although the feathers on her dress continued their frantic rustling, evidence of how agitated she was.

Raks shared a look with his wife. It was one thing to attempt to outbid Devlin, as everyone knew there was bad blood between the families, but Minister Sinclair was another story. Raks didn't need to best him to prove anything, and it might not be a good idea to go against the most powerful healer in our realm.

"Do I hear five hundred and fifty thousand?" asked the auctioneer, looking between Devlin and Raks.

Devlin shook his head. "My mother doesn't need a decorative book that much."

Raks raised his hands in a gesture of surrender. "Perhaps I was carried away in the thrill of the moment."

"Five hundred thousand going once. Going twice. Sold to Minister Tayden Sinclair!"

The crowd leaped to its feet, applauding furiously as Minister Sinclair stood and took a bow, his carefully styled black hair not so much as moving.

Contact the minister's Cypher, I instructed Batty. *Get his banking information so we can transfer funds. We also need to figure out how to take possession of the Chronicles.*

Batty tossed a date into the air and for once managed to catch it in his mouth. As the next item came up for bidding, he said, *I am ready with the minister's bank information. Archeron—the minister's Cypher—said he will be glad to deliver the book once we are in the carriage.*

I clenched my jaw, wondering if I'd underestimated the minister. I understood he couldn't simply hand me the Chronicles in full view of the Nemoyas and their guests, but I didn't like the idea of leaving the auction without the book securely in my hands. The longer it took for me to take possession of the Chronicles, the more opportunities there were for things to go wrong. Much as it irked me, I also wasn't in a position to make demands, which meant I would have to continue trusting the minister a while longer.

That's fine, I said, even though the situation was anything but fine.

Pulling out my peerin, I moved to a shadowed corner of the room and began transferring the funds to Minister Sinclair's account, glad there were only a couple of auction items left to get through. Spending such a large amount of money was so uncharacteristic for me I worried I might need to visit a bank, but thankfully the transaction went through without difficulty. Then there was nothing left to do but bide my time and wait.

At last, the auctioneer announced the end of the auction, and everyone clapped as Win'Din directed them to restocked tables of food and beverages. I watched Minister Sinclair make his way through the crowd, nodding at the congratulations and impressed exclamations over his purchase. He stopped before a gloved attendant, who escorted him into another room, no doubt to complete paperwork before he took ownership of the book. My heart pounded as if I'd just completed a hard run. There was no reason for the minister not to follow through with our plan. He'd been repaid, and he had to know I'd personally come take the book from him if he failed to give it to me, likely taking his life along with it. Even so, I had no way of predicting what he might do, and I hated the uncertainty almost as much as I hated being near the Nemoyas.

Thankfully, Devlin didn't protest when I caught his eye and used my head to gesture towards the door. Making his way to Win'Din, he gave her a hug and whispered something that made her giggle even as she nodded eagerly. It was a relief to step outside into the cold night air, and I was glad our transportation arrived quickly.

"What in the burning realm was that?" exclaimed Devlin once we were situated inside the carriage. "Why did you tell me to stop? Did you not want to go up against a government official? Or do you plan on stealing the book from him?"

From his position on the floor, Onyx glared at me, unhappy I'd upset Devlin.

"Sebastian, please tell me you have a plan," cried LeBehr, fanning her face and making the feathers on her dress wave in the manufactured breeze. "We have to get that book!"

"We will. We are." I shared the conversation I'd had with

Minister Sinclair. "I didn't tell you sooner because I needed your surprise to seem real." While I'd made the best strategic choice given the circumstances, I still felt a twinge of guilt for not telling Devlin and LeBehr the truth earlier, given all they'd done to help me.

"Oh, my surprise was real, alright!" Devlin assured me, sinking back against the plush seat with a loud exhale. "So how do we get the book from Minister Sinclair?"

"We wait for his Cypher to deliver it." While my voice was steady, the rest of me was unnerved. We were in the carriage . . . why hadn't the minister's Cypher appeared yet? If he didn't materialize soon, we'd reach the town and return the carriage and then what? Without entirely meaning to, I cracked my knuckles. If Sinclair attempted to double-cross me, the Fates themselves would weep over the pain and suffering I would inflict on him. There was no place he could hide, nowhere he—

Batty materialized on the seat beside me, interrupting my rising fury. "Archeron is ready to deliver the book."

I forced my muscles to relax as I nodded. A moment later, an enormous reticulated python appeared next to Batty. I could just see the edge of the Chronicles' cover peeking out through the creature's stunning black and brown coils.

"Thank you for your assistance," I said, trying to sound friendlier than I felt and not as if I'd just been picturing myself torturing the man the snake was paired with. "May I?"

"You may," the python replied. As he loosened his hold, I carefully reached over and picked up the book, momentarily wishing I could pet the creature. I'd always been fond of reptiles, especially snakes, but of course I would never do such a thing to a Cypher.

"Minister Sinclair would like you to know he is available to participate in future undertakings involving improved relationships between the realms," Archeron hissed, his tawny eyes glinting brightly. "He also sends his regards to Kyra."

"I'll pass them on, and please give my thanks to the minister."

The Cypher dipped his diamond-shaped head before rippling his muscular body and dematerializing.

Gazing down at the book in my hand, I ran the pads of my fingers over the cover, reassuring myself the book was really there. Pride and relief filled me as they always did after a successful operation, but in this case, they were accompanied by no small amount of disbelief that we'd really done it.

"Open it!" urged LeBehr, pushing herself to the edge of her seat.

I turned to Batty, who waddled closer and rubbed his wings together before placing one on the book. He began speaking in the old Astral language of Praxum before switching to the ancient Daevalic language of Shthornan. As he recited the spell, the book trembled, then lay still.

"One final thing," said the bat, pulling the page he'd removed from the Chronicles centuries ago out of a wing pocket. Pressing the tip of his wing against the book, the pages flipped forward; when they stopped, Batty placed his single page on top of the open book and the volume shimmered, the page rejoining with the others as if it had always been there. Even though I'd learned the bat wasn't as dim-witted or ridiculous as I'd once thought him to be, the fact that he'd managed to preserve the page from the Chronicles all these years was undeniably impressive. Kyra likely would have hugged him or kissed his head. I wasn't comfortable offering that much affection, so I patted his back before opening a cabinet and giving him a tin of chocolate-covered walnuts, which he accepted with a happy screech.

Flipping through the book, I hadn't expected the ink to look so freshly applied and ready to smear if my hand touched it. Gazing at the pages of Kareth's handwriting, I read a few lines of what she'd written. She'd chronicled major events in the kingdom, from the drafting of the Blood Treaty to important decisions we'd made, as well as anecdotes about daily life as Astrals and Daevals worked at living peacefully with one another.

I was surprised to feel my chest tightening. While I knew from my own memories my past life as the Felserpent King was real, this text proved what Kyra and I had shared beyond any doubt or question, as the age of the book could easily be authenticated. Not only would the Chronicles rewrite the history of Aeles and Nocens, upending everything Astrals and Daevals currently believed about their pasts, it would allow Kyra and me to change the future by reuniting the divided realms and giving those with gold and silver blood the chance to live in peace again. I thought back to the last words the Felserpent had said to me in his cave after giving me his blessing to rule Aeles-Nocens: "Serve well, Felserpent King."

Gazing at the Chronicles, resolve swept through me.

I will.

I was the Felserpent King, and that would never change, no matter how many lives I lived and no matter what other professions I pursued. I had both the power and the responsibility to care for Aeles and Nocens. While I still would have preferred to work from behind the scenes, I'd been a public figure before and I could—and would—do it again.

Knowing I could read the book in greater detail later, I handed it to LeBehr, and tears filled her eyes as she accepted it. Placing it on her lap, she ran a hand reverently over the cover. I knew she had a passion for books, particularly ancient ones, but I hadn't expected her to be so emotional.

"You'll have to forgive me," she said with a wobbly smile. "You see, I don't just view myself as a bookseller—I strive to be a book preserver. One we've lost a written text, we've not only lost a book someone took the time to create, we've lost knowledge. We've lost history. We've lost a part of our own story, and that can never be replaced. To know what this book contains and what it represents . . ." Her voice trailed off, and she sniffled as she smiled. "This is the reason I do what I do."

She carefully opened the book, and I momentarily wished I could capture the sheer awe that spread across her face as she began reading.

"Well, I for one think that was incredibly successful!" said Devlin as LeBehr lost herself in the Chronicles.

"Thank you again for your help."

He smirked. "Words you probably never imagined saying to me."

"Definitely not," I agreed, which only caused him to laugh.

As the stars shone through the windows, I pressed a fingertip against the gold bracelet, and Kyra immediately opened the connection.

We've got the Chronicles, and we'll be back soon.

Kyra was waiting in the foyer, practically hopping from one foot to the other in her excitement. I handed her the Chronicles, and she hugged the book to her chest before opening it, taking in words she'd written over a thousand years ago.

"I can't believe we've got it back," she said before turning to Devlin and LeBehr. "Thank you both so much!" Cradling the book in one arm, she hugged each of them in turn. "Everyone's dying to hear how you did it." She led the way into the Driftwood Lounge, and I was surprised to see almost everyone gathered; the only one missing was her youngest brother Deneb, who must have already gone to bed. Seren was sitting beside Minerva, but her eyes followed Kyra as if drawn by an invisible force.

"What a night!" LeBehr exclaimed, sweeping into the center of the room and striking a dramatic pose. I was more than happy to let her share what had happened. I sank onto a small sofa beside Kyra, who I could tell was torn between listening to LeBehr and reading the Chronicles.

When LeBehr reached the part where Raks started to bid against Devlin, there was a general chorus of raised voices protesting such behavior. Rennej looked ready to go to Jaasfar and personally tell the Nemoyas what she thought of her son being treated in such a manner. Dunston gripped the arms of his chair so hard, his knuckles started to turn white as Caz crossed his arms and shook his head.

"Devlin was marvelous!" praised LeBehr. "He had everyone eating out of the palm of his hand. Oh, you should have seen it. It was like being at the theater, the performance he put on!"

Devlin beamed, enjoying the accolades, although I noticed his eyes dart towards his father at one point. Was he hoping for a compliment from Dunston? The two of them had never been close, and Devlin had recently shared his desire to live outside his father's shadow, possibly relocating to Aeles once the realms were united. I'd never thought he cared about Dunston's approval, but I also knew relationships with your parents could be far more complicated than they appeared.

Dunston reached around Eslee, who was sitting beside him, and gave Devlin's leg a good-natured slap. "When I'm wrong, I'm wrong," he said. "Well done, son. You made the family proud today."

"Proving there's a first time for everything," replied Devlin breezily, but I didn't miss the way he held his head a bit higher as his chest puffed out ever so slightly.

"So, what happens next?" asked Skandhar.

"Now that we have the spell to reunite the realms, we need to deal with Tallus," said Kyra.

"And what will that look like?" asked Caz, interest filling his violet-tinged blue eyes.

"We're still working that out," Kyra admitted. "Batty and Aurelius uncovered the spell he cast on himself. But we need to find a way to break it; otherwise, he'll continue being reborn with the same hatreds and the same goal of ending the existence of Daevals. I'll share more once I know more, but it's going to take some figuring out."

"LeBehr, I do hope you'll stay the night," offered Minerva. "There's plenty of room."

"Oh, I wouldn't want to be a nuisance," said LeBehr. "Sebastian can open a portal right to my doorstep."

"Actually, I think you should stay," I said. Minerva appeared pleased I had agreed with her, while everyone else seemed surprised I had an opinion on LeBehr's lodging. I didn't want to sound dramatic, but we also had to be realistic. "I think everyone involved in helping Kyra and me should plan on staying at Sea'Brik until Tallus has been stopped. It's the best way to ensure you're all as safe as possible until the worst has passed."

"Well," said LeBehr as Mischief materialized near her feet, "when you put it that way, I'd be delighted to stay."

19

Dear Journal,

It has been ten years since the signing of the Blood Treaty, and there are moments I fear our determined regents might actually make this forced togetherness work. But then I remember Astrals and Daevals are fundamentally different creatures who cannot coexist, meaning it's only a matter of time until this experiment becomes too unstable to proceed. I continue to support rebellions and uprisings where I can, but it's challenging—there are far more folks than I'd anticipated who are eager to put aside our pasts and our differences and happily live next door to those with silver blood. If I am frustrated the monarchy continues to exist, I can only hope the monarchy is equally frustrated at least some Astrals and Daevals continue to challenge them, refusing to live in a peace that cannot be sustained.

I must find a way to bring together those Astrals who believe our fate should not be determined by anyone with silver blood. It will not be an easy undertaking, but one good thing that has come from this blasted regime is a truly remarkable castle library. Books are freely available to all, and I am certain I will find something to help me put Aeles-Nocens back on its proper course.

T

20

KYRA

Walking up the stairs to Sebastian's room, the peerin Caz had acquired for me vibrated in my pocket. While normally I loved hearing from Demitri, given our current circumstances I couldn't imagine he was reaching out with good news. I stopped at the top of the staircase and accepted the call, Sebastian at my side, searching Demitri's face for an indication of what was happening.

"All government offices were closed this morning until further notice," Demitri explained. "Everyone in Celenia has been ordered to appear at the Puhlcra Amphitheater at exactly three o'clock this afternoon." Fear flickered across his eyes. "Tallus announced he's developed a weapon capable of killing every Daeval in Nocens, and he's going to unveil it in a public demonstration."

My skin flashed hot, then cold, and I felt heavy and immobile as a statue.

Tallus controlled the Aelian government. He controlled the Aelian military. He wanted a war with Nocens. And now he had a weapon he claimed was capable of winning such a war.

I looked at Sebastian. While his expression was skeptical, I could also sense his unease.

"Do you know any details about the weapon?" he asked Demitri.

Demitri shook his head. "A government brief went out, saying what I just shared, and also letting folks know the event will be broadcast live so everyone in the realm can watch. Adonis, do you know more?"

I'd been so focused on Demitri I hadn't even recognized Adonis's kitchen in the background.

My surprise must have registered on my face because Demitri cleared his throat. "When I got to work and learned the office was closed, I was going to go back home, but I ran into Adonis and he invited me over for breakfast." The tips of his ears were turning a furious shade of red, and he quickly handed the peerin to Adonis before stepping out of view.

"Unfortunately, I don't know more than Demitri shared." Adonis ruffled his long mahogany hair. "I've never seen Celenia in such a state. It's difficult because Tallus seems to have evidence of Kyra being kidnapped, but folks still have a lot of questions. Most soldiers favor a diplomatic solution and don't support an invasion, but Tallus doesn't seem to care."

"He can't launch a full-scale invasion until the realms are reunited," said Sebastian. "How many Astral soldiers have portaling abilities?"

"Two," said Adonis. "Which means they would provide a very slow entry into Nocens the Daeval military could easily handle. Maybe Tallus assumes the realms will be reunited by the time he's ready to invade?"

"I can't imagine him thinking we'd reunite the realms before dealing with him," frowned Sebastian. "If I were him, I'd try to force us into reuniting the realms sooner rather than later, possibly using whatever weapon he's developed."

I shared my plan to remove Tallus's shade and force him into Vaneklus before his appointed time. While I knew Demitri could hear me, part of me felt better speaking to Adonis. My best friend would support me no matter what, but I still didn't like owning up to performing such an act with his eyes on me. Adonis was a soldier, however, and would judge what I intended to do solely on the effectiveness of the measure and not the cruelty of the act itself. "The only problem is, I have to be close to Tallus to do such a thing," I explained. "Do you know anything about his schedule and if there's a good time or place to catch him alone?"

"He's been keeping to himself lately," said Adonis, "and he's been making more broadcasts than public appearances. They look like they're coming from his office, but honestly, he could be anywhere in Aeles."

"The only place we know he'll be at for sure is the amphitheater, to reveal his weapon," said Sebastian. "That's our best place to get close to him. He probably knows that, too, which means he'll be expecting us."

"I can cast a glamour on you," offered Adonis. "Even if he suspects you'll hear about his weapon demonstration and sneak in to watch it, he won't recognize you if we use a glamour to change your appearance."

"Won't it disappear as soon as we step into the amphitheater?" asked Sebastian.

"Why would it disappear?" Adonis looked confused.

"In Nocens, every building is constructed with revelation spells cast directly into the foundation," explained Sebastian. "Anything you do to alter your appearance will disappear the instant you cross the threshold."

"Oh." Adonis appeared impressed but also surprised folks would start any interaction with the assumption that others wouldn't be truthful about something like their appearance. "No, that's definitely not the case in Aeles. Remember, Astrals don't expect to be deceived by one another. We give one another the benefit of the doubt. Nigel's working security on the amphitheater today, so he can check for revelation spells, but I don't think we'll find any. If Tallus casts one before he begins his demonstration, well, we'll cross that bridge if we come to it."

Adonis clicked the peerin lens a few times. "I just sent you architectural renderings for the Puhlcra Amphitheater so you'll know the layout," he said to Sebastian. "Should we try to get Tallus before or after his weapon demonstration?"

"Before," I said.

"After," said Sebastian at the same time.

"The entire government will be at the amphitheater," I pointed out. "All of Aeles will be watching. You, Adonis, and Nigel can kidnap Tallus, and I can tell everyone the truth, just like we're doing with the Nocenian government." *Finally* those with golden blood would know the real story of who Tallus was.

"I want to know about his weapon," Sebastian countered. "Just because we're going to destroy Tallus doesn't mean someone else can't come along and use whatever he created against Daevals. We need to know what we're even potentially up against."

Once Tallus was dealt with and the realms had been reunited, Aeles and Nocens wouldn't be so close to war with one another, which I hoped would make any such weapon obsolete, but Sebastian's assessment made sense. If Tallus had been able to develop something deadly to those with silver blood, there was always the chance another Astral who didn't support better relations with Daevals might decide to use such a device. Knowing what we were up against would better prepare us to deal with it, if such action was needed.

"We should plan on catching Tallus as soon as he's done with his demonstration," continued Sebastian. "He'll be pleased with himself and thinking about attacking Nocens, which might make him distracted or at least paying less attention to his surroundings than usual. We'll grab him and portal him to your house, Adonis.

That way Kyra can take as long as she needs to remove his shade without the military or any of his supporters interrupting."

I nodded, trying to appear brave as fear raced up my chest, burning my throat. I could do this. I *had* to do this. Then something occurred to me. "Won't Tallus's Cypher tell the Aelian military where he's being held? It won't take them long to show up at Adonis's cottage."

"That's where Nerudian comes in," said Sebastian. "Nerudian is a dragon," he explained to Adonis, whose mouth dropped open. "Once we've got Tallus secured, I'll open a portal and bring Nerudian to Aeles. His presence outside your house should give the Aelian military pause. Since there haven't been dragons in Aeles for hundreds of years, I doubt they have any weapon that could harm one—although I'd appreciate you looking into that, Adonis—and as they're trying to figure out how to deal with him, that will give us the time we need."

I hated putting Nerudian in danger, just as I hated the thought of Aelian soldiers potentially becoming the dragon's next meal, but hopefully I could remove Tallus's shade quickly enough that we wouldn't need to engage the military for long. Telling Adonis we'd discuss additional details when we arrived at his cottage later, Sebastian closed the peerin and handed it back to me as Batty dematerialized to speak with Nerudian about our plan.

"Did Tallus mention anything else he was working on when you were with him in Rynstyn?" Sebastian asked. "Anything he could have turned into a weapon?"

"No. He was completely focused on altering Daevals through their blood." I reminded him about Demitri's encounter with Healer Omnurion and how she'd been taking golden blood to Tallus. "Maybe his weapon uses golden blood somehow? But I can't see why, because golden blood alone isn't enough to turn a Daeval into an Astral."

Sebastian's expression hardened. "If he's developed a weapon, I think he's decided not to change Daevals after all."

"I wish we could find out more before he shares it publicly." I massaged my forehead. "But it has to be heavily guarded."

"I think we'll have to learn about it along with everyone else in Aeles," agreed Sebastian. "Adonis and Nigel could look into it, but if Tallus thinks they're snooping, he might send them off to the farthest reaches of your realm or assign them to the barracks for the evening. We need them to help us kidnap him. If I were Tallus, I'd be keeping a close eye on Demitri, too, so we can't involve him."

I didn't enjoy trying to think like Tallus in order to stay one step ahead of him, and I was grateful envisioning scenarios from our enemy's perspective didn't seem as taxing for Sebastian as it was to me. As I nodded my assent, I heard the soft patter of feet moving down the carpeted hallway, followed by a door closing.

Sebastian heard it, too, but shook his head. "We'll share this with everyone later. I'm exhausted, and we need to get a few hours of sleep before we go to Aeles and deal with Tallus." As we headed into his bedroom, he asked, "How were things here while I was gone?"

I told him about my conversation with Minerva, and he agreed holding a series of votes after reuniting the realms was a wise course of action. Climbing into bed, we set an alarm for a few hours later, giving ourselves time to portal to Celenia just before Tallus's scheduled weapon demonstration.

Dawn was still hours away when Sebastian and I woke. He went off to speak with Dunston, and I hurried to my mother's room, waking her and telling her what Sebastian and I were going to do. She gave me a strong hug, and while I knew she was worried, I appreciated her words of encouragement. I kissed Deneb's head as he slept, and my mother woke Enif so I could tell him goodbye. But when we knocked on Seren's door, there was no answer. My mother frowned and moved to open it, but I stopped her.

"I'll speak with her when I return," I said, trying to appear as if I weren't heartbroken over my sister's refusal to see me, especially since I was headed off to do something incredibly dangerous that could result in my being injured—or worse. I'd thought the bond Seren and I shared as family, as sisters, would ultimately prove stronger than her resentment towards me, but apparently I'd been wrong. I couldn't help feeling like an irreparable crack was spreading across my heart.

Pushing aside my sadness, I focused on Rhannu's hilt gleaming over Sebastian's shoulder and reviewed our preparation. The Chronicles was safely in our room. Sebastian was wearing the suppressor medallion so he wouldn't set off the Blood Alarm. Aurelius was at my side, Batty was on Sebastian's shoulder, and our friends were waiting for us in Aeles. It was time.

"Are you ready?" Sebastian asked.

I nodded, and we shared a brief kiss before he opened a portal and we stepped into Aeles.

After the night sky darkening the innumerable windows of Sea'Brik, it took my eyes a moment to adjust to the bright afternoon sunlight shining down on Adonis's cottage. The flowers in his window boxes seemed to bob their colorful heads in a greeting I wished I could enjoy as the soldier quickly ushered us inside.

"I spoke with Demitri earlier," said Adonis. "He's attending the event with some of his colleagues from the *Donec Auctoritus*, so he shouldn't draw any unwanted attention from Tallus. Nigel's already in Celenia, and he'll meet us outside the amphitheater." He turned to Sebastian. "What's the plan?"

"You, Nigel, and I will attend Tallus's weapon demonstration so we know exactly what he's developed. When he leaves the stage, Batty will follow him. When he's in a good location, I'll open a portal and we'll kidnap him. If there are anti-portal wards in place, we'll use this."

Sebastian pulled a small box from his pocket, and I recognized what had once been Nigel's portal disruptor. Thanks to alterations by Batty and Nigel, it now allowed for the creation of portals, which was how Sebastian had made it inside the experimentation center in Rynstyn and rescued me.

Sebastian looked at me, and I could tell he wasn't certain how I would respond to whatever he was about to say. "I think you should wait here, and we'll bring Tallus to you."

"That's fine with me," I assured him, feeling relief buzz through him at my quickly given agreement. Attending the weapon demonstration wasn't something I felt especially passionate about, not like recovering the Chronicles, which meant there was no reason for me to be present at the unveiling beyond satisfying my own curiosity. Plus, there was absolutely nothing I could do to help kidnap Tallus. It would be easier for Sebastian to focus exclusively on capturing him if I remained in the cottage, hundreds of miles from the Aelian capitol of Celenia.

Sebastian replaced the portal creator before withdrawing a smaller device and handing it to Adonis. "Tallus has the ability to make you face your worst fears," he explained. "If you see purple smoke coming from his hands, clip this in your nose. It'll filter the air long enough for you to get away. I've got one for Nigel too."

He offered me one of the tiny filters. "You weren't affected by his manipulation before. I don't plan on him casting any spells once we've captured him, but better safe than sorry."

I agreed and tucked the filter into a pocket.

"Where did you get this?" Adonis turned the tiny device over in his hands, inspecting it with an appreciative eye.

"I made it," replied Sebastian. "What Tallus is able to do"—he shook his head—"it's not something anyone should experience."

As Adonis put the filter away, I noticed the concern that rose in Sebastian's eyes, a brief moment of unguarded worry as he studied the Astral soldier who had unexpectedly become his friend. We both believed Adonis had been Farent, Schatten's best friend in a previous life, and I knew Sebastian was replaying how Tallus had murdered him in front of us. While it had been Farent's time to die, that hadn't made the loss any easier, and I felt Sebastian's resolve that this time would be different. I reached over and squeezed his hand as Batty dematerialized, then reappeared a moment later.

"Nerudian is ready," Batty said.

Sebastian and Adonis arranged a heavy chair in the middle of the room. Sebastian demonstrated how to apply spells to a rope to make it unbreakable, which would keep Tallus secured while I removed his shade. I mentally ran through the spells I would use until Aurelius tapped my leg with a paw.

Dova just reached out to me. The lynx tilted his head to one side, listening to my mother's Cypher. *Your mother couldn't sleep, so she went back to speak with Seren, but when she checked the room, your sister wasn't there.*

She's probably hiding somewhere in a secret room and doesn't want to be disturbed, I said, unable to keep the anger I felt towards my sister from my voice.

Dova thought that might be the case, so she reached out to Sappho, but your sister's Cypher isn't responding. Aurelius pricked his tufted ears. *When your mother asked the house to locate Seren, it said she was not currently at Sea'Brik.*

I stared at my Cypher, air rushing from my lungs as if someone had unexpectedly tightened a vice around my chest. *Where else could she be?*

Sebastian sensed my rising distress through our connection and moved closer. "What's wrong?"

"Seren's gone." I shared what I knew, and we looked at one another, dread building like storm clouds inside me, ready to break open any moment. This was a horrible turn of events. I couldn't afford to be distracted worrying about my sister when I needed to focus every ounce of my concentration on removing Tallus's shade.

"Do you know if Minerva's intersector is like Caz's?" I asked. "Could Seren have used it to go home?"

We both looked at Batty, who briefly closed his eyes, and I assumed he was reaching out to Minerva's Cypher.

"Minerva's intersector is exactly like Caz's," the bat said a moment later, gazing at me with concern. "It allows travel between the realms and does not record comings and goings."

Aurelius stiffened. "Sappho just reached out. Seren isn't in Nocens. She's in Celenia—with Tallus."

21

KYRA

"What?" I grabbed Sebastian's arm to steady myself.

"She used Minerva's intersector in the middle of the night," said Aurelius, passing along information as Sappho shared it. "She took it to Celenia."

"Why would she go there? Why wouldn't she go to our house in Montem?"

"She overheard you talking about Tallus's weapon, and she wanted to do something important—to prove herself."

Regret washed over me as I thought back to my fight with Seren and how determined she'd been to make a name for herself, desperate to perform an act that would eclipse anything I'd ever done. I wished to the Gifters she'd never attempted such a thing, but unfortunately neither regret nor wishes would get my sister back.

Aurelius continued. "Aside from Tallus, Demitri, and Demitri's parents, no one in Aeles knows your family has fled the realm, so Seren assumed anyone she encountered wouldn't be surprised to see her. Unfortunately, Tallus became aware of her presence just as she was preparing to return to Sea'Brik, which is why Sappho contacted me." Aurelius's gaze was troubled. "Seren is attending the weapon demonstration as Tallus's guest."

This couldn't be happening. How in the falling stars were we going to rescue Seren *and* kidnap Tallus? This made everything so much more difficult, if not completely impossible.

Sebastian put a hand on my shoulder and gave me a gentle shake until I looked at him.

"We'll change the plan," he said. "We'll kidnap Tallus before the weapon demonstration. We can learn more about whatever he created later."

"But what if he hurts Seren before we can get to him?" I felt a sob forming in my chest and tried to push it down even as I struggled to breathe.

"Tallus isn't going to harm another Astral in front of your entire realm, especially not when that Astral is your sister and all of Aeles is worried about your safety," Sebastian reasoned as Adonis nodded his agreement. "We know Tallus isn't above torturing children, but right now Seren is valuable to him without him needing anything from her beyond her presence."

"I'm coming to Celenia with you," I said. Sebastian opened his mouth, but I shook my head. "I'm not asking. You can kidnap Tallus before he goes on stage and bring him here. I'll find Seren. You can come back for us and open a portal to Sea'Brik. Once she's safe, I'll come here and deal with Tallus."

Aware there would be no changing my mind, Sebastian ran a hand through his hair. "Locating Tallus before he unveils his weapon is going to be more challenging. He'll probably be in a locked room until he goes on stage." He turned to Batty. "Can you do what you did in Rynstyn and materialize in and out of different parts of the amphitheater? Once you locate him, I'll open a portal and we'll kidnap him like we planned."

Batty nodded vigorously. While I hoped it would be that straightforward, I couldn't help feeling like something else terrible was about to happen, another shoe I couldn't foresee about to come crashing down to crush me.

"Has Seren told Tallus where I am or what Sebastian and I are planning?" I asked Aurelius, speaking out loud so Sebastian and Adonis had as much information as possible. "Did she tell him we recovered the Chronicles?"

The lynx consulted Sappho, and my heart thudded wildly, each beat vibrating through my entire body. "She has not told him anything," he finally replied, making my legs tremble with relief. "Tallus wasn't alone when he discovered her. He was with Senator Barmly, who was surprised to see her in Celenia without the rest of your family. Seren said they were too distraught over what had happened to you and were watching the broadcast from home, but she wanted to be present, especially if this weapon could help bring you back to Aeles. Tallus had to know she was trying to learn about his weapon to share information with you, but he invited her to the demonstration as his honored guest. Senator Barmly has kept Seren at her side, which is likely the only reason Tallus hasn't questioned her."

I hoped the Gifters would rain down blessings on Montem's senior senator, who had been good friends with my father. When I next saw her, I would give her the hug her kindness deserved. I didn't know if she was keeping Seren close because she distrusted Tallus or because caring for others was simply in her nature, but either way, her standing between Seren and Tallus, even unwittingly, was the single bright spot in the otherwise terrible news.

At the same time, Tallus's actions towards Seren simply reinforced my worst fears . . . the only reason he hadn't immediately tried to get her alone to interrogate her was because he didn't plan on letting her leave Celenia.

"Sappho should tell Seren to keep playing along and stay close to Senator Barmly," I instructed Aurelius. "But make sure Seren knows Sebastian and I are coming to get her." Even though

I was furious at the mess my sister had made, I couldn't help wanting to comfort her where I could.

Adonis stepped closer and flexed his fingers before saying the spell to cast a glamour. I could feel his words settling on my skin, and when he'd finished, I crossed the room to look in the mirror. A slight gasp escaped my lips. My dark skin was now pale, and my hair hung in long red curls. Grey eyes stared back at me, and I blinked at my unfamiliar reflection before turning to inspect Sebastian. He'd been completely transformed as well, and appeared to possess a round, boyish face with messy brown hair and green eyes.

"You cast amazing glamours," I said to Adonis, thoroughly impressed at his skill. I'd used the spell a handful of times while playing with my siblings, but I'd certainly never put effort into mastering the finer points of it.

"I have a lot of practice." Adonis pulled up the sleeve of his uniform before whispering the words to a revelation spell, and I was shocked to see inked markings appear on his forearm. He concealed them again before I could study each one in detail, although I'd definitely seen a rendering of his Cypher, a toad named Gordon, as well as the words *Aeles Invictus*, which I assumed was a military motto. Decorating your skin in such a manner was seen as uncouth in Aeles and something only Daevals did; I'd never met someone with golden blood bold enough to do what Adonis had done, but perhaps there were others—like Demitri—hiding parts of their selves deemed unacceptable by my realm. While I'd never expected Adonis to be such a rebel, it also explained a lot about his growing friendship with Sebastian and his desire to see things improve between Astrals and Daevals.

Bending down, I wrapped my arms around Aurelius. He was going to stay at the cottage, given that my Cypher would instantly be recognized in Celenia and would prompt questions as to my whereabouts. I knew he would pass along anything important from Sappho and keep me updated on Seren, but I still hated not having him right beside me. Batty would remain with him until we reached the amphitheater, at which point he would join us and begin searching for Tallus. Tallus and Batty hadn't worked closely together back when Batty had been my royal advisor, but that didn't mean Tallus had no memories of him. The bat had kept out of sight when helping free me from the experimentation facility. But there was a still a chance Tallus had seen him and would recognize him, and the less Tallus thought about anyone associated with Sebastian and me, the better.

Sebastian opened a portal, and I was glad Aurelius had given him coordinates to bring us out near the statue of Acies, my favorite Gifter. Pressing a hand against the base of the towering marble statue I'd visited more times than I could count, I offered a quick prayer to the Gifter of Wisdom. We then joined the other Astrals walking along the wide boulevard towards the amphitheater located where the twin rows of *Donec* buildings ended. We hadn't gone far when Nigel fell into step beside Adonis, who quickly filled him in on the change of plans. While Nigel knew Sebastian and I were wearing glamours, he was clearly still surprised to see us looking so unlike ourselves. Thankfully, he quickly recovered.

"I just came from the amphitheater," he said in a low voice, "and no revelation wards have been cast. We'll keep checking, but so far, we're good to go."

Sebastian handed him one of the devices he'd given Adonis earlier and explained about Tallus's ability to use your own fears against you. As we neared the imposing white marble arches towering over the outdoor seating area, I sensed a certain excitement in the air, although there was also a noticeable undercurrent of tension. I tried to listen to the conversations around us. Based on the snippets I managed to overhear, Astrals were curious about

Tallus's weapon but also wary of how quickly he'd assumed emergency powers and taken control of the military, as well as his plan to attack Nocens. I heard my name mentioned a few times. Folks wondered if I was still alive and if I'd really been kidnapped and who would become the realm's next *Princeps Shaman* if I'd been killed. I desperately wanted to cast off my disguise and tell everyone the truth, but now wasn't the time.

We stopped just outside the amphitheater, and Sebastian placed a hand on my arm.

"I don't want you looking for your sister by yourself," he said in a low voice, prompting Nigel and Adonis to move closer so they didn't miss anything.

"I'm completely disguised, so everyone here will see me as just another Astral attending the demonstration," I reminded him. "You should focus on finding Tallus. He poses a much greater danger than anything I'll encounter looking for Seren."

Conflicting emotions warred in Sebastian's eyes, and he pressed his lips together before turning to Nigel. "Adonis and I will go after Tallus—Batty's already searching for him—but I want you to stay with Kyra." His gaze was unblinking. "I'm counting on you to protect her if something goes wrong."

Nigel's grey eyes grew wide, but he nevertheless nodded. I understood Sebastian not wanting me to search for Seren by myself, but it was a mark of how much more comfortable he was trusting others that he would suggest me going off with anyone other than him. His confidence in Nigel's ability to keep me safe until he could reach me was impressive evidence of how much he'd grown, and I gave him a quick hug before the four of us split up.

"If Seren is here as Tallus's guest, I'm betting she'll be seated somewhere close to the stage," I whispered to Nigel, even though there was so much chatter around us we were in no danger of being overhead. "Let's go inside and we can look for her while making it seem like we're just finding seats."

"I'll be right behind you," said Nigel.

Walking under a curved marble archway, I ignored my pounding heart, which felt in danger of exploding, and instead focused on searching through the gathered Astrals for Seren. Making my way down the aisle, my breath caught every time I saw a head of blonde hair, only to be disappointed when it turned out not to be Seren. It was taking a significant amount of control not to call my sister's name or run up and down the rows of seats searching for her, but I couldn't draw attention to myself.

After what felt like an eternity, we neared the stage, and I shaded my eyes with my hands, silently whispering a repeated refrain to the Gifter of Victory. *Please, please, please, let me find her.*

When my eyes finally landed on Seren, it was all I could do to stay where I was. I bit down hard on my lip to keep myself from crying out. Seren was sitting in the front row two sections over. Senator Barmly was on her right, and Colonel Vonyas, a high-ranking military official, sat on her left. Her face was pale and her eyes were wide, but other than appearing scared she seemed unharmed.

"I see her," I said to Nigel, who quickly found us seats at the end of a nearby row as I reached out to Sebastian. *I found Seren. Has Batty located Tallus?*

No. Sebastian's voice was strained. *He saw his Cypher backstage, but there's no sign of Tallus himself. Adonis and I haven't found him either. We've still got a few minutes, so we'll keep looking.*

I told Nigel what Sebastian had shared, then did the last thing in the realm I wanted to do and sat quietly, waiting to hear Tallus had been successfully captured so I could run to my sister. Time had never passed so slowly before. When I saw Nigel glance at his watch, I couldn't stand it any longer.

It's almost time for the demonstration to start, I said to Sebastian, apprehension tingling through me. *What should we do?*

Go back to the original plan. Batty will follow Tallus off stage after he unveils his weapon, and we'll kidnap him then. Sebastian was clearly frustrated at being forced to modify his chosen course of action midway through a mission. *Where are you seated?*

I described my location. When Adonis arrived a few moments later, it took me a moment to remember the unfamiliar man with him was Sebastian. He sat down next to me. I took his hand, trying to maintain hope even though it seemed things were falling to pieces around us faster than we could repair them.

While no weather was right for learning about a weapon capable of destroying every Daeval in Nocens, the day couldn't have been more lovely. The warm sun, cool breeze, and twitter of birdsong somehow made what we were there to witness all the more disturbing. As everyone directed their attention to the stage at the bottom of the theater, a recording of the Aelian anthem began to play. Despite the terrible occasion, the powerful drums and rising chords never failed to make my heart swell with pride. Astrals were capable of so much good, and once Tallus had been dealt with and those in Aeles knew the truth, they could choose to act based off facts rather than fear.

As the music ended, a shadow fell across the stage, and, a moment later, Tallus emerged.

22

KYRA

Tallus's appearance immediately squelched the good feelings I'd momentarily enjoyed. For the first time in my life, I understood why animals bared their teeth when they were angry, words being insufficient to convey the fury they felt. Tallus's Cypher, a beautiful barn owl named Mendax, rode on his shoulder. The crowd burst into applause, and although much of it was genuine, I noticed at least some Astrals doing little more than pantomiming a clap or two to keep up appearances. I'd done the same during Tallus's internship orientation speech. While offering hesitant support was a far cry from public disagreement or protesting, I was grateful for any uncertainty among my fellow Astrals when it came to Tallus.

Tallus was his usual polished and poised self. His jacket looked as if someone had melted gold bars then molded the liquid into something wearable, and it set off the highlights in his reddish-blonde hair. Tiny pearls dotted the jacket, catching and reflecting the sunlight pouring into the open-air theater, and even from where I sat, I could see the excitement on his face. Beaming with a benevolent confidence he wore all too well, he gestured for an end to the applause as Mendax flew to perch on a crate on one side of the stage.

"Ladies and gentlemen, citizens of our beloved Aeles, thank

you for being here for what I know is an unprecedented gathering," began Tallus, spells projecting his voice. "Unfortunately, these are unprecedented times. When faced with challenges, we have but two options . . . we can allow ourselves to be trampled into oblivion, or we can rise to the occasion and charge forward into a glorious future of our own making. Creating such a future will not be easy, but I'm not certain it should be. We appreciate the things we've worked for far more than things that were simply given to us. As our dear former *Princeps Shaman* Arakiss Valorian once said, 'Place one pebble in a river and it might be washed away. But keep placing pebbles in a river and eventually, you'll change the course of the river.'"

My hands began to shake. I clenched them into fists, powerless to do anything other than despise Tallus for daring to use my father's words.

"There is still no response from Nocens on the whereabouts or well-being of Kyra Valorian." Sadness swept over Tallus's face and, knowing how much he wanted me to work with him to alter Daevals, his demeanor was likely a genuine reflection of his feelings. "While I fear the worst, I shall continue to hope for the best. But I also intend to do far more than hope. I'm so pleased to have Kyra's sister, Seren, here with us today." He gestured towards Seren, who sat perfectly still, although she wasn't able to completely hide how frightened she was. Thankfully, a sympathetic murmur rose from the crowd as everyone turned their attention to her, and given that Tallus had been mentioning my absence, Seren's reaction wouldn't seem of place.

"Seren, I say this to you, your family, and everyone in Aeles," continued Tallus. "If Nocens will not return Kyra, we will do everything in our power to rescue her."

I felt ill watching Tallus address my sister, and I briefly imagined using some sort of silencing spell to stop the lies pouring from his mouth, even though I didn't know any such spell. Seren's presence would make it seem as if my family supported Tallus's plan of invading Nocens. Nothing could be further from the truth, but clearly Tallus was only concerned with the truth when it suited him.

"Over the centuries, those with silver blood have shown they cannot be content to leave us alone." Tallus gazed at the crowd. "Our history is littered with their attempts to invade our realm, and while it seemed as if the Blood Alarm would put a stop to such behavior, Daevals have worked tirelessly to find a way around it. If a silver-blooded mercenary can enter Aeles and kidnap one of our own, what's to stop the entire Daeval military from catching us unawares and destroying all we hold dear before we can even mount a counterattack?"

Astrals shifted in their seats as they exchanged worried looks or whispers.

"We have been patient long enough." Tallus's voice resonated with determination. "No longer will our kindness be mistaken for apathy, and no longer will we sit by while everything and everyone we love is threatened. To that end, I have developed a weapon capable of eliminating every Daeval in Nocens. I call it Aurum powder."

Sebastian tensed beside me, and I pressed my leg against his, offering support where I could. While I wished we could dismiss Tallus's words as the exaggerations of a madman, we both knew what he was capable of. He wasn't to be underestimated.

"Allow me to demonstrate," said Tallus. The floor of the stage slid back in two places, and twin glass chambers rose upwards, miniature rooms made of four clear walls and a ceiling. A black tube hung down the side of each chamber. While one end dangled freely on the outside of the glass, the other end had been threaded through a small opening so it emptied inside the walls.

A chair had been placed in the center of each see-through box, and I couldn't keep from shuddering as I recognized them from my time in the experimentation facility. They weren't the same chairs, as those had been destroyed by Sebastian's fire, but they boasted the same arm and leg restraints I'd seen on the seats Daevals had been confined to while their blood had been forcibly taken.

Sebastian's nostrils flared, the only outward indication of the anger I felt stirring inside him.

"While Aurum powder is deadly to Daevals, it poses no threat to those with golden blood," explained Tallus. "Bring him out!"

Two soldiers appeared from one side of the stage, dragging a man between them who attempted to brace his feet against the floor. His hands were bound in front of him, and a gag was tied across his mouth. His eyes were wide; although he struggled, his efforts were to no avail, as he was forced into one of the chambers where his arms and legs were quickly fitted into the restraints.

The crowd reacted quickly, gasps and whispers becoming cries and shouts as Astrals sensed the man's silver blood. The more I'd been around Daevals, the less my body responded to them as a threat, but others in my realm hadn't had such opportunities, meaning their internal alarms were urging them to flee. A few folks stood, pulling their children close as if they were about to run, but Tallus raised his hands in a calming gesture, assuring everyone they were perfectly safe.

Sebastian leaned forward, studying the restrained Daeval. *That's Raks Nemoya.*

What? I tried to see the man's face better. *Are you sure?*

I'm positive. I just saw him last night at his auction.

Before we could speculate on how such a prominent Daeval had ended up a prisoner in Aeles—a Daeval Sebastian had *just* interacted with—Tallus spoke again.

"We have someone with silver blood, which means we need an Astral for comparison. And here's our charming volunteer."

He smiled and motioned for someone to join him onstage. A moment later, out walked Demitri.

My heart stopped. I couldn't breathe. Sebastian placed a hand on my leg as Adonis made a strangled noise and started to rise before sitting back down. It was clearly taking a great effort for him to control himself, and he dug his fingertips into his knees so hard his knuckles threatened to burst through his skin.

Demitri couldn't be there willingly. What had Tallus threatened him with to make him participate? Was I about to watch my best friend die? My heartbeat rang in my ears even as I tried to focus on Sebastian's voice in my head.

Tallus is doing this because he either assumes you're watching or he wants word of it to reach you. He could have ended Demitri's life anytime he wanted over the past few days, and he hasn't. Same as with your sister. He's not going to harm an Astral in an amphitheater full of other Astrals.

Even though Sebastian's words made sense, they didn't make me feel any better.

Demitri stood with his head cocked jauntily to one side, his hands in his pockets as Tallus thanked him for his dedication. "Your willingness to participate in our little experiment is a testament of your commitment to Aeles," praised Tallus.

Demitri looked out at the audience and grinned as he flashed a wink. "Once I knew my presence was required, I was more than happy to participate."

Tallus laughed and clapped Demitri on the shoulder as a few audience members offered tentative chuckles of their own. Demitri brushed his hair from his eyes with his fingertips, and anyone watching would think the two men were old friends engaging in light banter. I knew better, of course, and could see what others couldn't—the fear and fury behind the mask Demitri always kept in place out in public.

"Besides," added my best friend, his expression turning melancholy, "being here is a way I can stay busy, which helps keep my mind off things with Kyra."

Tallus placed a hand on Demitri's arm and nodded sympathetically, every inch the concerned government official. "You're closer to Ms. Valorian than just about anyone else in Aeles," he noted. "You must miss her terribly."

"I do," replied Demitri, "and I can't wait until she's home and can tell us all the truth about everything that's been going on."

A shadow passed over Tallus's face, but it was gone almost as fast as I noted it.

"We are doing everything in our power to ensure she returns home," he said. "That, I can promise you." He then offered a few more words of comfort before gesturing towards the empty chamber. "Whenever you're ready," he said with a bright smile.

Demitri walked into the small space and sat down in the chair, his expression perfectly pleasant. Thankfully, no one came to restrain him, as I wasn't certain I could have kept from running onto the stage and freeing him before attacking Tallus with my bare hands.

Tallus closed the door to Demitri's chamber before pulling a cylinder from his jacket pocket and inserting one end into the black tube snaking down the glass wall. He then moved to Raks's chamber and connected another cylinder to the tubing before striding to the far side of the stage, ensuring he wasn't blocking anyone's view.

"Aurum powder is airborne," he said, "and only takes a few minutes to affect those with silver blood. Let's watch, shall we?"

I couldn't have looked away even if I'd wanted to. Tallus had said Aurum powder wouldn't hurt Astrals, but what if he was lying? If my best friend was going to suffer for his association with me, the least I could do was bear witness to his torture before avenging him.

Something hissed as whatever was in the cylinders was pumped into the chambers. I thought I saw a slight golden shimmer above Raks's head, but it happened so fast I couldn't be sure. The Daeval stiffened. His eyes bulged, and he fought against his restraints, screaming unintelligible pleas or threats behind his gag. The crowd, already uneasy, began speaking in low voices. Just because Astrals feared or even hated Daevals didn't mean they wanted to watch someone with silver blood be tortured before their very eyes.

Raks's body began to spasm, and blood trickled from his nose as he gasped for breath, even though whatever he was breathing was clearly killing him. A few folks called out in protest while others covered their children's eyes or turned them away from the stage.

In the other chamber, Demitri continued to sit perfectly still, hands folded in his lap, gazing straight ahead and looking slightly bored.

Raks made a final strangled sound, then his body relaxed as his head lolled to one side, eyes open and unblinking.

"He's dead!" someone shouted, and the amphitheater was suddenly filled with a cacophony of voices. While a handful of Astrals were applauding or cheering, I was pleased to see most of my kind were unhappy, calling for an explanation, complaining that their children shouldn't have been forced to witness such a thing, or shouting out other distressed remarks. While I was no longer surprised at the lengths Tallus was willing to go to, I couldn't help but feel sorry for Raks. Despite how the Dekarais felt about the Nemoyas, the man didn't deserve to die in such a brutal manner, restrained and terrified while forced to serve as part of a public experiment.

To my great relief, Demitri appeared unharmed, although I wished Tallus would open his chamber and free him. Tallus raised his hands for silence, but it took a moment for the crowd to comply.

"This is our message to those in Nocens," he announced in a loud voice. "If Kyra Valorian is not returned to us within twenty-four hours, you will find the Aelian military on your doorstep, prepared to end our fight between those with gold and silver blood once and for all."

He then looked directly at me. Crooking two fingers so they resembled the fangs of a serpent, he pressed them against his heart in a gesture that shook me down to my very shade. I hadn't seen that gesture in more than a thousand years . . . it was the sign Astrals and Daevals had developed to pay their respects to the Felserpent King and Queen.

It was impossible. How had he recognized me through Adonis's glamour? Before I could think more about it, Mendax cocked his head and peered at the sky. "Look out!" he cried just before a few metal canisters fell from overhead, landing with sharp *plinks* at various points throughout the amphitheater. Different colored smoke began to spill from the containers as Astrals gasped and rose to their feet.

Is it Nocens? I asked Sebastian.

No. Batty checked, and it's not the Daevalic military.

I looked at Tallus just in time to see purple smoke streaming from his fingers, but given the confusion in the stands, I doubted anyone else noticed it. Those in the front rows were affected first, and folks started screaming, which only served to heighten the panic of those further back. Some attempted to run, while others fought things only they could see. As the purple smoke spread, chaos broke out in the amphitheater, Astrals screaming, shoving one another, clawing at the air, and tripping over the stone benches. Seren had her hands over her ears and was rocking back and forth in her seat. Demitri, in his air-tight chamber, wasn't affected, but he appeared terrified nonetheless, watching as those he lived and worked with seemed to lose their minds.

Tallus is going to make it seem like Nocens attacked everyone here with some sort of fear-inducing gas, snarled Sebastian before turning to Adonis and Nigel. "Use the devices I gave you!" he instructed the soldiers, who quickly reached into their pockets and inserted the tiny contraptions into their noses. I felt Death stir through our shared connection, ready to flood my mind with gruesome images as it had done before when Tallus had attempted to manipulate my fears, and once again I appreciated its all-consuming nature.

Surveying the pandemonium he'd wrought, Tallus nodded and began to make his way off the stage.

"We can't let him get away!" Sebastian shouted, pushing aside a man who'd stumbled into him, shrieking over an internal terror. "Batty's in position to follow him."

"I can't leave Seren!" My sister had crawled under one of the heavy stone benches and curled into a fetal position, and even from a distance I could tell she was crying.

"Nigel, take Kyra to get Seren. Adonis and I will go after Tallus," said Sebastian.

"We have to free Demitri!" insisted Adonis. "There's no telling what Tallus will do to him if we leave him behind."

Sebastian swore but must have realized there simply wasn't a way to rescue Seren, save Demitri, and stop Tallus all at the same time.

"You and Nigel get Demitri," he said. "Kyra and I will save Seren, and we'll deal with Tallus another day."

Sebastian grabbed my hand and began carving a path towards my sister, guiding us around Astrals trapped inside their worst nightmares. As I watched Tallus disappear from sight, I wanted to scream and cry and summon a bolt of lightning to strike him dead. We'd lost our best chance to stop him, and I had no idea how we were going to get close to him again, especially since we now had to do it before the deadline he'd given.

Making our way through the crowd of flailing, frightened Astrals was no easy feat, but I was glad Sebastian didn't treat them as enemies. Rather than pulling out Rhannu or knocking folks unconscious, he settled for shoving them aside, sometimes pulling me up onto one of the stone benches so we could move more freely. We had to duck a few times to miss punches thrown by Astrals fighting off some personal nightmare, but after running, crouching, and leaping across seats, we finally reached Seren.

Leaning down, I wrapped my arms around her. Pulling her to her feet, I held her close as Sebastian opened a portal. Dragging Seren through the crackling gateway, I lost my balance, causing the two of us to collapse onto the tiled floor of Sea'Brik.

23

KYRA

Sebastian hurried over, but I'd already untangled myself and was kneeling beside Seren. I said the words to a revelation spell and felt my skin tingle as my disguise disappeared. Shaking my sister's shoulder, I hoped the effects of Tallus's cruel gift were starting to wear off.

"Seren? It's me. You're back at Sea'Brik, and you're safe. Just keep breathing, deep breaths, in and out."

Slowly, the terror faded from her eyes, and she blinked before pushing herself into a sitting position, pressing a hand against her head. Sebastian, who had done away with his disguise as well, helped us both to our feet. As Seren stood before me, the fear I'd felt at the thought of Tallus harming her was swiftly replaced by anger.

"How could you sneak off like that?" I yelled, causing Seren to jump. "You could have been killed! You're lucky Sappho was able to reach out to Aurelius. Why in the falling stars would you do such a thing?"

"I just wanted to do something important—something you would do!" cried Seren, tears glistening in her eyes. "I overheard you talking in the hall, and I thought if I could find out something about Tallus's weapon, I could help you and then you'd include me more."

She buried her face in her hands, her body shaking as she sobbed, and while I was still furious with her, I also couldn't stand seeing her so upset. I stepped forward and drew her into a hug, smoothing her disheveled hair and holding her close as she wrapped her arms around me.

"I'm so sorry!" she cried, her words muffled against my shoulder. "I didn't mean to make things worse. I just wanted to help you."

"The best way you can help me right now is to stay safe," I said, but I couldn't force any real heat into my words. Pulling away enough to look directly in her eyes, my heart ached with each shuddering beat. "I don't know what I'd do if something happened to you. I can't lose you."

"I'm sorry," she sniffled, running a sleeve over her face. "For going into Celenia and for how I've been acting."

"I'm sorry too," I said. "Being your sister means more to me than any title I'll ever have or any spell I'm able to perform. Whatever happens moving forward, there will *always* be a place for you in my life. I love you, and you have to know that."

"I know," she said, the edges of her mouth rising as a bit of the usual happy shine returned to her eyes. "I love you too."

It wasn't at all the way I'd imagined healing with my sister, but I would take it. Mending my relationship with her, or at least starting the process of mending it, filled me with an additional strength I would unquestionably need in the coming days.

By now, the other occupants of Sea'Brik had joined us, no doubt drawn by my shouting. While I appreciated them letting me finish my conversation with Seren, they also needed to know what had just occurred. According to Caz, Tallus's message had already been seen by certain members of the Nocenian government, and they were understandably concerned.

"Some officials are saying we should hand you over, but of

course we'll do no such thing." Dunston patted my arm. "We've assured them you'll answer all their questions when you address them in a few hours."

As Sebastian shared what we'd learned of Aurum powder, Aurelius nudged my knee with his head. *Halo said Adonis and Nigel freed Demitri from the chamber, but before they could escape Celenia, they were ordered to escort Demitri to his apartment along with other soldiers who support Tallus. Demitri is not allowed to go anywhere without a military escort, but he's physically unharmed.*

Thank the Gifters. While I hated to think of Demitri trapped inside his apartment, being alive and held prisoner was far better than many other outcomes I could too easily imagine.

Needing a moment alone, I excused myself and made my way to Sebastian's room. I paced over the thick rug as I waited for my body to calm down, then rested my hands on the back of the sofa, closing my eyes and willing my heart to slow its frantic pace as I focused on taking controlled breaths.

Demitri was safe.

Adonis and Nigel hadn't been compromised or imprisoned by Tallus.

Sebastian, Seren, and I were safe and unreachable inside Sea'Brik.

At the same time, I had no idea how we would get near Tallus before his deadline. Even if Sebastian and I continued to hold off on reuniting the realms, just one soldier portaling into Nocens and opening a canister of Aurum powder would cause Daevals to die.

The peerin Caz had gifted me buzzed, and I quickly pulled it from my breeches, glad I could see with my own eyes Demitri was unharmed. Flipping open the hinged lids, the words I'd been about to speak died in my mouth as I found myself gazing at Tallus's smiling face.

"How . . . how do you have Demitri's peerin?" I managed to ask.

"I took it from him before he participated in my demonstration," Tallus replied. "I knew he had to be keeping in touch with you somehow. And speaking of my demonstration, I was so pleased to see you there." He crooked his fingers in front of his heart again. "Hail the Felserpent Queen."

Are you alright? Sebastian's voice was sharp in my head.

Tallus contacted me through Demitri's peerin.

I'll be right there.

It wasn't the most important question to ask Tallus, but I wanted to keep him talking until Sebastian arrived. "How did you recognize me?"

"I told you before; while there are limits to what I can do with others' minds, I am in excellent control of my own. I mastered seeing through glamours three life cycles ago, and I haven't been fooled since." He chuckled. "While I enjoyed your efforts, red hair most certainly does *not* suit you."

I wasn't certain whether Tallus had contacted me for a reason or simply to unsettle me by demonstrating what he was capable of. Even though I worried I might accidentally let something slip I hadn't intended to share, I also wanted to learn something useful.

"Aurum powder uses golden blood, doesn't it?" It was the only thing that made sense based on what I knew of Tallus's previous work. "It settles in Daevals' lungs, and since their bodies can't process anything related to golden blood, they die within minutes. How did you ever discover such a thing?"

Part of me wasn't certain Tallus would share anything about his weapon, but he'd always been a stickler for facts. He'd also demonstrated a tendency to want to talk about his work, to have his creations appreciated. While vanity seemed like an insignificant character flaw, I'd learned from Sebastian any weakness could ultimately prove useful.

Tallus nodded excitedly. "I knew no one other than you would truly appreciate my work. You see, I never abandoned studying gold and silver blood, and I'd already started on this project when Sebastian destroyed my facility. If something happened to you or you continued refusing to work with me, I needed another way to eliminate Daevals. I admit, I thought I'd hit a stopping point once we realized Daevals couldn't process golden blood, when really, that discovery was the key to extinguishing them once and for all." His expression radiated a deep satisfaction over what he considered a job well done. "That's the whole point of research—developing increasingly better options from the remnants of our failures." He leaned closer to the peerin screen. "I really should thank you. If you'd agreed to work with me, I never would have developed Aurum powder."

That was the thing about Tallus; he knew how to make you feel like something was your fault even when it wasn't and even if you'd been actively working against him. I shook my head, refusing to let his words settle in my mind where they might exert any sort of effect on me. Thankfully, the door flew open and Sebastian rushed in, coming to stand behind me.

"How did you kidnap Raks Nemoya?" he demanded.

"I didn't kidnap him." Disdain clouded Tallus's face. "The man was an enterprising Daeval looking to make a profit. He was aware Kyra had supposedly been taken from Aeles by one Sebastian Sayre, the very same assassin who showed up to his antiques auction alongside a Devlin Dekarai and a bookseller named LeBehr." Tallus's gaze was unwavering. "I'm assuming you were there to retrieve the Chronicles, and I *do* hope you were able to get that book back."

I stared at him, uncertain exactly how much he knew but determined not to give anything away.

"I also hope you realize I didn't have to reveal my Aurum

powder," he continued. "My demonstration was intended as a warning. Reunite the realms, and I won't release the powder."

"Reuniting the realms will just make it easier for you to invade Nocens and use your weapon," I scoffed.

"Kyra, Daevals are already living on borrowed time." Tallus spoke as if he was lecturing a stubborn child. "You can't stop their demise, but you *can* control how much they suffer. My original offer still stands: after you reunite the realms, we can work together to painlessly change Daevals from the inside out."

"I will *never* work with you." My voice was as unflinching as the glare I leveled at Tallus, and eventually he shook his head.

"I've given you my deadline. What you choose to do with the information is up to you."

He ended the call, and I closed the peerin, dropping it on the sofa before pressing my hands against my eyes. Sebastian wrapped his arms around me, and I sank against his chest.

"What are we going to do?" I whispered.

"We're going to come up with a new plan," said Sebastian. "We'll address the Nocenian government, and then we'll figure out another way to kidnap Tallus."

A knock sounded at the door, and even though I wasn't in the mood to speak with anyone, I dutifully answered as Sebastian headed to the shower.

LeBehr offered me an apologetic smile.

"I'm sorry to bother you," she said, "but seeing how we're all up . . . I'm assuming you'll be taking the Chronicles with you when you speak to the government, but if you're not using it until then, I'd love to start making copies. Mischief is gathering the supplies I keep at the shop, and Minerva said she can provide anything else I need."

Picking up the Chronicles from Sebastian's nightstand, I offered it to LeBehr, who hugged it excitedly to her chest.

"Will you be able to make any copies we can share with the Nocenian government?" I asked.

"Unfortunately, the process isn't quite that fast," she replied. "Thankfully, I won't need to sit and copy every word in the Chronicles myself, but it's also not as if I can just point a stick at the book and command it to replicate itself." She patted the green cover. "The fastest way to create multiple copies of a volume is to use myself as a conduit. I'll assemble some empty volumes and then recite the *Exscribend* spell. When I put one hand on the Chronicles and the other on the newly bound book, everything inside the Chronicles will transfer to the waiting pages."

"I'm surprised there isn't a spell that doesn't require your personal involvement," I said.

LeBehr smiled. "When it comes to putting words on a page, I think an Astral or Daeval should always be involved. Creation is never easy, nor do I think it should be, even if we're simply creating another version of something that already exists. It's the effort that makes the outcome worthwhile."

I thought of all the effort I'd expended against Tallus in Rynstyn, only to ultimately fail at taking control of his mind. It had taken a concerted effort to coordinate with Adonis and Nigel, disguise ourselves, and sneak into Celenia for Tallus's weapon demonstration, and while we'd rescued Seren, our efforts hadn't resulted in capturing Tallus. In spite of my best efforts, failures were mounting around me.

"What if you make every effort you can and it's still not enough?" I hadn't meant to ask the question out loud, but it slipped out of my mouth, opening the way for more questions to follow. "What if I'm not strong enough to stop Tallus? What if I'm not able to reunite the realms? And what if I can't recover Grace?"

My last words were little more than a whisper, and LeBehr

placed a hand on my shoulder. "You're not alone when it comes to stopping Tallus. You have Sebastian, your family, your friends in Aeles, and many of us here in Nocens ready to support you however we can. And you'll reunite the realms because you're one of two individuals who possess the authority to do so. As for recovering Grace, do you have to do that by any particular time?"

"No," I admitted, "which is good because before I recover her, I have to find a Daeval who died at their appointed time, who knew Grace when she was alive, and who is willing to let Grace's shade have their body."

LeBehr's eyes widened. "Oh, well, if that's all you have to do . . ." Her voice trailed off, and she shook her head before squeezing my shoulder. "Best to focus on one thing at a time," she said gently.

I mustered a smile and gave her a hug. While I appreciated her belief in me—I appreciated the support of everyone helping Sebastian and me—I still worried it wouldn't be enough, that *I* wouldn't be enough. Tallus was always one step ahead of us, and at this moment, I didn't see how we could catch up with him, much less defeat him. Try as I did to stop it, I couldn't prevent a crippling fear from winding a slow, painful course through me, leaving nothing but despair in its wake.

24

KYRA

I closed *The Book of Recovrancy* and placed it on the table beside me, rubbing my eyes before looking out one of the numerous windows. Sebastian and I hadn't attempted to go back to sleep after returning to Sea'Brik. The sun had just risen, although I didn't have the energy to appreciate the warm yellow light dappling the surface of the ocean. I'd searched for other ways to remove Tallus's shade without needing to be so close to him, but the book had made it clear such a thing simply wasn't possible.

Sebastian was sitting at a large table across the room where he'd been using the peerin Caz had given me to speak on and off with Adonis as he studied maps and schematics of buildings in Celenia, trying to decide when and how we should make our next move against Tallus. He'd also been in communication with Camus, with whom he'd shared how to create a portable air purifier like the devices he'd given Adonis and Nigel. While Tallus's weapon wasn't common knowledge in Nocens yet—and hopefully wouldn't be, so long as we stopped him—the Dekarais had quietly shifted priorities at a few of their factories and begun manufacturing the filtration devices on the terrible chance even a single canister of Aurum powder made its way into Nocens.

I was about to ask Sebastian if he'd had any breakthroughs or new ideas when my mind was suddenly filled with gruesome images—folks drowning, burning, suffocating, or worse. I felt as if my very shade was being shaken, and I gasped, leaning forward and pressing a hand against my chest. Sebastian jumped up from the table and pulled a dagger from the holster on his boot, settling into a fighting stance as his eyes scanned the room. Aurelius rose to all fours from his position on the rug, the fur on his back raised as he let out a low growl, and Batty peered at me from the back of Sebastian's chair, his dark eyes filled with concern.

"It's Death," I said, working to catch my breath, which had all but run away from me. Sebastian looked around as if Laycus might suddenly appear in the room with us, which was admittedly a terrifying thought. "Vaneklus just reached out to me through our connection," I hurried to explain. I'd become so much better at managing our connection, it had been a while since Death's memories had caught me off guard. And even then, I'd never experienced such an insistent demand for my attention before, which meant something important had to be happening.

Sebastian replaced his dagger. "Any idea what Laycus might want?"

"No, but I better find out." I hurried to the wardrobe and grabbed my shifter cloak. Settling it over my shoulders, I made my way to the middle of the room and lowered into a cross-legged position on the thick green and grey rug. "I'll be back once I know more."

Laycus was already waiting for me near the dock when I arrived in Vaneklus.

"That was a terrifying way to be summoned," I chided him.

"Then be glad I don't make it a habit of summoning you," he retorted. Scowling at me, he nevertheless extended a skeletal hand. "Suryal has requested a meeting with you."

Any annoyance I had at being contacted in such a manner immediately disappeared. I quickly took Laycus's hand, allowing him to help me into his boat even as I wished I'd worn something more appropriate than tan breeches and a dark blue tunic for meeting with someone as important as Suryal. At least my cloak looked nice.

Arranging it as I took a seat, I couldn't keep from asking, "Do you know what she wants to speak with me about?" Perhaps she had such good news about my bond with Sebastian, she wanted to share it with me directly. On the other hand, perhaps the news was so terrible, she felt it was best delivered face-to-face.

"The sooner we meet with her, the sooner you will know," replied Laycus.

I clutched the edge of the hard bench seat as Laycus turned the boat around and began guiding us down the river. No matter what time I came to Vaneklus, the landscape always looked the same, lit by a muted light whose source I had given up trying to determine. While I'd originally thought the large boulders lining the sides of the river appeared ominous, I'd grown to appreciate them, the mottled black and grey stone shaped into smooth curves and sharp edges by . . . time? There was no wind in Vaneklus, no storms or other elements for the stones to battle. Perhaps they'd simply always existed as they were and would continue to do so for eternity. The river lapped against the boat as the oars moved us forward, but even the pleasant sound of the water wasn't enough to soothe me.

"Is the reason Suryal wants to meet with me good or bad?" I asked Laycus.

As I'd half-anticipated, he merely grinned. "Patience has never been your strong suit," he said. "Perhaps you should consider working on that, either in this life or the next."

He wasn't entirely wrong, but that didn't stop indignation

from flickering in my chest. "Sebastian and I have the Chronicles back in our possession," I said, preferring to talk about a success rather than a shortcoming. While I was never certain what Laycus knew of events in the realm of the living, either through his own special powers or because Batty visited and shared news with him, I was happy to tell him of our accomplishment. His eyes glowed with interest, and as I told him about the events at the book auction, he let out a raspy laugh.

"In Vaneklus, we refer to traits shades demonstrate across more than one life cycle as *constants*," he said. I nodded eagerly, always excited when Laycus shared something about his realm or work with me. "No matter what else changes about LeBehr, she always maintains a passion for books. Her love for them is as much a part of her as your recovrancy is a part of you."

I grinned, thinking how delighted LeBehr would be to hear such a thing. "May I tell her you said that?"

Laycus shrugged. "I will never understand your kind's fascination with learning about their past lives, but I see no harm in her knowing."

I tried to consider things from Laycus's point of view. "Perhaps it's different because you're immortal," I said. "Compared to you, the lives of Astrals and Daevals are so short. There's no way we can accomplish everything we want in a single lifetime. I think we like hearing about our past lives because we hope to discover we did something good or exciting . . . we want to know that we made a difference or, at the very least, that we were happy. Learning who we've been helps us understand ourselves in ways we'd otherwise need hundreds of years to do. Plus," I added, "we're so used to a finite amount of time, to things beginning and ending, it's nice to know that even if our bodies don't live forever, our shades do—or at least for a very long time."

Laycus nodded slowly, considering my words. "The very

concept of immortality isn't nearly as straightforward as it might first appear," he admitted. "There are different types, you see. Some eternities—such as mine—are continuous. I remember everything, each experience stacked on top of the previous."

"Like Tallus," I said, and Laycus scowled, although I hadn't meant it as an insult. "I'm just trying to understand what you're saying in terms of things I can personally relate to," I assured him, which thankfully served to restore his talkative mood.

"Most shades have an unrecognized eternity," he continued. "They exist without end, but they have no knowledge of previous lives and experiences, making each life cycle seem like the first. The system promotes learning and choice, but on a smaller scale —one hundred years versus one hundred thousand. There are benefits and losses to any life system, and while it's certainly not perfect, it's seen as the most sustainable option, at least for now."

I wanted to ask him who had instituted this life system or made the decision that an unrecognized eternity was the best option for Astrals and Daevals, but I doubted he would give me an answer. If Gifters or Fates existed, Laycus didn't appear to interact with them, or at least he'd never mentioned interacting with them.

"What about Sebastian and me?" I asked instead. "We don't seem to fall into either category."

Laycus snorted. "That is an understatement. You two have created your own category."

"Schatten and I were immortal at one time," I reminded him. "It was a gift that came with assuming the Felserpent's position as caretakers of the realm. When Tallus divided the realm, he not only destroyed the peace between Astrals and Daevals, he destroyed our chance to live together forever."

"He destroyed your ability to have a continuous eternity," corrected Laycus. "But you seem to have found a way around that."

"Perhaps the two of us have an interrupted eternity," I suggested.

Laycus grinned, a rare occasion when his demeanor was completely free of sarcasm or spite. "I rather like that," he said. "Although I'm also glad it doesn't seem to have caught on. It's enough dealing with the two of you."

I fell silent as he guided us through the three gates preventing shades from traveling back up the river if they changed their mind about being reborn. The scenery on either side of the boat was becoming noticeably different, grey boulders giving way to white trees, crystals swaying like icicles from their branches as pearls dotted the riverbank, clustered together like glistening sea anemones. Quartz formations rose elegantly upwards, creating a shimmering fence-like structure that was almost too lovely to be a boundary, even though I suspected it was.

We neared the spot where I'd spoken with Suryal before, and I sat up straighter at seeing her boat of bleached wood already waiting in the middle of the river. Sweat dampened my palms, and I rubbed them over my pants as I did my best to prepare myself for whatever was about to be revealed.

"Welcome, Kyra," the ruler of Karnis greeted me with a smile. "Thank you for meeting with me."

"The pleasure is mine," I assured her, heart pounding.

"My brother told me the lengths you are willing to go to in order to ensure Tallus is no longer a destructive presence in the realm of the living," she began. "You are very brave to make such a sacrifice, willing to live with the knowledge you chose to take a life."

"Thank you," I said, not having expected this to be the topic of conversation. "I certainly don't relish performing such an act, but I can't allow him to continue harming those I love or ruining any attempts at peace between Astrals and Daevals. He has to be stopped, and as I've told Laycus, I'll do whatever is required."

"My brother said as much," nodded Suryal, "and while I have no doubt you are more than capable, I do not wish for you to live the rest of your life carrying such a burden. Taking a life, regardless of the reason, is not something that ever leaves you, particularly since, as a Recovrancer, you are charged with saving lives."

"I don't wish to live with such a burden either," I admitted, "but I don't know what else to do. Batty and Aurelius discovered that Tallus used the *Memoria Aeterna* spell on himself, but there's no record of a counterspell to break it. I'm not strong enough to take control of his mind and make him forget his past life memories, so removing his shade and bringing him to Vaneklus is the only option I have."

"It is the only option you've had until now," smiled Suryal.

I grabbed the side of the boat, part of me not daring to believe there was another way to stop Tallus even as hope stirred deep inside me.

"There is a way to remove the spell Tallus cast to preserve his memories that does not require ending the existence of his shade," said Suryal, reaching up one of her billowing white sleeves and withdrawing a scroll, which she handed to me.

I carefully accepted the shimmering parchment and unrolled the document.

> *In order to break the* Memoria Aeterna *spell, the shade who cast it must appear in Vaneklus; this can be at their appointed time to die or they may be brought to the realm early by a Recovrancer. Once the shade is safely in Vaneklus, the following individuals must be gathered:*
>
> * *The Shade Transporter*
> * *The Shade Restorer*
> * *A Recovrancer*

- *The rightful wielder of Rhannu*
- *A Great Beast*

The words to break the *Memoria Aeterna* spell followed, but I stopped, my heart so heavy, it might as well have been replaced by a boulder.

"I'm a Recovrancer," I said. "Laycus, you're the Shade Transporter, and Suryal, you must be the Shade Restorer." She inclined her head. "Sebastian is the rightful wielder of Rhannu, but"—I swallowed, hating to be the bearer of such terrible news it seemed those in Vaneklus weren't aware of—"there are no more Great Beasts. The Felserpent was the last of them, and he died, or at least vanished, when Schatten assumed his title as King of Aeles-Nocens."

Laycus shook his head. "The Felserpent was not the last of the Great Beasts."

I stared up at him in disbelief. There was no reason for him to lie, but how had I not known this?

"One still remains," he said. "Speak with Bartholomew. He knows where to find the creature."

Some part of me wasn't the least bit surprised to discover Batty was involved, and I tried to imagine who the last remaining Great Beast might be. Was the animal hidden away in the furthest reaches of the realms, far from the daily lives of Astrals and Daevals? Hidden away—in a cave, perhaps? Could Nerudian be the last Great Beast? But even as I considered the possibility, I recalled Batty saying he'd known Nerudian back when he was an egg waiting to be hatched, which meant the black dragon couldn't be an immortal creature. Perhaps the Great Beast was another dragon, though, a member of Nerudian's family. Excitement filled me at such a thought, but at the same time . . .

"What if the last Great Beast doesn't want to help?" I asked, my fingers fidgeting with the serpent-shaped clasp of my cloak.

"Let us hope they will." Suryal's normally kind expression turned somber. "We need their power." While she didn't say as much, I suspected there weren't many—or any—other options available to us, should the creature not wish to become involved.

"I'll do my best to convince them," I said. "Thank you so much for this, Suryal. I had no idea such a thing was even possible."

"You are more than welcome," she replied, dipping her head and causing her long white hair to cascade over one shoulder. "When you bring Tallus's shade to Vaneklus, know I shall be ready to do my part."

I nodded, and she waved goodbye as Laycus turned his boat around. I held the scroll carefully as he guided us along the river, excitement sending a tingling sensation all the way to the tips of my fingers and toes.

"Thank you, Laycus," I said once we'd made our way through the gates requiring his concentration. I shifted on the bench to see him better, standing behind me as he steered the boat. "You didn't have to do that."

"I didn't," he agreed. "But if you were willing to do whatever it took to stop Tallus, the least I could do was see if there was a way to assist you—although I am mildly disappointed I won't have the chance to consume his shade."

"Well, if the last Great Beast doesn't want to help us, that might be our only option," I reminded him. "I wouldn't count it out just yet."

We reached the area near the dock, and I hopped over the side of the boat, my bare feet making contact with the smooth stones lining the riverbed. "After we've addressed the Nocenian government, I'll bring Tallus here as soon as I can."

"I shall be ready," he said, his garnet-red eyes flashing with a devilish anticipation.

Returning to my body, I rose from my position on the floor and darted to where Sebastian was still working at the table.

"Suryal gave me something incredibly important." I held up the scroll. "I'll tell you everything, but we need to include Nerudian."

After throwing on boots, we stepped through a portal directly into Nerudian's cavern. As Sebastian raised the lever to turn on the lights in the otherwise dark space, the dragon lifted his head over the edge of his canyon and blinked sleepily at us, coins, gems, and other treasures falling from his black scales.

"I'm so sorry," I said, "but I promise it will be worth the disruption." I explained about Suryal wanting to meet with me and sharing how to break the spell Tallus had cast on himself. "If we can do it, Laycus won't need to consume his shade—Tallus can be reborn with no knowledge of who he used to be or what he planned on doing to Daevals." Still struggling to believe there might be a solution that didn't require me to end Tallus's life, I unrolled the scroll and read it out loud before letting the parchment curl back in on itself.

"When I reminded Laycus all the Great Beasts were dead, he said that wasn't true and one still remained. He also said I should speak with *you*, Batty." I knelt in front of the bat, who was perched on a low rock. "Where is the last Great Beast? Who are they? And more importantly, do you think they'll help us?"

Batty shared a long look with Nerudian. The dragon cocked his head to one side, arching the bony ridge over one eye, and Batty eventually nodded before wrapping his wings around himself.

"I know they will help," the bat said. "As for where the last Great Beast is and who they are," he grinned up at me, "I am right here."

25

KYRA

I stared at the bat, not believing what I'd just heard him say.

"But . . . you're a Cypher!" Disbelief exploded across Sebastian's face, one of the rare times I'd seen him too caught off guard to control his expression.

Batty's smile grew wider. "I said before, a Cypher is only one of many things I have been in my life. In addition to being a Cypher and a royal advisor, I am also the last of the Great Beasts."

Aurelius slowly lowered his haunches to the stone floor. "I always sensed there was something different about you," he admitted, "but I never imagined *this*."

Batty hopped down from the rock. "Let us get comfortable," he suggested. "This is worth taking some time to explain."

We settled around him as Nerudian peered over the edge of the chasm. The dragon wasn't the least bit surprised, clearly having known the truth about Batty all along, and as he caught me looking at him, he offered a toothy grin.

"It was not my secret to share," he explained.

"I understand," I assured him. "I'm just trying to believe it."

Batty sneezed, ran a wing under his nose, and began his tale.

"As Astrals and Daevals became more prominent in Aeles-Nocens, the time of the Great Beasts ended, prompting them to leave for the Fertile Grounds. Now, a Great Beast leaving behind the realm of the living is not like a shade dying, and there were no Shade Transporters for Great Beasts; instead, the creatures assembled in Vaneklus where they were carried away on specific ships, taking the animals to their eternal home where they would never experience death. When your reign was established and you accepted responsibility for the realm from the Felserpent, I had a choice. I could join him on the last ship to the Fertile Grounds, hoping for the best after my departure, or I could remain, doing what I could to ensure Aeles-Nocens grew and thrived." He smiled first at Sebastian, then at me. "I chose to stay."

"You chose to forgo an eternity of rest with others like you to stay here and look out for the realm?" Sebastian stared at the small creature. "Why?"

"Because my place is here in the world I love," said Batty, "surrounded by those I love." He gazed fondly at each of us before adding, "Besides, there is no food in the Fertile Grounds, since the creatures do not need to eat, so I did not give up much."

Even as the bat pulled a caramel from a wing pocket, content with his choice, I still couldn't comprehend what he'd done, and I sensed Sebastian struggling to come to terms with this newest revelation. While he'd apologized for his less-than-kind treatment of Batty and had been doing an admirable job of being more patient with the creature, I knew how I would feel if Aurelius suddenly made such a realm-shattering announcement.

"Why didn't you tell us—or at least me—sooner?" Sebastian asked.

"I didn't see how it would make a difference to the realms," shrugged the bat. "I have assisted where I could, but my powers cannot fix the problems we face. You two have done the truly important things. You bound your shades together. You returned and found one another. You recovered your past life memories. You reclaimed Rhannu. You've started bringing peace between

Astrals and Daevals. And you have everything you need to reunite the realms."

I wanted to protest the bat had done far more than he was claiming credit for, but he wasn't finished.

"The way I saw it, even as a Great Beast, there was nothing I could do that you are not already doing—or so I thought until you read Suryal's scroll." The grin that slid across his furry face was far more wicked than I was used to seeing on the sweet-natured creature. "While I hoped I could be useful in defeating Tallus, I had no idea my presence would be considered *necessary*." He stood up straighter and proudly smoothed the golden mantle of fur around his neck.

"Since you chose to forgo the Fertile Grounds, are you still immortal?" I asked as Sebastian ran a hand over his face, desperately trying to process everything his Cypher had shared.

"I am not entirely certain," Batty admitted. "A Great Beast choosing to forgo the Fertile Grounds in favor of remaining in Aeles-Nocens is unprecedented, so I have no idea what to expect." He grinned. "As Laycus is fond of saying, it is nice to have lived for so long and know I can still be surprised. I suspect my end will come at some point, and when it does, I shall make my way to Vaneklus, where Laycus has kindly offered me a position as second-in-command on his boat."

I smiled picturing such a thing: Laycus's boat cutting through the ever-present fog with Batty perched on the bow, popping candies into his mouth and waving a wing in greeting to a newly arrived shade. He would certainly provide a more welcoming presence than the Shade Transporter alone, pulling up to the dock in his shadow-black shroud as his red eyes flashed in his skull-like face. Given how much Laycus preferred his privacy and his routines, his offer to share his boat spoke volumes of how much he cared for Batty, and I was grateful for his unexpected kindness. I leaned towards the bat. "I can only hope one day, Astrals and Daevals will be worthy of the sacrifice you made. Thank you for everything, Batty." I kissed the top of his head, then looked at Sebastian. "That means we have everything we need to break Tallus's spell . . . aside from Tallus himself."

"It is most unfortunate things did not work out when you attempted to capture him before." Nerudian shook his head, obviously having been updated on the situation by Batty. "But I remain available to assist you however I can."

"Thank you," replied Sebastian. "We'll finalize a plan after we address the Nocenian government, but we're definitely going to need your help. And speaking of addressing the government, I want to get my cloak before we go back to Sea'Brik." Annoyance flashed across his face. "I'm certain Devlin will have ideas about how I should dress for our speech, but if I'm wearing something I wore as king, it might be enough to keep me out of a suit." His eyes met mine and behind the annoyance, I saw a rare vulnerability. "I also thought wearing it might . . . I don't know, exactly . . . make me feel better about what I'm telling everyone."

"I'm in no hurry to leave." I gazed around the cavern and smiled at the pink quartz walls. "I've missed this place."

Aurelius waved an oversized paw at me.

"You two go retrieve Sebastian's cloak," he said. "It seems even at my age, there is still much for me to learn, and I have more than a few questions for Bartholomew." His tufted ears pricked as he glanced hopefully at Batty.

"Oh, ask him how Cyphers are descended from Great Beasts!" suggested Nerudian eagerly as he propped his chin on the edge of the chasm. "I always love hearing that one."

Aurelius's mouth dropped open, and I felt the shock that ran through him. "How Cyphers are *what*?"

"The process of pairing a Cypher with an Astral or Daeval

began shortly after the realms were divided," Batty explained. "It was started as a way to offer comfort to folks after everything they'd been through. But the endeavor was so successful, it quickly became standard practice in both Aeles and Nocens. Unfortunately, not just any mortal animal could become a Cypher, even though many wished to. Researchers were never able to figure out why some animals could form a connection with Astrals and Daevals that allowed them to speak into each other's minds while other animals couldn't, but such an opportunity was seen as a blessing from the Gifters or the Fates, so no one delved too deeply into the hows or whys.

"What the researchers did *not* know was that each of the animals who became a Cypher could trace their lineage back to a particular creature in their unique species. While tales of these creatures' powers were no doubt exaggerated, truth lies at the heart of every exaggeration. Those animals who were able to become Cyphers were directly descended from the Great Beasts. And so it remains, to this day."

Aurelius looked as if the slightest breeze would topple him, and I didn't blame him. While part of me wanted to stay and hear more of what Batty knew, Sebastian was waiting for me at the mouth of the tunnel.

Aurelius, will you remember any other interesting stories Batty shares so you can tell me later? I asked.

Of course, replied the lynx, gazing at the bat in a manner that suggested my normally opinionated Cypher was too stunned for words.

Leaving the creatures to talk amongst themselves, Sebastian and I made our way down the tunnel to his living quarters.

"I still can't believe Batty is a Great Beast," he said as we walked. "So many incredible things have happened, I keep thinking I'll stop being surprised at some point, but it hasn't happened yet."

"I know what you mean," I agreed, slipping my hand into his and feeling more relaxed than I had in weeks. There was something about being back here, where so much had transpired, that made me feel like everything was going to work out and that, just for this moment, I didn't need to do anything but be right where I was.

"It feels like forever since we've been alone," noted Sebastian. He, too, was calmer than I'd seen him of late, and one side of his mouth rose as he looked at me. "I'm glad it can be just the two of us for a while before we address the government."

He was right . . . it had been a while since it had been just the two of us, and his words made me realize something else.

"I think this is the first time we've been alone without our Cyphers close by," I said, something tickling the inside of my stomach as a shiver zipped up my spine. "Aurelius must have finally decided it's not dangerous for me to be around you unsupervised."

"That's quite a compliment, coming from him," replied Sebastian. "But I'll never fault his devotion to you."

We made our way to the sleeping alcove, and I ran my hand over the dresser Sebastian had purchased for me.

"It'll be nice to have a chance to use this," I said. "Sometimes it's hard to imagine there will actually be a time when we aren't doing big, important things, like stopping Tallus and preventing the realms from imminent destruction. But I keep telling myself at some point, we'll be able to focus on just living our lives."

Sebastian pulled his cloak from his wardrobe. "Do you see yourself keeping your apartment in Celenia after the realms are reunited?" he asked.

I looked at him, sensing there was more to the question.

He dropped his gaze to his cloak, turning it over in his hands. "I mean, do you see yourself staying mostly in Aeles, or"—he raised his eyes to mine—"are you open to dividing your time between Aeles and Nocens?"

"I hoped we would divide our time," I replied. "Since my family has already started planning our wedding, it seems only right we would live together. At least, that's what I want, but only when you're comfortable with it. I know what a huge change it's been to let me into your life and your space, and I don't want to rush you."

"I can't imagine not seeing you every day," Sebastian said. "I want us to be together as often as possible. I'm not certain what your family would think of coming to visit you in a cave, but we could find a house wherever you like in Nocens."

I very much liked the idea of picking out a place to live with Sebastian that belonged to the two of us. Plus, dividing our time between Aeles and Nocens would help avoid any charges that might be leveraged at us for favoring one realm over the other. "That's a wonderful idea." I smiled at him. "But I still want to keep the cave so we have a place to go where no one can find us. And so Nerudian always has a home."

Sebastian returned my smile, and the happiness in his expression made me feel like I'd stepped into a warm bath.

"I've never thought of any place I've lived as 'home' before," he said. "Not since I was a child, anyway. But when you say it, I like how it sounds."

"My home is wherever you are." I moved towards him, wrapping my arms around him and rising on my tiptoes to press my lips against his. Sebastian's mouth met mine with a force I hadn't expected but was glad to receive, and I hugged him closer, feeling his firm muscles and sharp shoulder blades beneath my hands. He tossed his cloak onto the dresser, and his kisses became more insistent as he ran a hand through my hair, pulling me against him.

My heart began to beat faster. The other times Sebastian and I had attempted to be intimate, I'd accidentally kept recovering memories of our past life together. While I'd loved being able to recall things that made me blush, I'd also been ready to make new memories with the man I loved. Now, with no past memories resurfacing, it seemed the time was finally right, and eagerness sped through me. It was just us, Sebastian and me, as we were in this life, in this moment. Given that everything in our lives was about to change, this time alone with Sebastian felt even more special and something to be savored for as long as it lasted. Sliding my hand under the hem of his tunic, I let my fingertips trace their way up his spine.

He stiffened and pulled back just enough to look at me.

I'm . . . self-conscious about my scars. His voice was strained in my mind.

Do you want me to stop?

No, I just . . . I don't want them to bother you or for you to—

Sebastian, those scars are not your fault, and they're nothing to be ashamed of. I can heal them for you, if you want, but to me, they just mean you're a survivor. And I'm glad of it, because I can't imagine my life without you.

Sebastian gazed so deeply into my eyes I wondered what he was searching for. Whatever it was, he must have found it, because his stiff posture relaxed, and then he was kissing me again, sliding his hand under the hem of my tunic before pressing his fingertips against my back. Never in my life had I imagined the simple act of being touched could make me feel like I might explode into a million pieces of pure happiness. I wasn't sure how I managed to remain standing when I seemed to be melting into Sebastian, losing all sense of where I ended and he began.

Both of my hands were under his shirt now, grasping his back, but I still wasn't close enough, so I began tugging his shirt over his head. That required us to stop kissing, and I took the opportunity to pull off my own tunic. I'd never seen Sebastian's eyes so wide. Heat rose to my cheeks, but knowing how much he cared about me made me feel safe enough to act with such boldness.

Running my hand over Sebastian's chest, I marveled at his smooth, cool skin, a sharp contrast to the fire that burned in his veins. When I met his gaze, his dark eyes resembled flame-laced embers as a look I'd only seen glimpses of before spread across his face, a look that spoke of hunger and desire and *wanting*.

I wasn't certain which of us took the first step towards the bed, but I found myself lying on my side, my mouth against Sebastian's, the bare skin of our chests pressed against one another as our hands explored everything that had previously been covered.

"I want you," he murmured between kisses. "I want to know every inch of you, in this body, in this life. But I'll only do what you're comfortable with."

"I want you too," I said, kicking off my boots. "I want us to know each other like we used to."

Sebastian stood up and tugged off his boots and, even though his hands hesitated for the smallest beat, he undid his belt and slipped off the rest of his clothes. I could have lain there staring at him for days, but the rest of my body wasn't as content as my eyes, and I quickly began undoing my own breeches. Sebastian moved to the foot of the bed, grabbed the legs of my pants, and pulled them off me in a single movement, although I wouldn't have cared if he'd ripped them off at that point.

And then we were pressed against one another, and I'd never felt anything as good or as right as our bodies intertwined with nothing between us. At one point, I'd been worried my lack of experience would be embarrassingly obvious, but it seemed I'd worried for nothing, as my body instinctively knew what to do.

I love you, I said, a thousand new pleasures coursing through me as time stopped and nothing existed except Sebastian and me, past and present coming together in a world of our own creation.

I love you too, he replied, and when our movements finally slowed, he rested his forehead against my collarbone, allowing his breathing to return to normal. After a moment I wished would never end, he kissed me before reaching over and pulling the blanket around us. He shifted onto his back before wrapping his arms around me. Lying there with my head on his chest, I thanked the Gifters I'd said yes when asked to marry an unknown Daeval to stop the warfare in Aeles-Nocens. Meeting, marrying, and falling in love with Schatten hadn't just brought peace to the realms—it had helped make me who I was, who I was meant to be, and was without a doubt the best decision I'd ever made. I wished everyone had the chance to experience such love.

"I've been thinking." Sebastian's deep voice tickled my ear where it was pressed against his chest, and I lifted my head to look at him. "I really appreciate you offering to remove my worst memories. Obviously there's no one I would trust to do it other than you." He gave me a wry smile. "I still can't fully imagine what it would be like going to sleep without worrying what nightmares I'll revisit."

I nodded, encouraging him to continue.

"But I'm scared," he admitted, using a word I'd never heard leave his lips before. "I'm scared I might forget something about you or us or our shared past. Not because you would do anything wrong," he hurried to add, "but because all my memories are just too connected. I don't know how memory making and storage works, but part of me pictures it like a game I played as a child with Devlin and Eslee. You stacked small blocks into a tower and then removed them one by one, hoping you didn't cause the entire structure to fall. There were blocks you could easily remove without affecting the others, but eventually you couldn't move a block without risking the entire stack collapsing."

He brushed his hair off his forehead. "I'm not opposed to you removing my worst memories. I'd love to not be so affected by them. But I think I want to keep that as a last resort. I've always tried to just deal with them myself, and by deal with them, I mean ignore them and pretend they don't exist, which hasn't helped. One thing I haven't tried is working through them with someone who loves and supports me."

His eyes searched mine. "If you're willing to be patient and . . . reassure me when I need it . . . I might be able to recognize that even though those things happened, and even though they were terrible, they aren't happening now. I think, with your help, I might be able to change my perspective on the memories and then perhaps they won't affect me so much. Does that make sense?"

"It does," I nodded.

"I've just seen how much I've been able to grow and change as a result of being with you," he explained. "And I'm not saying I'm glad those things happened to me, because I'm not. I didn't deserve to suffer like that. But those experiences *did* contribute to who I am today. I'm afraid if I tamper with them, I'll change something about who I am, and who I am is completely in love with you. I'd suffer far worse than I already have as long as it ended like this, with us together."

I rested my fingers over Sebastian's heart, and he covered my hand with his.

"So, for now, that's what I'd like, if you're alright with interrupted sleep and possibly being woken by me screaming and thrashing," he said. "And later, if things don't get better because it's just too much for me to work through, I'll have you remove certain memories for good."

"It's whatever you want," I assured him. "I just want you to be happy."

Sebastian offered a contented smile that only served to highlight how handsome he was. "I've never been happier. In fact, I didn't know it was possible to be so happy."

We stayed there, holding one another, drifting in and out of sleep and occasionally talking, but after a while, as much as I would have loved to pretend we had no pressing cares or responsibilities, it was time to address the Nocenian government.

26

Dear Journal,

It is not enough to include Astrals in my plans to bring an end to the reign of the Felserpent King and Queen. If I truly want to change the course of the realm, I must be willing to work with Daevals who also despise the monarchy and want no part in a united society. While I derive no enjoyment from partnering with such inferior individuals, I will do whatever is necessary to protect those with golden blood, and if this is the sacrifice I must make, I make it willingly.

I know what I must do.

While I claim no revelation from the Gifters, they must have lent their blessings to my efforts, as I recently discovered a rare book in the castle library. In it, I encountered a remarkable spell known as the Fragmen Incanta, or Breaking Incantation. I will use it to divide the realms. Aeles will become home to Astrals, a safe haven free from the corrupting influence of those with silver blood. Daevals will be given their own realm where they can live as they please, which will most likely result in them descending into anarchy and ending their own existence within a generation or two. Whatever happens, their behavior will no longer be a cause for our concern.

What I am planning will be viewed as unthinkable treason by some and a welcome revolution by others. I did not survive the massacre that took my parents from me to sit idly by and offer commentary on the actions of others. I owe it to those I lost to do everything in my power to make things better for all Astrals. In my frustration, in my fury, in my moments of quiet grief, I have discovered my purpose, and I will not stop until Aeles is free from every last drop of silver blood.

T

27

SEBASTIAN

Standing beside Kyra near the intersector in Minerva's receiving room, I listened closely to Caz.

"You'll be speaking at the Territorial *Adran*," he explained. "Dunston keeps an office at the Trades and Tariffs *Adran*, but we thought meeting there might make it seem like we were trying to send a message. This isn't about us or the relationships we have with you; this is about all of Nocens. We'll be meeting in the *Undod* Auditorium, a place where officials from all five territories regularly discuss important events or resolve disputes."

I nodded, forcing myself to take slow, controlled breaths. This was no different from completing a contract. I knew the environment, I knew the timeline, and I knew the objective. Thanks to Kyra, I wouldn't really need to do much, although as far as I was concerned, standing silently at her side as she divulged the truth about our past was the same as standing naked in the middle of Vartox shouting the truth at the top of my lungs.

Dunston and Caz took their turns on Minerva's intersector. Batty was perched on my shoulder, and while it was still odd going out in public with him, I found myself glad to have him nearby, particularly in case someone asked a question about the past Kyra and I couldn't answer.

You will do fine. Batty patted the back of my head. *I know you are doing this for Kyra, but the choice was still yours to make, and I am very proud of you.*

It doesn't feel like something to be proud of, I admitted. *Giving up something isn't the same as accomplishing a goal.*

Giving up something is a huge accomplishment, Batty protested. *We are defined by the things we choose not to do as much as the things we actively pursue. It is no secret I never liked what you did for a living, but you were very good at it. It served you well, and now you are saying goodbye to that. While I have no doubt you made the right decision, it is still a sacrifice, and your ability to make it is why you will always be the Felserpent King.*

I wasn't prepared for my throat to tighten, and I quickly blinked away the unexpected burning at the back of my eyes. Reaching up, I stroked Batty's leathery wings as I stepped onto the intersector, arriving in a receiving room at the Territorial *Adran*. After inspecting the space, I let Kyra know through the bracelets it was safe for her to join us. A moment later, she appeared on the intersector, Aurelius at her side.

"Right this way," beckoned Caz, leading us into a corridor lined with glowing sconces hung at regular intervals along the wood-paneled walls.

"How many Daevals do you think will come?" Kyra asked Dunston. While she was certainly the more gifted public speaker between us, I could feel the fear unspooling through her. The bag slung over her shoulder contained the Chronicles, and she placed a hand against it as if to reassure herself.

"Only those who play an essential role in governing the realm were invited," Dunston replied. "I wouldn't expect more than a hundred, give or take a few."

"A *hundred?*" Kyra repeated. I looked over just in time to see her blue eyes widen. "That's a lot of essential government positions."

"Daevals do love their bureaucracy," chuckled Dunston. "But don't worry. Given the seriousness of the situation, I've asked them to keep the pomp and circumstance to a minimum. Everyone will already be seated when you begin, which means we won't have to sit through the traditional arrival ceremonies. There'll be no musical interludes and no elemental performances. We'll accept a few questions at the end, but Caz will handle that so you won't be seen as favoring one Daeval over another."

"Won't those in attendance be upset if I can't answer all their questions?" Kyra worried.

"It's the government," said Caz with a wave of his hand. "They're used to things being parceled out on a need-to-know basis. Plus, even if they aren't happy about what you're saying, they'll *love* knowing they're hearing about things before the Aelian government."

That was true, and while I could tell Kyra wasn't so certain, she nodded anyway.

"We'll enter from the side of the stage," explained Dunston. "I'll go out and say a few words, and then it'll be all yours."

We wound a course through the hallway until Caz took a sharp left and opened a door; I motioned for Kyra to wait until I'd investigated. Satisfied the space was secure, I tried to slow my rising heart rate as she joined me in a small room off to one side of a large stage. I couldn't see the front of the stage since a heavy red curtain hung across it, blocking my view of the audience and their view of me, but I could hear the hum of nearby conversations. I reached over and took Kyra's hand, trying to encourage her but also wanting to distract myself. *It's no different than the Dekarais' party*, I said. *You were amazing there, and you'll be amazing here.*

It seems so much more serious meeting in a government building, she fretted. *I wish we were in a house where I could speak with folks individually.*

The door we'd come through suddenly opened, and I dropped Kyra's hand to step in front of her. Dunston hurried forward to greet the new arrival, who was wearing a smart red and black outfit that looked a bit like a uniform, although not a military one.

"That's our rule keeper, Ikan," whispered Caz. "He makes sure the rules of order are followed in government proceedings."

"We have a parliamentarian in Aeles," Kyra shared. "She calls out anytime someone does something out of order. What should I do if he tells me to stop?"

"He won't tell you anything," replied Caz. "First and foremost because we've told him not to, but also because that's not how he works. If you were to get out of line, you'd find yourself receiving an uncomfortable tingle somewhere in your body. If that didn't deter you, you'd eventually find yourself shocked into unconsciousness."

Kyra gaped at Caz, and I had to admit, even I was impressed. I'd heard of Ikan and others like him, but only in passing.

"Ikan is a channeler," Caz explained. "He has an intimate connection to lightning, which means it doesn't need to be storming in Vartox for him to channel a bolt or two into a target of his choice."

Kyra was clearly trying to picture how such a thing would be received in Aeles, and Caz patted her shoulder.

"It makes those in attendance think very seriously before they speak or act," he said in a voice I could tell was meant to be reassuring before stepping over to speak with Ikan.

I took the opportunity to peek through an opening where the curtain didn't quite touch the wall, although I immediately wished I hadn't, as my stomach dropped almost to my boots. The auditorium was huge; the stage appeared so small all the way down at the bottom, the only furniture on it a shiny black obsidian podium. Sensing my anxiety, Kyra stepped closer, pressing against my side.

I couldn't believe so many Daevals had gathered to hear what we had to say, although I supposed I should have been grateful for their interest. Kyra was afraid of driving a wedge even deeper between those with silver and gold blood, but my fears were far more personal; while I didn't care what others thought about me, that wasn't to say what they thought didn't matter. It mattered greatly. Just because I didn't want a role as a leader or figurehead didn't mean I was fine being barred from assuming such a role, particularly since that's what Kyra would be doing for the foreseeable future.

A tall silver-trimmed mirror stood in the corner so those about to go on stage could give themselves a once-over, and I glanced at my reflection. As I'd suspected would happen, Devlin had shown up at my Sea'Brik bedroom to help me choose what to wear while addressing the government. While he'd begrudgingly agreed my black breeches and grey tunic were "acceptable," he'd been thrilled over my cloak. "Cloaks are a great way to have a signature look," he'd said as he'd run his fingers appreciatively over the smooth scales. "They're stylish, but they're also functional. You'll look regal without screaming, 'I'm here to take back my kingdom, peasants!'"

Kyra was wearing her shifter cloak, and she smiled at our reflections before placing a hand against the thick velvet falling from her shoulders. The garment shivered, and the swirling pinks, purples, and blues transformed into black and grey scales, making her cloak appear identical to mine.

At some invisible cue, Ikan straightened his shoulders and strode out onto the stage, where the red curtains parted with a flourish. He bowed before the assembled Daevals to polite applause.

"He's reminding them he's here and won't hesitate to act as

he usually does, should anyone get out of line," explained Dunston.

"That's . . . kind of him," Kyra said.

"Perhaps." A knowing smile tugged at Dunston's lips. "Or he might simply be repaying the favor he owed Caz."

Caz batted his eyelashes at his brother but didn't deny the possibility, and Dunston clapped his hands together before striding out onto the stage. The applause was noticeably louder for him, either because the gathered Daevals genuinely liked him or because they were afraid of offending him. Dunston quickly waved away the fanfare.

"Thank you all for being here today," he said, spells amplifying his voice evenly across the space. "I know I'm not the one you want to hear from for a change, so I'll keep my introduction brief. Many of you know Sebastian Sayre, and quite a few of you recently had the chance to meet Kyra Valorian at a little gathering Rennej and I hosted. We're going to let the two of them speak without interruption, and we'll have time for questions at the end."

I felt so nauseous that for a moment I was afraid I might faint, but I focused on taking evenly spaced breaths even as my knees shook. Dangerous situations didn't usually elicit such a physical response from me; when I knew my life was on the line, I did whatever was required to preserve it. While this situation didn't technically herald the end of my life, it still felt like facing a kind of death, one everyone would watch play out on a very public stage.

"It's my great honor and pleasure to bring out Kyra and Sebastian," said Dunston, turning towards the back of the stage and waving us out.

Holding Kyra's hand as if my life depended on it, I took a step forward, the lights so blinding it was difficult to make out individual audience members. The applause was more restrained than it had been for Dunston, but at least no one was booing us. Aurelius walked at Kyra's side with his head held high, and Batty rode silently on my shoulder, his behavior for once appropriate to the setting.

I stopped near the side of the podium, allowing Kyra to stand directly behind it since she would be doing most of the talking. Blinking against the annoying stage lights, my gaze landed on a familiar face in the front row, and Minister Sinclair dipped his head in greeting as relief pulsed through Kyra.

This makes things so much easier, she said, sounding almost happy. *I can just imagine I'm speaking with Minister Sinclair.*

I didn't see how that changed anything, as we were still standing on a stage in plain sight of everyone gathered, but if such thinking made Kyra feel better, I was glad. And, out of all the Daevals in attendance, Minister Sinclair was probably the most likely to support us, which counted for something.

"Thank you so much for letting us speak to you," Kyra began, pushing her shoulders back and offering a friendly smile. I swept my eyes around the room, searching for any potential threats while also gathering a sense of the overall mood. "We have a lot to tell you, and some of it will truly sound like something from a bedtime story, but I promise everything we're about to share is true."

A murmur rippled through the crowd, acknowledging the importance of such a pledge, particularly one made voluntarily.

"Members of this distinguished audience might be surprised to know there weren't always two separate realms," Kyra said. "Thousands of years ago, there was only one realm, known as Aeles-Nocens, ruled by creatures called the Great Beasts. As Astrals and Daevals grew in numbers, they claimed more territory for themselves. The age of the Great Beasts ended, ushering in a new era under the dominion of Astrals and Daevals. As often happens when resources are limited, fighting broke out between those with gold and silver blood, each claiming land or water or food for themselves. The fighting became so terrible leaders on both sides came together and called for a truce, determined to find a way forward that didn't involve bloodshed. The reign of Astrals and Daevals began with the reign of the Felserpent King and Queen."

Even though I knew Kyra spoke the truth, it was surreal to hear her share it so openly. I remembered the choice I'd made as Schatten to accept a political marriage and become the Felserpent King, but hearing Kyra describe our pasts was like listening to her speak about someone else. She shared how a golden-blooded healer and Recovrancer named Kareth had wed a silver-blood warrior and Pyromancer named Schatten, establishing a kingdom where everyone, regardless of the color of their blood, was welcome.

She then pulled the Chronicles from her bag and began reading the Blood Treaty. As she spoke, the room was so silent, my heartbeat was the loudest thing I could hear.

"Unfortunately," she said when she'd finished reading, "there were some who weren't happy about Astrals and Daevals living peacefully together." She told them about Tallus, his use of the *Fragmen Incanta*, and the dividing of the realms. "Before they fled, Schatten and Kareth bound their shades together, promising to return and find one another when the time was right to reunite the realms. Centuries passed, and relations between Aeles and Nocens became worse. Hatred, distrust, and fear made it impossible to even imagine peace and unity. But eventually, Kareth and Schatten returned."

Kyra smiled at me before gazing out at the assembled Daevals. "Sebastian and I were Schatten and Kareth." She held up the Chronicles. "When I was Kareth, I kept a record of the events in the kingdom. Experts can authenticate how old this book is, and the leading bookseller in Nocens has already started making copies so everyone can read the history of the realms for themselves. This book also contains the spell to reunite the realms, which is why the two of us have returned."

A clamor rose, such that I couldn't make out individual questions, and while part of me wanted to run and duck behind the curtain, I forced myself to remain where I was. As Schatten, I had spoken to unhappy crowds before; in fact, being the Felserpent King had required me to make many decisions that hadn't initially been popular. And now, just like then, I wasn't alone.

Kyra returned the Chronicles to her bag before raising her hands to calm the crowd. "Before we address your specific questions, there are two important facts you need to know. The first is we aren't the only ones who have returned. Tallus is back, as well, although everyone knows him as Senator Tenebris Rex, the very same senator who recently assumed emergency powers in Aeles and announced the development of a weapon capable of killing anyone with silver blood."

She described the experimentation program Tallus had been running in Rynstyn, part of his unending desire to do away with Daevals for good, and explained how he'd learned Daevals' bodies couldn't process anything related to golden blood, resulting in the creation of Aurum powder. While those gathered were of a sufficient status that they'd already seen recordings of Tallus's weapon demonstration, shock still spread over their faces, along with fear and no small amount of doubt and suspicion. Kyra also shared how Raks Nemoya had ended up in Aeles, and I could tell those in the auditorium were conflicted. On the one hand, Raks had been a newer addition to Nocenian society and not an especially liked one, but at the same time, he'd still been one of us, and many would see his murder as justification for a retaliatory attack against Aeles.

"And the second thing you need to know," continued Kyra, "is that if Aeles and Nocens aren't reunited, there will be no future for either realm." She explained why natural disasters were happening so much more frequently, a direct result of the realms' increasing instability the longer they were apart.

"Sebastian and I have no desire to reinstate a monarchy," she said in a clear, firm voice. "Our desire is to one day see a coalition government formed, made up of both Astrals and Daevals." Daevals shifted in their seats, some appearing interested as others crossed their arms or shook their heads, but Kyra wasn't deterred. "Just as the realms aren't meant to exist apart from one another, neither are Astrals and Daevals. We're strongest together, and while it certainly won't be easy, Sebastian and I are living proof Astrals and Daevals aren't destined to be enemies. We can't do it alone, but with your support, we can work together to ensure those with silver and gold blood live happily, peacefully, and prosperously. And now, we'll take questions."

At her invitation, hands exploded into the air.

28

SEBASTIAN

As I gazed out at the mass of waving arms, I was grateful Caz came to stand near us, absolving us of the responsibility of choosing who to call on. Given Minister Sinclair's government position, as well as how he'd helped us acquire the Chronicles, I wasn't surprised to see Caz point to him first.

"As the Minister of the Meddygol *Adran*, my utmost responsibility is the health and well-being of Daevals," the minister began. "I am certainly open to sharing what I know with Astrals and learning from healers with golden blood, such as yourself, Ms. Valorian. I understand the need to reunite the realms to ensure a future for all who live here, but what if there are Astrals and Daevals who simply do not wish to live in close proximity to one another? Do you plan to enforce a united society?"

I heard calls of "hear, hear!" and scattered applause, many of those present not so ready to willingly associate with those who had barred us from their realm for centuries.

"No one will be forced to do anything they don't wish to do," Kyra assured Minister Sinclair. "I expect the transition to be a slow one, and many things will have to be figured out along the way, but it's not as if there's no precedent. Astrals and Daevals lived together before, and I'm confident they can do it again. However, that choice will be up to them, and I propose a series of votes be held after the realms are reunited. Citizens should have the final say on things like a unified government, creating cities where you can live regardless of the color of your blood, or creating cities strictly for Daevals or exclusive to Astrals. It's only right those who live in the realms be the ones to decide their future."

Minister Sinclair nodded his agreement, and Caz pointed to another Daeval farther back in the crowd.

"When do you plan to reunite the realms, and what will the process be like?" the woman asked, her half-glasses perched precariously on the tip of her nose.

"We need to deal with Tallus first," replied Kyra. "If we reunite the realms now, it'll make it too easy for him to send the Aelian military into Nocens with canisters of Aurum powder. But once we've dealt with him, Sebastian and I will return to the ruins of our former home, which remain in Aeles, and cast the *Ligarum Incanta.* Nothing will visibly change in either realm, but the rejoining will exert a healing effect, in addition to allowing travel between the realms by way of the sea, which will offer exciting new trade opportunities between Aeles and Nocens."

The idea of new business ventures brought eager smiles to many officials' faces, but while those gathered seemed open to accepting the truth about the past, I could see folks struggling to imagine a future where Astrals and Daevals voluntarily interacted with one another. Given how those with silver blood had been treated by Astrals since the division of the realms, I didn't blame them.

Caz pointed to another Daeval. As the man stood up, I recognized Camus's curly blonde ponytail and felt myself relax a bit. While I'd initially met him during my brief time at the Nocenian military academy as a child, we'd remained in touch over the years, and I was glad to see not only a familiar face, but someone I genuinely liked and respected.

"What's your plan for stopping Tallus before his deadline?"

Camus asked. While he hadn't specifically directed the question to me, Kyra stepped away from the podium, allowing me to answer.

"My plan is to enter Aeles, catch him unawares, and ensure he's never a threat again," I replied.

In the silence following my words, I sensed an uneasiness spreading through the crowd, and my stomach clenched. Was it because I'd reminded them what I was capable of or because they didn't trust me to stop Tallus?

"Perhaps I should have phrased that differently," Camus smiled. "Would military support be helpful for what you're planning?"

"No," I said. "That would only draw attention. I don't want to say too much and risk anything getting back to Tallus, but I'm confident in our plan."

Kyra stepped up beside me. "You have to remember, Tallus is the enemy here, not those with golden blood. I don't want my kind harmed or thrown into a fight they didn't choose. It's Tallus who wants a war with Nocens, not Astrals."

Caz called on another Daeval who I recognized as Minister Travers, an elderly man with a white beard and headful of white hair who oversaw banking in Nocens. He and Dunston were friends, and I'd completed a significant number of contracts for him over the years.

"From the little news we've managed to glean from Aeles, it sounds as if this Tallus has amassed a following." Minister Travers shook his head. "That means not everyone in Aeles will be in favor of improving relations with us. I think we should reconsider the major's offer of military intervention and send you with them, Mr. Sayre."

A representative of the territory of Oexiss, Madame Jocelyn Eskar, raised a gloved hand but didn't wait to be called on. "What exactly do those in Aeles know about what you've shared with us?"

"Aside from my closest loved ones, no one in Aeles knows the truth about who Tallus really is," Kyra said. "I don't have a way to communicate any of this to them right now. But I trust those in my realm. My father was Arakiss Valorian, the *Princeps Shaman* of Aeles, and it's no secret Astrals are waiting for me to take his place. While I certainly can't guarantee everyone with golden blood will be excited about a reunited realm, I do know a great many of them will listen to what I have to say and respect my decision to move forward in good faith with Daevals. It's *your* support I need. I can't force you to do anything, and I wouldn't even if I could. But, even if no one here thinks improving relations with my kind is good for personal reasons, expanding trade and commerce with Aeles presents countless business opportunities. And if I've learned anything about Daevals, it's that those with silver blood are incredibly gifted at seizing opportunities and turning small successes into remarkable—and profitable—victories."

Dunston caught my eye and winked as heads nodded and smiles sprang to faces that had previously been disbelieving or simply uncertain. Kyra was a born diplomat, and I felt like I was back in Velaire, watching her hold court. Things seemed to have taken a good turn, skillfully directed by the brilliant woman at my side, and as Caz called on another man, I hoped he would be the last government official we spoke with.

"Am I the only one who thinks it's precisely because *you* have a plan, Mr. Sayre, that we might have a problem?" The man pressed his lips into a thin scowl. "I can't be the only one here who knows what you do for a living. I suspect more than half of the attendees in this room have purchased your particular services at one time or another. How can someone who deals in fear and death possibly be trusted with something as important as reuniting the realms or a task as delicate as fostering peace between Daevals and Astrals? For all I know, if I don't agree with you, I'll wake up with a knife at my throat—*if* I wake up at all."

I saw Ikan look at Caz, the man's fingers twitching lightly against his thighs as if impatient to send a bolt of lightning into the Daeval who'd spoken. I didn't blame him; I wanted to send my fire directly at the man too. Caz, in turn, looked at me. He knew I wasn't impulsive, but he also knew I didn't stand for being denigrated. Kyra clasped the edges of her cloak, and while I appreciated the anger speeding through her on my behalf, this wasn't something she could fix. I'd known this was likely to happen, and I would have to handle it myself. I brought my hands to either side of the podium, letting my palms rest on the cold, black obsidian as I considered what I wanted to say.

"It's true I've completed contracts for many of you in here," I began. "Obviously, I won't be moving forward with the same career I've had these past few years; no one could be expected to trust someone who acts as they please. I can't change who I've been or the work I've done, but I can choose who I am and what I do moving forward." I gazed out at the crowd, my eyes having adjusted to the lights. "By the same thinking, we can't change the past, but we can learn from it and try to do better as we know better."

I hadn't stammered or repeated myself, which was good, and I forced myself to keep going. "It was a shock to learn who I'd been in a past life—who I still am, in some ways—but I'm not only putting aside the work I used to do because I'm intent on helping the realms. First and foremost, I'm changing careers for *me*."

I turned to look at Kyra. "I would have fallen in love with Kyra even if we hadn't bound our shades together in a previous life. When I first started imagining the possibility of a relationship between the two of us, the one thing I knew was that a future with her would require changes on my part. I could never be with her and continue to work as an assassin. If giving up the business I've built helps the realms, that's all well and good. But make no mistake . . . I'm doing this for me so I can spend the rest of my life with the woman I love, who makes me a better man and deserves nothing less than me doing everything I can to take care of her every single day."

I could tell Kyra was stunned by my words, which was understandable. She knew how I felt about her, but much of that was due to our connection and our ability to sense one another's thoughts and feelings without needing to put them into words. It was huge for me to say such things, and the fact that I'd just done so in a packed auditorium was even more unexpected.

The crowd obviously wasn't certain how to respond to such sentiment being expressed by me, of all Daevals, but I could only speak my piece. I couldn't control their reactions. Having said what I wanted, I moved aside, knowing Kyra would find a way to eloquently close out the gathering.

"We're not asking you to make any decisions now," she said. "Please just think about what you've heard. More will be forthcoming in the next few days, but Sebastian and I need you. We'll never have a chance at convincing the average citizen to change their minds about Astrals or Daevals if those in power don't support such change. With influence and wealth comes responsibility to those who work for you, who create the comforts you enjoy, and who ensure your society functions on a daily basis. I want a united Aeles-Nocens to prosper to an extent no one has ever seen before, but Sebastian and I can't do that on our own. Your knowledge, insights, and connections are more valuable than you know, and we look forward to working with you however we can. Thank you for your time."

While we had barely scratched the surface of the questions the Daevals had, no one made a fuss when the gathering came to an end. Dunston and Caz were right that those in the Nocenian government were fine receiving information in bits and pieces and would make what decisions they could in a given moment. When more was shared, they would reevaluate and go from there.

The applause as we left was much more robust than when Kyra and I had first set foot on stage, and a few Daevals—led by Minister Sinclair—even rose to their feet. Kyra waved one final time before we took our leave, and as the curtain fell, Caz pulled her into a hug.

"Brilliant, just brilliant!" he exclaimed. "That couldn't have gone better!"

He released Kyra just as Dunston burst into the room. I'd seen him angry plenty of times, and I'd even seen him worried, but I'd never seen fear in his eyes. My fire flickered uncertainly beneath my skin.

"Tallus attacked Sea'Brik!" he shouted. "We've got to stop him!"

29

SEBASTIAN

"But Sea'Brik is unbreachable." Caz's eyes were wide with disbelief.

"Minerva just reached out." Dunston withdrew his handkerchief and mopped it across his forehead. "What should we do? What if he has Aurum powder?"

"Rhannu's in my room," I said, already running through tactical scenarios. I'd left the sword behind in order to appear less threatening while addressing the government, but I should have just worn it and let the officials react as they would. "I'll take us there. What else did Minerva say?"

"Tallus came in through a portal with members of the Aelian military," said Dunston. "That's all I know."

There was obviously more to it, but my questions could wait. Right now, the only thing that mattered was protecting those at Sea'Brik. Opening a portal, I stepped into my borrowed bedroom, and while I would have preferred for Kyra and the Dekarai brothers to stay where they were, I knew there'd be no convincing them—not with their loved ones' lives at risk. The room was empty and nothing had been disturbed, so I gestured for the others to join me. Motioning for everyone to stay back and be quiet, I tossed my cloak onto a chair and pulled Rhannu from its scabbard. Darting across the room, I grabbed the doorknob, preparing to slip into the hallway.

The door wouldn't budge.

I tried to turn the knob again before directing my fire at the hinges. The wood and metal absorbed the flames with a hiss, powerful spells keeping the room cordoned off and protected.

"Some of Sea'Brik's defenses," whispered Caz.

Something crashed outside the room, and someone screamed. Running footsteps sounded on the other side of the door just before a groaning noise rang out, like the clang of metal pieces grinding against one another. I hoped it was more of the house's defenses, but trapped inside the room, I had no way of knowing.

Before I could ask Aurelius and Batty to communicate with the other Cyphers to give us an idea of how everyone in the house was doing, Batty flapped his wings and sprang into the air. "Mischief said Tallus is in LeBehr's room! We must hurry!"

The bat dematerialized, and, without another thought, I opened a portal and charged into the hallway. Whispering for the house to direct me to LeBehr's room, I followed the blinking lights, moving as quickly and quietly as I could, wishing I knew how many soldiers Tallus had brought with him. Glancing over the railing as I crossed the second-floor landing, I saw an Astral soldier pinned to the wall, one of Eslee's metal sculptures piercing his chest. Caz had mentioned the house's defenses, and using artwork as a weapon must have been one of them. Rounding a corner, an Astral soldier jumped out at me, but I ran Rhannu through him and tossed his body away, barely breaking my stride.

Tallus has Aurum powder! Batty shouted in my head.

I'm almost there!

As I turned another corner, two more Astral soldiers were lying in wait, but I sent my fire roaring at one while using Rhannu to make swift work of the other. Reaching LeBehr's room, I took a deep breath, gathering as much air as I could, then portaled inside, letting the fire from my hands wind upwards to cover

Rhannu's blade. An empty canister lay on the ground, and Batty stood on the mantle. Raising his wings, he shot a bolt of white light at Tallus, which made the man shout and double over. Batty flew at him, causing Tallus to cover his face with his arms as the bat's claws sliced at anything they could find.

LeBehr lay crumpled in a heap across the room, but I couldn't tell if she was breathing. Two soldiers were with Tallus, and one of them conjured a portal as the other brought the blade of his sword against mine. Tallus stumbled towards the portal, managing to right himself as he reached it. As I plunged Rhannu into the soldier's chest and shoved him aside, Tallus paused just long enough to smile at me. I was pleased to see Batty had cut a deep gash along his cheek, and I darted forward, but the portal winked out of sight just before I reached it. Running across the room, I threw open the balcony doors, hoping the fresh air would disperse any remaining Aurum powder since I didn't have my air purifier on me.

Kneeling down beside LeBehr, I refused to imagine the worst and searched for a pulse. Thankfully, I found one, and as I let out a soft sigh, something sharp stung the inside of my chest. I pressed a hand against my sternum and tried to draw a deep breath, but I couldn't. It was as if my lungs had shrunk, becoming too small to hold the air I needed. It had to be Tallus's Aurum powder. My heart beat faster, and my head throbbed as I tried to focus on taking smaller breaths. The sips of air I managed weren't enough, and my body clamored for more, causing a growing panic to swirl through me. I glanced at the balcony and the promise of fresh air, but my limbs weren't responding to my commands to move.

This couldn't be happening. I couldn't die here, not now when I had so much to do and so much to live for.

At the same time, a terrifying thought nudged its way into my consciousness: I'd died before in the unicorn sanctuary, but it hadn't been my time. Was that because *this* was how I was fated to die? Was it my time now?

Sebastian, what's wrong? Kyra could sense my distress, and her voice was sharp with fear.

Aurum powder, I managed to reply, shocked at the effort it took to form the simple thought.

Batty landed on a chair in front of me, but I couldn't focus and kept seeing two bats instead of one. He was saying something, but I could only make out his last two words: ". . . hold on!"

I tried to assure him I was holding onto life with everything inside me, but black spots appeared in front of my eyes. I slumped forward, catching myself with one hand and barely keeping my face from smacking against the floor. The pounding in my head was growing louder . . . no, it wasn't in my head . . . someone was pounding on LeBehr's door.

"Sebastian!" It was Kyra. "Hold on, we're coming!"

I collapsed onto the cool tile floor, aware my chest was no longer rising and falling because my lungs were no longer functioning. Something creaked and groaned in the hallway, and then the door fell into the room with a crash that reverberated across the floor. Kyra ran across the fallen door, dropping to her knees when she reached me.

"We can heal him," said Batty, "the same way he and Adonis healed you when you were injured recovering Rhannu." The bat hopped down from the chair and scurried closer to my face, pressing the tip of a wing against my cheek. "Direct your fire to cleanse your lungs. Kyra will use her *alera* to keep the rest of you protected."

I wasn't certain how I would manage to do such a thing, given that I could almost hear the Shade Transporter's boat gliding across the river to claim my shade, but perhaps knowing my survival was on the line, the fire inside me roared to life. As Kyra pressed her hands against my chest and poured her healing *alera* into me, I imagined the fire moving beneath my skin, seeking out the golden blood infecting my lungs and destroying it. My chest was suddenly awash with heat, and if I'd had any breath to spare, I would have gasped and possibly screamed. Seconds passed, and even as I worried about lighting myself on fire from the inside out, I found I could breathe the slightest bit easier.

It's working, I said, although I wasn't certain if I was speaking to Batty or Kyra. As my vision cleared, I could see Eslee in the hallway. She was holding the twisted remains of the door's hinges in her hands, having used her gift for manipulating metal to remove them. After a moment, I could draw a full breath.

"I'm fine," I assured Kyra, although the tremor in my voice was at odds with my words. Lying on the floor, gazing up at her, I was reminded of the first time I'd seen her, when Batty had rerouted my portal and I'd stumbled into a grove near Kyra's childhood home, sick with the effects of the potion I'd taken to disguise my silver blood. Kyra had healed me, and staring up at her, I'd been surprised at how familiar she'd seemed, even though I'd never met her before. Now, just like then, I felt like I would happily drown in the depths of her deep blue eyes.

My lungs once again functioning as they should, I drew a deep breath and pushed myself into a sitting position as Kyra threw her arms around me. I hugged her back, feeling her tremble, but rather than focusing on what might have befallen me, we needed to help LeBehr.

"See what you can do for LeBehr," I said, prompting Kyra to turn her attention to the fallen bookseller. As she placed her hands on LeBehr's chest, Batty launched himself at me, clinging to me in a hug I was, for perhaps the first time in my life, more than happy to return.

By now, all the Dekarais were in the hallway, peering

through the opening where the door had previously been but uncertain if the air in the room was safe to breathe. Kyra's family arrived, and while Deneb was instructed to wait with Eslee, Skandhar, Seren, and Enif rushed into the bedroom without hesitation. As Astrals, they were immune to the effects of Aurum powder, and I appreciated them heading straight to LeBehr.

"Can she be moved?" Skandhar asked Kyra, who lifted her hands from the bookseller's chest and nodded. "Let's get her into bed," directed Skandhar. LeBehr's eyes fluttered open, and while she tried to help, Kyra and her family did most of the work relocating her.

"I'll burn out the Aurum powder," I said to Kyra, pushing myself to my feet. Kyra moved to one side of the bed while I stood on the other, and as golden light poured from her hands into LeBehr's body, I pressed my hands against LeBehr's torso, directing the fire to seek out and destroy every last trace of golden blood. When we stopped, Kyra assessed the results of our efforts.

Her lungs are clear, but the Aurum powder caused significant damage. I'm trying to heal it, but her body isn't responding the way I'd like it to, Kyra said, her worried expression prompting a new rush of anxiety to sweep through me.

LeBehr moaned, and the sound made my heart feel as if it were being ripped in two.

Needing something else to focus on as Kyra tended to LeBehr, I turned to Minerva. "What happened?"

"Tallus arrived through a portal with a group of soldiers." Her grey eyes were hard as flint. "The only portal signature authorized entry into the house is yours, so I have to assume he managed to forge it. Obviously the blood sensors reacted the instant they detected Astrals other than Kyra and her family, but by that point Tallus and the soldiers were already inside."

Given everything Tallus had proven himself capable of, I

wouldn't put it past him to have somehow recreated my portal signature, even though I'd never heard of such a thing before.

LeBehr stirred on the bed, prompting everyone to move towards her.

"Tallus . . . wanted . . . the Chronicles," she said weakly.

"He must have gotten tired of waiting for us to reunite the realms and decided he'd attempt it himself," said Kyra, her eyes snapping with barely contained fury.

Even with the *Ligarum Incanta*, Tallus would never have been able to do such a thing; reuniting the realms could only be accomplished by the Felserpent King and Queen, as it required our blood, as well as the use of Rhannu. But it was clear he didn't know that, and if LeBehr's life hadn't been on the line, I might have enjoyed the rare instance where we knew something he didn't.

As the Dekarais turned to dealing with the bodies of the dead Astral soldiers scattered throughout the house, both those I'd killed and those the house itself had attacked, Kyra looked at me across LeBehr's bed.

I was wrong. Her voice, even in my mind, was colder and harder than I'd ever heard it. *Tallus doesn't deserve the chance to be reborn. What he's done to you and those we love . . .* She clenched her jaw. *He deserves to have Laycus consume his shade, and that's exactly what's going to happen once I get him to Vaneklus.*

As her eyes burned like twin flames of cerulean fire, I couldn't disagree with her. Tallus didn't deserve a second chance. But as furious as I was with him for harming LeBehr, we needed to focus on capturing Tallus before we made any decisions about what to do with him. LeBehr grimaced, and I reached out and took her hand in mine as Mischief curled up beside her shoulder.

She's stable now, said Kyra, her lips pressed together in a decidedly unhappy manner even as she smoothed LeBehr's hair off her brow. *We destroyed any remaining Aurum powder, but I can't seem to reverse its effects. She's not getting any worse, but she's not healing as fast as I'd like. I think we should have Minister Sinclair come and stay with her, just in case her condition changes while we go after Tallus.*

Leaving LeBehr to rest under her Cypher's watchful care, we joined the others downstairs. Batty reached out to Archeron, and Minister Sinclair soon arrived on Minerva's intersector, happy to stay with LeBehr while Kyra and I pursued Tallus. After goodbyes and assurances we'd update everyone when we could, Kyra and I hurried to gather what we needed before going to Aeles. I tightened Rhannu's scabbard across my chest and slung my weapons belt around my hips before pinning the suppressor medallion to my tunic. Kyra tied her hair back and grabbed the bag containing the Chronicles from where she'd dropped it on the bedroom floor. Slinging it over one shoulder, she turned to me, nodding that she was ready.

"Batty, go to Aeles and locate Tallus," I said. "Kyra and I will go to Adonis's, and then Adonis, Nigel, and I will portal to wherever Tallus is and bring him back to the cottage."

The bat offered a salute that would have embarrassed a soldier but made one side of my mouth rise in a smile as he dematerialized.

Kyra used her peerin to contact Adonis, who thankfully answered even though it was hours before dawn in Aeles. As I stepped through the portal into Adonis's home, I was surprised to see Demitri there. Kyra made a strangled noise and ran forward, hugging Demitri so hard I thought there was a very real chance she might injure the slight man.

"I'm fine," he assured her, returning the hug.

"How did you escape your apartment?" I asked when Kyra finally released him.

Adonis stepped forward. "Nigel and I used glamours and

told the guards we were taking Demitri somewhere else, per Tallus's orders. I didn't want to leave him unprotected and at the mercy of Tallus's supporters while we were dealing with Tallus."

"Thank you," Kyra said to Adonis and Nigel, her voice thick with emotion. "Demitri and I are so lucky to have you as friends."

Nigel grinned proudly, but while Adonis nodded at Kyra's appreciation, he didn't appear quite as enthusiastic. Thinking back to the exchange I'd seen between him and Demitri before we'd gone to Rynstyn, I wondered if perhaps the soldier wasn't content being just friends with Demitri or if there was something else going on. Well, whatever it was, social interactions weren't my area of expertise, and this could wait until after Tallus had been dealt with.

"While Batty's searching Celenia, I'm going to get Nerudian," I explained. "I want him in position guarding the house when we return with Tallus."

Portaling to the cave, I let Nerudian know we were ready to accept his offer of help.

"I shall meet you up top," he said. "It will be easier for me to go through a portal there."

Relocating to the woods above the cave, I watched as the ground opened and Nerudian flew upwards, his crimson-tinted wings spreading majestically before he landed nearby. His own unique method of coming and going was how I'd discovered the cave in the first place: he had just entered the cavern and the ground had been knitting itself back together, but not before I'd accidentally fallen through the opening into the dragon's treasure trove.

I'd never attempted to change the size of my portal before, and it took me a moment to figure out how to do so. But once I did, I easily expanded the shimmering gateway. Nerudian flashed an excited grin before hurrying through to where Kyra waited to welcome him. Following after the enormous creature, I didn't miss the awestruck expression on the faces of Adonis, Nigel, and Demitri.

"I can't believe dragons still exist!" exclaimed Adonis. "We've always been told they'd gone extinct."

"Not in Nocens," I said.

Nigel kept shaking his head. "I don't believe it. This is incredible!"

As the Astrals introduced themselves to Nerudian, Batty reached out.

Tallus is in a room at the Donec Legibus, offered the bat. *It seems to be a laboratory, and only a few other Astrals have been coming and going.*

"It's time," I said, waving the others over and looking at Kyra. "We'll be back with Tallus."

The single nod she gave me radiated a cold fury. "I'll be ready."

30

KYRA

I flexed my fingers, waiting impatiently for a portal to reappear and sending a silent prayer to all the Gifters and Fates for the safety of Sebastian, Nigel, and Adonis. Demitri was sitting near me on the sofa, and Aurelius was standing close by. I leaned down and ran a hand over his silky fur, the familiar softness of his coat never failing to soothe me. A crackling sound caused me to jump to my feet, and a portal sprang open as my heart pounded and Demitri made a frightened noise. Tallus stepped into the living room, Adonis and Nigel on one side of him, Sebastian on the other. The three men dragged him to a chair, careful to keep his hands apart so he couldn't form any spell-casting gestures, and made quick work of using the spelled rope and a host of other enchantments to secure him before Sebastian withdrew Rhannu and pointed the tip against Tallus's chest.

The fact that Tallus didn't seem the slightest bit upset about being kidnapped only served to infuriate me more.

"My Cypher has alerted the military to my whereabouts," he said as calmly as if we were discussing the weather. "You had to have known he would do such a thing, so I'm curious as to what you have planned."

"We plan to let the dragon outside deal with the military," growled Sebastian. "How did you know LeBehr was at Sea'Brik?"

I wasn't surprised at his question. I knew how much LeBehr meant to him, and he wanted to know exactly how she'd been harmed in spite of him doing everything he could to protect her.

Tallus looked as if he couldn't decide whether Sebastian was telling the truth about a dragon being outside, but he gave his head a slight shake and focused on Sebastian's question.

"It was a calculated guess. When Raks informed me of LeBehr's presence at his auction, I assumed you would want to keep her close to ensure her safety—and because as a bookseller, she could make copies of the Chronicles. Raks told me what he knew of the Dekarais. When he described Minerva as the most private of the siblings, that made wherever she lived a good place to start searching for both the bookseller and the Chronicles. I would have targeted another Dekarai residence next; I simply chose to start at Sea'Brik. While you were addressing the Nocenian government, I paid LeBehr a visit." He sighed. "Unfortunately, she was less than helpful."

I glared at Tallus, trying not to be overcome by the anger pounding inside me as he turned his gaze towards me.

"I take it you haven't changed your mind about *aleric* shade alteration and turning Daevals into Astrals?"

"No."

Tallus shook his head. "Then you leave me no choice. Whether it happens in this life or another, I *will* invade Nocens and release my Aurum powder. One thing I won't do, though, is make the mistake of attempting to work with you again. The next time I encounter you, I'll end your life."

"I have no doubt you'll try," I said, running a finger over Rheolath. "But you forget that, between the two of us, I'm much more familiar with Death."

Rheolath sprang to life, the red carnelian bead always eager to be of use, and Tallus shuddered, then stiffened in his seat. I could feel him fighting me. As he clenched his jaw, purple smoke began to stream from his fingers, which was more impressive than I wanted to admit given that he couldn't move his hands.

"It isn't like you not to learn from your past failures," he chided, obviously expecting me to seek control of his mind.

"*Permitte mihi videre quod est absconditum,*" I said, Rheolath singing loudly from my wrist.

The purple smoke disappeared from Tallus's hands as if it had been forcibly pulled back inside him.

"What are you . . ." His voice trailed off as his mouth fell open, his eyes widening. Slowly, the contours of his shade began to emerge, his very essence glowing brighter and brighter before me. While part of me couldn't believe I was seeing a shade in the realm of the living, now was not the time to be distracted. Carefully, I drew Tallus's shade out into the space between us, and golden light formed a silhouette in front of him until I could barely see his seated body behind his shade.

Now came the more complicated part, but I spoke clearly:

"Pono imperium tuum et umbram tuam
Praecipio animae tuae ut facias mandata mea."

I stretched out my fingers, placing one on Zerstoren and another on Tawazun while keeping contact with Rheolath. Managing three beads at once was challenging, and Rheolath pulled against my will, straining to be freed so she could assume control of everything around her. I focused on the even tone of Tawazun, sounding against the deep, melancholy peal of Zerstoren, a sound that made my own shade tremble ever so slightly.

Focusing on the edges of Tallus's shade as I held him immobile before me, I recalled excising a tumor from a patient's body under my father's supervision. I'd used my *alera* like a glowing scalpel, carefully cutting away the diseased growth, severing its connection to the otherwise healthy body. *Tallus's shade is no different*, I told myself. The more *alera* I sent towards the shade, the more the edges began to waver, pulling away from the body that had housed it.

And then with a snap, the shade was free, hovering in front of Tallus's body, which was still tied to the chair. I reached out and grabbed the shade's glowing hand, moving my fingers to Rheolath and Tawazun as I shouted, "*Bidh mi a'dohl a-steach!*" before dropping into a seated position so my own body wouldn't fall over when my shade left it.

Arriving in the grey river of Vaneklus, Tallus jerked his hand from mine, and I didn't attempt to hold him. Here in the realm of the dead, there was no place he could go, no escape he could make, and no way he could return to his body. The river lapped happily around my knees, pleased I'd brought a shade with me and excited to see what would happen next.

I wasn't certain whether Tallus's ability to keep his past life memories intact extended to remembering all the times he'd been to Vaneklus, but regardless, introductions were in order.

"Welcome to Vaneklus," I said, reaching down and trailing my fingers affectionately through the water.

Tallus ran his hands over himself as it to ensure no part of him had been lost in the transition from the realm of the living. "What did you do?"

"I removed your shade from your body. If I'm being honest, the fact that I was able to do such a thing is really *your* fault." I felt an immense satisfaction at using words he'd said to me before, when he'd told me it was my fault he'd created the experimentation facility in Rynstyn.

Tallus raised an eyebrow.

"Your desire to turn Daevals into Astrals forced me to think about *aleric* alteration of a shade," I explained. "But I took it one step further. I learned how to assume control of a shade—such control, in fact, that I could remove the shade from a body and command it into Vaneklus. Don't go anywhere," I instructed. "I'll be right back."

Returning to my body, I saw Sebastian had already lowered himself into a cross-legged position beside me. Nerves tingled all the way to the tips of my hair, excitement and hope colliding with fear and doubt and creating a veritable maelstrom inside me. I took Sebastian's hand, interlacing my fingers through his. Everything we'd planned, everything we'd worked so hard to set in motion, our sacrifices, our dreams—not to mention the very future of Aeles-Nocens—all came down to this.

Tallus scowled as I reappeared in Vaneklus with Sebastian, although I didn't miss the spark of curiosity that flared in his eyes.

"How is he here without having died?" he demanded.

"His shade is bound to mine, so he can go wherever I go," I replied.

Tallus's gaze landed on Rhannu's hilt gleaming over Sebastian's shoulder, and he exhaled loudly, frustrated but also resigned. "I suspected the price of creating Aurum powder might be my life, at least in this life cycle," he admitted. "I suppose removing my shade before running my body through with that cursed sword was the only way to ensure I didn't immediately head to Karnis before you could offer whatever threats you've no doubt prepared." He shook his head. "You must be truly desperate to stop me if you've resorted to such a temporary measure."

"I am desperate to stop you," I agreed, "but this isn't a temporary measure."

The prow of Laycus's boat broke through the fog bank, and as the grey curtains pulled back to allow him admittance, he flashed a sinister grin, his garnet-red eyes fastening hungrily on Tallus.

"If you remember anything about Vaneklus from your past lives, you'll certainly remember Laycus," I said, feeling much better having the powerful figure close by.

"Of course," Tallus replied, although I didn't miss the way his shoulders stiffened. "Well, Shade Transporter, clearly it's my time, so let's get on with it. The sooner I'm reborn, the sooner I can continue with my plans."

"In the interest of accuracy, it's actually *not* your time," I said.

Tallus turned to stare at me, questions rising amidst the disdain in his pale blue eyes.

"You're not here because it was your time to die," I explained. "You're here because I brought you." I tilted my head to one side. "You've accumulated so much knowledge over the centuries, I wonder—do you know what happens to a shade who appears in Vaneklus before their appointed time of death?"

Tallus's confidence began to slip away as if it was being drawn from him by the swift current of the river.

"The shade belongs to Laycus." I gestured to the Shade Transporter. "By all rights and natural laws, they become his property, subject to whatever he decides to do with them. Laycus, please enlighten Tallus on what you do with shades who arrive early in your domain."

Laycus's smile vanished, his entire countenance darkening as shadows rose from his cloak to swirl around him. If I hadn't known he was on our side, I would have found him a frightful specter to behold. "I consume them," he said. "And by consuming them, I end not only their life but their existence, ensuring there is no way they can ever be reborn again."

Tallus's face paled, and he took a step back, looking from Laycus to me.

"You wouldn't let him destroy me," he said in a voice that sounded more confident than he currently appeared. "You couldn't live with yourself for orchestrating such a thing."

"At one time I would have agreed with you," I said, "but that was before your Aurum powder. Before you attacked LeBehr. Before you almost made me watch the man I love suffocate to death." My voice rang with the authority I'd possessed as the Felserpent Queen. "You have to be stopped, and I will do whatever is necessary to protect Aeles-Nocens and those who live in it."

Laycus's boat edged closer to Tallus. "I've watched as you've harmed those I care for most in the land of the living," said the Shade Transporter. His voice was rough and low, grating against my ears in a way that made me want to run and hide, even though I knew he wouldn't harm me. "I always hoped you would appear in my domain before your time, allowing me to put an end to you once and for all, but alas, such a thing never happened—until Kyra learned how to control your shade, forcing you to appear here at a time of her choosing."

Tallus looked wildly from one side of the river to the other, but there was no place for him to run, much less hide. The boulders lining the riverbanks prevented a shade from wandering too far from the dock. There was no going back—this time, there was only going forward.

Laycus raised his staff and pointed the tip towards Tallus. Grey smoke rose from the river, entwining itself around Tallus's legs and wrists and creating chains to hold him in place. He screamed and fought against the shifting restraints, but the fog and water simply moved with him, writhing as he did. I sensed Death's excitement, its hunger for new memories to savor, and part of me wished Tallus could feel it, too, forcing him to acknowledge how truly helpless he was.

"You can't do this!" Tallus shouted, splashing water on himself as he struggled.

"Oh, I assure you, I can," replied Laycus.

Another boat broke through the fog, and the bleached white vessel came to a stop beside Laycus. Suryal gave her brother a fond smile before lowering her cowl and turning a cold gaze to Tallus.

Tallus made a sound that was half snarling, half whimpering. When no escape from his terrible predicament presented itself, he fell silent, fury and fear chasing one another across his face as his chest rose and fell in short bursts.

Laycus turned to me, questions in his eyes. Was he to consume Tallus, or were we going to break the spell Tallus had cast?

Given the harm Tallus had caused, the lives he had ended and the destruction he had sown—not to mention what he'd forced Sebastian to endure, both at his experimentation center and as a result of his Aurum powder—there was a part of me that truly did want Laycus to end the evil man's existence forever. I swallowed, watching the ripples on the river's surface as I struggled to find the dividing line between justice and vengeance.

Sebastian moved in front of me.

Tallus doesn't deserve a second chance, he said, following along with my thoughts. *But neither did I, and I'm living proof that, deserved or not, a second chance gives someone the opportunity to make better choices.*

I thought back to recovering Sebastian when I'd only known him as an assassin, long before we'd been aware of our shared past. I'd made that exact argument to Laycus, insisting Sebastian could use his second chance at life to make better choices. Not ready to put aside the idea of retribution just yet, I nevertheless nodded at the wisdom in Sebastian's words.

Whether Tallus's shade is destroyed or he's reborn without memories of who he used to be, he won't remember any of this, continued Sebastian.

We're the ones who will have to live with the knowledge of our actions. Ultimately, I don't think this is about what Tallus deserves . . . it's about what we choose to do.

He was right. I was a healer and a Recovrancer. I didn't do good for others because they deserved it; I helped them because I had the power to do so, the ability to ease their suffering and make their lives better. Just as my actions didn't depend on how good someone else was, neither should they depend on how selfish or cruel someone chose to be. My actions should be about *me* and who I was. The realization swept over me like a strong gust of wind, driving away the dark thoughts clouding my mind and removing any lingering desire for revenge.

Thank you. I brought my gaze to Sebastian's. *You're right.*

Turning back to Laycus, who was watching me expectantly, I gave my head a gentle shake, and while he scowled, he also didn't seem surprised. Tallus had closed his eyes, and Laycus flicked a skeletal finger, causing the chains around his wrists to shake and prompting him to peer out hesitantly from half-closed lids.

"You are fortunate Kyra is here to stay my hand," hissed Laycus. "If it were up to me, I would consume you in an instant."

It took Tallus a moment to register the Shade Transporter's words, but his eyes quickly found mine, his previous terror pushed aside in favor of calculating how he could make the most of this unexpected reprieve.

"I'm going to end our fight with you once and for all," I said, "but not in that particular way. We're going to break the *Memoria Aeterna* spell."

Tallus let out a sharp laugh. "It's not possible. I chose that spell because breaking it requires the presence of a Great Beast, and Schatten killed the last one before assuming control of the realm."

"Fortunately for us, the Felserpent wasn't the last Great Beast," said Sebastian as Batty materialized on his shoulder.

Tallus blinked as he stared at the bat, terrible understanding spreading across his face.

"The royal advisor—it's not—you can't be!" he spat.

"It is certainly unexpected," agreed Batty, "as I am not nearly as impressive as the Felserpent or most of the other Great Beasts. But my size does not make me any less powerful."

The bat reached into a wing pocket and pulled out the scroll Suryal had given me. I accepted it and reviewed the spell one last time before tucking the scroll into my bag. Batty raised his wings and pointed them at Tallus, an amber-colored light flowing from his small claws. Laycus and Suryal raised their staffs, directing them towards the chained man, and black and white light joined Batty's amber glow. Sebastian gripped Rhannu's hilt with both hands, widening his stance as he pointed the tip of the sword at our enemy, adding a bright silver beam to the mix. I summoned my *alera* before running a finger over Zerstoren, the grey bead cold beneath my finger. As golden light flowed out from my hands, I began the spell from Suryal's parchment.

Tallus shrieked and attempted to wrench his arms free, but his struggle was to no avail. The chains of water and fog held him firmly in place. If Death wasn't going to be permitted to savor Tallus's shade, it would extract whatever pleasure it could from him, and I didn't begrudge the realm its enjoyment. Our combined powers struck Tallus with a force that shook his body. As we directed our collective might towards him, I spoke the words of the spell, repeating them over and over as the parchment had directed:

"Simul nos fortes (Together we are strong)
Ligatus victus est (What was bound is broken)

Tallus thrashed against his restraints. "No!" he wailed. His entire shade began to glow with a faint purple light, as if a mist had settled on him. Cracks spread over the surface of the pulsing light before the sound of breaking glass filled the air. I jumped where I stood, then watched as thousands of tiny lights fell away from him, disappearing into the water waiting hungrily below.

Tallus collapsed to his knees.

His shoulders were bent, and his head was bowed.

We'd done it. Tallus was defeated.

His past life memories were no more, nor would he be able to keep the memories he'd made in this most recent life cycle. Daevals were safe, and Aeles and Nocens could finally become a realm at peace.

Slowly, our vanquished adversary lifted his head. "What now?"

"Now you're going straight to Karnis for rebirth," I said, "without any memory of me or Schatten or Velaire or how much you despise Daevals. You've been given a second chance even though you most certainly don't deserve one, but perhaps there's hope for you yet. What you do with that chance is up to you."

The chains fell from Tallus's wrists, and a particularly strong wave lifted him up, sweeping him forward and depositing him unceremoniously in Laycus's boat. As he pushed himself upright, sputtering and wiping water from his face, Laycus glared down at him.

"I would love *any* reason to consume you rather than ferrying you," the Shade Transporter growled, "so let that guide how you choose to act in my presence."

Turning around, Laycus flashed me a quick grin. While I couldn't tell if he was simply trying to scare Tallus or if he was being serious, I smiled back, some part of me wishing I could go along and watch Tallus's discomfort during the boat ride. "Thank you for everything, Laycus."

He nodded as his boat turned around, slipping across the water as the current sped up, Vaneklus clearly eager to be rid of Tallus.

"I suppose that means I'd best go too," smiled Suryal. I thanked her for her help, and she waved a cheerful goodbye before following Laycus down the grey river.

Sebastian returned Rhannu to its scabbard, and we stood facing one another. My limbs felt so weak, I was surprised to find myself still standing. We both stepped forward at the same time, falling into each other's arms and holding one another close.

By defeating Tallus, we'd given Astrals and Daevals the best possible chance of living peacefully with one another. Now it was time to return to our former home, to the ruins of Velaire, retracing the footsteps of our past to give the realms the future Aeles-Nocens deserved.

31

SEBASTIAN

Back at Adonis's cottage, we shared our good news and enjoyed a moment of celebration, complete with handshakes, hugs, cheers, and more than a few exclamations of relief.

"Did anything happen while we were gone?" I asked.

"A squadron of soldiers showed up," said Adonis, "but when they saw Nerudian, they hurried back through their portal, and we haven't seen them since."

That was good to hear, and while I wished we could savor our victory a little longer, there was still one more task we needed to complete. I caught Batty's eye where he was perched on the back of the sofa. "Would you scout out Velaire before we go, just to make sure Tallus didn't send soldiers there?"

Batty dematerialized, and I addressed the others.

"Once we reach the ruins, Kyra and I will follow Batty to the Cor'Lapis stone. Adonis and Nigel, you can serve as lookouts."

"I'm coming too," volunteered Demitri. "I can't fight, but I can certainly raise the alarm if I see anyone from the Aelian military."

"That's fine," I replied. "I think—"

"Wait." Adonis's interruption surprised me, and I studied him as a look I couldn't decipher crossed his face. "I don't know what's going to happen," he continued, "but I know if I don't say something and things go badly, I'll regret it forever."

Turning to Demitri, he drew a deep breath before taking the

man's hands in his own. Demitri's eyes widened, and for a moment, I thought he might wrench his hands free and back away, although he ultimately stayed where he was.

"Demitri, if you never want to speak to me again after what I'm about to say, I will completely respect your choice, but it's only right I tell you the truth." Adonis's sea green eyes were bright. "I've tried to content myself with just being your friend because that was the only way I could spend time with you. But the more time I spent with you, the more I knew I didn't want to be *just* friends. You are, without a doubt, the most incredible man I've ever met. I love your smile and your laugh and how witty you are. I love that you can't tell the difference between a spoon and a spatula but are always so excited over anything I cook."

Well, that certainly answered my previous question about whether Adonis might possess romantic feelings for Demitri. The captain's cheeks were flushed, and his words spilled out one after the other.

"You're the most talented artist I've ever met, and I've saved a copy of every single poster you've designed for government campaigns. When Kyra first told us about the experimentation program in Rynstyn, the only reason I agreed to look into it was because I thought by helping Kyra, I would also be doing something for you. I fall asleep every night thinking about what it would feel like to kiss you, and I wake up every morning thinking of how I can arrange my day to see you, even if it's just for a few minutes."

Adonis must have run out of air because he gulped before saying, "In case it's not obvious from everything I just said, I love you, Demitri. After the realms are united and all relationships are welcomed in Aeles, it would be a dream come true to court you. But, I also understand if you don't feel—"

Whatever he was going to say was cut short by Demitri stepping forward and pressing his lips to Adonis's mouth. Kyra grabbed my hand as Nigel pumped a fist into the air. When the two men separated, Demitri's face was multiple shades of scarlet, but his smile was almost as wide as Adonis's.

"Kyra has listened to me pine over you for years," Demitri said. "I've always wanted to be more than friends, and after the realms are reunited, if Aeles won't accept us being together, we'll move to Nocens!"

If Adonis's grin stretched any wider, there was a chance his face might split in two. "I have so much more to tell you," he said, "and I desperately want to hear what you've been saying to Kyra about me, but I've shared the most important part, which means the rest can wait."

I extended my hand to him. "Congratulations." As Adonis shook my hand, I did the last thing he likely expected and pulled him into a hug, clapping him soundly on the back. He laughed and returned the embrace. While I wasn't quite ready to hug Demitri, I inclined my head respectfully towards him. "I'm happy for you. Everyone deserves to love someone and be loved in return."

Demitri offered me the first genuine smile I'd ever received from him. "Thank you," he said as Kyra squealed and rushed to embrace him.

Batty materialized on the back of Adonis's sofa. "There is a squadron of soldiers waiting in the forest surrounding Velaire. Most likely, Tallus was going to let you reunite the realms and then attempt to capture you and take possession of the Chronicles."

"Well, it looks like we won't be the only ones revisiting our old home," I said.

Heading outside, we explained the situation to Nerudian, who immediately offered to disperse the gathered soldiers so Kyra and I could follow Batty into the ruins of Velaire. Dawn was just breaking as I opened a portal using the coordinates Batty shared, and Nerudian winked a boulder-sized eye at me before hurrying through the portal, moving with surprising speed for such a large creature. Shouts of terror followed his arrival, and I watched as he charged into the clearing, scattering soldiers before taking to the skies and bellowing fire, a terrifyingly majestic spectacle to behold.

"Let's go!" I waved the others through, then closed the portal and assessed our surroundings.

We'd emerged just inside the tree line of an enormous grove. At one time, the area around the castle had been cleared out much farther than this, but over the centuries, trees and shrubbery had worked to reclaim the land. Tangled briars sporting sharp thorns formed a natural barrier in places. You could still see glimpses of the Nebosa River where the trees were thinner, and I recalled standing on the balcony off the bedroom Kareth and I had shared, watching boats float along the water as the sun sank behind the distant mountains.

Breaking into a run, Kyra and I followed Batty as he flew ahead of us. When he disappeared into the darkness between two crumbling rock formations, I paused just long enough to cast an orb of light into the air before hurrying after him.

Many of the rocks surrounding us were taller than me and had fallen on top of one another, creating precarious tunnels and archways I hoped remained sturdy after all these years. Just to be safe, I offered a quick prayer to Rhide, the Fate responsible for the future, asking for their assistance in keeping the collapsing structure from collapsing further.

Carefully placing one foot in front of the other, I sought anything that could serve as a foothold. Thankfully, broken stones and gnarled roots were embedded deep into the ground, forming makeshift stairs. The air became cooler as we descended, and I could hear water dripping in the distance.

"Careful," I said to Kyra, who was walking a few feet behind me as we picked our way over, around, and sometimes under stones, snapped branches, and tangled vines. Judging by the pauses between her steps, she was choosing her footing as best she could. It was jarring to think we'd lived here at one point. I let my gaze roam over the piles of debris, some small, some large, the edges of quite a few rocks still blackened from the fire that had destroyed our home. I could see the castle overlaid across the space as it had existed in its prime, the magnificent, solid structure a sharp contrast to the weed-infested, rock-strewn ruins in front of me. Sadness blossomed in my chest.

"Why did so little of the castle survive?" I asked Batty, walking as quickly as I could without stumbling or sliding.

"After the realms were divided, much of the castle collapsed, falling into sinkholes like this one that were created during the breaking," he said.

As we descended deeper, the walls of the sinkhole rose around us. Cracks overhead let in thin shafts of early morning sunlight, the beams illuminating pools of dark water and moss growing on slick rocks.

We finally reached what seemed to be the bottom of the hole, or at least the bottom that had been formed during the division of the realms. I tested my weight on the makeshift floor before nodding for Kyra to join me. The rocks were different here, smooth stones similar in shape and size, making me think they might have formed part of the courtyard before the castle had come crashing down. The sinkhole was so large, I couldn't see where the earthquake-formed cavern ended. Stunted vegetation grew in the places where sunlight was able to shine through, some plants staying low to the ground while others stretched their fronds upwards, as if hopeful they might somehow be transported to the surface.

"The Cor'Lapis was used in the castle's foundation," said Batty, perched on a lichen-covered rock. "We are not far now."

Stepping over a section of uneven ground, I felt as if I'd accidentally walked into a corridor of the castle: handwoven carpets covered the stone floor, paintings and embroidered tapestries lined the walls, racks of weapons filled the armory as cooks bustled about the kitchen, and sunlight streamed through the stained-glass windows. The images came rushing back so strongly, I swayed where I stood, overwhelmed by the memories of my past.

Kyra came to a stop beside me. As our eyes met, I was glad she was having the same experience, since no one else could possibly relate to the simultaneous sense of discovery and loss I was feeling.

Aurelius's eyes flashed in the dark, his whiskers twitching disapprovingly at being so far underground. "I never thought I would say this"—he pinned his ears against his head—"but I actually miss your cavern, Sebastian. At least it's a proper cave." He shook his head. "This feels as if it could all come tumbling down at any moment."

"Thank goodness for portals," said Kyra, shooting me a smile before running her hand reassuringly over the lynx's head.

Batty flew a few yards ahead, then came back, fluttering his wings excitedly. "It is just over there!" he cried before darting off again.

Kyra and I followed, our boots sloshing over sections of spongy ground.

When we reached him, Batty pointed to a cluster of rocks. "Under there."

I studied the stones, some of which were far too large to move by hand. I could use Rhannu's powers to eviscerate them, although there was a chance the small explosion would bring the entire sinkhole crashing down. I looked around, searching for another option, but when nothing presented itself, I withdrew

Rhannu. We had to reach the Cor'Lapis stone, which made using the sword a risk worth taking.

"Stay here," I said to Kyra before casting a protective ward around her and Aurelius. Walking forward, I pressed the tip of Rhannu to the pile of stones.

"*Frry'doe*," I said, hating to destroy any part of our former home even though I knew it was necessary. The stones exploded into tiny pieces, arcing away from me, the powers inherent to Rhannu keeping me protected. As the dust settled, Batty scurried forward and dropped down into a crevice before popping back into view, a grin on his face.

"It is here!" he crowed.

I removed the protective spell, and Kyra and I brushed the dust and pebbles aside until a single rock, roughly half my height, stood before us. There was nothing remarkable about the black and grey stone. In fact, if Batty hadn't been there to point it out, I never would have looked twice at it.

The bat clapped his wings gleefully. I'd expected there to be some sort of opening in the stone, a gap to slide Rhannu's blade into, but the surface was smooth and unbroken.

"We will start by reminding the stone who you are," said Batty. "A small bit of blood from each of you will suffice."

I held Rhannu out, and Kyra used the edge of the blade to make a cut along her palm. Before I did the same, I unpinned the suppressor medallion from my shirt, since we knew from experience it would keep my blood from being recognized. The Blood Alarm immediately began to wail, but I ignored it, and Kyra and I pressed our palms against the stone. As we lifted our hands, the surface of the stone rippled, and we watched as our silver and gold blood disappeared, absorbed into the rock. Kyra healed our hands, and I replaced the medallion, which thankfully served to quiet the alarm. I then stared at the Cor'Lapis stone, having no idea what to expect.

The stone began to move, causing Kyra to startle, and it groaned as it shifted to reveal an opening across the top. Judging by the length, it was just long and wide enough to hold Rhannu's blade.

"You will place Rhannu inside the stone," instructed Batty. He turned to Kyra. "You will read the reunification spell. And then we will all brace ourselves."

I hopped on top of the rock, and Kyra pulled the Chronicles from her bag and opened it to the *Ligarum Incanta.* Turning Rhannu upside down, I carefully slid the sword's blade into the Cor'Lapis stone.

Kyra began reading from the Chronicles, her voice echoing in the open air:

> *Quod confractum est, integrum sit, (Let that which was broken be made whole,)*
>
> *Et quod divisum est reunietur. (Let that which was divided be reunited.)*

As she spoke, the stone began to glow. Light emanated from Rhannu's hilt, brighter than the Aelian sunbeams streaming down around us. The rock began to tremble beneath my feet, and I reached down and grabbed Kyra's hand, pulling her up beside me and wrapping an arm around her. Holding onto Rhannu with my other hand, I trusted the power of the sword to protect the two of us as Aurelius materialized by my feet.

Dirt sifted down, and we swayed on top of the rock, trembling so violently I heard Kyra's teeth chatter until she clamped her jaw shut. The walls of the sinkhole creaked and shuddered, although they seemed to be holding, and stones grated loudly against one another as vines snapped and roots writhed.

This had to work. We'd come so far and survived so much in the name of resuming a responsibility we'd accepted lifetimes ago. This was for all Astrals and Daevals, proof that what had formerly been broken and divided could be rejoined and made whole again. But it was also for Kyra and me, ensuring we had a realm to return to in all the future lives we would live together.

And then, as swiftly as the shaking had started, it stopped. Soil and twigs continued to sift down from overhead, but the quaking was no more. My ears rang with the sudden quiet, and I looked at Batty.

His dark eyes gleamed. "You have done it!" he said, clasping his wings together. "The realms are reunited."

Pulling Rhannu free, I returned the sword to my scabbard before hopping off the stone and lifting my arms to Kyra's waist, helping her down. As I lowered her feet to the ground, she pressed her lips against mine, her kiss full of joy and triumph and more than a little disbelief.

"We did it!" Her face glowed with happiness. "We reunited the realms!"

I wrapped my arms around her and pulled her against me, letting my excitement and relief flow into my embrace. Much as I enjoyed holding Kyra, however, I quickly opened a portal back to the surface, not wanting to be in an unstable sinkhole any longer than necessary.

Adonis, Nigel, and Demitri gazed at us in awe as we rejoined them.

"Was that it?" asked Nigel. "That earthquake—it was the realms coming back together, wasn't it?"

"It was," grinned Kyra.

Before we could bask in our accomplishment, Batty stiffened on the tree stump where he was perched. "Mischief just reached out." The sadness in his eyes made me feel as if I'd been kicked in the stomach. "She fears LeBehr does not have much time left."

32

KYRA

Batty caught up with Nerudian, who returned to the grove and disappeared through the portal Sebastian opened back to the cave. Once Nigel, Adonis, and Demitri had been returned to Adonis's cottage, Sebastian and I made our way to Sea'Brik. My heart clenched painfully as we stepped inside LeBehr's room. We couldn't defeat Tallus only to lose LeBehr. I had to save her.

LeBehr opened her eyes at our arrival.

"We did it," I said, answering her unspoken question. "The realms are reunited. And we broke Tallus's spell. His memories are no more, and he'll never be a threat to Daevals again."

"That's a relief," smiled LeBehr.

I caught Minister Sinclair's eye. He gave his head an unhappy shake, his frown indicating the bookseller's condition hadn't improved. Stepping forward, I placed my hands on LeBehr, letting my *alera* stream into her body. As I did my best to improve her condition, I experienced the same sense of helplessness I had with my father . . . I'd stopped bleeding and mended bruises, but my patient wasn't truly healing.

I did my best to ignore the sinking sensation in my stomach, the small voice suggesting she might not be getting better because it was her appointed time to die, and instead summoned all my healing abilities and used every spell I knew from my time as

Kareth, as well as those I'd been taught by my father. When I finally lifted my hands, LeBehr offered me a smile. I wasn't certain whether my recovrancy skills were becoming stronger or if my connection with Death had improved my abilities, but I sensed it truly was her time, even without being in Vaneklus and using my *sana* bracelet.

"I think I'd like to spend my remaining time at my own home," she said. "Near the creek."

Sebastian's face was hard as stone, but his eyes shone with unshed tears. I felt his devastation at being forced to tell LeBehr goodbye. She was a link to his past, a stalwart figure who had always been there for him, and now he was being forced to let her go, powerless to protect her further.

Sebastian leaned forward and scooped the bookseller into his arms, holding her blanketed body close as he made his way through a portal. I grabbed a pillow and followed, Minister Sinclair, Aurelius, Batty, and Mischief right behind me. LeBehr coughed as her body began to shake, and Sebastian set her down gently beside a bubbling creek, adjusting the blanket as I tucked the pillow beneath her head. The sun had set in Nocens and dusk was falling, fireflies winking in and out of sight as birds sang their evening songs from the trees. LeBehr closed her eyes, and Mischief curled up near her head, purring loudly as Sebastian took one of the bookseller's hands in his own.

It couldn't be LeBehr's time. It just couldn't. I knew better than anyone that death was a natural part of life, but right now I didn't care, too consumed by sadness and anger and a refusal to suffer such a loss. I ran my hands through my hair, digging my fingertips into my scalp just as LeBehr opened her eyes and looked at me.

"I've had a wonderful life," she said, comforting me even though I should have been the one comforting her. "I'll miss not getting to live in a united Aeles-Nocens, but"—she grimaced, a rattling cough making her curl in on herself until the moment had passed and her shoulders relaxed—"there's one last thing I need you to do for me."

She held out the hand Sebastian wasn't holding, and I took it. "Of course," I croaked.

She smiled up at me, her mismatched green and yellow eyes clear. "I need you to use my body to house Grace's shade when you recover her."

I gaped at the bookseller, trying to make sense of what she'd just said as her words floated around my mind, falling in and out of any particular order. LeBehr squeezed my hand, but before I could reply, her eyes closed, and a soft breath escaped her lips. Her hand went limp. I looked at Sebastian, whose dark eyes were filled with grief, even though a tiny flame of hope trembled against all odds. Blinking through my own tears, I shifted into a seated position before heading to Vaneklus.

LeBehr was there, standing on the dock and gazing around in awe. As I joined her, I ran a finger over Glir, even though I knew what I would find. Everything felt peaceful, balanced and settled and just as it should be. The bookseller had been right.

"I meet all the qualifications," LeBehr said, continuing the conversation she'd started in the realm of the living. "I have silver blood. It's my time to die. I choose to have my body used in this way. And I knew Grace for years."

Hope and fear intermingled inside me. I would likely never have a better candidate than LeBehr, but that didn't automatically mean the recovery would be successful. If anything, it meant if this didn't work, I might never have another chance to bring Grace back to life.

All you can do is your best, Aurelius reminded me through our connection. *The result is out of your control.*

He was right, and I turned to LeBehr. "If that's what you want, I'll do my best," I said. "Sebastian should be here for this, though. Let me get him."

I returned to the creek side and held Sebastian's hand as we entered Vaneklus. LeBehr told him what she'd told me, and he stepped forward, hugging her with a fierceness that spoke of his love for her.

I drew a steadying breath, trying to remember everything I'd read in *The Book of Recovrancy*. Running my fingers over Rheolath and Tawazun, I spoke the spell to summon Grace's shade from Ceelum:

"Quiete te accerso (From rest I summon you)
De morte mittam te (From Death I will send you)
In terra viventium (To the land of the living)
Tibet licet redire (You are allowed to return)."

A moment passed, and the only sound in Vaneklus was the river lapping against my legs—until I heard the slap of oars rising and falling against the water.

33

SEBASTIAN

My heart pounded in time with the slapping oars, each rise and fall bringing Laycus's boat closer. I'd been so focused on stopping Tallus and reuniting the realms, I hadn't given hardly any thought to the possibility of seeing my mother again, and it was all I could do to keep breathing as the curtains of fog parted and Laycus's boat pulled into view. Laycus wasn't alone, though, and at the sight of his passenger, everything inside me went still. My mother saw me at the same time I saw her, and her brown eyes widened as she pressed a hand to her mouth.

"Mother!" I shouted, running into the river without waiting for Laycus's boat to reach the dock.

"Sebastian!"

My mother hopped nimbly over the side of the boat, landing in the water and moving forward as fast as her dress would allow. Reaching one another, I threw my arms around her, resting my cheek against her shoulder as thirteen years' worth of emotions rushed through me—thirteen years of grief and loss and blaming myself for her death and wishing she'd been there to see me grow up. I'd spent most of my life missing the only parent who had truly loved me, who had done everything she could to protect me. While I'd wished circumstances could have been different, I'd forced myself to face each day knowing my mother would never again be part of my life. Pulling back, I gazed down at her as she raised her hands to cup my face. It was odd to be looking down at my mother, but then again, my last memories of her had been as a seven-year-old child.

"My son," she whispered, joy shining from her eyes.

I couldn't contain the sobs bubbling in my chest as I embraced her again, feeling exactly like I used to in her arms—safe and secure and certain that, even if I didn't understand how, everything would turn out alright.

After a moment, we separated. "Look how you've grown!" She beamed at me. "You're so handsome . . . and tall!"

"You look exactly the same," I said, causing her to laugh.

"I never stopped thinking about you." Her eyes studied my face as if she were memorizing every feature. "I told myself, somehow, some way, there would be a chance of being reunited with you, and when it finally presented itself, I would take it, no matter what."

Grabbing her hand, I guided her to the dock, and she joined Kyra and LeBehr, offering hugs to both women.

"But, LeBehr, if you're *here*, that can't be good," she said, casting a worried look at Kyra.

Kyra gave her a sad smile. "As much as I don't like it, it's LeBehr's time."

"And because it's my time, I have one final request," said LeBehr. She explained about wanting her body used to house my mother's shade, and my mother's eyes widened.

"You don't have to do this," she said.

LeBehr reached out and patted her arm. "I know. I want to, which makes it so much better." She turned to Kyra. "Whatever's meant to happen will happen. All I'm doing is offering a chance, and if it doesn't work, that's not your fault."

Kyra gave a shaky nod then hugged LeBehr close. "Thank you for everything. I love you, and I'll miss you. Nocens won't be the same without you."

"I should hope not!" LeBehr chuckled. "Since this is quite unprecedented, please make sure Mischief is looked after."

Kyra and I promised we'd take care of the Cypher, and LeBehr and my mother said their goodbyes as Laycus guided his boat beside the dock and extended a hand. I hugged LeBehr with all my might, struggling to find words for feelings I'd never attempted to express.

"Thank you," I said. "You helped take care of me all these years, and I didn't even recognize it. Your door was always open, and you always had a kind word and supported anything I was interested in. You were the first to believe us about being the Felserpent King and Queen. You're the reason we found the Chronicles." A lump formed in my throat, but I pushed my next words around it. "I love you."

She hugged me back with a fierce strength. "I love you too. And it was my pleasure to help where I could. I always saw you as family."

The realization of how much LeBehr had been a part of my life made me feel grateful for having known her but also made losing her all the more painful. Pouring my feelings into my hug, I eventually forced myself to let her go. LeBehr squared her shoulders, excitement spreading across her face as she stepped forward and accepted Laycus's hand. Arranging herself on the single wooden seat, she grinned up at the Shade Transporter.

"I can only imagine the stories you must be able to tell," she said. "Oh, I wish I could remember them so I could write them down and share them!" Her smile turned embarrassed around the edges. "As much as I love sharing works by others, it's always been a secret ambition of mine to write a book. And what better subject than the life of the illustrious Shade Transporter? I've sensed more speculation than accuracy in anything I've ever read about you."

"Shades normally don't recall anything from previous life cycles," admitted Laycus before glancing between Kyra and me. "However, as everyone here knows, there *are* exceptions. I have always hated the things the living continue to get wrong about me." He tapped his fingertips against his black shroud, then shrugged. "Perhaps some of what I tell you will linger, providing the basis for a book or two in your next life."

I was glad to see LeBehr was still wearing the oversized purple and pink shawl she'd had on while taking her last breaths, and she tossed one end excitedly over her shoulder before giving us a farewell wave. Laycus turned his boat around and directed it down the river before clearing his throat.

"Now," he began, "the first thing Astrals and Daevals most often get wrong about being the Shade Transporter is . . ."

While I strained my ears, I couldn't hear what he said next, his words swallowed up by the fog, but I would certainly keep a lookout. If anyone wrote a book about the Shade Transporter in the next few decades, they might be LeBehr returned, which was a very comforting thought indeed.

As Laycus's boat disappeared, carrying LeBehr on to her next grand adventure, I turned my attention to Kyra.

"You'll need to hold on to me," she directed my mother, "since I'm going to be focused on using my *sana* bracelet."

My mother kissed my cheek before stepping forward and placing a hand on Kyra's shoulder. It was a wonder no one commented on how loudly my heart was beating, and I hoped it wasn't possible to pass out in the realm of the dead from sheer anticipation.

"Thank you for trying this," my mother said to Kyra, giving her arm an encouraging squeeze. "Whether it works or not, you've given me the greatest gift anyone could ask for. You let me see my son again."

Kyra smiled, but I could sense the fear running through her from her desire to give me and my mother more than just the chance to see one another again.

Whatever happens, I love you, I said to her. *All you can do is try.*

She swallowed, focusing on her *sana* bracelet and arranging her fingers across four beads. I'd memorized her bracelet by now and recognized the ones she touched—Rheolath, for control; Tawazun, for balance; Saund, for peace; and Lleiaf, so my mother's memories would remain intact. Kyra moved her fingers across the beads, and I let the four-note melody wash over me, echoing off the boulders behind us and floating over the surface of the river.

Kyra spoke in a clear, strong voice, sounding like the queen she would always be:

"Id quod mihi permittitur facere (That which I am permitted to do)

Libenter facio (I do willingly)

Ut haec umbra iungere cum hoc corpore (May this shade join with this body)

Cursus vitae, ubi mors (Ensuring life where there is death)."

My mother's eyes widened, and then she disappeared, vanishing before my eyes. Kyra quickly took my hand and returned us to the creek side.

LeBehr's body lay still on the ground before us, just as I'd last seen it, and I willed myself to be calm even though it felt like my fire might pour through my skin at any moment.

"What now?" I asked Kyra.

"Now we wait," she said, her voice tight.

I continued to hold Kyra's hand, watching for the slightest

movement of LeBehr's chest to indicate my mother's shade was starting to form a successful tether. For a moment, there was nothing beyond the gurgle of the creek, the evening chorus of crickets and frogs, and my own ragged breathing, but then I saw it—the rise and fall of LeBehr's chest. I squeezed Kyra's hand. It had to be a good sign if LeBehr's lungs were functioning the way they were supposed to . . . but a step in the right direction wasn't the same as a completed journey. Would my mother's shade truly take to being housed in a new body?

I had no idea what to expect or how long we might be waiting, and I nearly fell over backwards when LeBehr's body began to stir, fingers twitching, followed by one hand moving, then the other.

And then the body before us blinked, revealing mismatched green and yellow eyes gazing up at me. The body wouldn't have been able to move if my mother's shade hadn't established at least some sort of a connection . . . but how strong was that connection? And had my mother's memories survived the journey? Would she remember who she was, or who I was, for that matter?

"Mother?" I whispered, the part of me that was still a heart-broken child hardly daring to hope.

A smile stretched across the face that had been LeBehr's. "I'm here, sweetheart."

While the voice was LeBehr's, the words were my mother's. As she placed a hand against my check, I pulled her into a hug, hoping I wasn't gripping her too tightly but in no hurry to let her go.

Once she felt ready, I helped her to her feet, and she looked around, still a bit unsteady, pressing a hand to her head, then her face as she tried to become acquainted with her new body. Everything seemed like it was going well, and my heart hammered in my chest as I desperately hoped something terrible didn't happen and ruin the amazing moment.

"Kyra, look!" shouted Aurelius as Minister Sinclair made a startled noise. Kyra and I spun around just in time to see two forms rising from the creek. The shimmering outlines slowly solidified until I could make out two shrouds: one black and one white.

I stared at Laycus and Suryal, shocked to see the two of them standing before me in the realm of the living, even though I recalled meeting with Laycus in the Nebosa River before marrying Kareth.

"You did it, Recovrancer." Laycus smiled at Kyra, and there was no hiding the pride in his gaze. "As I knew you would. And now my sister and I have two gifts for you." To my surprise, he turned to me before adding, "For *both* of you."

The two beings clasped hands and began chanting in a language I didn't know. Black and white light swirled around LeBehr's body, and I watched in amazement as the body began to change, features rearranging, hair growing, limbs lengthening, until I found myself looking at my mother the way she'd appeared in Vaneklus and in her last life: tall, lithe, with shoulder-length blonde hair. Her eyes, however, were still those of LeBehr.

"Something to remember your friend and her gift by," said Suryal with a smile.

I hugged my mother, marveling over the change that shouldn't have been possible but had been made so by beings whose powers I would never understand and would certainly never forget.

Letting go of my mother, I walked to the edge of the creek. "I truly can't thank you enough," I said, bowing low. Given how much Laycus disliked me, I suspected he'd done this more for Kyra, but I was grateful, nonetheless. If Demitri and I could learn to get along, it was at least possible I might develop a friendlier relationship with the Shade Transporter, who never seemed to think anyone was good enough for the Felserpent Queen.

While part of me had expected Laycus to make a snide remark, I was grateful he merely nodded and accepted my thanks.

Kyra joined me on the edge of the creek, shaking her head in amazement. "I had no idea such a transformation was possible!" she exclaimed. "*The Book of Recovrancy* never even hinted at it. Recovrancers are encouraged to record their own experiences in the book, and I can't wait to document this."

A genuine smile stretched across Laycus's face, although it quickly settled into what I assumed was his usual smirk. "It's good to know my knowledge is still far superior to that book's," he quipped, his fiery eyes flickering with pleasure.

Suryal gave an exasperated shake of her head but didn't admonish him. "As for the second gift we have," she said, refocusing the conversation, "I have news about what reuniting the realms means for your bond."

My breath caught, and Kyra and I looked at one another. We'd both accepted reuniting the realm had likely cost us our bond and made peace with it the best we could, mostly because I trusted Kyra's ability to somehow bind our shades together again.

"You bound your shades so you would always find one another," Suryal said. "Reuniting the realm was an action you planned to take, but your desire to restore Aeles-Nocens is not what made the binding successful. It was your love for one another. That is separate and sacred and not something that can be affected by completing or not completing a task, even one as important as reuniting the realms. Your bond is unaffected; if anything, it is stronger than ever and will only continue to grow."

Relief flooded my chest as Kyra made an indecipherable sound and threw herself against me, wrapping her arms around me and hugging me tight.

"Thank you, Suryal!" she said as we separated. "Oh, I'm so

relieved! After everything that's happened, it's wonderful to be surprised by good news for a change."

"Aeles-Nocens is fortunate to have the two of you," replied Suryal. "Enjoy your life together."

And with that, she took Laycus's hand. The two waved goodbye, their forms shimmering brightly before they melted away, leaving us on the banks of the creek struggling to comprehend everything that had happened. Wrapping my arms around Kyra, I rested my cheek against the top of her head.

Against all odds, she and I had found one another again. Tallus had been defeated, the realms had been reunited, and my mother had been successfully recovered. Kyra wasn't the only one who had grown and changed since we'd reconnected. I'd spent years living solely for myself, certain the only way to ensure my safety was to avoid relationships. While that mindset had served me for a time, it no longer fit with who I had become. I was ready to leave behind the instincts that no longer served me while also keeping those parts of my past—my many pasts—that had brought me to the point of being able to choose who I wanted to be.

And who I wanted to be was, and always would be, in love with Kyra. As she'd so perfectly said, the two of us had overcome death and outlasted time, and I would never live a life without her again.

34

KYRA

"You may now seal your union with a kiss!"

The crowd burst into applause punctuated by happy cheers, and a few in attendance even went so far as to whistle and shout. Over the veritable roar of the enthusiastic guests, I grinned at Sebastian. He smiled back, and I wondered if it were possible for your heart to explode from sheer happiness. It certainly wouldn't be the worst way to enter Vaneklus, although Laycus would undoubtedly have something snide to say about such an undignified death.

Guiding my attention back to where it belonged, I joined in the clapping and cheering as Demitri cupped Adonis's face in his hands and pulled him close. The kiss was so passionate that when the two separated, Adonis was the one blushing for a change.

The wedding officiant spoke again. "It is my great honor to introduce Adonis and Demitri Forenza-Prior!"

The two faced the crowd and interlaced their fingers before raising their clasped hands, prompting the cheering to grow all the louder. The musicians struck up a cheerful song, and Adonis and Demitri practically floated up the petal-strewn aisle towards the large white tent that had been set up next to Adonis's cottage.

Eslee, standing beside me, gave me a sharp bump with her hip. "You're next," she whispered, wiggling her eyebrows in a manner that reminded me of her father. "Demitri and I have already decided we're creating a special piece of art for you and Sebastian once you announce your engagement."

I smiled at her, glad she and Demitri had become such good friends. I'd wasted no time introducing the two of them, and they'd immediately begun collaborating on art projects in Aeles and Nocens. Demitri had arranged a showcase for Eslee in Celenia, and her sculptures proved so popular she was in the process of opening a gallery there. Demitri had invited her to join me in standing with him as part of his wedding party, and Nigel and Sebastian had stood with Adonis.

Nigel offered his arm to Eslee, and I watched the two glide up the aisle before threading my arm through Sebastian's and following, some part of me still not entirely believing I was participating in a wedding between two men in Aeles attended by both Astrals and Daevals.

Defeating Tallus and reuniting the realms had been the first steps towards peace, but even so, it was going to take time and a willingness to accept change before those with silver and gold blood could truly live comfortably alongside one another. As Minerva had suggested, a vote had been held, and while it hadn't been the unanimous decision I'd hoped for, fortunately the majority of citizens wanted a chance to interact with those they'd been kept apart from their entire lives. Trade and commerce would go a long way towards uniting Astrals and Daevals, and the more they interacted, the more they would see how wrong they'd been about one another, replacing biases with firsthand experiences directly contradicting the terrible things they'd been taught to believe.

Laughter at the edge of the tent caught my ear, and I looked over to see Devlin surrounded by a group of Astrals, each vying to be closer to the charming Daeval and clearly doing their best to entertain him by saying something clever. He waved excitedly at us and managed to extricate himself from the adoring group before hurrying over.

"You look radiant as always," he said, giving me a hug, "but I have to say, Sebastian, a Nocenian wedding suit really does suit you. I never thought I'd see you in a vest and a jacket—and wearing cufflinks!"

Devlin was right. The formal suit looked fantastic on Sebastian, and the bright pink carnation in the buttonhole of the dark blue suit matched the rose quartz cufflinks Demitri and Adonis had given Sebastian and Nigel as wedding attendant gifts.

Sebastian ran a hand through his hair. "Thanks to you, I can't help but pay at least some attention to what I wear now. You've ruined me."

While his words might have sounded like a complaint, he smiled as he spoke, causing Devlin to laugh.

"If I can help *you* become interested in fashion, clearly I'm capable of far more than even I imagined," he said. "It's good to know I have other career options if matchmaking doesn't work out."

"From the look of things, business is going well." I nodded towards the group waiting impatiently for Devlin to return.

"Incredibly well!" Devlin agreed. "My appointment calendar is overflowing. In fact, my biggest problem these days is figuring out how many events I can attend in one evening, which isn't really a problem, since there's more than enough of me to go around." His pleased smirk softened into a kinder smile. "Thank you both for your support. Moving here and going out on my own was one of the best decisions I've ever made, which I know might not be saying much, but still . . ." His eyes glowed with happiness. "Who knew having a job could actually be fun?"

Devlin had moved to Celenia with far less fanfare than I'd

expected from the attention-loving Daeval, and he'd been almost immediately approached by Adeline, the foremost matchmaker in Aeles. She'd wanted to be the first to offer Astrals the opportunity to meet, court, and wed those with silver blood, and Devlin had readily accepted the position. The work required constant socializing and kept him squarely in the public eye, which he loved, and he'd begun to build quite the successful business, to his mother's delight and his father's growing pride.

Devlin returned to his clamoring mob of hopeful clients, and Sebastian and I continued into the tent as the sounds of musicians settling in with their instruments provided a gentle backdrop to the laughter and conversations already filling the air. Healer Omnurion hurried towards me, a smile on her face.

"I know this isn't the time or the place to talk about work," she said, "but I wanted to let you know I finished drafting an outline of our proposed internship exchange program." Her smile grew wider. "Who would have ever thought we'd host Daeval students in Aeles and send Astral students to Nocens? I'd love your thoughts, so I'll send it to you before the next Unity Council meeting."

"That sounds wonderful. Thank you." I hugged my former mentor, thrilled over her willingness to welcome and teach students with silver blood and grateful she'd accepted a position on the fledgling Unity Council.

While Aeles and Nocens each wanted to retain their own individual systems of governance for the near future, a coalition had been formed to help the newly reunited realm move forward, made up of an equal number of Astrals and Daevals. I had accepted a position on the Unity Council on the condition I not be solely responsible for anything, and while Sebastian had also been offered a position, no one was particularly surprised or upset when he politely declined.

Healer Omnurion bustled away, citing a need to speak with

Senator Barmly, and we made our way to where Nigel and Camus were getting drinks.

". . . nice to have an evening off," Nigel was saying. "And tomorrow, too! We should have weddings more often."

Camus laughed and heartily agreed, and it made my heart swell to see Astral and Daeval soldiers interacting peacefully. Integrating the full Aelian and Nocenian militaries had been deemed too much just yet, so military officials had started by creating a single integrated squadron comprised of Astrals and Daevals. Adonis and Nigel had been the first to volunteer, and Camus had assumed command on the condition Sebastian regularly participate in the group's training, which he was more than happy to do.

"How's the consulting business, Mr. Sayre?" asked Camus, giving Sebastian a welcoming handshake. "Doing poorly enough you'd consider joining the military full-time?"

Sebastian shook his head. "Not a chance. Even if I wasn't booked for the foreseeable future, I'm happiest being my own boss."

While Sebastian still worked for himself, he'd opened a new business that didn't have to be discussed behind closed doors, establishing himself as the foremost independent security consultant in Aeles-Nocens and helping others ensure their homes, businesses, and valuables were protected. While some Daevals were still skeptical of hiring him given his past profession, I was pleased at how many folks were eager to secure his services, although he likely could have made a comfortable living solely from working with the Dekarais.

"How's the dragon reintroduction program going, Nigel?" asked Sebastian.

"Nerudian's been fantastic!" exclaimed Nigel. "Four of his extended family members are relocating to Aravost next week, and we're all set for them. Once they're settled in, we have a unicorn family moving to Eisig, and we're putting the final touches on their new home."

Plans had been put into place to welcome dragons back to Aeles, and Nocens was eager to rebuild their unicorn population, creating sanctuaries for the creatures where they could live without fear of being hunted for their prized horns. Nerudian and Nigel were in charge of the joint effort, and of all the things Aeles and Nocens had to be happy about, welcoming creatures believed to be extinct had proven to be very near the top of the list.

Shortly after the establishment of the Unity Council, Astrals had argued strongly for better treatment towards animals in Nocens, including more planterian food options and moving away from using animals for entertainment or labor. I'd learned diplomacy was an artful mixture of concessions and triumphs. While things didn't always move as quickly as I'd have liked, I was nonetheless pleased over the improvements in animal welfare taking place throughout the Nocenian territories. In exchange for such changes, Daevals had demanded Aeles do away with any and all laws regulating relationships. I'd been a nervous wreck the day of the vote, but thankfully it had passed, leading Adonis and Demitri to announce their engagement shortly after.

As the men continued to talk, I headed towards where Minerva and Seren were standing and watched as a girl with braided black hair tapped Seren on the shoulder. I couldn't hear what the girl said, but Seren appeared surprised, although a huge smile quickly broke out over her face. She nodded before taking the girl's hand and following her to the dance floor. Seeing my little sister dancing with someone with silver blood filled me with happiness, and Minerva and I shared a smile just as her peerin buzzed. Clicking it open, she read whatever was on the screen before giving a single nod and returning the device to her pocket.

"Business never sleeps," she said, "but in this case, it's also personal." She fixed her penetrating eyes on mine. "I want you to know, I've altered my will. I'm leaving everything, including Sea'Brik and my portion of the family business, to Seren."

"That's . . . incredibly generous," I stammered, completely caught off guard by her revelation.

"Or merely selfish," she replied. "I like knowing my work will live on long after I'm gone. While I don't plan on meeting your Shade Transporter anytime soon, should I be the first in the family to go, I can only imagine the mistakes my brothers would make. Seren is growing into an exceptional financier, and she'll catch things Dunston and Caz wouldn't even think to miss."

While her words weren't exactly kind, she nevertheless cast a fond glance at her brothers, both of whom were on the dance floor. Caz was dancing with my mother, his gold and silver sequined suit flashing brightly every time he moved, and Dunston and Rennej were laughing and swaying in place with their arms around one another. The Dekarais had been the loudest and most ardent supporters of opening official trade between Aeles and Nocens and played a central role in drafting legislation to make such trade possible—legislation that favored them generously, of course. While I had no doubt they would always find a way to circumvent regulations when it was convenient, I was thrilled to see commerce taking shape between the formerly divided realms but even happier to see Seren forging her own path and earning accolades that had nothing to do with being my sister.

Someone tapped my shoulder, and I turned to find Minister Sinclair.

"And how is everyone's favorite *Princeps Shaman?*" he asked. A broad smile broke out over my face at *finally* hearing myself referred to by a title I'd dreamed of holding for so long—and not just in this life cycle.

"Incredibly grateful there's nothing for me to do except enjoy myself," I said. "Folks in the *Donec Medicinae* are still talking about the lecture you gave at the healing conference. Your work on using *alera* to improve emotional healing is groundbreaking!"

The first thing I'd done upon being named Aeles's *Princeps Shaman* had been to organize a conference on healing open to both Astral and Daeval healers, with a keynote address by Minister Sinclair. He'd kept his word and immediately begun championing cooperation between those with healing abilities regardless of the color of their blood, and my only regret was that my father hadn't been able to attend the conference. He would have been so proud. Even though I knew my healing abilities weren't solely due to being his daughter, since I'd possessed them as Kareth, it was still nice to know we'd shared the ability. I would always think of him when I healed someone.

Minister Sinclair smiled. "The Fates favor the bold, and I'm pleased the annals of history will remember me as the Daeval who shared such knowledge with Aeles."

While humility would never be one of his defining traits, I'd genuinely enjoyed working alongside him and getting to know him better, so I let his words pass without comment.

"I'm also pleased to have a new line of study to pursue," he continued. "After seeing how those children suffered at the hands of Tallus during their time in Rynstyn, I find myself more than a little motivated to uncover ways to ease emotional suffering." He shifted his champagne flute from one hand to the other. "Most of them have made significant improvements, but the youngest one, Raethe—some of the things she says continue to trouble me. I was hoping you might meet with her and see what you can make of it."

"What sort of things is she saying?"

"I'm sure she's doing her best to make sense of events that

are far too terrible for such a young mind to process," said the minister, "but when she describes her dreams, she talks about feeling as if she's falling out of her own body. There's always water—which isn't surprising, given how frequently Tallus's followers used near-drownings as a form of torture—and sometimes there is a figure dressed in black." He shook his head. "The things that child must have endured."

I stared at him, the hair on my arms prickling. What he'd described reminded me of the first time I had visited the realm of the dead. I'd felt as if my shade had been ripped from my body, and I'd fallen blindly through what seemed to be endless space before landing in the grey waters of Vaneklus, where I'd encountered the Shade Transporter in his black shroud. I knew every Recovrancer's path to learning about her gift was unique, but according to things I'd read in *The Book of Recovrancy*, at least some girls with the gift took their first trip to Vaneklus during their sleep, making the experience seem like a dream.

But that was impossible. Raethe was a Daeval, and all the Recovrancers I'd ever read about had been Astrals.

The realms being reunited changed many things, noted Aurelius, speaking through our connection as he enjoyed time with other Cyphers away from the crowded dance floor. *You have only to look around you to know that. A gathering like this hasn't occurred in more than a thousand years. Things once believed to be impossible have proven to be* quite *possible.*

"I'd love to meet with Raethe," I assured Minister Sinclair. Now that recovrancy was no longer outlawed, I often thought about how there was always one senior and one junior Recovrancer. I couldn't wait until the girl who would be my protégé would be revealed, especially since she would live in a realm that not only needed, but wanted, her, and would welcome her unique powers.

I was on the verge of asking the minister more, but Sebastian and his mother were walking towards us. My questions could wait until I met with Raethe.

"You look beautiful!" I said to Grace as we hugged one another. She blushed and ran her hands over her dress, the warm peach color complementing her fair skin and making her green and gold eyes positively glow.

"I can't believe I have the chance to dress up and attend a celebration again!" she laughed. "Everything tastes, feels, and smells so much better than I remember."

"Being alive unquestionably suits you," agreed Minister Sinclair, earning himself a sharp scowl from Sebastian as I bit my bottom lip and tried not to smile. The minister cleared his throat. "What I meant was, no one would ever believe you spent the past thirteen years in Vaneklus," he said, his voice assuming a more clinical tone. "Any changes in your connection with Mischief?"

"None, I'm happy to report," replied Grace. "She's the most darling creature, and she's been so helpful as I'm adjusting to life again."

After recovering Grace, we'd faced the question of what would happen to Mischief, since the shade of her former pairing was gone even though the body continued to live. While I hadn't initially liked Minister Sinclair's idea of involving Nocen's Cypher *Adran*, this was completely unprecedented, and I didn't want anything bad to happen to Grace or Mischief. Thankfully, the black cat had retained at least part of her connection to the body that had belonged to LeBehr, and it had been an easy fix to ensure she and Grace were properly bonded. Those at the Cypher *Adran* had been incredibly helpful, possibly because everyone across Aeles-Nocens had been thrilled to learn I was a Recovrancer, but more likely due to Dunston making a generous donation for a new *Adran* building and Caz calling in a few well-placed favors.

"How are things at the bookstore?" I asked Grace. She had

assumed responsibility for LeBehr's Bookshop, retaining the name as an homage to the book-loving woman Sebastian and I still missed but would always remember fondly.

"They couldn't be better," said Grace. "One of the dragons relocating to Aeles was going through her treasure trove and found a crate of books at least three hundred years old. They arrived this morning, and I can't wait to go through them! I also can't keep copies of the Chronicles on the shelves." She smiled. "It's a good thing you made a recording of it so everyone can listen on their peerins."

"All credit for that idea goes directly to Batty," I said as the bat appeared on Sebastian's shoulder, his fur shining from the bath Deneb had given him earlier. "Just like it was his idea to create a guided tour folks could listen to while visiting Velaire."

The ruins of Velaire had been left as they were, with the addition of a few spells for stability—a hallowed ground where anyone could come and see the Cor'Lapis stone and learn about the past, either from what I'd recorded or from Batty, who occasionally offered guided tours that filled up almost as quickly as they were announced.

Looking around, Sebastian's fingers intertwined with mine, it seemed impossible to believe we'd accomplished everything we'd set out to do. But this moment was proof we'd done it, a reminder the impossible could indeed become possible. Surrounded by those I loved, with the knowledge of my past to guide me, I felt fortunate and more than a little excited to be part of creating a better future for everyone, a future that wouldn't be divided by gold or silver blood. Astrals and Daevals might have their differences, but we were one realm, with one future.

Following along with my thoughts, Sebastian leaned over and brushed his lips against my ear.

"Hail the Felserpent Queen," he whispered.

EPILOGUE

KYRA

Lying on a thick blanket, I marveled as another burning star streaked past. Sebastian had brought us to the desert of Jaasfar to watch the Rhai Lla'khar meteor shower, partly because he knew how much I'd love it but also because LeBehr had suggested it to him a few weeks back, and he wanted to honor the memory of the beloved bookseller. The air was crisp and cold, and the sky was alive with twinkling lights.

"Oh, there goes another one!" called Nerudian, his yellow eyes following the glowing light enviously. "I do wish I could fly that high."

Aurelius was curled up beside me, his paws tucked underneath him, and Batty was lying on Sebastian's chest, gazing upwards, his wings folded over his belly. It was still difficult to believe we were doing something as ordinary as watching falling stars, but I was more than happy to work to believe it.

As if on some unspoken signal, Nerudian swiveled his head towards us as Aurelius shifted to sit on his haunches. Batty waved a wing, causing an orb of light to appear.

"We have something for the two of you," said Aurelius as Nerudian nodded excitedly. "For whenever you're ready to use them. Bartholomew, if you please."

Batty grinned and pulled two small boxes from a pocket of his wing, handing one to me and one to Sebastian.

"Open them!" he exclaimed.

Sebastian and I looked at one another before pushing ourselves into sitting positions, neither of us having any idea what was happening. When I opened the box, my breath caught . . . Inside was a ring, shaped like a crown. The jewelry was made of both silver and gold, and each tine of the miniature crown was decorated with a different gem.

"I told you crowns could be reforged," smiled Batty. "Everyone helped. Aurelius and Demitri designed the rings. Eslee and Nerudian created them. The Dekarais donated the materials. Seren, Enif, and Deneb selected the gems. And I," the bat stood up straighter, "supervised everyone very closely."

Overwhelmed by the thoughtfulness of the creatures, as well as our loved ones who had helped them, it took me a moment to realize Sebastian had repositioned himself down on one knee.

"I realize this isn't necessary," he said, "given that our shades are bound together forever, but I was married to you once before and I'd love to be married to you in this life cycle. Would you do me the honor of marrying me . . . again?"

"Yes," I smiled, leaning forward and wrapping my arms around him. "In this life, the next, and every one that will come after, my answer will always be yes."

I'd become so used to being guided by the past, to having at least some idea of what needed to be done, it was odd considering an unknown future. But even though I didn't know what the future held, I knew who I would face it with.

And that was all I needed to know.

The End

Acknowledgments

I can't believe this series has come to an end . . . although the end of writing a book also means the beginning of readers turning the pages and meeting Kyra and Sebastian, so I'll choose to focus on how exciting that is rather than how sad I am to leave this world.

Thank you to my publisher, SparkPress, and to book champion Brooke Warner for supporting this trilogy. Many thanks to Lauren Wise for expertly guiding this book every step of the way. Julie Metz, you once again outdid yourself with a book cover I want to dive into and never leave.

Deep and heartfelt thanks to my phenomenal BookSparks PR team: Crystal Patriarche, Hanna Lindsley, and Rylee Warner. It's an honor to be part of the BookSparks family, and you all have worked magic that would make any YA fantasy character green with envy. Thank you for the guidance, for always making me feel like a "real" author, and for your unflagging enthusiasm for what I've created.

A. R. Capetta, I am so fortunate that a bit of your writing magic lives in the pages of this book. Having you as an editor was a dream come true. I will be forever grateful for your love of my characters and for the way you saw things I couldn't. You've helped me grow as a writer, and I still read back over your editorial letters when I need encouragement and worry I'll never write anything worth reading again.

Jen Braaksma, Lenore Borja, Sathya Achia, and Anastasia Zadeik: I'm so happy to know each of you, and I can't thank you enough for your support and your championing of my writing.

KX Song, I'm so glad we connected through a Highlights Foundation retreat, and here's to many more panels and author events together!

To every reader, blogger, influencer, Bookstagrammer, Booktoker, and book lover who shared posts, wrote reviews, and created character art, you have my eternal gratitude. Connecting with readers is the best part of being an author, and I'm beyond lucky to have been welcomed so warmly into the intense world of YA fantasy.

To my family and friends who bought my books, showed up for events, sent encouraging messages, and celebrated even the smallest of successes with me, thank you. Special shout-outs to Carol Kruger, Marjorie Pezzoli, and Shreya Shrikumar for the kind of support most authors only dream of receiving.

To my husband, Cameron: thank you for being the inspiration for Kyra and Sebastian's love story. As Kyra says, "But even though I didn't know what the future held, I knew who I would face it with. And that was all I needed to know." I couldn't have said it better myself. Thank you for making it safe for me to believe in magic.

And finally, to the person who is reading this and dreaming of one day holding their own book in their hands: to paraphrase William Jennings Bryan, "Destiny is not a matter of chance, but a matter of choice. It is not a thing to be waited for; it is a thing to be achieved." Believe in yourself. Choose yourself. Achieve your destiny. And let me know what you're working on so I can cheer for you every step of the way.

About the Author

Photo credit: Cameron Bowman

KATIE KERIDAN has written all her life—from childhood, through college and graduate school, and during her career as a pediatric neuropsychologist. She enjoyed being a doctor, but creating her own characters and worlds brought her far more joy, so she slowly left the medical world behind to focus exclusively on writing. She has written two other novels in the Felserpent Chronicles series, *Reign Returned* and *Blood Divided*, and her work has been featured in *Highlights Hello Magazine, The Blue Nib, Youth Imagination Magazine, Red Fez, The Red Penguin Review, Sand Canyon Review*, and *Every Day Fiction*. She loves sharing her writing with others who feel different, misunderstood, or alone. Katie lives in Northern California with her husband and two very demanding cats.